Landscape with Landscape

Landscape with Landscape

Gerald Murnane

SHEFFIELD - LONDON - NEW YORK

This edition first published in the UK in 2026 by
And Other Stories and first published by Giramondo in 2016.
First published in 1985 by Norstrilia Press.
Sheffield – London – New York
www.andotherstories.org

1 3 5 7 9 8 6 4 2

ISBN: 9781916751378
eBook ISBN: 9781916751385

Offset by Tetragon, London; Series Cover Design: Elisa von Randow, Alles Blau
Studio, Brazil, after a concept by And Other Stories; Author Photo: Ian Hill.

And Other Stories books are printed and bound in the UK on
FSC-certified paper by the CPI Group (UK) Ltd, Croydon.

A catalogue record for this book is available from the British Library.

And Other Stories' Authorized Representative within the EU
GPSR legal framework is: Logos Europe, 9 rue Nicolas Poussin,
17000 La Rochelle, France. (Logos Europe do not represent to publishers
the rights to this title.) E-mail: Contact@logoseurope.eu

And Other Stories gratefully acknowledge that our work is
supported using public funding by Arts Council.

Contents

AUTHOR'S FOREWORD

I'll admit it's a trite comparison, but I sometimes compare my books as a father might compare his children; I claim to feel for each an equal *quantity* of affection but a different *quality*. My affection for *Landscape with Landscape* includes much sympathy. I feel sorry for my fourth-eldest, which of all my book-children was the most brutally treated in its early years.

I have no overall sales figures for my books but I strongly suspect that *Landscape with Landscape* and *Emerald Blue* sold the fewest copies. Both are often described by booksellers as scarce or rare. I can hardly believe a few obsessive collectors are hoarding large numbers – it seems obvious that these are the two of my books that were least bought and read. *Emerald Blue* was hardly publicised and little reviewed. *Landscape with Landscape* was widely reviewed but not with much sympathy or understanding and sometimes harshly or even unfairly.

About five years after the book's publication, I received a letter from a well-regarded Australian novelist of that era. He told me that he had just read and had greatly admired *Landscape with Landscape* and that he regretted not having read it earlier. He had not done so, he explained, because he had been turned away from the book by the first review of it that he had read – a most unfavourable review in the *Bulletin*.

Some writers may claim not to be affected by reviews or not even to read them. I make no such claim. During my forty and more years as a published author, I've received every possible sort of review, from the unreservedly adulatory to the utterly dismissive. I tend to forget those from the middle of the range, but I can't help recalling those from either extreme and when I set out to write this paragraph I didn't need to look through my files for the *Bulletin* review of *Landscape with Landscape* – I called to mind easily some of the nastiest passages.

I've never engaged in public or private with any reviewer and I'm not about to do so now, but I'm going to wonder aloud what it was in *Landscape With Landscape* that provoked the *Bulletin* reviewer to include in his piece a malicious attack on me, the author, and to invoke, of all things, the outworn Sydney versus Melbourne thing, he being the sophisticated Sydneysider, of course, and I being the upstart from Melbourne.

I could only wonder, after I had read the novelist's warm letter, how many other potential readers and/or buyers of my book had been put off, perhaps for ever, by the review in the *Bulletin*. I had already suspected that one prominent reviewer and critic had had the wind put up her by the strong stuff in the *Bulletin*. She is no longer alive, but in her day she was a much-published reviewer and the author of at least one book of criticism that I can recall. Hers was the first review of *Landscape with Landscape* to be published. It was a long, detailed review in the *Age*, in June, 1985, and I was elated by it. My fourth book, so I read, was a work of extraordinary power and vision, which would surely be an outstanding novel of the decade. The review was about a thousand words of detailed commentary, almost all of it highly favourable. I was especially pleased that the reviewer had been most impressed by 'The Battle of Acosta Nu', which I've always considered a piece of writing at least as dense and accomplished as *The Plains*.

The *Age* review had been published for only a few weeks when the *Bulletin* review appeared. During the rest of the year, a number of other reviews expressed the usual range of opinions that my books attracted in those days. I had the usual range of feelings while I read them, and if I needed to cheer myself up I had only to recall the unqualified praise that the *Age* reviewer had come out with. Then, towards Christmas, the *Age* filled a couple of pages in its books section with lists compiled by its reviewers of the books that had most impressed them during the past year. My reviewer of six months before, she who had filled three columns with unstinting praise for *Landscape with Landscape*, did not include my book in her list. The lesson that I got from this was that I should never expect any reviewer to stray too far from the herd.

The book took five years to write. I'm sometimes dismayed to hear my body of work described as some sort of orderly program that I devised early in my career and followed faithfully afterwards. The fourteen filing-cabinet drawers of my literary archive are filled with failed beginnings, wrong turnings and abandoned drafts, and elaborate plans that came to nothing. I had been at work on *Landscape with Landscape* for three years before I devised the plan of the whole. For a long time, I had thought of it only as a collection of short fiction or of novellas. I had started work in 1980 as a full-time teacher of fiction writing in a college of advanced education. I required my students to write short fiction, but I had written hardly any myself and I decided to turn my hand to it. In 1980, I finished a piece of about 2,000 words titled 'The president was freckled', which later became the beginnings of 'Landscape with Freckled Woman', although that piece, the first in the finished book, was the last to be written and almost defied me to find its final shape. In my files are more than two hundred pages of early drafts of 'Landscape with Freckled Woman'. The final draft was my *fourteenth* attempt to get the thing right. Thirteen times previously, I had given up and begun again.

Landscape with Landscape has had its share of modest successes. It was shortlisted for the major fiction award at the Adelaide Festival in 1986, and it was included in the *Classic Australian Works* series published by Sydney University Press and supported by other prestigious bodies. Now, here it is being republished thirty years after its harsh early life and when it's old enough to stand up for itself.

Gerald Murnane, 2016

LANDSCAPE WITH FRECKLED WOMAN

I was the only man among nine women. Together we formed a committee of ten, with myself as treasurer. I sat beside the president and the secretary while the seven others sat facing me. I was not comfortable.

I knew none of the women, although all of them lived in my own suburb. The only name I knew was the president's. She had phoned me a few hours before this, the first meeting of the committee, and persuaded me to serve as treasurer. Then she had asked me to tell her a little about myself so that she could introduce me properly at the meeting. And the warmth in her voice had prompted me to say more than I meant to.

Sitting at the table and waiting to be introduced, I glanced at each of the committee in turn. I tried to apportion my glances so that each woman got an equal share. But if anyone met my eyes I looked calmly away. I did not want to be locked into a long exchange of stares like a character in one of the films I supposed the women watched every evening. Yet I wanted each woman to wonder; when the president introduced me and they learned I was a writer, whether I might have been quietly observing her for some time before she caught me at it.

The women were all a few years younger than me – in their early or middle thirties. But they were not too young to have been, fifteen or twenty years before, the young women I had tried to impress by telling them I was going to become a writer. Those young women had always stopped listening – sometimes politely, sometimes not – when I reached a certain stage of drunkenness and began long, elaborate sentences and then could not finish them. Yet I had never been wholly discouraged when some young woman turned away and left me talking to myself; she added one more to the number of women who might meet me years later and learn that I had become a published writer after all and regret that she had not listened more closely to me.

Even as a young drunk, devising petty dreams of my vindication, I had no grounds for believing a woman would remember for ten or twenty years what she had heard one night in a corner of a crowded room. But sometimes after I had sounded especially eloquent, and after I had seen something more than tolerance in the look of the young woman listening, I thought she might have gone away with at least one word fixed in her mind. Somewhere in Melbourne there ought to have been, I decided in the committee-room, one woman who would remember me as the man who talked about his landscape.

I would have preferred that woman not to remember in detail what I had once told her about my landscape. In my notebooks of those days I had boasted that I was privileged to see what no one else could see: that all I had to do as a writer was to describe the far-reaching vistas and the intricate topography continually before my eyes: that I need not be curious about what were called real people because I had already made out certain dim figures in my landscape. Nearly twenty years later I would have been satisfied for the woman to concede that I might have seen, over the years, just a little more than people such as herself.

The time came for the president to welcome me formally. I prepared to sit with my eyes lowered for as long as I was the centre of their attention. The last I saw of my surroundings was the president shifting a little in her seat as she mentioned my name. (Was she herself already wondering where she might have met me before and turned away from me?)

The president tried for a little humour. She said they were honoured to have a man on their committee for once: a rose among the thorns, to coin a phrase. For his sake they would try to be more businesslike and not gossip too much at their meetings. And then she said, trying to sound more serious, that their new treasurer wanted to be just as involved as the ladies of the committee. He would be available at any time of the day or evening if any committee member needed him urgently.

If she paused at this it was noticeable only, perhaps, to me. And without looking up I could not tell whether she was in the least embarrassed or confused, or whether any of the others had moved in their chairs or smiled weakly. But the president's next words bothered me more. Their treasurer was available, she said, because he worked at home all day. He was a writer. He was hard at work on a book right now, and it might turn out to be about a suburb very like their own little corner of the world.

That should have been the time for me to lift my head boldly and to look through their faces towards some subject for fiction that was out of their sight. But I managed only a glance that did not quite cross the distance between the women and me. And while the president went on talking of other things, I could only wonder whether the women who looked briefly at me during the rest of the evening saw a man whose eye had ranged widely over the world but who now chose to scrutinise their quiet streets for his own purposes, or a man who had failed somewhat in the world at large and who now came humbly to learn from them what they saw beyond their kitchen windows all day or in the greyness of their television tubes late at night after the last image had dwindled to nothing. And I wondered too how I might have described myself or the book I was supposed to be writing: whether I could still claim that what passed in front of my eyes deserved to be distinguished from what others called the world, or whether I had only used the word 'landscape' (and still resorted to it occasionally) to console myself for failing to see what others saw quite clearly.

At some time during the evening I found myself staring at two freckles low on the neck of one of the committee women. I called the brown marks freckles, but I did not confuse them with commonplace specks that sunlight produced on most pale faces and forearms. The woman was marked below her throat with the deep-brown dots that appeared infrequently on the least exposed parts of bodies. I preferred to think that these marks were not caused by sunlight but grew inevitably outwards from the depths beneath the skin. Their sites were therefore not the chance results of weather but signs of the distinctiveness of a body: landmarks of a particular skin.

I did first what I always did when I saw those marks on a woman's chest or legs: wondered where else on her body the marks might have appeared and in what patterns. And then I got from my sight of the freckles the reassurance that I was looking for the moment at a real woman – someone mildly flawed and therefore nobody's dream.

For most of my life, I would have admitted, I had dreamed of women instead of looking at them. I had even decided more than once that I was only a writer because I dreamed rather than looked – not only at women but at anything else I had claimed to see.

Ten years before, when I was about to be married, I had got ready to burn the collection of pictures of women I had clipped from magazines for years past. But I had hesitated over the few pictures that had been my favourites. Each was of a woman with at least one of the marks I looked for. I said goodbye easily to the women who were uniformly gold or beige; only when I had been unusually drunk or despairing had they meant anything to me. But the freckled women had always seem peculiarly my own. I liked to think that readers of the magazines mostly passed over these women because their freckles seemed to mar them, to disqualify them from the world of satin cushions and marble bathtubs. I knew I would never miss the women whose surfaces were no more varied than the golden drapes and creamy carpets they posed against. But I did not want to crumple the pictures of the freckled women.

I had paused over those women because they might have proved I was no ordinary dreamer. Other young men, admirers of white or tanned skin, could dream only of what they supposed ideal: of an unclouded sky or an unspeckled skin or an untroubled smile. I, the admirer of freckled women, had taken to dreaming not because the world

I saw by daylight was not enough for me but because it was too much. Even half-alert, I saw its rippled and mottled and freckled surfaces as promising too many meanings. I had never tried to imagine what was perfect, to work my way through gradually merging variations towards one ideal. I wanted to go in the opposite direction, to wander among the branching capillaries of the changeable world until I found instead of the One the Once-only. I wanted to possess, in some unthought-of sense of that word, a woman subtly and uniquely marked out from all others.

But there was more to my dreaming than the search for a woman. I had always noted carefully the background behind each posed body. Usually it was some narrow view of walls or drapes or tree-trunks – nothing that would take the admirer's eyes for too long from the figure in the foreground. What I looked for, but hardly ever found, was a doorway in the wall or a window between the drapes or a gap among the foliage. When I saw such an opening, I thought of it as giving onto a place beyond the crudely imagined dreamlands of the average man. To see into that place might have brought on the same pleasant confusion that came from hearing in a dream the voice saying, 'All this so far has been a dream, but what follows is real.' And I could imagine no one but a freckled woman leading me to the window overlooking the hidden courtyard or to the glade deep among the trees. Only a woman marked unpredictably above her breasts or on her thigh could have persuaded me that until that moment I had been dreaming and then led me to a place that she and I could agree was peculiarly real.

When the nameless woman of the committee stretched a freckled knee in my view or leaned her chin on a freckled wrist, I should have been able to admire her easily, knowing she was no mere sign of some other woman I was yet to meet. I should have told myself calmly that I would see her again in some front garden of my neighbourhood in days to come. But I could hardly forget that I had not yet burnt, after all, those few pictures that had been my favourites as a young man. The slender folio of freckled women was still at the back of my filing cabinet. And whenever I stored in that cabinet some more of the hundreds of pages of discarded drafts of my fiction, I seemed to be writing my way towards a woman I would never see because every page I filled with words only added to the distance between her and myself.

The president went on talking of committee business. The other women talked at intervals. I was not asked to speak. I had all the time I needed for rehearsing my speech to the woman I expected to approach me after the meeting. I saw nothing absurd in what I was doing – sitting at the heart of the scene I had dreamed of fifteen years before and yet dreaming further of another scene that would lead me at last into the real world. I had the pleasant suspicion that I was about to complete a neat pattern I had often admired as a subject for fiction. I might have been about to demonstrate that at the heart of every scene assumed to be real was at least one character imagining further scenes that would be closer still to reality.

The scene I assumed to be real had at its heart the unfolding of the landscape I had talked of and thought of so often. After the committee meeting had ended, the freckled woman had brought me a cup of milky tea with a sugar-speckled biscuit resting on the saucer and had asked me what sort of writer I was and where I found the subjects for my writing. I told her that the scene we were enacting just then – her approaching me with those questions and my answering them with feigned authority – was a scene I had often imagined as a drunken young man who dreamed of becoming a writer. In that scene, I said, she was the same woman who had once turned away from me fifteen years earlier. But of course she, the woman standing with me at the supper-table, had never seen me before tonight. She was therefore both the woman who woke me from a long dream and (because I was still at my table and the committee meeting still proceeding) a woman in quite a different sort of dream.

The drunken young man had not always been drunk and babbling, I told the freckled woman in one of my dreams. On four or five nights each week he was alone and sober and trying to write fiction. Perhaps he was not quite sober, even though he was not drinking. He believed in those days that he could only write in a certain mood, and alone in his rented room he tried to bring on that mood. He had a private word for it; he called it his *ginestran* mood. The word came from the title of Giacomo Leopardi's poem *La Ginestra*, which the young man had not read but whose author he believed to have been the most solitary of all great writers. From the little he had learned of Leopardi, the man imagined the poet all but imprisoned in his parents' house; sitting at his desk in deep shadow but in sight of a distant rectangle of white sunlight that was all he saw all day of some far-ranging view of Italian hills with somewhere among their tufts of treetops the flowering branches of the broom – *la ginestra* – which the poet had probably never touched or smelled but which kept him at his desk in the shadowy room day after day until he had laid out in metre and rhyme a landscape that would outlast by centuries the many-coloured scenery around his window.

Where was I? – dreaming of remembering a dream,

I might have interrupted myself just then to let the freckled woman see that I could mock myself as a narrator. I might even have told her that if I were a writer of a certain fashionable sort of fiction my standing at the supper table and saying those words to her could later have become part of a story of redoubled complexity, but that since I was a writer interested only in what was real, the scope of my question encompassed no one but my real self.

That young man had been sure, I went on to say, that a writer needed no more than a landscape of his own. The young man's mistake was to believe that his landscape already contained all the scenery and figures he would ever want to write about. He had been so sure of this that he used to contrive certain rituals for turning his back on the landscapes of others.

His rented room was in a south-eastern suburb of Melbourne. Every Sunday, soon after midday, he walked to an intersection of two main roads to buy his milk and bread. He stood afterwards for five minutes or so beside the traffic lights, pretending to wait for someone but actually watching for any car that had a young man as driver and a young woman as its only passenger. (There were many such cars. It was 1960 and the young man's generation had discovered the secondhand Holden and the new Volkswagen.) When one of these cars stopped at the lights, he watched the driver's fingers drumming on the steering wheel and the young woman's head turning restlessly about. She was the driver's steady girl friend. They had been out together on the Saturday night and now he had called around at her house to take her for a drive. She had not been told exactly where he was taking her but she was not surprised to find herself being driven eastwards. All the people she knew in Melbourne looked east or south-east when they thought of travelling towards the pleasant places that waited all week on the edges of their thoughts. In the east was Mount Dandenong, a blue-black hump that served as a not-too-distant goal for those who liked to keep a goal in view. Short of the mountain were gentler folds of hills, the furthest looking like true countryside from a distance and the nearest already marked out with rows of newly built houses such as a young woman and her boy friend could peer into quite innocently as though they were merely curious about the kinds of home their married friends were choosing and not secretly dreaming of living there themselves.

All this waited in the east for the young couples in their cars, and the young man with his milk and bread under his arm hoped they would explore it thoroughly, so that they would be all the more dissatisfied at dusk that day when they waited again at the same intersection, still twitching their fingers and staring around them. He himself would spend all the afternoon in his room, reading and writing and trying to define his landscape. At dusk he might be almost as tired and discontented as the young couples. But while they wondered how many miles further they would have to travel on some Sunday to come before they saw the landscape they were really looking for, he would never have doubted that he had looked all day in the right place.

Yes, I said, anticipating the question in the face of the freckled woman. Yes, she might well ask what exactly was this landscape of his that had allowed him to jeer at landscapeless young couples. The young man would have described it in detail if only she had taken him aside and asked him earnestly on the night of the party. He would have told her which eastern landmark was its equivalent of Mount Dandenong and what strange contours filled its nearer distances. But now it was too late. I could only tell her that when the young man had sat alone in his room with what he called his *ginestran* mood on him, the blank page between himself and his window had seemed the foreground of a remarkable tract of country.

But surely, the committee woman would have asked, I had kept the notes or drafts that the young man had written. Yes, I would have told her, I had kept every page. They were safe, stacked far back in my filing cabinet against a collection of pictures that had once seemed to offer access to his landscape from quite a different direction. But whenever I tried to read what the young man had written I saw only a vista of dim rooms, each with a table where a man (a few years older in each case) sat over a blank page. And the last page of all was more blurred and misty than any horizon the young man could have dreamed of.

The young man had decided in time, I said, that the south-eastern suburbs were distracting him from his landscape. On some Sundays in his room, facing his sheet of paper, he saw simple patterns like rectangles of roads where much more complex shapes should have been; and a single blue mountainous hump came between him and his sky. He decided he was only trying to outdo the Sunday drivers, as though he could show some wide-eyed young woman what she had always wanted to see. And so he resolved to live in a suburb of Melbourne that offered nothing to the eye: a suburb from which a writer could see only what he himself devised. And he fixed on an inner suburb.

At that time he had never heard of anyone wanting to settle in an inner suburb. In those far-off days of 1960, I said to the freckled woman in 1975, most inner suburbs were called slums. Young people were expected to buy blocks of land in new suburbs, in Chelsea Heights or Forest Hill or Banyule. Some couples when they were first married did live in South Yarra or Hawthorn, but only in rented flats in tree-lined streets while they saved for their newly built houses far away to the east. The young man looked for his inner suburb in the true slums north of the city. And of those slums he chose what he believed to be the least regarded – a suburb almost bare of trees, where front doors were an arm's length from the footpath and walls of factories kept whole neighbourhoods in shadow all day; a suburb where some people still lived without cars and without distant views of Mount Dandenong; a suburb that he knew from his newspapers was an underworld haunt with sly-grog joints and shooting incidents. He moved his suitcase of books and his grocery carton of notes and manuscripts to a room with use of bath (two pounds, five shillings per week) above the kitchen of a single-fronted house in Argyle Street, Fitzroy.

The young man asked one of his few friends, a school teacher like himself, to drive him and his belongings from Malvern to Fitzroy on a Sunday morning. The friend helped to carry the young man's baggage across the tiny backyard, through a kitchen where a woman and three men were drinking beer in front of a television set, and up a narrow staircase that began near the kitchen stove and ended at the young man's door. When the carrying was done the friend looked at the bed with its bare, stained mattress. He looked at the cupboard and the table and chair and then he walked to the uncurtained window and looked across the backyards towards MacRobertson's chocolate factory. He asked the young man rather awkwardly did he know what he was doing. The young man knew at once that his friend suspected he was about to have what his friend would have called a nervous breakdown. The young man decided that his friend was no friend but only one more of the thousands who knew nothing of true landscapes because they had grown up in the belt of neat suburbs between Port Phillip Bay and Mount Dandenong. The young man decided too that he had wasted his time trying to explain to such people (even to the young women among them) that true landscapes were not bounded by such obvious features as mountains and seashores. But he was too tired to rebuke the man from the south-east and a little alarmed that the man might go back to his bayside suburb thinking the young man's mind had given way. So he told the friend that he had come to Fitzroy to write about reality – about the sort of people in the kitchen downstairs; people who lived lives of elemental passion unhindered by the conventions of the suburbs by the sea.

You would not have met the young man during the three months that he spent in Fitzroy, I told the freckled woman. (By now the cups of tea would have been emptied and some of the committee women would have been edging towards the door. The rest of the story ought to have been told a week or so later on the freckled woman's front doorstep. I should have said lightly to the woman as we rinsed and dried our teacups that I might call on her some afternoon to finish the story of my landscape. But in that case the woman might have suspected me of wanting to get closer to her, of wanting to get past her front door and into the empty house with her. And even if I stood at the farthest corner of her front porch, leaning against her white-painted wrought iron and fingering the gloss on her camellia leaves and not glancing past her shoulder into the hallway and towards the bedroom doors opening off it – even then she could still reasonably suppose that the long, rambling story of the landscape was only my peculiar way of approaching her. Sitting quietly beside the president, I knew I could never tell the freckled woman the ending of my story. And if I could not tell her, then I myself could hardly foresee the end of it. I could not even foresee the ending of a much simpler story – the story I had wanted to assure the woman I would never write about my standing with her at the supper table. Even if I had tried years afterwards to write such a trivial story, and even if, years later still, the freckled woman read a certain published story of mine and stopped at the words 'and stopped at the words…' she ought to know that before the story she was reading had come to an end there would have been nothing left of my landscape.)

You would not have met him then, I would probably not have told her, because on Saturday nights he was miles away from the parties that you and your friends went to. He still taught by day in a primary school south-east of the city, but at other times he kept to his room. He had read a little about Arthur Rimbaud and he wanted to disorder his senses. He had read somewhere too of a reassuring experiment in psychology: of people lying in warm baths with their eyes hooded and their ears stopped until they saw odd visions. The young man believed he might draw a map of a city beyond the reach of normal perception and only faintly recalling the city where he had lived his early life. The suburbs and districts in the new city would be sized and spaced according to the intensity of the poetic feeling he had once felt in this or that part of another Melbourne. Thus, a huge glowing core of what he called vivid imagery – with its centre where Fitzroy might have been – would spread outwards and drive to the farthest margins the shrivelled remains of places where a young man had once tried and failed to feel what was expected of him. For a few days, with his back to the window and the chocolate factory, he felt that he himself might have had the shape of a far-reaching city. What had once seemed the vaguest parts of him – his dreams and imaginings – were the hub of its intricate network, and he only had to shrug his shoulders or wag his fingers to upset the tiny mountains or to stop the trickle of sea at its edges. But before he could find the words for his city he had to defend it against the people from the Fitzroy of the former city.

He had not been able to pass in and out of the kitchen downstairs without speaking to the woman who seemed the chief tenant of the house. (He was never sure which of the several men who drank with her every evening actually lived in the house.) He drank in his own room every night, but having no refrigerator he was forced to keep flagons of cheap wine instead of the beer he preferred. On Melbourne Cup eve the woman climbed the stairs and called out to him to come down and be sociable. The young man sat in the kitchen with the woman and her men-friends and accepted their beer. When they asked him what he did for a living he said he was a teacher by day and a writer in the evening. They became uneasy, and he wondered which part of his answer had not convinced them. He said he had moved to their suburb to be among real people. They sat and looked at him. He thought they might have resented his coming empty-handed to drink with them, so he climbed up to his room to bring back what he called his grog. When the woman saw his flagon of hock she ordered him to get it out of her house that minute. Paint was what she called it. No one, she said, had ever insulted her by bringing paint like that into her house before. He explained that he only drank wine because he had no fridge for beer. She wanted to know why he hadn't asked to keep his beer in her own perfectly good fridge in the kitchen.

He took the wine outside and poured it down the gully-trap. One of the men told the woman to take it easy and offered the young man more beer, and he stayed drinking with them until after midnight. But from that day he could no longer write in Fitzroy. For two weeks he went on drinking wine – taking his flagon to work each morning in his bag in case the woman broke into his room and searched it while he was out. But each night instead of working on his landscape he lay with his ear to the floor trying to hear what was being said in the kitchen. He no longer walked through the kitchen to the toilet in the backyard but urinated into a bottle and poured it out of the window onto a patch of weeds. But he began to believe that the woman in the kitchen could hear his water splashing on the ground in the lulls of the television.

He had heard of a few people who lived in rooms above warehouses and shops in the city itself, in the central business district. If he could have found such a room he would have moved there at once. He wanted a room without windows if possible and with a door that he could enter and leave through unseen by any other human being. He saw the central city as a blank space from which the true patterns of the suburbs would be visible; he compared it to the centre of some spiral galaxy; he wanted to hide there and begin a new study of his landscape. He imagined himself as crouching at night on the floor in front of his pages – white pages in a dark room in a city white with lights in the darkness of the universe – having given up desk and chair because they brought his eyes to a height that might have shown him some unwanted sight from outside.

He had to settle for a block of flats about a mile

from the city, in St Kilda Road. Although he knew nothing of architecture, the outside of the building recalled something he could only have seen in the American films of his childhood (before he had stopped watching films for fear of their intruding on his landscape).

St Kilda Road could hardly have been called a suburb, and most of his windows overlooked the elms and Moreton Bay figs of Fawkner Park, so he allowed himself during his first weeks there to look occasionally around the edges of his drawn blinds. The weekly rent was half his teacher's salary and he could not afford furniture. He slept on an inflatable mattress on the floor and ate his meals (milk, boiled eggs, bananas and oatmeal) standing at the sink. Walking in each day from St Kilda Road, into the vaguely Californian building and then further in again to his bare rooms, he began to form a new notion of his landscape. He thought of it as lying within himself – within some broad but invisible zone composed of his memories (which were mostly memories of dreams). If he could begin some fresh pages, he thought, describing first a view of himself from twenty years earlier when he had dreamed in detail of the scenery that would surround him twenty years later, then he might create a horizon that was clearly within his reach.

He began to write, expecting to recall some of his earliest dreams of landscapes. He recalled clearly the actual places where he had dreamed – a patch of gritty soil overhung by a lilac bush with leaves sombre-green and shaped like the spades on his mother's playing cards; a back veranda where the cement was so old that he prised out easily with his fingers the chips of stone called blue metal and fitted them back loosely into their sockets. He recalled the mood that he had dreamed in – the taste of a lilac leaf on his tongue or the feel of a blue metal chip dropped into his trousers would make him want to weep with rage because they told him nothing and yet he had folded the leaf under his tongue and gripped the stone between his legs because the leaf and the stone had seemed to promise him something precious from a world more solid than his own thoughts. He recalled the weather he had most often dreamed in – the afternoons in late summer when huge domed thunder-clouds arrived from inland and his father's hens flopped under the tamarisks with their beaks gaping and the loudest sound in the silence before the storm came from some radio in a house over the back fence giving out the faint and rhythmic thumping that he privately called Great Plains music because it might have come from the loneliest district in the farthest country on earth. He recalled all of these things and wrote about them, but when he tried to recall the places he had dreamed of as a child he found himself looking into the same blankness that had so often crept into his landscapes.

Perhaps, the young man thought, the child's landscapes were out of sight because the man trying to see them was in the very spot where the landscapes should have been – standing in place of the man the child had dreamed about. If that was so, then whenever the man had failed (in the past year) to see his landscape clearly he had been standing in the very places that he should have been dreaming about. He had been trying to write about places that he himself could never write about: places that must wait until some undreamed-of man came across them quite by chance.

He could never recall (he would probably never have time to tell the freckled woman) the month or even the year when he had first noticed people from the outer suburbs finding their way into the inner parts of Melbourne. Perhaps in his own confused way he had been aware years beforehand of the prevailing mood of the late 1960s. Perhaps, blundering into Fitzroy in 1960 with his flagons of sickly hock and sherry, he had been something of a pioneer. He might even have scribbled somewhere in his notes of those days a phrase that came into vogue much later: he might have written that he wanted to explore *inner space*. But if he had wanted to establish any of these claims he left it too late. While he was writing the hundreds of pages of notes for a novel about his childhood he hardly noticed that what he had thought was the fixed shape of Melbourne was changing. The inner suburbs, the slums that he had wanted to walk through as a solitary writer waiting for his true city to appear to him – the shabby houses were here and there occupied by teachers and lecturers and what were called business and professional couples. On his walks through suburbs where he had once felt safely alone and far from anyone who might one day read his fiction (and perhaps then confuse the inner suburbs with his private landscape) he saw the trails and outposts of the people who would soon be called trendies and who were going to change their surroundings without reading his or anyone else's fiction. After he had been inside a few of the houses of these people and heard their talk and sipped their wine, he realised that the man who had dreamed vaguely of a landscape somehow appearing within the hollow spaces in Melbourne was now a vague figure in the remotest of landscapes.

At about this time he married and had to decide where in all of Melbourne he would buy a house. Being one of a married couple he found himself invited into still more of the terrace houses and he saw more clearly how the people in them had shaped their surroundings to suit themselves. On summer nights, sitting on seats made from railway sleepers in backyards paved with bluestone and planted with gum saplings, he heard from couples who had bought miners' cottages or disused hotels and churches in the decayed towns between Ballarat and Bendigo. These people talked of restoration and heritage and boasted of tracing back their family trees to great-grandfathers who had dug on the goldfields.

At that time he was still trying to finish his first novel before he reached the age of thirty. It was the novel of his childhood. He had been born in a northern suburb of Melbourne. His parents had taken him inland to Bendigo at the age of five and moved back to Melbourne four years later. He had lived in Melbourne ever since, sometimes thinking of his own history as a kind of landscape. The foreground hardly mattered. It was too brightly lit, or he stood too close to it to wonder how else it might have been arranged. The background lay under a strange light that brought out surprising details in its surface; it was like a distant quarter of a wide plain picked out late in the afternoon by a single shaft of sunlight from a threatening sky. The middle ground was vague and obscure, as though a range of shadowy hills or even a dark gulf lay between the far, distant horizon-lands and the confusing foreground.

Living with his wife in a cream-brick block of flats in Brunswick and writing all Saturday and Sunday with his face to a large translucent rectangle of sealed venetian blinds, he saw himself confronting the map of Victoria. The Bendigo he wrote about – the Bendigo of twenty years before – was a miniscule patch of brightly lit land far out of his reach. Between Bendigo and Melbourne was something he felt himself forbidden to cross. No map-maker could have found a name or a sign for this blank middle-distance of his. But the more he wrote, the more he thought of it as something fixed not only in every map he imagined but in every view he took of his life.

Yet the people of the terrace houses were at ease in their landscapes. He never heard them talking of maps or wishing some writer of fiction would reveal to them what lay on the far side of some barrier blocking their vision. And whereas he refused to travel past the northern edge of Melbourne, and once had even refused to look at photographs his brother had taken of Castlemaine and Bendigo, those people dined on Saturday nights in restaurants in Chewton or Maldon and admired paintings and pottery in converted miners' cottages on Sunday afternoons and then drove easily home to Abbotsford or North Carlton, satisfied that they had looked all weekend deep into their own territory.

One Saturday night in 1970 he found himself the only beer-drinker among a group sampling wines from Victorian vineyards and talking of the grapes they themselves were planting in Central Victoria. He kept at his beer until he had to stumble to a far corner of the backyard and vomit into a bed of *hardenbergia*. Standing up afterwards, wiping the water from his eyes and hiding behind blue-gum leaves from the last few couples left on the lighted patio, he saw that the inner suburbs had become part of a far-reaching landscape such as he had once wanted to write about. The trees around him were part of a forest that had grown over Victoria while he had been hiding indoors. If it was not exactly a true forest it was still, for the people on the patio, the only landscape they needed: clumps of observed and imagined treetops linking their chosen suburbs with the treetops they saw or imagined in Gisborne and Castlemaine and further still to the north.

Soon afterwards he persuaded his wife to buy a house in the last place left for him, the only place that the dreamers of the new Victoria had disregarded. It was a mere clearing in their extensive forest although it had once seemed likely to spread for fifty miles and more around Melbourne. It was the narrow belt of newer suburbs where all the houses were said to look the same.

Now he wrote in a brick veneer house, in a side room whose window looked out towards the side window of another house with a few leaves and twigs between. His street was in a narrow valley. He assured himself that someone looking from the highest point in Carlton across the northern suburbs would see nothing of his insignificant hollow in the land. He had gone to earth. He had found for a hiding-place a clearing in the landscape of others, a real corner in an imaginary Victoria – unless the creators of the new landscape had already decreed that theirs alone was real and that the suburbs he had once avoided were now only imagined by a few young people too poor or too stupid to dream of the right places.

Writing in his side room and seldom going out of his valley, he tried not to think of himself as cut off from whatever wide spaces had once been ahead of him. In his notebooks he described a theory of time as a kind of space. He wrote about a universe moving constantly but erratically so that a man or a street or a suburb on a given day is separated by an incalculable distance from what might have seemed the same man or street or suburb on another day. He was not really interested in revolving planets or elliptical orbits. All he wanted was the scope for thinking of some unclaimed land around him. And for a few months he saw a long road, silvery like a snail's path, winding away from his desk and disappearing far back in the twilit wake of his native country where a man sat at his desk believing that time was space and that any unexceptional afternoon was a remote and desolate territory.

After his first novel had been written he would not show it to any publisher. He felt he did not deserve to be called a writer of fiction. In all the pages of his manuscript there was no description of the landscape he had always wanted to see. The chief consolation he got from the novel was that sometimes, talking to a man or women who might never read it, he could see between himself and that person an expanse of pages like the patchwork he had arranged around himself on the floor of his room while he put his manuscript in order. His novel was not itself a landscape but it marked out the space around him where a landscape could have been.

He made notes for a second novel – nearly a hundred pages of notes written on bright afternoons when he had pulled down the blind and stuck masking-tape around its edges. He wondered how he had ever considered himself a man of any city or suburb. Now he seemed almost defined by the long shapely sentences in the pages on his desk, by the strange varieties of sunlight in his shaded room, by the shifting patterns of shadows of foliage on his sealed blind.

Someone took pity on him and looked through his manuscripts and told a publisher about them. The publisher agreed to have them read. Much later the publisher and the man who had taken pity invited him to lunch in a restaurant in Bourke Street. When the meal was finished none of the three men wanted to stop drinking. They went on ordering bottles of port. They were still at their table drinking, alone in the restaurant, when the tables around them were being set for the evening meal. All afternoon the unpublished writer had been staring at the panels of coloured glass at the front of the restaurant. As a child he had peered every afternoon through coloured glass at the few people passing in his street. When he had written in his first novel about those afternoons, he had supposed that coloured glass was no longer used in houses and that his writing about it helped to establish the quaintness of his parents' rented house and the Edwardian tints of his childhood imaginings. But by the time his novel had been finished he had begun to notice coloured glass in the houses in the inner suburbs. And now in the fashionable restaurant at the centre of Melbourne the glass in the front windows seemed almost the same murky, clotted orange as the stuff he had looked through in Bendigo more than twenty years before.

He had already understood that the publisher did not want either of his novels, although both men at the table had claimed to be impressed by some of his writing. Now, however, he felt a surge of strength in himself. He put an arm around the publisher's shoulders and made the man look at the shapes of people passing in the street outside. He announced to the publisher that the prose of his mature period would be like the glass in front of them. Through its tints and textures the reader would see a world marvellously coloured and distorted.

The publisher emptied his last glass of port and paid the bill and led the writer outside onto the footpath. It was past five on a winter afternoon, yet the twilight seemed too bright for the writer after the hours he had spent on the other side of the glass. The crowd was moving too fast for him, and he could not focus his eyes on any face.

He stood, blinking and unsteady, against the glass panel of the restaurant with the publisher close beside him. People striding past left a little space around the two of them. The publisher told him slowly and distinctly that in his honest opinion the writer would never write anything publishable for so long as he avoided looking at the real world. He wanted to hear no more talk, the publisher said, of the writer's peeping at the world from behind drawn blinds. And by way of saying goodbye the publisher pointed a little east of north (which was exactly the direction of the writer's own suburb) and told him to spend every afternoon going from door to door in his suburb, introducing himself as a writer to every young woman who was at home alone, telling her he was looking for material for his next book of fiction, then having an affair with every one of the dozens who would volunteer, and finally urging each of the women to buy the book when it was published and to tell her friends to buy it.

Even if I could have been sure that I would never tell my story to the freckled woman, I would have left out of that story the advice from the drunken publisher. Yet I might have told the woman that when the president had said to me a few hours before the meeting that she had never dreamed a writer would be living in her own suburb and that the ladies of the committee would be very interested to know what I was writing about, I had suddenly decided it was time I spoke openly about myself and my writing to any woman who was interested. I had then told the president that after writing two novels I had now turned to the short story. I believed a story, five or ten thousand carefully chosen words, could describe better than a novel what I was trying to write about. The president had asked me again what I wrote about. I had told her I simply described the real world. Then she had asked me if any of my work had been published. I told her that my first story, *Sipping the Essence*, would almost certainly be published before I had finished with the committee; I had been putting the last touches to it when she phoned me.

Privately, to the freckled woman, I could say that I had been not quite honest with the president. I had hardly begun to write *Sipping the Essence*, although I could see it waiting for me like a wide landscape. Yet I was ready at last to write truthfully about my landscapes. I felt now like a man who for nearly twenty years had failed to keep his eyes open. The real world was by no means as simple and unlandscaped a place as I had once imagined. I could say more, I could say to her. I could even learn from her a little about the real world. But I preferred to speak with her alone. If she thought any others of the committee could overhear her she might be reluctant to reveal herself. This being so, I could imagine myself saying, I had better call at her front door on one of those afternoons that I usually gave up to writing.

As treasurer I could have invented any pretext for calling on her. But in the days after the first committee meeting I would have come to realise that seeing her alone could never achieve what I wanted. She knew, of course, that I was a writer; and the president's foolish words of introduction would have persuaded her that I was searching her suburb for characters in some work of fiction. I could have told her frankly at the supper table that all I wanted was to ask her what she thought the real world consisted of. But even then she might have thought I wanted her answer only for a passage of reported speech in a work of fiction.

I began to see, towards the end of the committee meeting (or I would have seen during the days that followed), the absurdity of talking to the freckled woman about the real world. However simply and earnestly I questioned her, she was not bound to answer truthfully. Believing that I was a certain kind of writer, she might say to me whatever she thought fit for a certain kind of fiction. Even if I persuaded her that nothing I wrote in future was likely to be published, the word 'fiction' alone would have made her own story seem, to her, too simple or even too complex for telling.

I understood then (or I would have understood later) what I should have understood years before, even before I first tried to write fiction: the simple fact that people speaking to one another or looking towards one another are thinking of how they might sound or appear in a work of fiction. I could never claim that any freckled woman had spoken truthfully to me about a real world. There was only one situation in which such a woman could be taken as speaking truthfully. If I were to write a work of fiction with a freckled woman as a character in it, then I, in the person of the narrator, might insert in the fiction such words as 'she answered truthfully, at last…'

Then I imagined myself (or I could have imagined myself) writing at last about the real world that the freckled woman would never describe to me. In the foreground of that world were the streets with prunus trees on their nature-strips and the houses with photinias and Japanese maples in their front gardens and camellias by their front porches. But somewhere among those streets, in the middle distance, was the house of the man who had been introduced to a committee of women as a writer of fiction. And what he was writing about, so the freckled woman saw, was a suburb very like her own. Someone very like herself appeared in its streets, perhaps freckled in surprising patterns on her breasts and thighs. And part of the man's story might be that woman's hearing from a man somewhat like himself a description of what he called his landscape.

But in the foreground of that landscape was a woman very like herself looking at what she took for the real world, with a man writing in its middle distance.

In the committee room, or wherever I was, I would have liked to accept this scheme because it seemed to mean that my landscape still existed and that it actually enclosed what I had once called the real world. (There was also the pleasant possibility that the freckled woman would approach me later with a cup of tea and a biscuit and ask me what sort of writer I was and where I found the subjects for my writing. In that case I was ready to tell her that I had foreseen someone like herself asking me that very question and my asking her in return what sort of character she was and what sort of fiction had given her that idea of herself.) If I could think about my landscape, then whenever I sat down to write a sentence of fiction I would seem to be extending still further the vistas of men like myself writing about women thinking about men writing.

Yet I could not have been finally satisfied with this – with the whole world for my landscape. At some time in my imagined future I would have wanted to see my landscape as a private place marked off from all others: a place that distinguished me as surely as a pattern of freckles could distinguish a woman.

There was such a place, although I did not recognise it for some years afterwards. By then it seemed less a landscape than the ending of the only fiction I could write. It was the space between myself and the nearest woman or man who seemed real to me.

SIPPING THE ESSENCE

Four of us were renting a unit of Orlando Holiday Flats at the end of a sandy track on the edge of Sorrento. None of us was much older than twenty and we were living away from home for the first time. Only two of us had cars, and we all had to share the one bedroom in the flat, but we talked often of bringing girls back to the place of an evening. And we planned to have a wild party on New Year's eve, the last day of the 1950s – of the decade that had seen us through our teens.

In the first week of our holiday we took to playing golf in the mornings and drinking beer in the afternoons. At six, when the hotels shut, we went back to our flat and sat around the portable record player, eating fish and chips and drinking more beer and trying to decide which dance to go to. At around nine o'clock one of us would announce that he was too drunk to go to any dance. This was the signal for us all to relax. Someone would turn up the record player and someone else would go to the fridge for another bottle. By midnight we would all be asleep, in singlets and underpants and socks, in our bunks that lacked for sheets because we hadn't bothered to bring any.

On New Year's Eve, though, we had to keep faith with ourselves. We played our usual early morning round of golf and drank as usual in the afternoon. But at dusk we plumped the cushions on our divan, straightened the blankets on our bunks, swept the floor, rinsed the stack of glasses in the sink, and wiped a damp rag around the toilet seat. Then we filled the fridge with beer and a variety of what we called ladies' drinks, and dressed in our best casual clothes.

It was agreed that we were going to the dance at the lifesavers' club. But at the last moment Kelvin Durkin said he needed a few hours' sleep to sober up for the party. Since he wasn't one of the car-owners he was allowed to go to his bunk. Then, when the engines of the two cars were already idling, I hung back. I had prepared a little speech to deliver to the man who was ready to drive me. I was going to say that I was still buggered from my twenty-seven holes of golf that morning; that I needed a little more alcohol to revive me; that I had better stay at the flat in any case to save Durkin from choking on his vomit if he happened to be sick in his bunk. But the two men at the wheels of their cars were not interested in any speeches from me. When I made no move to join them, they drove off into the dark tunnel of tea-tree scrub that was all I could see of the road to Sorrento.

I went to the fridge and chose not beer but a full bottle of a liqueur called gold wasser de Danzig. I turned off the record player and sprawled in my chair with the bottle at my elbow. I made sure that my face could not be seen through the open window. Then I held my glass up to the light and fished with my finger for the gold specks glinting in the liqueur.

According to the label on the bottle, the original recipe had called for real gold. I suspected I was drinking a poor imitation concocted by profiteers in some inner suburb of Melbourne, but it suited my mood to have motes of mysterious stuff drifting in my glass and to be linked to the burghers of old Danzig while beer bottles clanked unmusically in the darkness outside the fibro-cement holiday flats. I had been a regular drinker for only a few months, and although I was too timid to order anything but beer in crowded public bars I disliked the taste of it. In private I experimented with blends of spirits and soft drinks. If I could find a drink that I could swallow easily I was going to prepare it in the right proportion and take it in flasks to parties. I wanted to give my drink a colourful name and to compel my friends to accept me as a man with distinctive tastes. The gold wasser was my most recent experiment.

Snatches of laughter and music came to me from the other units of Orlando Holiday Flats. I turned off the light and sat drinking in the darkness. I would not have admitted it, but I was somewhat ashamed to be alone on that of all nights, with dances and parties all around me. And yet I did not want to be jammed against the wall of the crowded lifesavers' club or standing alone by the fridge in some flat filled with strangers. I wanted to take my pleasures in my own good time and in the places that suited me. Each afternoon when my three drinking companions left the beer garden and stumbled along the beach, trying to strike up conversations with girls, I stayed behind. I found a seat with a view of the sweep of Port Phillip Bay. I sat there and performed the exercise that I called 'holding Queensland up to the light'.

I believed in those days that I did not belong in Victoria. My peculiar hopes could only be fulfilled, I thought, in the far sunlight of Queensland which I knew – as yet – only from pictures in magazines. But I could enjoy in advance some of the pleasures of Queensland if I looked at Victoria from the right distance. And so I sat on the cliff-top at Sorrento while my mates inspected the beach. The distant arc of sand, closely speckled with the browned bodies of the girls I did not want to meet just yet; the far blurs of headlands above other beaches where other collections of girls were arranged; and behind me the close-set hills of Portsea, where the daughters of the wealthiest families of Melbourne sunned themselves by private pools in secluded gardens – all this belonged in my private Queensland so long as I did not walk down onto the sand and blunder among knots of bare legs and shoulders, and did not feel on my face the multiple gaze of hostile eyes, invisible behind dark discs of sunglasses. And at night when every car roaring through the scrub might have been carrying a couple towards some shadowy parking-spot in a dead-end street, I was able to contemplate without any unease the headlights dying away and the car-windows fogging up and lay-back seats being put to good use all over the Mornington Peninsula, even while I was falling asleep with only three drunken young men for company. I could do this because I believed I was destined to enjoy in due course the refined and long-lasting pleasures of Queensland.

Sometimes, while the others lay dead-drunk in their bunks, I would get up quietly and take out from the bottom of my suitcase what I called my Queensland notebook and jot down the theme of one of the poems I was going to write when I found myself at last in the shade of some rain-forest a thousand miles from Melbourne. On New Year's eve 1959, alone in the darkness and thinking of the gold specks stirring faintly in the bottle beside me and the countless points of light trembling in the warm night air for miles around, I was ready to make another note in my book if I could do it without waking Durkin in his bunk.

But then the light flashed on and Kelvin Durkin was in the bedroom doorway grinning at me. He went to the toilet and I listened for the sound of vomiting, but only heard him urinating long and fitfully. He came out and opened a bottle of beer from the fridge and sat down beside me. He asked why I wasn't at a dance somewhere. There was less than the usual flippancy in his manner and I thought he might still be in danger of throwing up.

All three of the men who shared that flat with me I called, swallowing my dislike of the word, mates. But Durkin was the only one I had ever tried to talk seriously with. He called himself a funny-man and talked mostly banter, saying things that made me laugh aloud although they seemed hardly funny when I repeated them afterwards to others. But he was the only person I knew who read *Time* and who knew who Vladimir Nabokov was, and Jack Kerouac. Seeing him pale and listless, I tried to talk sense to him. I knew I was not quite as drunk as he was, but I made sure to slur my words a little and wave my arms about. I hoped he would realise I was confiding in him at last.

I told him first about the hot summer afternoons in Bendigo when I was seven or eight years old. In our shabby weatherboard house we had no fridge. (The Durkins would not have had a fridge in those days either, but I was not trying to tell him a tale of hardship.) When my brothers and

I came inside with our wrists and shins marbled by sweat and dust, there was usually nothing but tepid water from the kitchen tap to cool us. A wooden ice-chest stood in the kitchen with its legs resting in jar-lids of water to baffle the ants. Sometimes my mother kept a poley jug of cool water in the zinc-lined chamber of the ice-chest, but we were never allowed to get at it. Every time we opened the ice-chest door, she said, the hot air rushed in and melted the ice to nothing. So my brothers and I guzzled the insipid tap-water and took off our shirts and lay with our bare bellies pressed against the dusty linoleum in the laundry and told each other we were freezing.

But once in a while my mother brought home from the grocer's a little bottle of red cordial extract. She tumbled cupfuls of sugar into saucepans of boiling water and stirred in the extract and went on stirring and simmering the mixture. When it was cool she poured it carefully into empty lemonade bottles, one for each child. She warned us to ration it, because sugar cost money, and never to use more than a half-inch of cordial to a cup of water because she wouldn't be making any more for weeks. And then it was ours to drink whenever we felt like it.

My brothers' bottles were empty before a week was out. But when they had gulped down their last cup each of cordial-and-water my bottle was still half full. And I told them I could have made it last for the whole summer if I had wanted to.

And what was my secret? I asked Durkin this, rhetorically. It was our custom to put such questions to one another. It gave the listener the opportunity to inject some nonsense into a conversation that was threatening to become too serious. But Durkin had no answer for me. He only said it was high time our mates arrived home with their cars full of girls. And he went into the bedroom, muttering that he had to get dressed for the party.

I went on talking with my face to the bedroom door. I described how once, leaning over a saucepan of cordial while my mother stirred, I had asked what caused the strands of richness that swayed in the wake of the spoon and she, who never cared for one word more than another or troubled herself to explain to her children anything beyond the names and appearances of things, told me that I was looking at the essence.

And that was it, I announced to Durkin, or supposed I announced. That one word had done something to me. Afterwards, when I mixed my cordial with water and saw the molten filaments of darker red spiralling through the milder colour, I pronounced the word 'essence' with more pleasure than I got from tasting the liquid that was its nearest sensible equivalent.

I tried to recall what I had set out to demonstrate by telling Durkin this story. It had seemed, when I began, something important to both of us: something that would make us easier with each other. But then Durkin came out from the bedroom and sat in his chair. He was wearing what I knew was his best sports shirt, with huge onyx cufflinks. He had put on calfskin moccasins and clean socks. But he had no trousers on. He posed in his chair with one leg resting easily over the other, smartly dressed except for trousers. Below his shirt he wore only some fancy underpants of a style I hadn't known men could wear.

He poured himself more beer and took two cigars from his shirt pocket and gave me one. When we were smoking he leaned far back in his chair and said in one of his funny-man voices, 'You see me now, boy, in my fornicating costume. Run down the road like a good fellow and find our friends and tell them to hurry up with those girls they're procuring for us.'

I was supposed to say something appropriate, but I said nothing and barely smiled. I believed I saw what was behind his posing. At the same time I thought he might have been trying to tell me his own story. I hadn't got to the point of my story of the essence, but he might have understood why I had set out to tell it. And now he was repaying my confidence in the way that came most easily to him – by putting on one of his acts.

He might have been telling me first that we were friends – not just drinking mates but friends, although we would never use that embarrassing word between us. And he might have been telling me too that he knew why I was sitting without a girl on New Year's eve. He understood my solitariness (I understood him to be telling me) because he, like me, was unqualified with girls. But this was not so much because he or I was ignorant or afraid. Each of us needed a certain setting before he could be himself. And although Durkin had often scoffed at my talk of Queensland and called the Mornington Peninsula his own stamping ground and the sex capital of Australia, yet (he might have been saying) he and I might one day sit together beneath flowering hibiscus in a hotel garden in a place not unlike Queensland with the girls we had waited for.

I still wanted to make my position clear to Durkin: to show him it was rather more complex than his own. But just then we heard cars turning in to the driveway, and soon afterwards voices – girls' voices as well as men's. Durkin heard the voices too, but still sat trouserless in his chair.

I tried to drag him towards the bedroom (and hated touching his body – even through his shirt; I thought of someone having watched us through the window for the past half-hour and now deciding that we were linked by an unnatural bond). He lay back and grinned at me and asked me what was I frightened of. I stumbled across the kitchen to keep the visitors at bay but the back door opened before I got my hand to it. Three girls stood blinking in the light. I felt myself smiling foolishly and trying to say something about the drunk who had fallen out of his trousers and hoping the girls were too innocent to have heard of homosexuality. The girls looked at each other and then at the two men behind them. I looked back over my shoulder and saw, of course, that Durkin had disappeared from the lounge room.

When the girls stepped into the big bare room they seemed to bunch together a little. One of them laughed aloud and the others made mild jeering noises. The men who had brought them asked me accusingly why the party had broken up so early, but I was too confused to think of a smart answer. I stood in the middle of the room feeling ashamed that three obliging girls had been shabbily tricked. And I couldn't look any of them in the eye for fear that two of them had already been paired off with my flatmates so that one girl now realised she had been brought there for a man who couldn't go out and win a female for himself.

Something like that had apparently happened. The two established couples sat down beside the record player while the unattached girl took the chair that I had been sitting in all evening. Durkin's empty chair was beside her but I chose not to sit in it. To flop down close to her and lay claim to her so soon was unseemly, I thought. I had to persuade her first that there was something special about me and about our meeting by chance in the last hours of the decade. So I sat on the floor at a decent distance from her and did what I always did when something important had to be explained – drank resolutely and talked too rapidly to be interrupted.

Whatever I began to say to her was inspired by my having read not long before that August Strindberg had begun his courtship of one of his wives by talking continuously to her for three hours on the subject of himself. The girl sat comfortably and listened, but after a few minutes Durkin strode out – properly dressed – from the bedroom, pushed the empty chair against her own, and sat down and asked her name.

She was Carolyn, she said, and she would like to talk to him but she happened at the moment to be very interested in what his friend on the floor had to say.

Durkin told her that I was no friend of his. I was an escaped lunatic who thought he was living in Queensland and who wandered around the Mornington Peninsula gate-crashing parties and preaching that Australia could only be saved by drinking liqueurs instead of beer and reading poetry instead of watching television.

This was meant to start one of the exchanges of nonsense that we called in those days our routines. We fell into them on the golf course and in hotels or alone together late at night, always feeling we deserved an audience of at least two intelligent young women to appreciate our wit. Every Friday night in 1959 I had walked two miles across the suburbs from my rented bungalow to sit with Durkin in his kitchen while his parents and his sister shut themselves away with their television set. Durkin would try to interest me in his jazz records. I would read to him from *On the Road*. Durkin didn't exactly read books, but he noted all the reviews in *Time* and he finished as a duty the short fiction in every issue of *Esquire*, which he read from cover to cover. If I thought I was Jack Kerouac, seeing a poetic glow around my Queensland-California whenever I had drunk two glasses of my mixture, Durkin thought he was Mort Sahl or Shelley Berman, one of the comedians in vogue just then in the USA – someone who could sidle up, faultlessly dressed, to a microphone and murmur into it a few words that brought forth from a vast audience a loud but disciplined laughter. And on those nights, when we went into a routine in the Durkins' quiet back rooms, I would submit to being the straight man, the fall guy. I believed that Jack Kerouac's blend of poetry and craziness would one day take over the world and that my own talents would then be acknowledged. But for the time being the Kelvin Durkins, the men who studied the features and the fashion ads in *Esquire*, had something over us poets; we would have to search a little longer for the words to prove that the truth of the future lay with us.

And so, while the funny-man sat beside Carolyn with his face needlessly close to her and I crouched at their feet, I obliged Durkin by saying that yes, I had escaped from an asylum, but I had been wrongfully confined there for preaching that Jack Kerouac was the Messiah and I was his disciple.

I said this because Carolyn Whatever-her-name-was had turned towards me with her eyes screwed into what seemed a tolerant smile. A contest was about to take place between the elegantly dressed man who saw himself posed against the shapely hills of the Mornington Peninsula or the ivied mansions of New England and the blunt, awkward man who was already exploring in his poetry the tangled greenery of Queensland or crossing flat Iowa or dusty Nebraska. Carolyn could decide between us.

I took heart from my having decided that very evening that Durkin was not what he seemed; was perhaps no more experienced with women than I was. And swallowing more of my gold wasser I may even have looked forward not just to winning over Carolyn but to persuading Durkin at last to drop his pose, to recognise as I did the mad splendour underlying the surfaces of life and to form, with Carolyn and myself and some other woman that his new-found honesty would surely impress, a little band of spiritual adventurers – the first of a new kind of Australian fit for the 1960s.

Sometimes sitting at Carolyn's feet and sometimes pacing up and down past her chair and Durkin's, I announced that the time for pretending was over. The 1950s were done with, and the world was about to be revealed in its true colours. I had wasted my teenage years worrying about the millions of Communist Chinese in their blue-grey costumes who might have overrun Australia, or the men in dark suits and grey hats who conferred in Washington or London and might have saved us by dropping hydrogen bombs on Peking and Moscow. The men who were going to save us in the 1960s would wear quite different colours. They would pose for the dust-jackets of their books in open-necked plait-patterned shirts. One such man had already travelled across North America and discovered in its landscapes the poetry that had been overlooked for so long and then written a best-selling book about his time on the road. Wonders were waiting to be discovered in Australia too by discerning travellers who would make pilgrimages across the orange-yellow expanse between its capital cities. These wonders, though, were only visible to those who saw as poets saw.

I had trained myself to see in this fashion I said. Durkin as yet had had only occasional glimmerings of revelation. Carolyn, to judge from the look of intelligent curiosity on her face, was eager to learn from me. I was, of course, prepared to teach her. I had seen wonders already that night, sitting alone with a glass in my hand and observing the flashing of the tropical sun on golden fruit in the poetic orchards of Queensland.

At that point I filled my glass with the liqueur and held it in front of me. I told the girl there were specks of pure gold swirling in it and invited her to study them. She leaned back and laughed and told me to fish out some of the marvellous stuff so she could sample the taste of poetry. I dipped a finger in the glass but I was bothered to think of holding my sticky finger up to her delicate mouth, if that was what she expected of me. I was stirring my drink a little and pretending the gold was too elusive for me when Kelvin Durkin snatched the glass and tossed down a mouthful. He affected a fit of coughing and held his stomach and pulled faces. Carolyn laughed again.

I went on explaining my theories to Carolyn with Durkin interrupting me to tell her about George Shearing or Dave Brubeck and, when he thought I was outdoing him, about a story by John O'Hara that he had read in *Esquire* and claimed he could never forget. Not long before midnight someone spoke of the kissing to be done when the New Year came in. I slipped out of the room soon afterwards and walked towards the beach. I did not want to be forced to kiss Carolyn or any woman just then. Mere kissing seemed unworthy at such a momentous point in my life. I wanted to hear the sound of the sea against some jagged cape of Queensland. In any case I had not learned how to kiss a woman and I did not want Carolyn to discover this until I had said much more to her.

Long before I reached the sand I heard the laughing of parties waiting on the beach for the New Year. I feared some gang of strangers might drag me in among them if they saw me alone there at that time. I hid in a patch of scrub and waited for the fuss to end. After midnight, when the car-horns had stopped blaring around the town, I went back to Orlando Holiday Flats and told Carolyn and Durkin simply that the beginning of 1960 meant so much to me that I had had to experience it in private.

When the other two men got ready to take the three girls home they told Durkin and me we would not be going with them. Durkin ordered me to hold the car door open for Carolyn and give her a boy scout's salute. I got what I thought was a smile full of meaning from Carolyn just before Durkin manoeuvred her away from the car and towards the shadows. I lowered my eyes as he flung himself against her in what I told myself was a last desperate attempt to equal me in her eyes. But I looked back at the two of them too soon and saw the fingers of her two hands interlocked for a moment at his back, so that I could not tell myself confidently afterwards she had suffered grudgingly the attentions of a drunk.

But I was at least as drunk as Durkin and proportionately as daring, measured in my own units of bravery with females. While Carolyn was settling herself in the car I told her I had much more to say to her. She said she was leaving Sorrento next day but she gave me her phone number in Melbourne. I hurried into the bedroom repeating the number aloud. I tore aside the last few clean socks and underpants in my suitcase and wrote Carolyn's phone number on the front cover of my Queensland notebook.

I remember little else from those first hours of the new decade. It seems that Durkin and I, full of bravado after entertaining girls at our flat, stayed up to drink until daybreak. At some hour when the sky was pale I leaned against a fence outside and vomited over and over. I would surely have tried to sneak away to hide my condition from

Durkin, for we had often argued over who was the better drinker. But I recall his standing beside me, cheering each of my spasms and pretending to see grains of gold in the puddles I made.

Durkin and I met no more girls at Sorrento that summer. In Melbourne after our holiday neither of us mentioned Carolyn, but I was sure he would have broken into my suitcase at Sorrento to learn her phone number. Yet even though I had no girl friend, even though Carolyn was the only young woman I had spoken to for months past, and even though I thought often of her smiling patiently at me while Durkin was trying to howl me down on New Year's eve, nevertheless I was reluctant to phone her. I wanted urgently to explain myself to a young woman, but I feared what seemed to me an absurd ritual of the suburbs I had grown up in – asking a woman out. Those very words made me squirm whenever I heard them from the girls in my office. 'And then he rang her up and asked her out…' 'And who was she going out with before him?'

Reading Kerouac had suggested a better way of approaching a woman than by asking her to dress in her best clothes and sit silently with me through some dreary film. I foresaw myself confronting my sort of woman on the outskirts of Bundaberg or Rockhampton. My hair would still be damp from the storms that had broken over me on the slopes of the Great Divide. There would be no false gentility between us – no asking out to some place ordained by society as more fitting than the hotel or the roadside cafe where we had first met. And instead of our staring at scenes devised by screenwriters whose only journey had been from Brooklyn to Los Angeles by aeroplane, she could hear from me how I had walked and hitch-hiked through the huge horizons of the Riverina and the steamy valleys of the Northern Rivers of New South Wales.

The Queensland woman and I would not be together for long. Even in my giddiest daydreams I knew it was preposterous to think of a young woman sharing the dirt of camping grounds with me or climbing beside me on to the dusty tray of a farmer's truck. And I would probably ask no more of her than to listen to my story and lean her head against my shoulder at certain points of that long, strange narrative. I would prefer not to kiss her. I had read *On the Road*, as I thought, shrewdly and observed that the narrator was by no means easy with women. The reckless, ecstatic man of the roads was, I believed, a man with a secret not unlike my own. When he glimpsed a certain girl through a windscreen and saw in her face all the poetry of the South Platte Valley, he was not just regretting that his road was about to take him away from her for ever; he knew that even if had flung open the car door and stepped into the street of whichever little prairie town it was and claimed the girl, he would have got from his night with her nothing to equal his mood as the miles of prairie drifting towards him slowly effaced the image of one more of the women he had done nothing about.

At least once every day I walked into a phone booth to ring Carolyn and then thought of a reason against it. One reason was that I had no car. I used to take pride in arriving at parties on foot or in a taxi. What I called my philosophy of life would have required me to spend hours on suburban trains with Carolyn if we went out together to conventional places. (I had learned that the prefix of her phone number belonged to a bayside district fifteen miles from my own suburb.) Another reason was my believing that every young woman of the suburbs was quietly hoping to marry the man she was going out with. It seemed unfair to ask Carolyn out when I was planning to leave my clerk's job in the public service some time in 1960 and to hitch-hike up and down the eastern States of Australia for the rest of my life, working sometimes as a labourer and writing an endless poem about my travels.

It was still only mid-February, but one night I sat staring at the map of Carolyn's suburb, moving my finger up and down the long straight lines of its streets and wondering where exactly was the site of my lost happiness: the home of the only woman in Melbourne who had listened to me and understood. I visited Durkin that night, hoping to forget my trouble, but he told me he had just bought a secondhand Volkswagen because his social life was blossoming.

I rang Carolyn next morning. I could not bear to think of her with her fingers once again clasped comfortably against Durkin's fashionable sports-shirt, or having to listen to his wisecracks. Telling me about his so-called social life, Durkin had had all the swagger of a man who learned the techniques of courtship from oral folklore instead of literature. I could never have given myself up to my travels if I had yielded a sweet-faced, intelligent young woman to a man who thought John O'Hara the greatest living American writer; if I had allowed Carolyn for the rest of her life to believe that there was only one Australia, a land peopled by glib Durkins, and that the eccentric poets and wanderers she sometimes heard rumours about were lost in a wilderness unconnected with the real world.

Carolyn was the first woman I had asked out, and I carefully rehearsed what I would say to her. I believed in those days that every unmarried female in Melbourne aged between fifteen and thirty had a regular boy friend who took her out on every Friday and Saturday night of the year and went driving with her on every Sunday, but that perhaps one in every thousand of those females kept an occasional Friday night free in the hope that some enterprising solitary male would dare to pit himself against her regular escort. Such a female (and I hoped Carolyn was one) would go out for a few weeks with both suitors before deciding between them. I therefore tried to make matters easier for Carolyn by asking to see her on a Friday night three weeks ahead.

She surprised me by saying she preferred to see me on a Saturday rather than a Friday. And she told me she had heard from my comedian friend, Kelvin Durkin, who had phoned her a week or two earlier. She answered my unspoken question by saying he had asked her out but she had been too busy to see him. And when I told her I had no car she said she had just bought a new Morris Minor that could take the two of us wherever I wanted to go. I had decided to adopt a conventional pose at first. And so, as much as I disliked having to sit silently with her in a cinema, I asked her to go with me to a Russian film: *The Idiot: Part One.*

On the night after my phonecall I visited Durkin again. I took with me a flask of gin mixed with lemon cordial. That was one night when I felt no need to counter his quips. While he talked about a wild party he had lately been to and the car he was going to buy, I sat quietly and congratulated myself because Carolyn had decided for me against that shallow man. I saw my victory over him as a blow for Jack Kerouac against Mort Sahl; for serious literature against the spurious art-form of jazz; for those aware of the essences of things against those preoccupied with appearances.

When the gleaming white Morris Minor stopped at the corner of my street and Carolyn leaned across and opened the passenger door, I told myself I was a bastard. I had tricked a good-natured girl from a respectable family into spending Saturday night with a man who wanted to tell her that the only good in life was poetic pleasure before he fled to the back roads of Queensland and mocked the conventional domestic life she was dreaming of. But sitting beside her and watching her I began to see quite a different future for us both.

She was wearing a caramel-coloured dress or suit that she must have carefully arranged when she first sat behind the steering wheel. The fabric fell away in graceful folds from her elbows and I guessed it might have cost her a week's wages. (I was wearing my only suit, bought three years before.) Her face was carefully made up. Whenever she had to concentrate on her driving I looked sideways at the faultless texture of her cheeks and the shiny spicules of silver under her eyebrows and saw into a part of Australia I had scarcely thought about.

I saw into ten thousand bathrooms all over Melbourne in the hot, slack hours of Saturday afternoon when young women were getting ready to go out with their regular boy friends. And then I saw thousands of arid cricket grounds or golf courses, or crowded hotel bars, or the betting ring at Flemington or Moonee Valley, where the young men of Melbourne were struggling in the heat for some small achievement to mark them out from their kind. I saw the young men threatened more often than not by failure but each one consoling himself by thinking for a moment of a bathroom where a young woman, loosely draped in her house-coat (if that was what an Australian woman called her negligee), peered into a mirror still steamy from her shower and plucked at her eyebrows or smeared soft stuff into her face, preparing for the evening ahead.

Seeing the half-witted young men of Melbourne enjoying this privilege would normally have irritated me, and for the young women I would have felt only a generalised sympathy that they should work so laboriously for such unworthy objects. But now I considered myself one of the privileged young men.

I looked once more at Carolyn – at her white, frail wrists and the interesting shapes of her ear and throat – and wondered how many hours she had spent that day ironing her slip or washing her hair to make it so fluffy. While she had been in her bathroom I was at my desk scribbling notes for my journey northwards. And then I dared to ask myself the question that might change my life: what if I did not go to Queensland?

At that moment we were in Dandenong Road, approaching St Kilda Junction. Before we had passed under the last plane trees near Princes Bridge, I had already foreseen myself staying in Melbourne and writing an epic poem set in an imagined Queensland (where much stranger places than Banana or Barcaldine might have been waiting for me); going out with Carolyn every night for a year; proposing marriage, becoming engaged, marrying, and making our home in a south-eastern suburb.

For days beforehand I had made notes of what I would talk about with Carolyn. I had estimated that she would go out with me perhaps four times before she discovered that I belonged in another country and could not be expected to delay much longer in hers. I had therefore planned a long argument in four parts. I thought of it as like one of Cicero's courtroom orations; it would be delivered in parts over the weeks that I was with her, but each part would build on what had gone before so that the four would make up a compelling whole. Each week I would talk about the life and work of a writer I greatly admired. The four writers in order were Raymond Roussel, Mikhail Artsybasheff, Leonid Andreev, and Jack Kerouac.

My deciding not to go to Queensland forced me to change my argument at short notice. I had planned to explain to her that I was a dedicated nihilist, to prepare her for my disappearing into the back roads of the north. But now, to prepare her to be the wife of a poet, I talked to her on our first night out about Frank Wedekind.

I began talking to her while she looked for a parking place in the city. I went on talking before the film began, then during the interval, and afterwards in a coffee lounge. I told her how Wedekind had lived for years as a bohemian, satirising the government and the middle classes of his day and having affairs with dancers and actresses in the cabarets where his early works were performed, but had later married and seemed to adopt a conventional way of life. In fact, though, Wedekind had only changed his tactics and not his beliefs when he married. Wedekind the husband still ridiculed fools and hypocrites, but now he attacked society from a secure position within it.

In telling all this to Carolyn I avoided the words 'marriage' and 'affair' and used in their place abstractions such as 'conventional morality' and 'loose living'. I believed that one of the strictest taboos of my society prevented me from using the word 'marriage' in the presence of the girl I was going out with. I believed that the customs of my society forbade young people from becoming serious, as the phrase had it, until they had gone out together for so long that their friends began making pointed remarks to them. What happened next I was not sure of; I supposed that the man summed up, late one evening, the reasons why the two of them ought to marry and at last revealed that he had been in love with the woman since their first meeting.

And something else I did not explain to Carolyn, but for rather different reasons, was that Wedekind had believed the worst hypocrisy of the middle classes was their refusing to acknowledge frankly the chief good in life: what he called unfeigned sensual pleasure.

Carolyn heard me out patiently until we were parked in my street after midnight. Then, with no warning that I could see, she pressed herself against me and put her face up to mine so that I was spared what had been bothering me all night: the decision whether I should try to kiss her after only our first night out together (and so prove myself no different from Durkin, who had grabbed at her body only hours after meeting her at Sorrento).

In the week after that Saturday I thought continually of the hour I had spent in the car with Carolyn, kissing her and telling myself that I need never leave Victoria after all. Yet I was not quite the fool I might have been; or, at least, I warned myself not to appear to Carolyn and Durkin as a fool. I wanted to keep on thinking of a place like Queensland and talking about it occasionally. I knew I must not seem to have dreamed of my travels only because I had never had a girl friend, and to have turned back from the north just because a young kindergarten teacher from a bayside suburb had taught me how to kiss. On the Saturday afternoon before my second outing with Carolyn I sat for three hours at my desk trying to explain in the pages of my notebook that even when Carolyn and I were busy in her car with one of our prolonged kisses, and even when we were finally husband and wife and enjoying unimaginable pleasures together, I would still see something richly coloured like Queensland that was not quite within my grasp.

On three successive Friday nights I visited Durkin and told him lightly that Carolyn had said such and such to me recently, or that my girl friend was interested in this or that. He asked me what he thought were witty questions: how Carolyn coped with two gear-sticks between the front seats of her car; whether it was Carolyn or myself who swerved at the last moment to avoid a child.

I let him talk. I no longer wanted to turn everything into the stuff of jokes, but I took care to laugh with him so that he could not accuse me of becoming absurdly serious about the woman he knew was my first girl friend. He urged me not to be satisfied with seeing Carolyn once a week. I should tidy my bungalow and buy a bedspread to cover my dirty blankets and some presentable mugs for serving coffee. Above all, I should pour disinfectant down my sink and stop using it as a urinal. And then, if Carolyn was any sort of woman, she would call on me regularly and minister to all my needs; she might even cook on my gas ring something more tasty than the porridge and sardines that I lived on.

On my fourth Saturday night with Carolyn I was ready to tell her about my own poetry after reaching the end of my talks about the literary giants who had inspired me. I had taken Durkin's advice and tidied my bungalow, but I had no thought of seducing her when I asked her to spend the following Friday night alone with me, just drinking and talking. And I trusted Carolyn to know this, since I had done no more than kiss her on our four nights together.

She told me it just wasn't possible at the moment for me to see her on any other night but Saturday. I panicked.

I forgot about Jack Kerouac and the roads of Queensland. I was a man of the suburbs of Melbourne, trying to hold on to his first steady girl friend. She told me I had been very sweet and she very much wanted to go on seeing me, but it so happened that on Friday nights – and sometimes on other nights as well – she saw another man, someone she had known for a long time before she met me at Sorrento.

I saw a man dressed like Kelvin Durkin, but far more sure of himself, steering a much larger car than Carolyn's Morris into a dead-end street beside a bushy park late at night. I saw him kissing Carolyn in ways I had still not yet learned, and perhaps putting his hand on those places I had so far made detours around.

Watching Carolyn calmly tap her cigarette into the ashtray of her car, I decided to leave for Queensland next morning. I was even composing the first lines of the letter she would receive from Tamworth or Lismore, after I had been a week on the road. Then, so that I could feel more intensely in years to come the pain of being a thousand miles from Melbourne, I demanded to know more about my rival. (I called him this, as though I wanted to duel with him for Carolyn's hand, but I had already privately yielded place to him.) I wanted to have a clearer image of the man I would think of while he put his hand over Carolyn's wristwatch and told her they could spend still another hour in his car and I tramped through the tropical rain towards the distant lights of Proserpine.

She said she had always believed in being frank with her boy friends, so I had better know that she had been seeing this other man for a year or so, even though he was married with two children. He had swept her off her feet when she first met him, but lately she had begun to think he was in no hurry to divorce his wife.

I sat for a long time at my desk that night. I had no doubt that I had been in love with Carolyn. I tried to persuade myself that losing a woman I had loved was an auspicious start to my career as poet of the lonely spaces of Australia. I began a poem set in my private Australia, but I ended by writing a letter to Carolyn telling her I could not see her again because our friendship was leading us nowhere. I said I would always be grateful to her for helping me to find my true bearings. I was sure now that I was a man of the roads of Queensland and if ever she wanted to find me in years to come, when she had learned at last the difference between poets and ordinary men, then she would have to set out for the north.

I called on Durkin during the week and said that Carolyn was making a fool of me. I told him a little about the married man. I was careful of my tone as I spoke. I put just enough concern into my voice to tell him, if he cared to understand, that I was a poor innocent fool like himself and in need of a friend to commiserate with me. I hoped he would put on one of his wailing jazz records and go to the fridge for a bottle and advise me to phone the bitch that very minute and to tell her to do what she liked with her married boy friend but to stop tormenting a serious-minded poet. If he had said something like that I would have responded by telling him all about my affair with Carolyn and quoting from the letter I had posted to her. I would have let him see that he and I were still what we had been at Sorrento – two solitary males on the fringe of a vast, baffling country.

But Durkin started to laugh one of his idiot-laughs. He told me I didn't have a worry in the world. I was going out with a woman who was fully experienced and qualified; she was even polishing up her technique on the nights when

I wasn't seeing her. Then I told him I had already written to her, saying I wouldn't be seeing her again. He told me he could hardly believe any man could be so stupid. I said he knew nothing about Carolyn; I had talked to her for hours and seen glimpses of a very different person from the frivolous woman he took her for. Durkin answered that I should have been looking for glimpses of something else about her instead of talking to her for so long. And he announced that he himself would be going out with her very soon.

Walking home that evening I wondered how I had ever thought of Durkin as a friend. Yet I wanted to keep visiting him. I wanted to learn how an ordinary Australian man who wrote no poems and never dreamed of Queensland could get what he wanted from a young woman. Already I saw Durkin and Carolyn trapped in a mere corner of a huge country that I was free to explore. But I decided that night not to leave for Queensland just yet. I could not rush away from Melbourne if Durkin was going to take my place with Carolyn. Even at that moment, in Durkin's suburb, the thought of the two of them together made me feel what I had thought I would not feel until I chanced to hear the word 'Melbourne' in the buzz of voices on some rainy evening in a hotel in the back streets of Home Hill. Suddenly I thought I might discover what I believed Jack Kerouac had discovered: the scope for endless journeys of exploration in what was supposed to be well-trodden territory. But the suburbs of Melbourne would be for me what the entire United States had been for Kerouac. Around me in the deserted streets the masses of trees and shrubs made a complex pattern of dark tunnels out of reach of the streetlights. There seemed space enough in Melbourne for a solitary to travel for years out of sight of those who huddled together. While Durkin and Carolyn clutched at one another in cars and loungerooms I could follow my winding routes all around them in the country they never saw.

I went home to my desk and my manuscripts and notebook. I sat down and tried to think of the first miles ahead of me. I was too stirred to write. I mixed a glass of gin and brandy and both lemon and raspberry cordial, dripping each as a tincture and watching the swirls of it subtly vary what was already a strange colour. I drank only enough to convince myself that never to touch or kiss Carolyn again was to claim all the young women of Queensland, and that to put the rest of the mixture away for another night was to take possession of them at last.

Durkin phoned Carolyn the next evening and within a month he was going out with her regularly – not just on Saturdays but on Fridays and on weeknights as well. I learned much later that Carolyn had asked him when he first phoned what on earth he meant by asking her out when he knew she was going out with me. Durkin told her that I had announced to all my friends that I was leaving for Queensland. In any case, he had said to her, I was much too serious and solemn to be hanging around a fun-loving woman like herself.

And then he had won her over with a phrase from the world that he thought he belonged in – the world of the coloured ads in *Esquire* or the PEOPLE page in *Time*. His exact words were, 'I want us to go out together *just for kicks*.'

I despised him for using that phrase. I believed he and his kind had stolen it from its rightful context. It belonged, I thought, to the language of the Beat Generation whose disciple I was still. While Kerouac and his soulmates were crossing and recrossing the heartland of the USA and trying to find the right words for their rich mixture of emotions, journalists and advertisers were already purloining and debasing the hard-won phrases of the Beats. Now Kelvin Durkin had presented himself to Carolyn as a man who knew better than I did the language of feeling.

I went on visiting Durkin each week, and for the first few months – while he and Carolyn really were doing things for kicks – I learned at last how two average people my own age conducted a steady relationship. I learned first of all that Carolyn's married friend had been dismissed very promptly. Durkin claimed to have ordered Carolyn to get rid of the bastard because he was only complicating her life. Durkin also claimed that Carolyn had been on the point of doing this anyway when she had told me about the man, and that she would have broken off with him at once if I had told her firmly to do so.

I expected to learn soon after this that Durkin and Carolyn, in pursuit of their kicks, had done lightly and easily what I called in my diary 'the ultimate'. Ten times a day I would call on my memories of the hours I had spent kissing Carolyn, and compose from such details as the quickening of her breath and the swishing noise of her stockinged legs being pressed together an imprecise image of her surrendering, as I put it, to Durkin. I wanted to imagine the scene clearly so that I could stand silent and knowing in any hotel bar in the far north while men talked of what they had done with women.

I wanted to take the news quite impassively when Durkin finally broke it to me. Before each of my visits I drank a long glass of my latest drink: equal parts of Bundaberg rum and lime cordial. And I went on sipping my mixture while Durkin told me about the parties and outings that kept him and Carolyn busy. But for nearly two months he insisted, in one of his funny voices, that despite all the whispered allegations the answer to the question being asked in a hundred saloon bars around Melbourne was in the negative: the red-blooded Kelvin Durkin and the lovely, passionate Carolyn Cottrell had so far done nothing they couldn't tell their mothers about.

On the night when he told me (as an aside in a story about his latest exhausting weekend) that he was not the same man who had last spoken to me, I was drinking beer. I had decided to force myself to like the taste of it. If I went to Queensland, or even if I lingered all my life around the hotels in the back streets of Melbourne, I had better not, I thought, be too conspicuously eccentric. Durkin told me, trying to sound weary, that nothing was ever what a man imagined it to be. I stared into my beer and tried to look as though I had known all along that he was pursuing the wrong goals. I even hoped he was going to renounce his pursuit of Carolyn and tell me he and I would leave together for the north within a week. And now that I could stomach a certain amount of beer I could see Durkin and myself sitting in terraced beer gardens, shielding our eyes against the dazzling blue Pacific with pots brimming with amber and telling one another that some other poor bastard was sitting just then beside Carolyn, while she drove her Morris through the drizzling Melbourne twilight, and waiting to learn that nothing was ever as a man imagined it to be.

But Durkin's reticence did not mean he was ready for Queensland. It was more a message to me announcing that he had gone so far beyond me it was pointless his describing the mysteries he and Carolyn celebrated together. I took his message humbly to heart. I still visited him each week and told him about the books I had read and poems I had written, but he only had to sigh and say that he had had another exhausting weekend with Carolyn and I would be reduced to staring into my beer and hoping he envied me one thing at least – that I never had to keep myself sober at weekends for the sake of some woman.

Although Durkin told me almost nothing about his sessions with Carolyn, he told me quite readily the story of Carolyn Cottrell in the years before she had turned up in our flat at Sorrento. Each week he told me some separate anecdote, usually with a name and a date. I pieced together a chronicle that astonished me, although I tried to hide my feelings from Durkin. In the years when Durkin and I had been hardly more than giggling schoolboys, Carolyn had had affairs such as I thought belonged only in novels. Just after her seventeenth birthday she had gone for a holiday to Queensland, to the so-called Gold Coast, determined to lose her virginity. She had met on her first night there a man willing to oblige her. For the next three years, while she travelled by day between her coastal suburb and the kindergarten teachers' training college (and could have been one of the demure-looking girls who took my eye each day in my railway carriage) Carolyn Cottrell had had never less than one and sometimes as many as three boy friends with the right to phone her at short notice and take her out. When she arrived at Orlando Holiday Flats on the last day of 1959 and listened patiently to me (who had never kissed a girl) and Durkin (who had kissed perhaps two or three), this quietly spoken young woman, the exact contemporary of Durkin and myself, had been intimate with seven or eight men. (The tally was Durkin's, perhaps kept vague from his loyalty to Carolyn or perhaps an accurate report of Carolyn's own vague recollections.)

Durkins' information often came to me with little bonuses: an anecdote would have a moral obviously meant for his solitary male friend; or he would pass on to me some brief advice sent openly from Carolyn herself. So it was that I learned how Carolyn still felt, as she put it, a little bit responsible for me. She had thought me (and Durkin tried not to sound too patronising when he reported this) by no means inept or backward as a boy friend. She would have me know that she had been engaged to be married for three months to a man who had been not much more forward with her than I had been in our four weeks together. In the long catalogue of her boy friends, those she had slept with were never the ones she had felt anything for. And if I hadn't gone all peculiar (her words to describe my change of heart when I had learned about her married friend) she and I might have got on very well together.

Usually I resented these moral tidbits that Durkin passed on to me. I could never hear them without imagining the moments when Carolyn and Durkin discussed me, which they seemed to do pretty often. I saw the two of them side by side in bed. (It was one more of Durkin's strokes of luck that a married friend of Carolyn's gave her the use at weekends of a holiday house at Somers.) While the morning light silvered the water of Westernport beyond their bedroom windows, they each spared a thought for the poor hermit waking up just then in his backyard bungalow with only his empty bottles for company. Carolyn, naked and languid, reminded herself to take me along with the two of them to their next party and Kelvin, reaching for a cigarette, made a note to pass on to me as a useful tip for the future his discovery that early morning was an excellent time for sexual activity. I, imagining the scene, could only resolve to keep an impassive face when Durkin next told me about one of his tiring weekends at the beach.

Sometimes I willingly tormented myself. I would

imagine the morning when Carolyn confided, not unkindly, to an incredulous Durkin that I had not even laid a hand on her breasts in our time together. Sometimes, when Durkin asked how my sex life was going (and I knew he would report my answer back to Carolyn), I told him exaggerated stories of how much I was drinking at weekends and how long it was since I had even spoken to a girl.

I was not trying to humiliate myself in their eyes. There were times when I felt far superior to Carolyn and Durkin. When I had written a few lines of poetry that seemed worthy of publication, and I was in the early stage of drunkenness before my thoughts shrank to nothing, I saw myself as a man who deliberately deprived himself of Durkinesque pleasures so that he could look into things as Kelvin and Carolyn could never look again. I was now thinking of a Queensland that I could visit without leaving my desk. And even when I could hardly see the outline of such a place, I thought that Carolyn and Durkin probably saw me already as living in a strange, metaphorical Queensland.

Sometimes I invited Durkin to my bungalow of a weeknight. I gave as my excuse that he could drink more freely away from his mother and sister, but in fact I wanted him to see for himself and to report back to Carolyn that my life was as cheerless as I described it. I poured him long glasses of beer from bottles kept in buckets of crushed ice on the floor (I had no fridge in my bungalow) and waited for the talk to veer towards what was most on our minds in the almost-bare room: my solitary condition.

Even drunk on tepid beer we could not talk honestly. Our messages for one another were obliquely worded, or hidden behind childish mimes and antics. At a certain point in the evening Durkin would make a show of examining the tangle of blankets on my bed and finding evidence that a man and a woman had shared it not long before. I would point out what I claimed were signs that a young adult male had recently masturbated there, using a heap of pillows as a surrogate woman and seeing the furthest wrinkles in his blankets as the coastal hills of the Mornington Peninsula. Durkin would then tidy the bedclothes and demonstrate what I ought to do on the bed as soon as I had come to my senses and invited home one of the thousands of girls in Melbourne who were waiting every night by their telephones as anxious to meet a new man as Carolyn had been at Sorrento. Then, if I was drunk enough, I would argue that all those women must have once been to the Gold Coast of Queensland as Carolyn had been and must have learned there too much for a beginner like myself. And if I saw that he was drunk enough I would announce that my last hope was his sixteen-year-old sister. Had he guarded her honour? I would shout at him. Could he keep her from setting out towards the Gold Coast and deliver her to me instead? I would treat her honourably and do no more than read my poems to her until our wedding night and be a fine, boozy brother-in-law to him for the rest of our lives.

When his sister was mentioned he would offer to fight me, and we would grapple on the floor until our buckets of bottles were in danger. Whenever I was on top of him and had him by the throat I boasted that my strength came from my celibate way of life. But whenever he had me pinned to the floor I begged him to procure me his sister or any girl who would give me a strength like his.

One night in September when a fine rain had been falling for hours on my suburb, Durkin started talking about the summer holidays to come. He said he needed a break from Carolyn; he wanted to enjoy the life of a single man again.

He lolled in my only armchair, with one hand curled around his glass and the other hand cupping his privates. He had the look of a man so glutted with bodily pleasures that the only enjoyment left for him was the pretence of being a solitary planner of journeys as I was. He even talked of staying with me again for a week at Sorrento and going to dances to look for girls or just playing golf and drinking.

I had a better plan in mind, although I could not tell him for fear of being misunderstood. He and I would go back to Orlando Holiday Flats, just the two of us at first. But I was not going to try myself with girls while he watched me critically. We would invite Carolyn to stay for a few days. She and Durkin would have the bedroom, of course, and I would sleep on the divan in the main room. (I knew that this scheme was preposterous. On the few occasions when I had seen Carolyn after she took up with Durkin, she had behaved as though he was courting her in my fashion. Once, when Durkin mentioned their staying at Somers, she had told me pointedly that their married friends had been with them for the whole weekend.)

After Durkin had gone home on that rainy night I imagined with great care the first night at Sorrento after Carolyn would have joined us. I had played golf with Durkin in the morning and drunk with him in the afternoon (not failing to notice that for once he refused to keep pace with me). After tea in the flat I politely excused myself and took out my poetry folder and wrote and drank steadily. When they suggested going to a dance I thanked them and said I was much too busy. When they sat themselves on either side of me and asked wasn't I being a little childish, burying my nose in my writing when they could have driven me to any dance on the Peninsula and arranged a little party for four in the flat afterwards, I made no sweeping declarations but simply repeated that I had other things to do. Later in the evening I closed my folder and poured instead of my usual beer a mixture of strangely coloured liqueurs blended for the occasion. Towards midnight Carolyn and Kelvin exchanged a glance that I seemed not to notice. Then, when the woman who hadn't lived up to my expectations and the man who had taken advantage of my confidences looked out for the last time before they closed their bedroom door and saw me with my glass to the light, staring at something in my peculiar mixture, I was content.

I was no voyeur or Peeping Tom. I was as anxious as they to have their bedroom door shut firmly. If any sound had reached me from their side of the wall I would have squeaked my mattress or cleared my throat to cover it. And in the hour before sunrise when I woke to hear Carolyn's bare feet on my floor as she passed on the way back from the bathroom, and when I heard her pause in the middle of my room and step very quietly towards my bed, and I knew she was standing only a little way from me in the grey half-light, shivering slightly in her thin shortie pyjamas, looking down on me and ready, if I opened my eyes, to sit on the edge of my bed and discuss seriously what she would have called my emotional problem, even then I went on breathing easily and kept my eyes closed until she understood that between the two of us was a broad zone of dreams she knew nothing about, and she turned and went back to her bed.

But a week later Durkin arrived at my door with an armful of bottles to tell me it was all off between him and Carolyn. He gave me no simple reason. But late that night he told me Carolyn took things too seriously instead of just looking for kicks. Still later he told me it was my turn now; I had better ring Carolyn and take her out and read poetry to her, since that was probably what she had wanted all along.

I described quite a different plan. Durkin and I could take our annual holidays together and spend Christmas and the New Year wandering through northern New South Wales and parts of Queensland. On sweltering afternoons we would sit together in beer gardens and plan a new future for ourselves. That was as much as I told him. I kept to myself my hope of hearing from him on those afternoons all the details that a drunken and disillusioned man would tell of his affair with a woman he would never see again in a city a thousand miles away. I would wheedle out of him all his recollections of those wintry Sunday mornings when he and Carolyn awoke in their bedroom overlooking Westernport and started on one another yet again. While the jacarandas overhead dropped dusky-blue blossoms onto the table between us he would describe all that I had missed out on. As he talked and drank he would look boldly around at the crowded tables overhung by hibiscus and tropical ferns. He would see two young women alone together and announce to me that they must have come from Victoria for the same reason that Carolyn had visited Queensland while he and I were still schoolboys. He would switch to one of his funny-man voices, expecting me to join him in one of our old routines. But when he stood up, steadied himself, and told me to follow him to the women's table, I would lean back in my chair and stare through the blue haze of the jacarandas at the nearest of a thousand green hills undulating towards the remote south-eastern corner of Australia where Durkin and I had grown up together and where I had first looked innocently towards the north. And while he drew up a chair beside the young women and began to talk to them, and while one or both of the women sometimes looked curiously towards me, I would go on drinking and looking to the south, back towards an insignificant peninsula, as though I saw even there the true Queensland that Durkin could never discover.

I was not very surprised when Durkin told me a week later that he and Carolyn had sorted everything out and were going to announce their engagement at Christmas. The wedding would not take place until a year afterwards, but Durkin made me write the date down because he wanted me as best man and Carolyn seemed to think I might leave for Queensland in the meanwhile and let them both down.

During the year of their engagement I politely avoided Carolyn and Durkin. I was beginning to think that my scheme for wandering in the north had been a bout of temporary madness. I moved from my backyard bungalow to a comfortable flat and dressed like the average public service clerk. I still wrote poetry but I told no one about it and used a pen-name whenever I sent a poem to a magazine. I had decided that alcohol could show me all I needed to see. I drank on six afternoons of the week with a group of men from my office. They were mostly twice my age and they talked of little else but racing and football. But when some girl in my office saw me hurrying down the stairs after work as though I had a fiancée or a girl friend to meet, I used to think of the ill-lit saloon bar ahead of me as my private Queensland. The bar had windows of thick, orange-gold frosted glass, and when I looked towards a window through my beer I felt at a safe distance from Melbourne, ready to go home to my bachelor's flat and write like a man in the depths of the north: at two removes from the unpoetic experiences of his early years.

A few weeks before the wedding Durkin told

me that he and Carolyn had agreed I must be kept from drinking before the ceremony. I decided that Carolyn was a timid bitch from the bayside suburbs, terrified of anything unconventional, who had smiled and listened to my ravings two years before for the same reason that she had spread her legs for Durkin and half a dozen men before him: because she would have tried any means of fulfilling her lifelong ambition to appear as a radiant bride on a sunny Saturday at her local Anglican church. I prepared small flasks of all my mixtures from my early drinking days – gold wasser, gin and lemon, rum and lime, vodka and tomato juice – and hid them a week before the wedding under shrubs and behind sheds and in the forks of trees in the backyard at Durkin's place, where I had to spend the morning of the wedding-day.

Durkin and I played backyard cricket on his wedding morning and I had plenty of opportunities to poke around in the bushes and swig from my flasks. I was glowing all over before we left for the church and I never remembered afterwards any detail of the ceremony, although Durkin's parents told me late that night that I had done a splendid job as best man. At the reception I was free to drink beer without offending the bride. My worst moment came when I found myself expected to kiss Carolyn with people watching. Drunk though I was, I could not forget that Carolyn was the only woman I had ever kissed and that she knew this because she had had to guide me, at the age of twenty-one, in the art of putting my open mouth against hers. Now, when she was Mrs Durkin, I had to give her a different sort of kiss – the ceremonial public kiss – and once again I was not sure of the correct movements. I hung back and let Carolyn guide me again and hoped she did not think I hesitated because I was choked with emotion.

Mr and Mrs Kelvin Durkin drove to Surfers Paradise

for their honeymoon. I hardly saw them for three years after their marriage. I excused myself whenever they invited me to a party at their flat. I believed they were trying to pair me off with Kelvin's young sister or with some other unattached girl they knew. And I supposed the Durkins would have described me to the young woman as a man who drank a bit too much and had a few strange ideas but only needed a kind-hearted woman to straighten him out.

In the fourth year of the Durkins' marriage I acquired my second girl friend. She was the daughter of one of my drinking companions who used to invite me home sometimes for a meal and a night of beer and cards. She was eight years younger than me, and she used to sit quietly reading while her father and his bachelor brother and I drank and played three-handed euchre. After she had caught me glancing at her one night I began to ask her father in the hotel what I hoped he took for casual questions about his daughter. When I learned that she had had no regular boy friend for two months and actually spent some weekends reading at home I decided we were perfectly matched.

I phoned the girl next day and asked her out. She made no objection. It seemed so simple. I felt comfortable with her because I had calculated that she was a child of thirteen when I spent New Year's eve at Sorrento. I looked forward to telling her a little about my old dreams of Queensland. But I knew I would end my stories by telling her I was ready now for a quiet life; all I wanted was to write the occasional poem, to drink in moderation, and to see in my glass the truth about the years I had wasted.

When I was satisfied that I had a regular girl friend at last, I took her to visit the Durkins. Kelvin and Carolyn had moved into a contemporary-style timber house in the cheapest subdivision of Mount Eliza. Carolyn was eight months pregnant with her first child. She walked languidly around her house with all the airs of an experienced wife and mother. Kelvin and I drank all afternoon and I assumed the women were getting on well together. But my girl friend told me on the way home that she considered Carolyn an empty-headed, stuck-up bitch.

I phoned the Durkins later to thank them for their hospitality but also, they both knew, to learn what they thought of my girl friend. Kelvin called her a delightful young thing, but Carolyn asked me had I had enough experience of women to realise that I was getting serious about someone who wasn't my intellectual equal. The smugness in her voice made me determined to marry the girl.

After we had announced our engagement I argued for a quiet civil service but my fiancée wanted a church wedding with a conventional reception and seventy guests. I agreed on condition that Durkin should be my best man, although she had said at first that she didn't even want the Durkins invited.

Kelvin arranged a bucks' night for me and promised to bring along a crowd of what he called our old boozing mates. No more than a dozen turned up, and some of them were Durkin's mates rather than mine. I suddenly realised how few friends I had made in all the years I had sat in rented rooms and flats, trying to write poetry with a bottle at my elbow. The guests sat with me around a keg all night and told dirty jokes. Durkin had to leave early because his wife was expecting her second child, but before he left I took him aside. I was worried that he might have thought I was rushing to marry the first girl I had managed to impress. I had foreseen his asking me how I could think of giving up all my dreams of writing and travelling for someone who seemed colourless compared with Carolyn.

I tried to explain to Durkin that my wife-to-be was the ideal partner for a man who was still trying to be a poet. Being so quiet and so much younger than me, she would not dare to intrude on me when I retired each night to my study with my typewriter and my bottles. Then I told Durkin about the many Saturday afternoons to come when our families would visit one another. He and I would sit drinking on back lawns or shadow-dappled patios, and I would hold up my glass in the afternoon sunlight and still see a sort of Queensland in it.

My wife and I seldom visited the Durkins after our marriage. We and they lived on opposite sides of Melbourne and my wife insisted that she had nothing to say to Carolyn. On one of our rare visits to the Durkins, Carolyn left the lounge room, where we were all sitting, and came back with a baby in her arms – her third child. She sat in a chair opposite me, opened the front of her dress, and gave the child her breast.

I did my best to turn away from her with no sudden jerk of the head while I went on talking to Kelvin and my wife. I even turned back now and then to aim a few words at Carolyn, and managed to lower my gaze as far as her eyes. Yet for days afterwards I could not forget what I had hardly seen.

I told myself I was a social retard, a case of arrested development, a man so confused in his feelings that he could spin absurd fantasies around a trifling incident. I accused myself of being a rare kind of pervert who could see an innocent function of motherhood as a signal from a woman who was quite indifferent to me. I called myself a monster of egotism who supposed that every event within range of his vision had been arranged to send him some special message. But I still could not give up my belief that Carolyn had been telling me something by sitting down in front of me and unbuttoning her dress. Yes, she might have been saying, this is a sign for your benefit. I could have stayed in the bedroom to feed my child but I chose to sit out here, almost within arm's reach of you. My breasts are a mother's breasts, certainly, and my message is not what you would call a sexual signal. But I am showing you that a bond of some kind remains between us. You who never saw or touched my breasts when we were alone together, you are still a man I trust.

I would have got tired of these imaginings soon enough if I had been sure that Kelvin and Carolyn were happily married. But I sometimes gathered from Durkin's talk that he and his wife were deeply divided. He met me two or three times a year in a city hotel. He still talked mostly in wisecracks but I noted carefully his unsmiling complaints about marrying in haste and repenting at leisure, and one day he told me that Carolyn was staying with the children at her parents' home until things improved and that he was half-inclined to piss off to Queensland for six months to sort his ideas out.

When Kelvin and Carolyn and I were all in our middle thirties, they with three children and my wife and I with two, the Durkins invited us to a farewell party at their home. They were selling everything and moving to Grafton, in northern New South Wales.

I had not seen Kelvin for nearly a year, and I noticed as soon as I walked into his house that he was drinking lemonade. He told me quietly that he was cutting down on his drinking. Carolyn told my wife during the evening that Kelvin had become an alcoholic, that she was sure he had had affairs with women in his office, and that she threatened to take the children away from him if he didn't swear off alcohol and spend more time at home. But then she and Kelvin had agreed that what they really needed was to start a new life far away from all his drinking friends.

This was the first time that Carolyn had confided anything to my wife, and I was sure it was a message for me although I wondered how I was supposed to act on it. In the last days before the Durkins left Melbourne I saw myself asking Carolyn to lunch. We said little, but each of us understood what had gone wrong in our lives. And a few days later it was Kelvin alone who went north to take up drinking again and to chase women among the jacaranda groves of Grafton, while Carolyn remained in Melbourne so that I could approach her again – but this time with a clear view of what I wanted.

When it was too late to think of detaining Carolyn in Melbourne, I drank myself into a mood in which my life from 1960 onwards suddenly appeared in a new light. I had been destined for the north after all. After a few weeks Carolyn would send Durkin back to Melbourne; back to his drinking and his lady-friends. I would join her in Grafton. In this mood I sat for an hour making notes for the letter that would tell Carolyn I now knew the difference between reality and illusion, between the real life I had abandoned when I walked out on her in 1960 and the dream-life I had thought was waiting for me in those days. After dreaming of the north for so many years I was now ready to begin my real life there.

The Durkins sent occasional letters. They wrote in the language of tourists about perpetual sunshine and golden beaches. Kelvin and Carolyn were managers and part-owners of a caravan park and a cluster of holiday cabins, and they boasted of wearing nothing but shorts and t-shirts all week. There was no mention of the troubles that had persuaded them to go north.

Carolyn told me in a postscript to one of their letters that northern New South Wales was just the country for a poet; people there lived spontaneously and untroubled by stuffy convention. In my reply I agreed that I had always talked of leaving Melbourne for the north, but I preferred, I wrote, to make the dazzling colours of Grafton more intense by delaying in Melbourne a little longer.

That was what I wrote. But every evening when I sat at my desk and opened the first of my bottles, I looked at the map above my desk and studied the huge quarter of Australia that still lay north of Grafton. The Durkins had not even reached the southern edge of Queensland. I could take my wife for a holiday in their cabins and the four of us could sit together late at night; and while Durkin sipped his lemonade I could drink whatever I chose and announce that our lives were half over and we had still travelled only half-way up the map of Australia. While I stared into my drink, Carolyn would understand that I was thinking of all the rain-forests and the glades of orchids still to the north of us where we could begin at last to live our real life – the life composed of all our imaginings since 1960.

Yet even while I imagined myself approaching Carolyn at last in Tully or Innisfail, I was trying not to feel that I had reached my furthest north. For a week after we had taken up together I would not sleep with her. I would drink myself to sleep in my chair, explaining to Carolyn that I still had to add the last touches to the poetic reality of her. And even after we had settled at the base of the last peninsula of Australia, I would still not give up drinking and dreaming. I would remain a poet to the end. I would fill the last corner of Queensland with an immense Australia still waiting for a man and a woman who would travel always north.

The letters from the Durkins dwindled as the years passed. My wife and I sent them a card each Christmas. We heard one year that they had visited their parents in Melbourne, but we supposed they had been too busy to call on us. We ourselves never left Melbourne. At the age of forty I had been no further north than Bendigo, where I had lived for four years as a child, and sipped while my brothers gulped.

In the twentieth year after our holiday at Sorrento I opened a letter from Kelvin Durkin telling me that Carolyn had left him. He said simply that his wife had gone off with a married man, one of his neighbours. She had taken her two daughters and left him with his son. He believed she and the man were in Brisbane, on their way further north. He, Durkin, intended to drink and fornicate himself to death with agonising slowness over the next ten years, but he would very much appreciate a long letter from me in the meanwhile.

I was flattered that Durkin had asked me for a letter. I believed he was acknowledging at last that I could put into words what he could only vaguely feel. I found myself filling the first pages of my letter with a diatribe against Carolyn Cottrell. I wrote that she was incapable of honesty or sincerity – as I had found out when I first went out with her and learned that she was using me to stimulate her mind and her married boy friend to stimulate certain other parts of her. But I did not believe what I was writing. I found I was actually delighted that Carolyn had realised after all those years that Durkin was worthless. I thought she must have dreamed often, under the jacarandas of Grafton, of a man at his desk far to the south whose dreams had been much more impressive than anything she had seen on her travels with her husband. I even wondered whether Durkin had lied to me about the married man so that I would not know that Carolyn had gone to Brisbane alone and was waiting for me to find her there. And even if a married man was with her, the escapade might have been only a frantic sign urging me to leave my own wife and come after her.

In the last pages of my letter I told him about my own marriage, and as I wrote I found myself thinking of Durkin as a friend: as the same man I wanted to talk to when we sat alone together on New Year's eve, 1959. I told him that I had never explained all my dreams to my wife and that I believed she would one day tire of my sullen silences and leave me as solitary as I had been before I first met Carolyn. If this happened, I wrote, he and I could go back to a place like Sorrento and begin all over again.

Durkin phoned me from Grafton a week later. He sounded more drunk than I had ever known him. He told me my letter was the greatest bit of writing I would ever do. He was keeping it by his bed. It had saved him from suicide. But my letter had done more than that. It had encouraged him to adopt a new policy towards women. He was declaring sexual war on them. And yet they seemed to approve of his policy. Women had found him out from the first day after Carolyn had left him. There were three who phoned him regularly and offered their services. They would wear him out – not that he minded. One of them was sitting in the next room while he was talking to me but he didn't care how much she heard.

Then he began urging me to leave Melbourne at once;

to leave my wife for a few weeks and join him in Grafton. He would put me up in the most luxurious of his holiday cabins and procure for me every night one of the hundreds of hard-drinking divorcees or separated wives who infested Grafton. He would even arrange a sexual foursome for me. But perhaps, he said, I had better bring my wife. There was nothing like being married. He would like to sleep on the floor of our cabin just to be near a happily married couple.

And then the phone went dead and I imagined Kelvin Durkin toppling to the floor and sleeping where he fell.

Six months after his wife had left him, Durkin phoned me on a Friday night to say that he was in Melbourne visiting his parents. He hoped I could give him a bed on the Saturday, after he had been to the football.

He arrived at six next evening with an overnight bag and two dozen cans. My wife had prepared a special meal, but Durkin told her he had drunk too much at the football to appreciate good food. He left half his main course on his plate and refused his sweets, but my wife did not seem offended. He had opened cans for himself and me as soon as he came inside, and he said he wasn't going to bed until he and I had drunk all his beer and solved all our problems. I thought I saw my wife wondering what I might have told Durkin about her and me.

It was the first time I had seen Durkin drunk without being in the same condition myself. Much of what he said seemed childish and unfunny. I drank hurriedly to catch up with him. He wanted to talk about the years before either of us was married. He said our holiday on the Mornington Peninsula had been the high point in our lives, the last time when we stood ready to sample all the pleasures that life had to offer. I told him he was talking bullshit. I was still far from drunk.

My wife listened patiently to Durkin until nearly midnight and then went to bed. By then I was nicely primed. I began to interrupt Durkin and to make him listen to me. We talked until three or four in the morning and emptied all his cans.

I remembered afterwards not much from those hours. I remembered telling Kelvin Durkin once again how I had hoarded my red cordial as a child, and then declaring that I had merely sipped at life ever since but that I was now ready to empty my flask. I told him I was now writing prose instead of poetry. I said I had finished a story about the New Australians, the men from Queensland who had set out for Paraguay to found a country of dreams. I must have tried to make him read the manuscript, because I found it on the table next morning: *The Battle of Acosta Nu.*

I remembered Durkin's telling me that on the night when he first read my long letter he had been sitting outside with one of his lady-friends, having a quiet beer as the sun went down. A blue blossom from his giant jacaranda tree had fallen into his glass. Floating there it had reminded him of the strange mixtures I used to drink in the old days. So he had told his lady-friend all about me – how I was a great drinker and clever with words but a bit too cautious with women – and they had toasted me there in the twilight, Durkin still with the blue petals in his beer.

I remembered hating Durkin for that story and swearing to myself that I would go back with him to Grafton and stay only long enough to learn where exactly Carolyn had gone or to find the message she must have left for me.

I slept late and woke so ill that I thought I must have

vomited in my sleep, although the bucket beside my bed was still empty. I heard Durkin talking to my wife in the kitchen, and stumbled there and found him eating toast and bacon and drinking a can from my emergency stock in the fridge. I sat down and stared around me and wished I had the courage to order Kelvin Durkin from my house.

After his breakfast Durkin opened two more cans and put one in front of me. I did not touch it. My two young sons came to me in their football clothes and reminded me that I had to take them to their match and serve as goal umpire. I asked Durkin what time he was due at his parents' house. He said he would set out as soon as I left with my sons for the football.

My wife sat down and took a cigarette from Durkin's packet. He lit it for her with his lighter. I wanted to get out of the house, but first I picked up the can in front of me and forced myself to drain it with hardly a pause for breath. Durkin and my wife watched me calmly.

I backed the car down the driveway with my sons in the rear seat. Durkin waved to me from the front gate. My wife was somewhere in the house alone. When my house was out of sight behind me I tried to see Carolyn Cottrell travelling steadily north towards Cairns. Then I tried to imagine the man I had described to her twenty years before and to see him still somewhere to the north of her. But I was distracted by the taste in my mouth of the last can I had drunk. The sensation was sickly and quite unfamiliar.

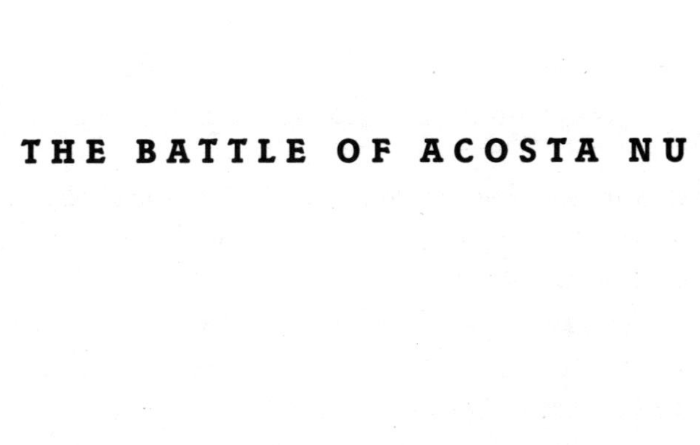

THE BATTLE OF ACOSTA NU

Re your repatriation idea, afraid it's too late. Speaking of New Australia nearly all the second generation have…married native Paraguayan women…and quite a few of the third generation cannot speak the language of their fathers. As for us oldtimers we are set in the ways of the country… But here we are, Australians who love Australia as few do who haven't left it.

Tom Martyn, writing in 1924 from New Australia, the Australian Settlement in Paraguay, to George Reeve in Sydney. Quoted by Gavin Souter in *A Peculiar People: The Australians in Paraguay.*

I stood on a hill northeast of Melbourne and looked across the folds of suburbs towards the Kinglake Ranges and almost believed I was in Australia after all. It was officially the first day of autumn but already, a few days earlier, I had noticed the onset of one of those spells of distinctive weather that pass for the true seasons with me. In early March in this country the sun loses some of its harshness, and the farthest distances are not so painful to look at. In the shallow valleys around me that day, each tree and roof and blank window seemed almost near or far enough to be a part of some remembered or looked-for suburb. Not that I was deceived. I knew the peculiar purity of the light was not about to reveal anything in those patterns of streets. Yet each year at that time, when the restrained sunlight promised to remove what usually separates observer and observed, I was able to visualise for a little what I should have seen all my life in Australia, the country where I belonged.

It was Saturday afternoon and I was one of a group of parents working in the grounds of our primary school. Most of the men had motor mowers and chainsaws but I was with the women, pulling weeds and pruning shrubs. The women were strangers to me, but after we had crouched together for an hour in the sunshine I sensed a fellow-feeling between us. And whenever I saw a brown arm groping near me, or a few inches of pale skin where a blouse had worked its way up a straining back, I thought once again of my old project of finding someone of Australian ancestry among the females of Paraguay.

I was not hoping to find such a woman in that unlikely setting. I only wanted to feel in touch with my own past; to be assured that a theme persisted through my confused and fragmented story. When I met the eyes of some woman bending and straining in unison with me I only pretended that my search of nearly twenty years was over. And when I made some remark in idiomatic Spanish or Guarani I only pretended that the women hearing me saw through my pretence: saw that I observed certain outward forms but was secretly an Australian, one of the little band of exiles from a land we had never seen.

The chance of my meeting an Australian woman in my own suburb was impossibly remote. And if that was not enough to discourage me I could have referred to something I had learned in the years before my marriage. Many women of Paraguay were able to feign an interest in Australia, and even to appear vaguely Australian, although they might have heard no more than the name of the country and that it was on the opposite side of the world from Paraguay.

In the years when I was still learning this, I used to arrive each Saturday night at the home of a married couple who were among my few friends. I would put my half-dozen of beer in their fridge and settle myself in front of their television set and hope for a quiet night with the man and woman who tolerated me as some sort of foreigner although they knew nothing about my homeland. But too often the husband would tell me they had been invited to a party and they wouldn't think of going without me. He had a way of sitting with his legs crossed and his upper foot kicking the air while he told me with relish that this could be the night when I won myself a woman. I saw all of Paraguayan manhood in his grinning face and his tensed muscles, and I recognised the poverty of Paraguayan culture in his form of words, which he had heard from his television set rather than in some far township of his land where the true culture should have grown out of the soil.

If I had still been sober I would have told the man politely that I preferred to live as a hermit rather than take part in the rites of a race so very different from my own. But usually I would have drunk enough to persuade me there could be no harm in the simpler pleasures of Paraguay. I would ask for an hour's grace, use the time to drink one or two of my bottles, and arrive at the party not overly aware of my Australianness.

It was always an hour or two before anyone noticed the young man alone in the corner pouring beer for himself. Then some young woman would perch on the arm of my chair and ask why I wasn't enjoying myself. I would say something that could only have seemed uncivil and nonsensical to a Paraguayan but might have alerted anyone with the least sympathy for Australia. More often than not the woman would want to hear more from me. Then, made hopeful by the beer, I would rush into supposing I had finally met a female of my own generation who was at least partly Australian.

I would test her further. I would make the most un-Paraguayan of remarks, and she would seem to accept them calmly. I would hint at preferences of mine or ambitions that would have seemed absurd to a thorough-going Paraguayan, and even if her answers were not quite what I wanted I could suppose she was confused by her shock at meeting a compatriot after so long. Eventually I would say too much; I would come out with one of the outrageous paradoxes that always occurred to me when I came close to defining the Australian character. Then either the woman would abruptly leave or she would betray herself by some typically Paraguayan answer.

Not all the women I met on those evenings were unmasked so easily. On many a Sunday morning I would weight up all that some woman had said to me only hours earlier and decide that I had still not finally established her race. But I would have walked off at the end of the party and left her to prove her Australianness by searching me out or writing to me in the weeks to come. And because I had probably not even told her my true name I could only wonder which suburb of our huge city had swallowed her and what sort of uncouth Paraguayan male had claimed the only eligible Australian woman I had so far met.

Yet, I could always console myself by recalling how ready this kind of woman had been to disregard my oddness. The very fact argued against her being an Australian, if I knew anything about my wary race. Although I might never have spoken to an Australian woman, I could not believe (at least when I was sober) that such a person would lightly reveal her true nationality – and certainly not for the trivial purpose of enjoying an hour of talk with a man met by chance at a Paraguayan party. Having been separated for so long from her compatriots, she would have devised elaborate and delicately poised theories about Australia. Even in the presence of a man she suspected of Australian connections, she would be reluctant to confide notions arrived at so arduously over so many years. It could never be done lightly – to compare a continent almost wholly conjectured with someone else's conjectures about a place of the same name; to risk discovering that her frosted plateaus were a waterless desert or that her ancestral city lay beneath an inland sea.

In any case, I was always able to conclude (on those Sunday mornings) that worse than turning away from a true Australian woman was the danger of falling in with someone who did not even care whether she or I was Australian or Paraguayan so long as we professed a vague sympathy for one another.

By the time when I knelt in the garden bed of my children's school, surrounded by Paraguayan women aged in their thirties as I was, I knew better than to expect anything from talking sincerely to them. And yet I had learned from my youth a way of conducting myself so that I seemed to share some small understanding with them. I behaved as someone with a secret that could not now be shared with any of them, but at the same time I tried to suggest that some of them might have shared a little with me if we had met fifteen years earlier in some country half-way between Paraguay and my own remote homeland.

The best of the women seemed to acknowledge with dignity this ambiguous tribute I paid them. There were moments in that delicate sunlight when I felt a little of the sympathy that binds the superior class of Paraguayans. But to keep myself from responding too warmly to what was a familiar temptation, I used some of my well-tried devices. I wondered what I should have been doing on precisely that afternoon of my other life – the life I might have led if I had been born in Australia; or I asked myself how many miles away at that moment was the nearest Australian man or woman, or how many days or weeks it had been since I had actually passed in the street and failed to recognise, as usual, one of my countrymen.

At that time I believed I had known two or three Australian men and perhaps one Australian woman. I had known them only briefly and seen none of them for many years. I suspected that this was the way with most Australians. We were even more cautious with one another than with the Paraguayans we professed to despise. We had all of us probably spent part of our youth hoping to meet fellow-exiles and to share all we knew of Australia. But the few of us who had actually attempted this had found it strangely difficult. Some of us might have decided it was by definition impossible.

The trouble had begun in our childhood. None of us had started life in Paraguay with anything more in common than a few scraps of legend about Australia. (Did our parents hide from us a body of sound knowledge, and if so why? Or did they know no more than what they passed on to us, bit by bit, over the years? Or did they know a great deal that they could never pass on to us because we were even further away than they from our original homes?) We knew at least that Australia was a vast place and that unlike Paraguay it offered all that we could want in a homeland. The rest we worked out for ourselves by reading and speculating. And the more ingeniously we interpreted texts and the more elaborately we embellished our dreams, the more we feared having our theories exposed as merely quaint or wilful. In our thoughts of our fellow-Australians we gradually abandoned the idea of meeting them in the land of Paraguay and looked forward to finding them years later under the skies of Australia where there would be no more need for pretending and we could smile together at how we had once avoided one another and preferred to dream of ideal Australians rather than risk meeting our actual countrymen.

Soon after my marriage I had begun to avoid needless meetings with Paraguayans. (By then, of course, I had no thought of meeting Australians.) I excused myself from social gatherings, kept mostly to my house, and adopted the dress and manners of one of the obscure classes of Paraguayans. In my free time I read and made notes about Australia. But while I told myself I despised all Paraguayans, I was not strong enough to appear to them as a friendless solitary. When I was forced to confront them I tried to hint that I had a small circle of allies and confidants. This was what I wanted the women to believe as I worked beside them in the school garden. Whenever one of them asked me an idle question about myself or my family I considered my answer carefully. I hoped to suggest that I shared with my wife and children a satisfying private lore.

The truth was that in my home I kept mostly silent about Australia. I had begun to fear that if ever my wife and I fell out she might betray to some Paraguayan what I had whispered to her, in the first years of our marriage, about Australia.

In the year when I first met her I was bothered by the doubts that probably trouble many an Australian exile. I was at an age when most of the Paraguayan men I knew had found wives for themselves. When I sat in their lounge rooms late at night I pretended not to notice how they drank one glass to my two and how they grew anxious to have me gone when their wives got ready for bed. And I only pretended to be annoyed whenever one of them told me I was turning into the sort of bachelor who adopts a posture of bluffness and makes a show of his drinking because he fears to approach a woman seriously. In those days I was sure I could only be comfortable with an Australian woman, and I was still hopeful of meeting one in my own time.

Alone in my rented room at night I felt reasonably at ease. I even read sometimes from the literature of Paraguay and listened to recordings of indigenous music, noting in both certain themes betraying an unspoken yearning for a land that no Paraguayan could hope to enter and telling myself that even Paraguayans were at heart no more content than I was. But moving by day among people of my own age I felt my isolation, and I began to doubt whether I could keep secret the truth about myself until the uncertain day when I somehow discovered an Australian woman. I tried murmuring under my breath what I thought were the central truths about Australia to keep myself from losing faith in a distant homeland awaiting me. But a year came when I no longer had the strength to survive as the only Australian among streets and suburbs filled with a race so different from my own. I convinced myself that I would not harm my country if I spoke of it in general terms and allowed the more perceptive of Paraguayans to understand a little the burden I carried.

For a few weeks, sometimes to friends but often to strangers who happened to be drinking with me, I spoke as I had decided an Australian exile should speak. I forbade myself to use the word 'Australia', but I used such words from Australian philosophy and theology that no sensitive listener, I thought, could fail to recognise me as the heir to a rich and outlandish tradition. One night after I had delivered one of my most eloquent speeches at a party, the Paraguayan man who probably knew me best asked me quietly whether I would care to go along with him to a discussion group he had once attended. The group met in the home of a doctor.

I was relieved that the issue had been clearly expressed at last – that a spokesman for Paraguay had told me my Australian ways were, by the standards of his countrymen, symptoms of mental illness. I declined to answer him directly, but from that night onwards I made a point of behaving more defiantly, of flaunting my foreignness in front of Paraguayans of all kinds.

Late one night I found myself in the garden of a house where a party was going on. A young woman was standing close beside me. The light from a distant window picked out the bones of her face and showed her as a caricature of the Paraguayan racial type. I seemed suddenly to be seeing things clearly after many hours or even days of drunkenness and confusion. I could not remember how the woman and I came to be where we were, but I understood that she wanted me to take her further into the bushes and to sit down with her on a blanket that I suddenly noticed under my arm. I realised that the time had come for me to stop playing at being a foreigner in Paraguay. I had to tell this woman whose name I did not even know that I was set apart from her race by the Australian blood in my veins. Yet I saw that even this announcement would mean nothing to her. She would not want to bandy words with me there in the darkness. I would have to do something, to perform some outward show to prove I came from a nation whose ways were strange to her. I stood there, using the last precious moments before she took me by the wrist and tried to lead me in among the Paraguayan ferns and evergreens. I asked myself what harm could come to me if I followed her, pretending to be an ordinary Paraguayan who had met and impressed a woman at a party. But I knew I had to stand my ground. I could not betray my country.

A worse complication occurred to me. What if I had already revealed my secret to her? In the hours I could not account for I might have blurted out the greater part of the story of why I kept myself apart. Now, even if I fled from her without another word she could go back to her Paraguayan friends – male and female – and tell them about the idiot she had met who didn't even know what country he belonged to.

But even that was not the worst I could think of. I asked myself whether the woman had confessed to me in the forgotten hours that despite her appearance she was partly Australian. (Surely nothing less than this could have persuaded me to follow her out into the darkness?) In that case she was testing me, and already I seemed to her hardly different from any Paraguayan male. In a moment she would run from me, and for weeks afterwards her Australian friends – the little band of exiles I had sometimes dreamed of meeting – would talk about the loud-mouth who boasted of being Australian but knew none of the country's passwords and rituals.

Whatever she was – Australian or Paraguayan – I saw I had no business to be there with her. I still could not decide how to break away without exposing my Australianness to ridicule. But by then my fear had got to my stomach. I blundered into the nearest clump of bushes, and while the woman stood just behind me asking what on earth was wrong, I doubled up and vomited.

I escaped around the side of the house and walked the four miles back to my room. I spent the rest of that night packing my books and clothes. I knew I had to go into hiding. After dark next day I visited the same friend who had wanted me to see a doctor. I told him calmly that I neither feared nor despised people of his race but that I wanted no more dealings with them. I proposed to clean the rubbish out of the shed in his backyard and to live there until I was ready to slip away to Australia. I would eat vegetables from a plot beside the shed and spend my time meditating and writing about my homeland. I wanted his and his wife's promise never to reveal that a foreign hermit was living behind their house.

My friend humoured me. I could move into his shed as soon as I had visited his doctor and got some tranquillisers. I agreed. I knew what a Paraguayan doctor would think of my condition, and I looked forward to justifying myself before a man trained in the dreary sciences of that benighted land.

The journey to the doctor's rooms exhausted me. I had to walk for two hours through the suburbs. I could not board any tram for fear that a woman of my generation was among the passengers. Even if she had not heard about me from the woman in the shrubbery, I believed now that something in my appearance gave me away; any Paraguayan woman could tell at a glance that I was separated from her by a cultural abyss.

The doctor was a large, calm man who sat forward with hands joined on the desk in front of him and tried to look as though nothing I might say could shock him. I told him at once that according to his science I was mentally ill but that in fact I was one of a handful of Australians still surviving years after our grandparents had arrived in

Paraguay to found an ideal settlement. I went on to explain that the settlement had failed because (as I understood but perhaps my grandparents had not) the Australians had foolishly abandoned the true source of their culture, the land of Australia itself. As I talked to him I understood, more clearly than ever before, the peculiar dilemma of the Australian exiles. We yearned for Australia but we dared not travel towards it for fear of finding it different entirely from our families' scant traditions and our own later conjectures. Our tension in the face of this dilemma, I boldly acknowledged to the doctor, fitted beautifully the Paraguayan definition of mental illness.

The doctor preferred not to discuss Australia. He considered me, he said, only a somewhat sensitive Paraguayan who had learned from his parents not to trust the land he had been born in. The doctor would not defend the Paraguayan culture that I scorned, nor would he dissuade me from dreaming occasionally of a more congenial homeland. But he urged me to make some compromises. I should realise that many Paraguayans were not very different from myself. If they did not exactly claim allegiance to a foreign nation, they at least admitted that some other land would be better suited to their natures than Paraguay.

I agreed to visit the doctor each week. I wanted to find out how far I could go in my talk of Australia without giving him grounds for declaring me quite unbalanced. At the same time I took the medicines he prescribed and slept on my friends' lounge instead of moving at once into their shed. But like many projects undertaken in Paraguay, the discussions between the doctor and myself soon petered out. He began to tell me there was no reason why I should see him so often; and at the same time I began to see that

I could survive a few more years away from Australia so long as I took tranquillisers or drank a couple of bottles of beer each evening and did not approach any Paraguayan woman. The doctor himself, on one of my last visits to him, predicted that my troubles would all be gone as soon as I met a woman who herself believed in her connections with some far away country. He even claimed there were thousands of such women in every large city of Paraguay. I knew my symptoms (as he would have called them) had died away when I allowed him to say this. A few weeks earlier I could not have tolerated his claim that any country beyond the borders of his land-locked republic were equally suitable for a dreamer.

I have never been sure what gave me the strength to quietly break off my visits to the doctor and to stop taking medicines. Perhaps it was my learning how ignorant the doctor was of geography – he had tried to look into the heart of me and yet he could not have named the capital city of my spiritual home. Somehow I must have become convinced of what I had only asserted to myself before then: that I was superior to most Paraguayans. I began at last to feel that a whole continent was spread out inside me. The feel of its immense prairies and its ten thousand lakes made me no longer anxious to impress the Paraguayans around me or to treat with their young women. I thought I could be content to wait for years until a few discerning people recognised me as a man with a vast and foreign land behind my face.

When I met the woman who became my wife I was calm enough not to rush at once into talk about places beyond Paraguay. I was able to question her cunningly about landscapes she had seen, or imagined, or supposed she had yet to discover. And I found with some astonishment that she was one of a breed I had not allowed for in my speculations. She was an Australian who had never been told about Australia. When I realised this I knew I had to marry her. I looked forward to the task that might take me years – my persuading her that despite all the falsehoods her parents might have told her and all the illusions she had created about herself, she was very much an Australian.

It was not easy. She talked to me for hours before our marriage about countries she thought more admirable than Paraguay. Often I made no effort to refute her, but watched with pleasure the play of expressions across her face as she described this or that land where she would have been more contented than in Paraguay. But when I tried to lead the conversation gently in the direction of Australia she gave no sign of knowing anything about the place. Sometimes I thought this was her way of protecting herself from disappointment: she refused to hope that there was in fact a far country she could claim allegiance to. Thinking this, I predicted that her joy when she finally came to believe in Australia would be even greater than mine as I convinced her of her true nationality.

In the first years of our marriage I became bolder, even contradicting her when she spoke as though we had all but achieved our goals by acquiring a house and a small piece of land in Paraguay and spending our leisure discussing pleasantly remote countries. But often I angered her. I could not tolerate her equating Australia with the country she had had sight of in church as a child or with some other nameless place that had come into her mind when she lay among the dunes of a deserted beach as a girl of thirteen and watched the wind making and unmaking patterns in the sand around her. Sometimes I had to cut her short and tell her that the places she described were mere hints of Australia, the country that her own parents would have told her about if they had not been ignorant renegades. But then she would demand to know by what right I could change the names of the countries of her world. And whether because she thought I was holding back something about Australia or because she perversely misunderstood my boasting of the strength I drew from my homeland, she would accuse me of not treating her as my equal.

After our quarrels I would keep silent for days and console myself by swearing to tell her no more about Australia until we finally reached our country, after which she could see with her own eyes that all I had hinted at was indeed true and thank me for being so patient with her years before. It would have been simpler for me if I could have decided that my wife was no more than an unusual sort of Paraguayan. But whenever I was on the point of deciding just that, she would startle me with a few words that took me back to the days when I had first admired her as an Australian in disguise. My hope of those days would return to me. I would look forward again to the rare pleasure of learning about Australia from another Australian; of resting from my endless struggle to visualise my homeland according to the little I had been able to learn, and taking heart from someone else's Australia; of listening while my wife described its folds of Alps and its countless archipelagoes.

Our differences became more serious after our son was born. The elder child, a daughter, I resigned to my wife's care. I acknowledged that I knew nothing about females except that they learned at an early age to appear as though they moved easily from country to country. If my daughter learned this from my wife, I decided, she might never need to rehearse any story – true or false – of some land she was devoted to beyond Paraguay. And yet wherever she travelled she might unwittingly inspire some poor exile to think he had met at last a woman from his far country. But I never doubted that my son would one day want to know why he could not feel at ease in Paraguay. And so, from his earliest childhood I prepared him for the revelation that he was an Australian.

Showing him his first picture books I quietly drew his attention to any path that wound away between hills towards a place beyond the reach of the characters in the story. I searched among collections of fairy stories and folktales for accounts of journeys or quests that seemed to demand more than a lifetime for their fulfilment. As soon as he began at school I tried to teach him the advantage of concealing his true allegiances. I still had not spoken seriously to him about Australia. I feared his repeating my words to some gaping school-friend or one of his ignorant teachers, or even his mother. In any case, I was cultivating in him a loyalty to something that could not be expressed in mere words. According to his mother I was only teaching the boy that he was different from others, or superior to them, and that his friends and teachers were not to be trusted. She sometimes accused me of using my position of father to strengthen my delusion that I had a secret message to impart to selected people in an unappreciative nation. I went on with my task but I was never sure what the boy thought of my advice, and I would not have dared ask him the name of any sprawling shape of land, studded with cities and veined with enormous river basins, that flashed past as he whirled the globe of the world I had bought for him.

Sometimes, if I found him idle of a weekend,

I would take him into Melbourne to the museum. His mother had bought a small television set for the boy and his sister, and I feared that my son would go the way of most Paraguayans and decide the world was no more than an infinite series of images, approaching but never quite coinciding with truth because one could always suppose that a cameraman had not positioned himself correctly or a producer had erred in his instructions or a government official had exercised an arbitrary censorship. I used to lead the boy to the cases of birds and stand beside him silently, hoping his eye might be taken by all those other eyes – tiny, dark, and staring fixedly at something that was in our world if only we could focus on it. Or I took him to the cases of insects and waited for the bright colours of the specimens to work on him, remembering the day in my own childhood when a boy had turned up at school with a glass case of mounted butterflies.

That boy's father had been away from home, fighting in one of the wars that had been the chief events in the history of Paraguay, and the boy showed the butterflies more from a wish to glory in his father's soldierhood than from any fondness for the colours of the insects. The only story he could tell about his treasures was that crowds of them fluttered around corpses of the invaders of Paraguay when they lay in the jungle, shot by the likes of his father. My classmates thronged around the case, at first only to escape from their schoolwork. But even the rougher boys were surprised by the butterflies. When I glimpsed between elbows and heads the huge black and blue and green wings outspread I despaired. Until that day I had believed there was nothing of outstanding beauty in Paraguay that was not recondite, difficult of access, to be found only after years of searching. (I did not yet know that I was an Australian.

I had heard my father talk occasionally of Australia, but I hoped my home was in a remote province of Paraguay.)

The children began what they called picking out their favourites. Even the teacher (who before that day had taught us nothing of natural history) joined in eagerly. Everyone chose one or other of the three largest butterflies – with wings glowing like enamel. No one asked me my choice, but I was ready to claim it was a creature not under the glass, not large or showy enough for the boy's father to have noticed it in the jungles of the borderlands. I could not accept that the father of one of my illiterate classmates, who played war-games in the schoolyard every day while I searched through books for some sign of where I belonged, could have travelled so easily to the edge of the country and picked up from the bodies of the men he had shot the richest colours in Paraguay.

I watched my son carefully while he stood in front of the glass cases, especially when some Paraguayan child strolled up and pointed to the largest and gaudiest beetle or parrot. I said nothing that might have made him think the Paraguayan was challenging him. I merely waited for him to ask me to lead him to the other birds and insects – to the unnoticed corners of almost-deserted alcoves where fragile specimens gripped their desiccated twigs or hung from their labelled pins, waiting for the few searchers who could make out the faded sheen on their feathers or wing-cases and wonder about a land where such things would dazzle the eye.

In the schoolground my son came up and complained to me that his leg was hurting. A little while before, I had noticed him lifting the leg with his hand as he swung himself into a wheelbarrow. Now he told me that even walking was painful and that he had felt hot and nauseous all day. He said this in the hearing of two nearest Paraguayan women, and I sensed that they were curious to know what I would say to the boy.

I had no doubt that he was in pain. His face was flushed and strained and I had never known him to feign sickness. While the eyes of the women were on me I did two things quite in character for an Australian exile: I told my son mildly to have a drink of water and to rest before he went back to his game; and I decided that he would die from his sickness, whatever it was.

I sent him away because I believed an Australian should seem imperturbable under the scrutiny of Paraguayans. A man who suffered the lifelong misfortune of exile should have been able to deal calmly with a child's passing illness.

I decided that he was going to die because the same thought had occurred to me every night for seven years while I stood listening to his breathing as he slept. He would die young before he could fulfil the hope I had had since his birth: before I could explain to him the importance of Australia and then wait to hear from him, before my own life was over, a form of words that told me our country was safe and that he understood the place in our lives of a land we might never see.

I decided he would die for another reason – because I had believed for many years that I would be punished at last for turning my back on Paraguay. I avoided all the common duties and responsibilities of a Paraguayan. My turning up at the school to pull weeds was my first meeting for two years with other parents and was meant to save my wife and children the embarrassment of explaining why I was never seen around the school. In my home of an evening I would never answer the telephone, and my wife was instructed to tell anyone inviting me to a meeting that I was out. (I could not bother with school affairs when I knew that only an accident of history had sent my son to a Paraguayan school, that his formal education would only result in his being able to pass himself off as one of the natives, and that I could teach him in a few minutes each night more of lasting value than he would learn in all his years at school and university. If things had gone better for our ancestors, the boy would have been growing up in a land where no distinction was made between custom and culture.) I irritated my wife by refusing to watch television or read newspapers, so that I never knew what personalities or issues mattered most to the few acquaintances who visited our home. While she helped the children with their homework on weeknights and arranged their sports and entertainments at weekends, I stayed in my room reading some little-known poem or novel because a comment in a review had suggested (perhaps to me alone) that the work was concerned less with Paraguay than with a nameless country that few readers would have sympathy with.

I was to be punished for another reason: because for many years I had half-hoped and half-believed that nothing could touch me – nothing, that is, of what Paraguayans took for reality. This was behind my not making a fuss while the women watched me in the schoolground. I was never sure what value to attach to what Paraguayans called the emotions. (How much, for example, of what I felt for my wife and children was truly derived from my Australianness and how much was derived from my being exposed all my life to overly demonstrative Paraguayans?) I preferred to seem untroubled by emotion than to risk being absorbed into some vaguely sentimental Family of Paraguay. I wanted to think that my strongest feeling was my attachment to Australia and that this feeling lay outside the spectrum of Paraguayan emotions. Sometimes, foreseeing clearly the early death of my son, I wondered if I would have the strength to demonstrate to the few who knew me that the loss of my child was not the worst of blows so long as I still had my true land to think about.

And so I listened coolly to my son's complaining, and probably shocked the Paraguayan women by sending him away. Yet I wondered how they would have felt towards me if they had known that I spent the rest of that afternoon thinking of the Battle of Acosta Nu.

I had never made a serious study of the history of the country that chanced to be my birthplace. I flinched a little whenever Paraguayans sang their national song or unfurled their flag, and I thought I detected something spurious in their occasional public expressions of patriotism. But I could hardly deny that thousands of Paraguayans had died fighting for their country even during my own lifetime. It hardly mattered whether or not the wars had been to save Paraguay from invasion or to gratify the ambitions of the dictator of the day. Hordes of barefoot Paraguayans had gone into battle against much stronger nations. We fought because we loved our land insanely – I had chanced on those words attributed to some nameless Paraguayan soldier and never forgotten them. They made me ask myself how much I would risk to defend my own country.

Acosta Nu is described in Paraguayan history books as a battle, the last engagement of a war that had ended only a few years before the first Australians arrived in Paraguay. In fact it was no more than a suicidal gesture of defiance by the last survivors of an army that had been almost wiped out. After the fighting the Paraguayan dead were found to be mostly boys, some only ten years old, still clutching as weapons their roughly sharpened sticks or their stones or broken glass, or even handfuls of soil. Often beside my son's bed while he slept I thought of those dead boys. I consoled myself by thinking that no Australian would ever have to suffer in that way for his country. But then I wonder whether an Australian could always expect to stay aloof from the affairs of Paraguay.

On that Saturday night my son refused his food and lay on his bed saying his leg was too sore for walking. My wife wanted to take him at once to the nearest hospital but I lapsed into one of my Australian moods and persuaded her to wait for a while. I told myself that my son had surely inherited my own toughness. (I had not had to consult a doctor since the troubled days before my marriage.) I believed that many illnesses were caused by spiritual uneasiness. This being so, my son – who had always seemed free of anxieties – would soon throw off a childish ailment. I dwelt on my dislike of that most Paraguayan of institutions, the hospital, where experiments were conducted on people regardless of their race in order to verify fashionable variations of the Paraguayan doctrine of materialism.

After tea I read to my children as usual. The girl sat at the foot of her brother's bed. I told her that the boy was not as sick as he seemed; that he was an Australian, one of a superior race who took no notice of troubles that would prompt most Paraguayans to scream for a doctor. (I occasionally used the word 'Australian' in this jocular way. It was part of my preparing my son for the day when I revealed that Australia was a serious matter. I had not used the word before to my daughter, but I trusted she would treat it lightly and not carry it back to her mother.) I read from a children's novel of that year, one of many popular children's books described as fantasy. When the first of these books had appeared I took them as a pleasing sign that even some Paraguayans wanted to read something other than accounts of countries like their own. But as more of these fantasies were published I began to worry that my own essays on Australia, when they were finally published, might seem mere modish invention or even whimsical stuff for children.

If my son had not been so drowsy I might have explained to him how the author I was reading from had used her imagination merely to embellish certain details of what she knew as real life, and that this was not the only means of arriving at a knowledge of places very different from Paraguay. But for that night I was content to show my respect for what I read. Probably neither child was ready to ask why it was that fantasy so satisfied them. But they were struck, I hoped, by their father's giving up, every evening, whatever work he had to do and reading fiction to them.

We called a doctor to the house next morning. He tossed his head when my wife suggested that our son was seriously ill. He examined the boy and found that his pain was located in his leg. A virus, the doctor said, had got into the child's muscles. My wife wanted to argue that the boy should go to hospital. I simply asked the man when he would call again and led him towards the front door. He would see the boy next day. Until then we should give him plenty to drink and sponge him to keep his temperature down.

When I deferred to the doctor I was following a policy I had devised soon after my father had first told me about Australia. I felt as a spy might feel, or a diplomat from a country not on friendly terms with Paraguay. In my private system of beliefs the land where I served my time counted for nothing. Yet although I could despise the place and its people, I was not so stupid as to commit acts of sabotage or speak out against the laws and customs or make a show of what Paraguayans would have called my eccentric ways. I did not want to lose my job or to have my children teased in the schoolground. And above all I wanted no one to brand me (if one day I became known as an Australian) as the kind of malcontent who praises some ideal foreign country and talks endlessly of settling there but only to excuse himself from being an active citizen of his own country.

So it was that my wife tried to dispute with the doctor and to struggle against circumstances whereas I heard out politely the man I privately scorned, and thanked him at our front door. But I made sure to take him past the room I called my library, where two of the walls were covered by shelves of books. I wanted to send him away wondering what sort of man would let his front lawn grow wild and would have bare wooden floors instead of carpets while he filled a room with books.

The boy seemed to sleep for most of that afternoon but whenever I tried to creep out of his room he would ask me, without opening his eyes, to bring him another drink or to rearrange his pillows. I stood once and looked at his closed eyes and said deliberately to myself that he was dead; that my only son had died ten thousand miles from Australia after hearing no more than the name of his true country.

I felt a surge of something like pride. I seemed for once the equal – by Paraguayan standards – of any swaggering Paraguayan. I could no longer be accused of wanting to escape any of the hardships of life in Paraguay.

My son had died within the borders of Paraguay. He had done as much as the boys who fell at Acosta Nu, and I had the right to share in the common fund of Paraguayan emotions – although I had as well deeper feelings of my own resulting from my Australianness.

But I still believed the boy was suffering from a virus in his muscles and that he would soon recover. And in fact he seemed rather more alert towards evening, sitting up and asking me to talk to him.

I got out a small puppet theatre that he and I had once made from grocery boxes. We had worked on the theatre on nights when I thought he was watching too many Paraguayan television programs. I used to take him quietly out of the room where his sister sat staring at the screen and tell him that with our imaginative prowess he and I could surely devise something more satisfying than the feeble pretences of television. At the time of his sickness we were still preparing conventional scenery, using pictures cut from some of his old books. But I was planning to paint for him sets of Australian landscapes.

I rested the theatre on his knees and propped his head higher against the pillows. The stage was bare; I had removed the pasted-down wings and backdrop, which had been meant for a fairy story. I began to tell him with all the eloquence I could call on that as soon as he had recovered he and I would enact on that empty stage a grand drama. There would be two chief characters – a father and a son. While he watched – intently, as I thought – I tried to suggest with my fingers the father striding backwards and forwards across the stage looking for his son. I wanted the boy in his bed to move his fingers as though the son came out of the body of the theatre to join the father on stage. I was then going to guide his hand so that father and son went off together into the wings (which I imagined decorated in the Australian style). But my son was too tired to follow my promptings.

I put away the cardboard theatre but not before my wife came into the room and told me to stop torturing the child. She had made up her mind, she said. Our son was gravely ill and she would take him to hospital that evening.

She bent over the boy and tried gently to lift his leg. He could not move it without crying out. She took me to the front room where he could not hear us and told me to phone the casualty department of a certain hospital while she packed a bag for the boy. I said it might be more diplomatic to call the doctor back to the house and to ask him to phone the hospital for us.

She lost patience with me. Our son, three rooms away, must have heard her. She accused me of being prepared to sit by and watch my son sink into a coma because I was too frightened to offend an arrogant young general practitioner. She had suspected for a long time, she said, that I was utterly impractical and self-centred; but she hadn't realised until now that I was cowardly as well and prepared to inflict suffering on my own child simply to spare myself a moment of embarrassment.

I wanted to defend myself of course, and as I stood silently in the face of her anger I heard myself confounding her with the supreme insult – telling her that I was an Australian while she was a Paraguayan, so that no communication between us was possible. For part of the time while she rebuked me I deliberately noted the ways in which she resembled some actress in one of the Paraguayan drama series, as they were called, that I had sometimes caught her watching on television. So detailed was my thinking while she stood with her face almost against my own that I began to compose a paragraph for one of my essays, asking whether it could properly be said that Paraguay was an actual country with a way of life or whether all Paraguayans thought themselves exiles from a vast and marvellous country – the land they glimpsed through the narrow apertures of their television screens. It seemed to me that my wife had learned from the people of that land that the illness of a child demanded a scene, by which she meant a display of frantic emotion.

I could not have refuted her claim that I had no feeling for the child. She saw only what was in front of her eyes: a child experiencing, for the time being, discomfort and pain. I believed I saw a wider view of things, not because my faculties were keener than hers but simply because I was an Australian who had stayed loyal to Australia. While she was compelled to express her grief suddenly and outwardly, I had not yet discovered the full range of my feelings; I had to consider the place of Australia in my son's life before I could estimate how much he suffered.

As for my fearing to offend the doctor, it was true that even after I had dwelt for so many years on the distinctiveness of being Australian I still quailed before certain Paraguayans. Perhaps I cringed in the presence of doctors because I feared they might somehow guess what I was writing in my essays. Perhaps I was in awe of their influence in Paraguayan society, the kind of influence that a writer of essays would enjoy in Australia.

My wife and I agreed on a compromise. She would take the boy to hospital that evening, but I would first call the doctor to the house for his final opinion and to have him phone the hospital.

While I waited for the doctor I sat with my son and told him quietly that his mother and I had decided to take him to hospital to find what was wrong with his leg. He seemed unafraid, but I suddenly realised that if his mother was to go with him and if he was seriously ill then this was my last chance to talk to him alone before his fight for his life.

I praised him for being so patient. Then I looked around to make sure that my wife could not hear – what I was about to say would seem to her quite inappropriate, and if things went badly for the boy (as I was beginning to fear) she might remind me for the rest of my life that I had used his last hours in our house to harangue him about my private obsessions. I told him quietly that he was luckier than other boys of his age. They were running around at that very moment, believing that life should offer them nothing but pleasure. He was learning already what they would not learn until they had endured much worse suffering than his: there was no real happiness in Paraguay.

At that point I hesitated. I wanted to assure him there was much more to the world than the disappointing country he and I had happened to be born into. Yet I was anxious not to suggest to him that we only had to settle in a certain other country to be rid of our troubles. The complex matter of our fate as exiles was too much to explain to him while he lay there dazed. I had planned to reveal to him gradually, over many years, the subtleties of our predicament: how we were bound to live as secret Australians and to learn all we could about Australia as though we were about to be restored to our homeland, although we must accept that we would probably spend our whole lives within the boundaries of Paraguay. From the time of my son's birth I had wondered how to put into words the paradox that overhung our lives. We knew we belonged in Australia, but we could not simply travel to any land of that name. It was almost certainly too late to retrace the journey our grandparents had made. To do so rashly would be to risk the unthinkable: our finding at last that Australia was not wide enough to contain our idea of it. Moreover, each of us learned in time that we could never know about Australia anything that could be verified. It would have been useless for us to hear or read what native Australians thought about their land. And if we turned to our own family lore we were relying on the imperfect memories of old men and women who had left Australia as youths or children. And in any case our traditions could only confuse us. The emigrants, the original Australian settlers in Paraguay, had once actually turned against Australia, called it unendurable, and then later remembered it as a far better place than Paraguay and taken to calling it before they died, their true home.

I had thought of other problems since the birth of my son. I did not want him to endure as a young child what I had endured: the feeling that almost everything I did was a mere rehearsal for my true life, which would begin as soon as my father was able to embark with me for Australia. My father had been too bitter. He had talked too much to me about his homeland and condemned too much of Paraguay. I wanted my own son to realise that there were things he might legitimately experience in Paraguay for what they could teach him about Australia; that he could even enjoy a little of Paraguay so long as he cultivated at the same time the more refined pleasure of knowing that he enjoyed it as an exile able to infer the existence of much finer and rarer pleasures in another land.

And I did not want my son to feel that things in Paraguay were somehow less than real or that the very land lacked substance because, unlike Australia, it was never dreamed about or wondered about by people far away. I had noticed as a child that as soon as a Paraguayan knew his country to be only one of many in the world, and saw it placed always on the edge of conventional maps, he no longer talked of Paraguay as though anything of note could happen there. He took to reading books or watching films whose settings were far away. I suspected that even in their dreams young Paraguayans saw nothing strange in Paraguay. (Wondering about this once as a young man I had worked out a theory that alarmed me. I began with the undeniable fact that sixty years before my time a band of Australians, still living in a land named Australia, had begun to dream of another country. The next step in the theory depended on the premise that any land dreamed about must exist somewhere. It may not be marked on maps – which themselves are a sort of dream – but if people can be described as moving nearer to, or further away from, a dreamed-of land then such a land must lie somewhere. This band of Australians had set out for a land more suited to them than their birthplace. They arrived in the land called Paraguay but to the district where they settled they gave the name New Australia. The settlement was soon disbanded, although my own forebears stayed for a long time afterwards around its site. Later, whenever the expatriate settlers talked about the land they belonged in but could never reach – and I had assumed they were talking about Australia – they were in fact describing New Australia. The heart of my theory was this: I had pledged myself as a boy to New Australia, thinking I had pledged myself to Australia; and if Australia was hard to reach, New Australia might be infinitely more remote. But what if the settlers had been not altogether wrong, I asked myself one day. New Australia might have been not far ahead of them when they set up their first camp. And although they went no further in their search for it, their descendants might still find New Australia somewhere in the backlands. For a few days I studied large-scale maps of the border provinces of Paraguay. I thought of my lost land lying just across this or that river, or somewhere along the path of the same wind that lifted the curtains of my room in Melbourne on summer afternoons. I was not planning to set out at once for the place if I happened to learn where it lay. On the contrary, I saw the routes of my journeys towards it during my lifetime as a pattern like those graphs of equations that tend towards but never reach a certain axis. I saw myself putting off year after year my entry into the landscape that should have drawn me to it but somewhere kept me at bay. Yet it was not long before I went a step further in my theorising. Assuming that New Australia and not Australia was the country that my father and I were meant to occupy, could it have happened that the men who first came looking for it in Paraguay were not misinformed or deluded, and that New Australia did lie in the very place they so named? If this was the case then perhaps it was only their faulty seeing that persuaded them not long afterwards that nothing but Paraguayan scenery surrounded them and that New Australia lay anywhere but among those tangled thickets and pathless grasslands where they had tried to build libraries and mark out cricket fields. I could not entertain this theory for long. I was only a young man when I first devised it. I could not bear the uncertainty of not being able to declare once and for all that nothing was concealed within the hinterland of Paraguay; that the land where I was born had failed me.)

While other children seemed cheerful aiming their thoughts and fancies far away from Paraguay I began to feel almost sorry for the landscape that seemed daily more desolate for lack of dreamed-of events. Even after I had heard from my father a little about Australia, I used to deliberately imagine myself a Paraguayan whenever I heard the children around me complaining that they never found in the bush outside their provincial city the adventures that children enjoyed in other lands. I argued for Paraguay purely from anger at their unthinking neglect of its quietness. I tried to defend the groves of listless ironbarks, the bare flinty soil, the sparse waxflowers and everlasting daisies, even while I was already giving them up for life.

There was more to feel sorry for and defend. I had never forgotten a certain afternoon in a schoolroom in that same provincial city in Lower Central Paraguay. It was the custom in the last hour of each day for any child who had finished the schoolwork early to read from the three shelves of books in the back corner. The books had brown paper pasted over their covers. They seemed to me very old; and because some of them had the names of previous owners on their fly-leaves and I could not believe that owners of books would willingly hand them over to be mauled by strangers, I thought of the previous owners as having died as children or been obliged to leave at a day's notice for distant parts of Paraguay. And because I found the books mostly dull I felt a vague sympathy for the dead children who had looked in vain during their last days for some memorable page or picture; or I supposed that the children who had gone away had deliberately left behind their drabbest books hoping that children trying to read them afterwards would be so discouraged they would take to dreaming instead of reading about places beyond their city.

I read those books every afternoon. I found in

them only stories set in the great countries of the world or accounts of what was called life in other lands – the other lands being strange and remote but never including Paraguay or Australia. I looked around at the slack faces of my classmates and wondered why they complained so often about the heat and the boredom of the schoolroom and their long uneventful walk home and yet never cared about the worst of their misfortunes: that no children in other countries were reading about Paraguay and adding details to the idea of the country. Sometimes I felt so sorry for Paraguay that I promised myself I would remember it often after I had arrived in Australia, imagining it as no Paraguayan could and making bearable the long afternoons of a boy such as I had been, who could have endured the dust and the silence of his backyard if he had known he was somewhere within the far-reaching boundaries of someone else's thoughts.

And then, on one of those hot afternoons, I turned the pages of one more of those disappointing books and saw in a murky half-tone plate three children of roughly my own age dressed as I understood my own parents had been dressed in their schooldays, with a horse beside them and part of a nondescript paddock behind them, and below them the caption that I never forgot: *Little children on a lonely sheep-ranch in far-off Paraguay.*

Looking at this picture made me profoundly miserable. Even before I began to consider the little children themselves and thought only of the people who had devised the caption, I saw I would have to question my beliefs about the countries of the world. I had always supposed – and so had my classmates unthinkingly – that countries other than Paraguay were written about and photographed so that Paraguayans could speculate more freely about them. In so speculating, Paraguayans were likely to find things that the actual inhabitants of those countries had overlooked. Readers of books were therefore enriching the landscapes of the countries they read about, and if some of those readers themselves wrote further books (or dreamed of writing books) describing their speculations, and if the readers of such books speculated freely in their turn, then the inhabitants of the countries that had first inspired the series of writings ought to find pleasure in being surrounded by a growing complexity.

That was what I had supposed. But the picture of the little children on the sheep-ranch warned me that something had gone wrong in the lands where books were written. I had never seen, and I never expected to see, any children in Paraguay dressed like the children in the picture. The world 'ranch' was never used in Paraguay. The people who were writing and reading about a land named Paraguay had speculated too freely. They had imagined a place so desolate and children so lonely that a reader could only imagine those children imagining themselves in a land where children crowded together in classrooms looking at pictures of still more lonely children in desolate lands.

I asked myself where exactly those little children were. I thought the true name of their country might be marked on no map of the world. I began to think of a land-between-lands, with its furthest districts impossibly far from all named countries but with others of its districts (thanks to a system of tenuous peninsulas and to improbable tricks of perspective and freakish weathers) offering access to the inmost parts of them. Sometimes as a child I thought this nameless land was the final destination of all those children who were dreamed of by dreamers of Paraguay. And when I remembered its grey skies and imprecise horizon and friendless inhabitants, I hoped the Australians in Paraguay had not imagined Australia too freely.

On the shelf above my son's bed I saw the books that my parents had given me as Christmas and birthday presents. I had kept them all carefully. I had once thought they were secret messages from my father, coded instructions telling me how to live as an Australian. But I learned in time that my father had never looked at the books. They had all been bought by my mother; my father was always too busy planning our next move to some other district of Paraguay. I had asked my father once why he never looked into books for hints about the land he valued above all others. He told me he knew in his heart all that an Australian needed to know about his land. I read even more intently after that; I was afraid my father might never explain to me what he claimed to know instinctively. In fact he died suddenly before I was twenty years old, leaving me with very little information about Australia – although I could still surmise that he would have told me much more if he had lived.

I had filled my son's shelves with books and spied on him to see how often he read them. Left to himself he read only for amusement. Either I would have to teach him all I had learned about Australia, or he would follow his grandfather and rely on his private insights. This disturbed me as often as I decided that each generation of our family ought to add to a growing body of traditions about Australia. But I could never be sure that I was not an oddity, even among Australians – a man who had to read hundreds of books in search of allusions to Australia because he could not trust his intuition.

The boy was resting with his eyes closed. His mother put beside him the bag he was to take to hospital. I slipped into it the only one of my childhood books that had been written and published in Paraguay: a handbook of Paraguayan birds. I knew I had done a cowardly thing. I was planning to sit beside the boy's bed in hospital while he was recovering and to take advantage of his discomfort. I was going to suggest to him that meditating on things rarely seen could compensate for unhappiness and suffering in Paraguay. I would interest him in little-known birds to train him in Australian ways of thought. I wanted to get at him soon after his illness and teach him the lesson I had learned early: it was better not to trust Paraguay. Left to himself he could pass as the equal of any Paraguayan of his age. But I believed he would take a greater interest in Australia if he thought he was somehow marked out by strangeness or by suffering.

As a boy I read my bird-book whenever I had been ridiculed or persecuted by my companions. Long before I understood the difference between Paraguay and Australia I realised I lacked some source of strength that was available to most others. I studied birds because I admired their furtive ways but also because I wanted to possess a private lore – to know the names and habits of creatures beyond the reach of the gangs that ambushed me in the streets and parks. I studied the rarest species of those that were reported to inhabit Lower Central Paraguay. I searched for them only in the pages of my book. I did not want to be observed myself peering into trees around my neighbourhood or wandering off the usual routes. In any case, I suspected I would never find the birds I admired most. I was learning already that my fate was to prefer what I could never point to.

The doctor visited us and agreed that perhaps the boy should go to hospital. My wife carried him at once to the car, but the doctor made a show of seeming unconcerned as he rang the hospital. When the house was quiet again I went into my daughter's room. She said she couldn't sleep; she wanted to know if her brother would die in hospital.

I told my daughter to remember the prayers her mother had taught her. My wife still took the girl to church each week. As a small child my son had gone with them, but he had since decided to stay home with me on Sundays. I had not influenced the boy deliberately, but my wife probably believed I had worked on him in secret. Not long before his illness she had overhead him telling his sister that a human being had no soul; that we were controlled by our brains, which functioned like enormous computers. My wife asked me, rather sadly, why I filled the boy's head with atheism.

I would have liked to explain to her at length that my son's childish nonsense dismayed me too – assuming that he was not merely baiting his sister and his mother. If religion was a devotion to the sacred then I was the most religious of our household. My wife and daughter held sacred the words of Jesus of Nazareth, a man who had never once expressed a love of his native land. (My wife's cousin, a priest who sometimes visited us, had told me his church took no account of a man's nationality – and had thereby excused me forever from taking his religion seriously.) I myself revered an entire country and its culture and history, its jungles and steppes – which made me, I would have claimed, more devout than any churchgoer. And I would have been prepared to leave Paraguay at a moment's notice if a way had been opened for me to go back to my sacred country, whereas I never heard my wife or daughter talk of setting out for the hills of Palestine or the plains of heaven.

On some Sunday mornings while my son and I were alone at home I would take him into the backyard to sit quietly among the shrubs and watch insects and birds. From where we sat we could hear the faint growl of cars on the busiest road of our suburb. I wanted the boy to sense the contrast between ourselves and the thousands of Paraguayans in their cars. They had posited some far suburb or country town as a worthy goal during the few hours of the week when they could go where they pleased (proving that the Paraguayan is at heart dimly aware that his salvation awaits him at the end of a long journey). He and I would undertake no frivolous journey along noisy roads, yet we would see further than any Paraguayan could travel that day if we saw ourselves as Australians.

One of my aims as I sat with my son under the wattle trees in the yard was to reassure him that we were not waiting, as his sister and mother might have been, to reach a better land after death. I wanted him to compare his sister's and his own situation of a Sunday morning: she inside a church with her eyes lowered and her hands pressed together and he among trees following trails of ants and fingering globules of amber sap. But I always took my son inside again before my wife and daughter arrived home from the church. I did not want to suggest a certain image to her – the image of a father and son among huge treetrunks with sunlight streaming down between them and the father singing the words of a song from the hit parades of the early 1950s: *Oh, the place where I worship is the wide open spaces*. And as I led my son away from the trees I cursed Paraguay for the banality of the images it had lodged in my mind.

Whenever my son saw me working on my essays and asked me why I spent so much time writing, I used to tell him I was making up stories about a place called Australia. If he asked me was I trying to make a book like those on my shelves I explained that no one in Paraguay could understand my stories; that perhaps only the people of Australia would want to read them. The danger with my saying such things was that he might conceive of our homeland as a sort of fairyland where all our desires were realised and our talents justly rewarded. I guessed he was thinking of such a place one day when I overhead him talking with his sister about heaven. Before I could stop him he said in the hearing of my wife that he did not want to wait until his death to reach the best country of all; he was going to travel soon with his father to a far better place than Paraguay.

My wife thought then it was time we sat down as a family to talk about heaven and other invisible places. I did not want my son to think that Australia was in any way like heaven or that he might reach his homeland only after his death. On the other hand I did not want my wife and daughter to persuade him that any attractive landscape offered equal scope for some kind of spiritual delight; that faith in God or the conviction of having been saved could turn a dewdrop into a diamond or a leaf into a miracle of intricacy, so that Paraguay or any other country was all that anyone could wish for. I wanted him to feel frequently throughout his life what I had felt so often in Paraguay (for instance, as the mild sunlight of autumn made every street around Melbourne seem like a vista leading towards some street in one of those somnolent Australian cities waiting for the return of its lost people): that we were almost but not quite ready to go back to where we belonged.

If I was going to have to talk about Australia to my family I was sure I would be asked why I did not simply set out for the place. I was ready to argue that Australians had somehow to make themselves worthy of their country. I could truthfully say that I had been preparing for my return to my homeland by writing the drafts of my essays every evening for years. (If pressed I might have conceded that the more I wrote the harder it was to say exactly what would meet my eyes in Australia.)

As it turned out, we discussed none of these issues. My wife quoted the saying of Jesus, 'The kingdom of heaven is within you,' and explained quite persuasively what she took it to mean. My son listened courteously and I said nothing. As we left the table I saw my wife and daughter as walking around with a zone of brightness inside where their hearts should have been, my son with an empty space waiting to be filled, and myself with Australia. Just then I felt it not as a precious possession but as a rather heavy load.

I sat with my daughter until she fell asleep. Looking at her face I wondered what I would tell my son if ever he asked me whether his sister and his mother would get to Australia some day. I thought I would tell him I had no right to answer that question. Even if my wife proved not to be Australian my daughter was partly so – as much so, I reminded myself, as my son. And disregarding for a moment the technical matter of pedigrees and their influence, I could not say for certain that some Paraguayans could not begin what my own ancestors had begun nearly a hundred years before. My own daughter could one day join a band who dreamed of New Paraguay, a place not utterly unlike New Australia. Remembering from my daughter's face how her mother had seemed to me when I first met her, I thought that what I had so often taken for a deceit practised by the women of Paraguay might have been their first awkward effort to tell me that this place, this New Paraguay, was already taking shape somewhere in the collective dreaming of Paraguayans. I could admit the idea even though any place of that name would be unthinkably remote from me: as far from Paraguay as Paraguay itself might have been from the place where my Australian ancestors had located their New Australia.

I fell asleep at midnight. The telephone woke me just before daylight. My wife told me in a strangely formal voice that I was to come as soon as possible to the hospital. Our son was seriously ill but not in immediate danger. She could tell me no more just then.

I wrote a note for my daughter and left it beside her bed. I wrote another note and poked it under my neighbours' front door. I rang for a taxi, and while I stood waiting at my front gate in the almost-Australian light of a Melbourne sunrise I thought how lucky I was to have typical Paraguayans for neighbours. They had no books in their house and they had never heard of Australia but they loved the challenge of practical tasks. They would cook my daughter a needlessly large breakfast and while she ate it feel quietly sorry that she had a father so foreign in his ways.

In the hospital my son had been put in a little room apart from the main ward. The room had glass walls but blinds had been pulled down to hide him from passersby. Two doctors were talking quietly at the door of his room. A nursing sister stood near them, waiting for some instruction. A younger nurse stood just inside the door of the boy's room. All four of them reacted faintly but distinctly as I walked towards them, yet none of them looked at me. I sensed at once that my wife had not exaggerated when she said the boy was seriously ill. But I thought too that my wife must have told someone in the hospital something about me. She might have said that the reason for the boy's reaching them so late was his father's streak of stubbornness, which he called his foreignness. The show of aloofness by the doctors and nurses, I decided, was to teach the father of the little half-breed boy to respect Paraguayan medicine and perhaps also to warn his foreign father not to bring into a temple of Paraguayan science any crazy notions he might have about faith healing or folk medicine.

Before I could prepare myself to approach the doctors and nurses with dignity, my wife saw me and took me aside. She told me the staff had been very kind to her. (I attributed this to their supposing she had a fool or a monster for a husband.) And she warned me not to bother the doctors with questions, as they had explained things fully to her already. Then she told me that the boy was desperately ill. He had septicaemia – blood-poisoning in layman's language. Somehow an infection had got into his bloodstream and spread all though his body without showing the signs of redness or swelling that usually warned people of blood-poisoning. The centre of infection was deep inside a hip-joint, and a surgeon had already operated to relieve the build-up of pus around the bone. But the boy's lungs and kidneys were also infected and he was now unconscious for most of the time. He was being given the maximum dose of a form of penicillin that was known to attack the agent of the infection. (I was disappointed to hear her using the stilted speech that Paraguayan doctors used when they spoke to laymen.) Nothing more could be done for the boy at present. We had to wait to see signs of gradual improvement. The registrar of the ward wanted a parent to stay with the boy day and night for the time being. There was a very real possibility that he would die. Unfortunately (my wife spoke slowly and pointedly) the boy had been left far too long without proper treatment. He should have been brought to the hospital when his symptoms were first noticed.

I said nothing to any of this. But I decided to show my wife I could be practical when I had to be. I told her to go home and sleep, and when she woke to take our daughter to an aunt and then to put a week's supply of food in the fridge so that the two of us could keep continuous watches in the hospital.

My wife left for home and I strode into my son's room. The doctors had gone away but a nurse was with him and I nodded to her. The boy was on his back with his eyes closed and his mouth gaping. He was breathing through his mouth and making a noise that filled the room. A tube dripped fluid into his wrist. Another tube came out from his pyjamas and dripped his urine into a plastic bag. One of his legs was kept outstretched by a dangling weight. He was lying on a sheepskin, and when I first saw him the nurse was rubbing grease into his shoulders and trying to move him into what she must have thought a more comfortable position. He struggled whenever he was touched but the only sound he made was his gasping for breath.

When the nurse left him alone for a moment I spoke softly to him and held his hand, but he seemed unaware of me. I might have sat there fairly calmly but I noticed, through the flap in his pyjamas, his scrotum swollen to the size of a tennis ball and its wrinkles all filled out by fluid. I dropped the boy's hand and stood up. I had to pace the room while I asked myself how much damage might have been done already to my son's testicles. Then two doctors arrived in the room.

The doctors nodded to me but I turned to the window while they examined my son. I could not give a

Paraguayan doctor the satisfaction of toying with my urgent question and then giving me no definite answer. I could only ask myself what would be the consequences of my son's surviving but having no son of his own. Could I bring myself to father another son from my wife, whose race I was still not sure of? Could I begin another long search for a woman who was at least part-Australian? Would I simply pass on to my son all I knew about Australia, knowing that a time would soon come when no descendant of mine was alive to dream about our homeland? Or would I never mention Australia to him again and leave him to speak and think and dream hardly differently from any Paraguayan, while some quiet town far out in the Great Rift Valley of Australia or some windy promontory among its Great Lakes remained empty forever of the people who might have found their way back to it after so long away?

The doctors talked quietly with their backs to me. I saw how absurd had been my thinking on the way to the hospital that some young doctor might take me aside when he met me and ask me could I explain some oddity he had found in my son: perhaps an unheard-of blood-group or an unusually well-developed heart or merely the boy's astonishing toughness in his fight against his infection. (I had thought at the time that I would tell the doctor the truth about my son and myself – not as a boast but simply to remind the medical man that his science overlooked much of importance: that if he wanted to know what enabled people to survive he had better ask himself what was the essence of a man and what distinguished one race of men from another and why years of exile could inure a body against lesser hardships.) But of course the doctors had nothing to ask me.

Standing awkwardly apart from them I felt compelled

to perform some Australian gesture in that room where the very air seemed oppressively Paraguayan. In the corner was a couch where a parent could sleep during a night watch. I sat down on this couch and took out of my bag the book of fiction that was my current reading. I found my bookmark and opened the pages and tried to read. I thought I noticed a sudden tension in the room as the doctors and nurses one by one noticed what I was doing and looked at me curiously. I hoped I was not mistaken; it would have cheered me just then to have those orthodox Paraguayans wondering what subject could be so important that a man would want to read about it while his own son lay fighting for his life near by. For once I would not have objected if one of them had put me through the barbaric ritual I had seen so often in Paraguay – a reader's having his book twisted in his hands and being forced to hear its title pronounced aloud in a tone of bafflement or suspicion. I would have said nothing and gone on reading. For once I would have savoured the pleasure of declaring my foreignness openly, and without even mentioning Australia, since a serious reader of fiction would be for most Paraguayans no less outlandish than a man calling himself an Australian. (In fact I had occasionally, in despairing moods, thought of giving up my quest for Australia and compensating myself with the lifelong task of reading and writing fiction. A certain sort of novel always seemed to me like a chapter of Australian history; many characters in fiction seemed to think like Australians; and sometimes the last pages of a novel affected me like a wind from a lost homeland. In one of these moods I had even written some drafts of fiction. *A Quieter Place than Clun* was a story such as an Australian might have written if he had had to give up thinking and writing about Australia.)

I kept my book in my hands for as long as my son lay still and sucked his air in evenly. As soon as he struggled or groaned or had to be held down while his blood was drawn out of him for the pathologists, I scrambled to his side. But I could only grasp his hand – and not even that if he was surrounded by doctors and nurses. I stood with my hands dangling foolishly at such times; I warned myself that it was mostly by disguise and cunning that an Australian survived in Paraguay, and I decided my son and I might be better helped if I put away my book and paced the room and wrung my hands. It might flatter the powerful Paraguayans around me if I appeared to believe, as they did, that the greatest good for my son was to recover and walk with me again in the landscape of Paraguay.

I was able to watch my own conduct while I believed that my son would either die suddenly or show clear signs of recovery within a few hours. But every hour or so something would suggest that he was only beginning a long and agonising struggle for his life. Some doctor I had never seen before would whisper with the registrar about the days to come. Or the specialist who watched the boy's urine would peer into the plastic bag and then tell me it was too early to comment on his long-term prospects. At one time my son sat up and stared around him and shouted that he was half-starved. I gave him a sip of water. He began to vomit a strange dark fluid and I thought his end had come. But the registrar only wrote *nil oral* on the boy's chart and my son lay down and went on with his regular gasping. At such times I found it hard to keep the idea of Australia in my thoughts. I found myself reciting under my breath, in the rhythm of a dead march, the names that had always made me tremble: Avay, Lomas Valentinas, Ytororo, and Acosta Nu.

I saw each of those river-crossings or swamps or crossroads in the Paraguayan blacklands as the site of my son's last hour on earth; saw him taking his stand in a huddle of ragged barefoot boys, with his sharpened stick in one hand and his shards of glass in the other. From somewhere in that absurd army I heard the words '... because we love our land insanely', and my eyes swelled with tears and I shuddered because my son was about to die for the wrong country and before I had taught him how to distinguish between the forests and grasslands that had beguiled him and our lost landscapes of Australia.

I tried to turn my mood into anger, to find fault with the doctors and nurses who watched the boy calmly and did not suspect what was at stake. But there was nothing I could blame them for, and I could not have trusted myself to speak calmly if I had complained of anything. I could only resolve not to ask them again how they thought my son was doing. I would give them no further opportunity to speak to me as though all that mattered was for my son to be restored to Paraguay.

And so I was silent and outwardly calm for most of the days and nights that I spent with my son. I weakened only once. I looked up from my book late one night and saw that a priest had come into the room. He was a stranger to me and he only nodded gravely and went on standing and watching my son from the foot of the bed. I knew so little of the routines of hospitals that I did not take this man for the chaplain visiting one of the latest patients on his list. I supposed my wife had sent for him because she had only just learned what I had still not heard because I would not speak to the doctors: that my son was about to begin his last struggle.

The priest made no move to speak, and the longer he kept silent the more I suspected he was waiting for my wife and that we would all three stand like devout Paraguayans around my son's bed until the end came. But then he turned to go, telling me he would pray for my son and all our family. I tried to say something polite but I made strange sobbing noises instead of words. I looked into the priest's face and wept, while he lowered his eyes and waited. Of all Paraguayans, this man was the last I would have wanted to see me break down. He and his kind were too much given to consoling bereaved Paraguayans by reminding them that Paraguay was not the only habitable land. I had talked with a few priests that my wife had received in our house, and whenever I led the conversation towards geography they nodded encouragingly at me as though anyone who had surmised that Paraguay was not the whole world was somehow on the road towards heaven; as though all thoughtful people were of their religion. I had never been able to attack their position; I even admired their way of moving easily through Paraguay as though they looked at each of its landscapes for the last time and yet were not regretful. I saw that I could not even begin to define Australia for any priest so long as he thought of it as my paradigm of heaven. The priests had very little to say about their heaven, their other country, although they assumed they would migrate to it after living rightly in Paraguay. I, on the other hand, could have talked endlessly about the glens or the downlands of Australia whose every detail I had meditated on since boyhood. But I could never have claimed I was sure of reaching them, before or after my death.

In the hospital room I thought the priest was waiting for me to concede that all of us – my wife and I, he, and all Paraguayans of good will – might resolve our different ways of thinking and agree that there was a land that would answer to all our needs: that heaven was in Australia or Australia in heaven and that both of these places were as near to us as Paraguay itself. And I thought afterwards that I had wept because I could never explain, even to that kind-hearted man, what I meant when I talked about Australia.

For three nights and days my wife and I watched our son and saw no clear sign that he was getting better or worse. Whenever my wife began her watch she asked the doctors what they thought. They told her only what they had told her on the first day: that the boy had been very ill when he arrived at the hospital, that he was being given the maximum dose of the best available drug, and that specialist doctors were watching his condition closely.

On the fourth evening, when I arrived for my watch, my wife told me she was beginning to be hopeful. The registrar of the ward had allowed himself to say that the boy's blood tests showed encouraging results. The special nursing sisters who had been assigned to the boy for the past three days had finished their term of duty and had not been replaced. And my wife herself had noticed the boy's urine flowing more freely.

And so, on the fourth evening, as I sat on the couch for my night's watch, I looked myself for encouraging signs. None of the usual specialists came to see the boy. I reasoned that they might have decided he was past the worst of his illness. I thought his urine seemed to drip more rapidly into the bag but I could not be certain. I watched the boy's face but it told me nothing. A nurse remarked that he looked more peaceful. I said he still seemed to be struggling for breath. She told me his airways might have been a little blocked with the remains of his infection.

I had a book with me as usual but I left it unopened. That night for the first time my son and I were alone together for long periods. If he opened his eyes and looked around I wanted to be ready for him. If the doctors were right and he was almost out of danger I wanted to be the first person he saw when he came to his senses. It seemed appropriate that he should see an Australian standing calmly by his bed rather than a Paraguayan ready to greet him with platitudes.

At some time before midnight the nurses changed shifts and a girl of about twenty, thin and plain-looking, began to hang around the boy. She was new to the ward and I resented her not having seen what the boy and his mother and I had so far endured. Whenever she saw me staring at my son she tried to make conversation, as though it was part of her job to cheer me up.

When I looked at her face I noticed two little half-ripe pimples on her chin. I was pleased to see them reddened from having been ineffectually squeezed not long before. I understood that while I had been watching over my dying son not all Paraguayans had been content with their land; this girl had been pinching her face in front of a mirror, trying to make herself fit for citizenship of the Paraguay she seemed to herself shut out of – the land made up of images from magazine photographs and television programs.

The nurse told me she had been out driving with her boyfriend all afternoon. I saw the two of them in his car – she peering at nothing through the hot windows and he drumming his fingers on the steering wheel whenever he had to stop in a line of traffic, and each of them silent and vaguely dissatisfied at having travelled for mile after mile and not seen even a minor accident or anything fit for the evening television news. I followed the couple back to the untidy room he called his flat and watched them sipping their coffee in front of his record player and then, still having found nothing to say, falling against one another and pressing their bodies together and (to reassure themselves that they were normal and healthy Paraguayans) making the gestures and noises they had learned from films.

The nurse, still chattering to me about her day out driving, leaned over my son's bed while I happened to be standing close behind her. I thought the sort of absurd thought that would have occurred to me at the age of fifteen: I saw myself grabbing the scrawny creature from behind, tearing aside whatever layers of clothing obstructed me, and relieving myself carelessly between her buttocks or thighs. I turned away at once and sat on the couch, but I was bothered by thoughts even more absurd. All the female Paraguayans who had ever caught my eye – from those I had believed myself in love with on account of their Australian appearance to those I had merely glanced at in the street – all these girls and women confronted me in a nubile throng and made me understand that if I would only consent to choose one of them there and then and take her behind the nearest tree and do to her what I had never done to any woman of Paraguay (they seemed to agree that my wife was not one of them), then I would be given the strength to bear whatever was ahead of me. I stood silent in front of them and tried to seem unmoved. But I was watching the nurse still leaning over my son, and for as long as her face was turned away from me her calves and even her bare wrists brought to me the message of the women of Paraguay. There is no such land as Australia, they told me; and even their voices worked on me. You dreamed of Australia only because you could not find your way to us. We are your true country.

The nurse turned around and I looked at her face and was myself again, knowing instinctively that what the woman had claimed was preposterous. The nurse was telling me that my son seemed to be coming along nicely and that it might be a good idea if I got a few hours' sleep. She reminded me that there was a proper bed in the children's playroom along the corridor.

I told her politely that I had not left my son alone for more than a few minutes in all the time I had watched over him. I said I was not tired but that I might lie down on the couch from time to time.

She said nothing more, but when she was next out of the room she spent a long time at the sister's desk and I imagined her telling the sister that the foreign-looking father of the boy in the isolation room was driving her crazy – staring at her complexion whenever she looked at him and breathing down her neck whenever her back was turned.

I lay on the couch and turned to the wall and closed my eyes. As I fell asleep I was struggling not to think of the nurse, who was still moving in and out of the room. I was afraid I would dream of her, of leaning my head against her insignificant breasts and telling her all about my son and my homeland, after which I would wake to find that the boy had died with no Australian beside him.

I woke and found I had slept for two hours and that my son had an oxygen mask over his face. The same nurse was beside him, looking hard at him. She told me nervously that nothing was the matter; my son had had a little trouble with his breathing and the resident doctor had ordered him to have a whiff or two of oxygen. Even from the couch I could hear the rattling of something in his breathing-pipes. And I saw how he stirred and fidgeted – although his eyes were still closed and he still seemed unconscious – and struggled for air.

At last, after nearly four days when for every premonition of his dying I was able to find some reason for thinking he would recover – at last I knew that my son was about to die.

The resident who had ordered the oxygen was, I remembered, a girl in jeans whose face had struck me as especially vapid, even for a Paraguayan. I had decided earlier in the night that she was avoiding my son's room, perhaps because she feared the responsibility of dealing alone with a patient who had had specialists with him for the past three nights, but perhaps too – I hoped – because she feared I might ask her some awkward question in my un-Paraguayan accent.

I left my son's room and went to find the resident. I was going to ask her whether it might not be time to phone for one of the boy's specialists or for a doctor from the intensive care unit that I knew was somewhere in the building. I walked only a few steps down the corridor and then stopped. I decided not to speak to the doctor. I would ask for no special consideration from Paraguayans. If they with all their intravenous drips and pathology tests and muttering together in corridors had chosen to leave my son with a girl in jeans and a teenager just back from her Sunday drive, they must have thought he was past his crisis. And if they were wrong they were not going to admit it to an Australian who had kept his nose in a novel when he should have been admiring them at their work. My wife, I knew, would have said I was affecting to despise the people I feared most. Perhaps I did fear them, but perhaps also it was right for an Australian to fear every member of the Paraguayan race because if ever the Australian gave himself up to their way of thinking then part of Australia would disappear for ever.

While I stood there a short, harsh cry came from my son's room. The nurse was calling urgently for the sister. In the lighted office further along the dark corridor the sister got to her feet unhurriedly and walked towards me. The resident, the girl in jeans, followed a few paces behind.

I knew what the cry meant and what was about to happen. I turned, every bit as deliberately as the sister and the resident, and walked ahead of them at an even pace towards my son – to watch him die in Paraguay. I tried to remind myself to be true to Australia, but I was so confused I could only repeat the word 'Australia' under my breath like a prayer.

I could not see the boy at first because the nurse was sitting over him. I walked around to the far side of the bed so that the sister and the doctor could get at him more easily. He had stopped breathing. He had raised his head up from the pillow and opened his eyes and fixed then intently on something ahead of him, but he was not breathing; and his face had gone grey.

Of all that happened in the next hours I remember only isolated moments with no sequence to them. I remember thinking how foolish my voice sounded as I told my son to breathe, not to be frightened, just to lie back and breathe – as though my urging was all he needed. I remember the sister or the resident getting him to breathe sometimes by poking a bit of thin plastic tube down his nose. I remember asking the resident, as though it hardly mattered any longer, whether the hospital's intensive care unit dealt with cases like my son's; her telling me she had already notified them by pressing the triple alert; and my wondering but not asking how urgent in the scale of alerts was a triple alert.

I did not see the two doctors who came from intensive care in answer to the triple alert. But one of them had shoes that squeaked as he loped along the polished floor of the corridor, and the other had shoes that merely thumped. The shoes went on squeaking and thumping past me because my son's bed had already been wheeled to some place called the treatment room at the far end of the corridor. I often wondered how I was persuaded to stay behind in my son's empty room while they wheeled him away. Perhaps I simply decided that he was past hearing whatever I could have said to him.

At some time when the sky was no longer dark outside, a cheerful Maltese man in overalls was standing beside me and mopping the floor where my son's bed had been. I wondered whether it was just a coincidence that he had come at that time or whether the hospital was so efficiently organised that they were already preparing my son's room for the next seriously ill child.

Once, I was standing in the staff kitchen with a cup of coffee in my hand, hearing the sister tell me that the doctors were still working on my boy and that she would keep me fully informed.

At another time again, I was at the window of my son's empty room and watching the daylight spread over Melbourne. I asked myself what sort of land my son might wake in after he had died. I could not forget the idea I had got from the religion of my childhood: that a person's fate after death was determined by his state of mind in his last moments on earth. I thought of forcing my way into the treatment room and hissing the word 'Australia' over and over at my son before it was too late. But I went on watching the grey shapes of the city, and I saw my son wandering in the nameless land-between-lands – the same grey place where three children had once wandered and been mistaken for little children on a lonely sheep ranch in far-off Paraguay. Then, while I was thinking of my son in a setting like an illustration for a book that no one but myself remembered, the squeaking shoes came towards me and a doctor whose face I have never been able to recall stood in front of me and said that he had come from the intensive care unit as soon as he had been summoned and that he and his colleague had done all that was medically possible. He then said something else. I took it to mean that my son had fought with amazing bravery against impossible odds but that he was now dead.

It was bright daylight when a woman calling herself the matron showed me to a chair in her office and gave me another cup of coffee and told me there was a private room waiting where I could break the news to my wife when she arrived at the hospital. I suspected I was being led into a Paraguayan trap. From the first day when I had realised that my son was close to death I had tried to fulfil my responsibility to Australia. I had stayed fairly calm, so far as I could recall, while my son had struggled for breath and even when the doctor had told me the boy had died. But I knew my wife, when I told her the news, could only react as a Paraguayan. I could hear already the precise sound of her sobbing and the very words of her questions about the boy's last hours. And I knew I would hear in every sound she made and every word she spoke the implied accusation that I had caused his death. I could see the matron too, bringing my wife a cup of coffee and trying to comfort her with Paraguayan advice.

I was finished with Paraguay. My only link with that country was broken for ever. Already I could see the bare room in an inner suburb of Melbourne where I would spend the rest of my life alone, reading and writing. What I wrote would probably be called madness by any Paraguayan who happened to read it. But for me it would be one letter after another to Australians whose names and addresses I would never know. In some of my letters I would seem to be pleading to be repatriated. In others I would seem to be saying I was afraid it was too late.

I had only one task left to do in Paraguay. I had to tell my wife what had happened to our son and to bear her accusations silently. I refused to do this in some corner of a Paraguayan hospital. I thanked the matron and told her I would go home by taxi to speak to my wife. The woman said something to me but I was already walking away.

Outside the hospital I walked beside a busy road that led into the centre of Melbourne. It was a cool cloudless morning that promised another of those autumn days more Australian than Paraguayan. People were already driving towards the city. I felt a savage satisfaction knowing I had at last a genuine reason for hating them all; for mocking their hunched bodies and half-witted stares as they drove and the lunatic rituals they were hurrying to perform in offices and factories. I was almost consoled to think that I – walking alone and asking myself what country my son now belonged to – was the only man in Melbourne engaged in a real task.

I saw ahead of me the empty spaces of a park I had sometimes stared at from my son's hospital room. There were no formal lawns and paths, only a roughly mown paddock with scattered native trees. The grass was wet with dew and the trees were faintly cobwebbed and the noise of cars grew milder as I turned from the road and walked into the park. I walked quickly, as though I had some destination in mind, but my eyes were fixed on the rough turf under my feet. Then, in a quiet place almost out of sight of the road, I began to hear noises.

The noises might have been coming from my own throat but they were not the noises of grief. They were the choking noises that my boy had made in the last hour of his life. I heard more noises – groans and grunts and short yelps of pain. Some might have come from my own son and some might have come from any dying boy. Then I heard what could only have been howls of defiance and I knew that I had come at last to the place I had dreaded since the day when I first became the father of a son in the land of Paraguay. I was on the battlefield of Acosta Nu, searching among the dying and the dead child-soldiers for the mutilated corpse of my only son.

When I knew where I was, I stopped and stared at the soil around me. It should have seemed no different from any expanse of soil that I had trodden during my lifetime in Paraguay. But then I knelt down and scraped together a small handful of dust and grass and fallen leaves and scraps of twigs and stood up again and flung my handful of soil away from me as the dead boys, in the last minutes of their lives, had flung their native soil against the enemies of Paraguay.

When I looked at it again, the soil all around me for as far as I could see had been changed. It was the soil that my son had died on. He had died in that place and had died fighting. He had fought because he loved his land insanely. And the land he loved was Paraguay. He had died for Paraguay. He was a Paraguayan.

Then I knew that if my son was a Paraguayan, so was I. And if he and I were Paraguayans, then the people in cars and trams passing a suburban park and glancing perhaps at a distant figure of a man and having no notion that that man stood among the dead after the sorriest battle in the history of an unhappy country – then those people must have been Australians. They were the exiles: the people whose ancestors had travelled in search of an illusion, the people who still dreamed of a vague land they believed themselves shut out of. They were the exiles and I was the man who had come to his senses after all and stood, sure at last of his whereabouts, in his native land – in Paraguay, the country he had thought for years was only a place he had read about.

A QUIETER PLACE THAN CLUN

For twenty-three years I was able to say that the most important event of my life had taken place on a frosty evening while I stood and shivered on a basketball court behind a Catholic church in an outer south-eastern suburb of Melbourne.

I was on a basketball court because I had joined the local branch of the Young Catholic Workers, and playing basketball was all they did on winter evenings. I had joined the YCW because my parents had told me it was high time I started mixing with other young people. (I had made a show of resisting my parents but I privately looked forward to meeting a female of my own age at last.)

Half an hour before the important event, I had learned that I was wasting my time at basketball. The president of our branch had announced that a picnic was being arranged: a bus trip to the snow at Mount Donna Buang. Our sister organisation – our local branch of the National Catholic Girls' Movement – was helping to arrange the picnic. Boys wanting tickets were advised to order them without delay.

I had watched quietly while every other member of my team ordered two tickets. Each YCW member, it seemed, had a girl friend from the NCGM to take to the snow. I had no girl friend. I had never had a girl friend. That was why I had joined the YCW. Yet I had still not spoken to a girl in all the months I had been playing basketball. I had never even seen the girls of the NCGM – although I had thought of them often enough. They too played basketball but they practised on Tuesday night. Every Wednesday night – the young men's night – I had enjoyed a keen pleasure to think that twenty-four hours earlier a throng of short-skirted young women had pressed the weight of their thighs and buttocks against the same asphalt that jarred my skinny, goose-fleshed legs. I had endured the practice sessions on freezing nights when clouds of breath hung above the grunting packs; the long trips by train to distant suburbs for competition matches where I sat with my overcoat around my shoulders on the reserves' bench; the captain's forced grin after each match when he praised me for being a great team-member – I had endured all this as a preparatory rite that would qualify me in due course to choose a girl friend from the shadowy team of females that I never saw. All through the winter I had imagined an end-of-season meeting between my team and the girls. Our parish priest would have urged us all to mingle freely. For once I would be able to inspect an assembly of eligible females without fearing that I might violate some unwritten rule of conduct between the sexes. And I would choose at last a quiet girl who obviously preferred reading at home to playing basketball; who had only joined the NCGM because she wanted to meet someone like herself.

But then the night had come when my team-mates calmly ordered their double tickets to the snow, and I saw I had been wasting my time. On other nights, when those same young men had changed into their basketball costumes, I had seen them tucking their privates carefully into their jockstraps and giving them a last, fond pat before they walked onto the court. But I had always assumed that the young men were thinking, as I thought, of a night far into the future – were trying, as I tried, to envisage the girls of the ghostly team who romped unseen on our asphalt. Now I saw that my parish was no different from the world at large, where all the desirable young women had been claimed already by men who had done none of the serious thinking that was my way of preparing to acquire a girl friend.

I stood on the basketball court that night and thought seriously. The ball was hard and cold, and it bounced with the sound of an outsized steel ball-bearing. Yet it seldom came near me. There were times when I could have walked away unnoticed from the court. Even when I seemed in full view of my team-mates, my thin body might have been as transparent as ice. I tried to think of myself as containing something solid and enduring.

I still imagined the space inside me as containing a soul. And even at the age of eighteen I still kept the image of my soul that I had first acquired as a small child. My soul was a buoyant object shaped like an Australian Rules football. Its surface should have been white and delicate like a petal but it was more often grey and soiled. Knowing from theology that my soul belonged to the spiritual order of things, I had come to imagine it as superimposed on my lungs and stomach and liver – a pale wash on a separate sheet overlaid on the full-colour diagram of my insides.

I got no reassurance from thinking of my soul. It belonged more to God than to me. And it was too little distinguished from the souls of others. When the basketball team had lined up to be photographed – all of us practising Catholics of the late 1950s – the men around me had thrust their chests at the camera as though they hoped the photograph would show the rows of white football-shapes floating inside rib-cages.

I had no intention in those days of rebelling against the teachings, as I respectfully called them, of my church. I could not imagine myself without my soul, grey and stained though it mostly was. But I had sometimes thought of a future version of myself who was rather more daring.

If the colour of orthodoxy was the translucent silver-white of a pure soul, then the colour of rebellion was the colour of skin. I usually thought of this colour as the golden-beige of the shoulders of young women who wore low-topped sun-frocks all though the summer. Sometimes, when that colour seemed too elusive to visualise clearly, I saw the flag of rebellion as purple-red like the bulb of my own sexual organ when it swelled with blood at the very thought of bare shoulders and the overthrow of the soul.

In my final year at secondary school – a year before my basketball venture – I had foreseen a lifelong struggle between my soul and my skin. Night after night, when I should have been studying, I used to contemplate alternate visions of my future.

I saw each of the two as a garden scene. The first was a view of the lawns and shrubs and curving gravel driveways around the seminary of the Archdiocese of Melbourne. Gusts of wind and rain bent the branches of this garden as my future self looked out from a window of the seminarians' library. I drew strength from thinking of the towering shelves of books behind me, and I felt a shower of silvery theology drenching my soul as the rain outside swept across the lawns.

The second vision was of the grounds of the University of Melbourne. The first term had just begun and the lawns were warmed by the clear sun of early autumn. My future self stood on the steps of the university library holding a book of philosophy or psychology. (When this scene had first appeared to me I knew nothing about philosophy or psychology, only that my teachers in secondary school had warned that many a Catholic lost his faith through studying them at university.) The book was full of convincing arguments against the existence of the soul. Feeling the weight of the book in my hands, I thought of myself as a skin-covered parcel of nerves and muscles and blood-vessels – and nothing more. I knew no obligation other than to obey the promptings of the densely packed nerve-endings beneath my skin. I looked out across the lawns and saw a group of young women baring their shoulders to the sun and waiting for me to approach them as soon as I had absorbed the doctrines of atheistic philosophy and psychology.

In the last weeks before my matriculation exams these two visions had driven me nearly crazy. Earlier, one or the other had provided a pleasant backdrop to my thoughts, each lasting a week or so before it gave way to its opposite. But as the time approached when I would have to decide finally between them, each of the two became more vivid and detailed. And they changed places daily, then hourly, then even more rapidly. Late on the eve of my first exam I sat alone in my parents' house trying to study, but all I could think of was myself in the seminary library, vowed to a lifetime as a priest. I saw myself-as-seminarian so haunted by the other vision that I went to a quiet corner among the shelves of theology and masturbated, then packed my suitcase and walked out of the seminary and enrolled at the university. I read volumes of philosophy and psychology and then strode across the lawns towards the young women. But only a few paces short of them I was so troubled by the other vision that I turned back and went in search of a priest who would hear my confession and help to get me back to the seminary, although I knew I would still remember there the colour of female skin under autumn light.

In the first weeks after school had ended, my parents understood that I was still deciding between a university course and a vocation to the priesthood. But then I learned that I had failed my matriculation exams. I joined the State Public Service and told my parents I would spend my evenings studying for a second try at matriculation. In my room of an evening, however, I simply read. Or I sat with a book in my hand and felt free at last from having to choose between visions of my future. My future had already been decided for me. For the rest of my life I was going to work by day at simple clerical jobs and to spend my evenings reading and perhaps, taking a few notes or writing a little poetry. I would go on reading until my thoughts ranged across hundreds of landscapes varied enough to satisfy any of my changeable moods.

I bought a book every Saturday morning in Cheshire's bookshop in Little Collins Street. I bought whatever took my fancy as I wandered among the islands of counters and shelves. Sometimes, when I was a little troubled by the prospect of living all my life in the same city, I bought back-issues of the *National Geographic* from Evans' bookshop in Swanston Street. If I felt suddenly regretful at having no girl friend I used to visit Sewards in Bourke Street to choose from their stacks of anthropology and psychology and to read for a night or two about sexual practices in Melanesia or the case studies of hysterics and nymphomaniacs.

My quiet life did not last long. One Saturday I took home from Cheshire's *Elected Silence* by Thomas Merton, the autobiography of an American poet and non-believer who had become a Catholic and later a Cistercian monk at a monastery in Kentucky. I had finished the book by Sunday night. On the Monday I took a day's sick leave from my work and searched all the secondhand bookshops I knew for *National Geographics* with pictures of the Kentucky landscape. I found few pictures of Kentucky itself, but then I extended my search to include any nearby States that might have looked vaguely like Kentucky. I went home with a stack of magazines and studied their illustrations.

Two separate landscapes lodged themselves in my thoughts and compelled me to choose between them. One was a hillside of leafless woods in Kentucky. The scene was an illustration for an article on folk musicians, but I saw the bare woods as part of the lands of a Cistercian monastery. As a monk, Merton sometimes walked and meditated in such a setting. I calculated that within two years I could save from my public servant's salary my boat fare to California and my train fare from there to Kentucky. Just as Merton had done, I could stay in the guest house of the monastery while my application was considered. A Cistercian monk was a priest as well. In Kentucky I could be the priest I had so often felt destined to be. And when I looked out across the leafless woods I would be too far from Melbourne to want to join the girls on the lawns of the university.

But in one of my magazines I had noticed a colour

plate in an article about the Outer Banks of North Carolina. A girl lay with a book in her hands in a sheltered spot between sand dunes under a blue sky edged with faint, feathery clouds. She was described as a college student at a summer camp. She wore shorts and a striped cotton top. When I looked at her face and her bare shoulders I was reminded that Melbourne's was not the only university in the world. As a student in America I could read and discuss atheistic philosophy all through the summer, at camps where female students took their books with them out into the mild sunshine.

From that day I could no longer see myself as a poet and book collector in Melbourne, filling his mind with scenes from his reading. I felt driven once more to choose between two landscapes from my possible future. Either I was the lean monk in his wooded monastery, despising the pleasures of the world; or I was the lecturer in atheistic philosophy at a university set among magnolia groves not far south of the Mason-Dixon line (and at summer camps on the Outer Banks). But as the monk stalked across the wintry hilltops of Kentucky under branches silvered by dripping rain, he saw the sky clearing away to the south over the Great Smoky mountains, and he could not keep out of his thoughts the image of himself strolling among festoons of Spanish moss with a young student whose religious faith he had undermined, although he might have known that the university lecturer on his way home from a day of pleasure (arranging for his summer camp in the philosophy of hedonism) would look towards the rim of grey cloud on the northern horizon and think for the rest of the evening of the solitary monk walking to his chapel in the drizzling rain.

I thought continually of these two landscapes. I read

only to look for details that would embellish one or the other landscape. (I found the phrase 'broad and generous' applied by Merton to the country near his monastery; I noted the branch of a flowering rhododendron in a corner of a photograph in a *National Geographic* article, 'Dixie Spins the Wheel of Industry'.) I suspected that I would never be able to choose finally between them. I could only hope to be distracted by some quite different landscape.

In those days I believed that people were distinguished mostly by the landscapes they thought about. I was sure I had not met a young woman whose landscapes could compare with mine. The public service typists in the office where I worked seemed made up of layers of streets in places like Elsternwick or Moorabbin or crowded beaches on the Mornington Peninsula. The young women I saw in church on Sunday gave onto the sandy plain south-east of Oakleigh where houses could be built with loans from the YCW Co-operative Housing Society.

Then, one Saturday morning, a young woman brushed past me in Cheshire's and reached down a small book from a shelf in Standard Authors and took it to the sales counter. When I saw her face I knew the landscapes behind it would lead me out of Kentucky and North Carolina. Watching her walk serenely out into the street, I decided she must have watched over places coloured neither soul-silver nor skin-gold.

I went back to Standard Authors and found that the young woman had taken one of Thomas Hardy's novels, almost certainly *The Woodlanders*. I bought a copy myself. It was a cheap edition without a dust-jacket, but the cover was a soothing dark-green. That night instead of reading the pages I stared at the cover and thought of the woman somewhere in Melbourne reading at that very moment the words behind the dark-green. I wanted to lose sight of my own unstable scenery and to look out over the young woman's landscape. I decided that falling in love was nothing else than wanting urgently to see a woman's landscape.

Every Saturday morning I hung around Cheshire's for nearly three hours but without seeing the young woman again. I bought, one by one, all the volumes in the green-covered edition of Hardy. They made a little moss-covered grove among the variegated spines of my library. I had still not read behind any of the green covers. I wanted first to speak to the young woman whose face had seemed like the foreground of a far-reaching vista. I wanted to ask her what she thought she saw while she read her green-covered books. Then, when I came to read Hardy I could suppose there was no end to the green valleys and hills ahead of me. Reading other books I had always been aware that the fictional scenery was surrounded on all sides by deep gulfs like seas or skies. But Hardy's country would be bordered all around, for me, by whatever I thought the young woman had seen in Hardy. And *that* country could seem never-ending because whenever I asked the woman about some corner of it, she would seem to tell me about some place a little further off.

There were other pleasant complications that I was too agitated to sort out at the time. When either of us thought of the other in the act of reading our green-covered fiction, or thought of the other's reading the same page of the same volume that was in front of our eyes, then a succession of landscapes would appear to each reader: a series of more or less green countries making the distance between us seem impossibly prolonged or absurdly foreshortened. Even more promising was my habit of giving a young woman in each novel I read the face of someone I admired. If I gave to some young woman of Hardy's the face of the young woman who read Hardy, and if I pictured that woman reading a page of Hardy and imagining the face of a female character…

In fact I never saw the young woman in the bookshop again. In the days while I still looked out for her I thought I noticed the stocks of Hardy's titles still decreasing. But I decided at last that she was more than likely safe in her comfortable home with the complete works of Hardy while a little band of her admirers went on buying the books that were their only way of reaching her.

In the last minutes before my revelation on the basketball court I asked myself what was the best I could have hoped for at Donna Buang with a girl who had trodden my own rectangle of asphalt. I had been to the mountain ten years before on an altar boys' picnic. I had climbed through mist and found the summit in bright sunlight. Then I had looked eastwards across ridge after ridge of forested ranges into the loneliest part of Victoria and felt solemn. Ten years later I could have shown those ridges to a young woman, but they would have comprised an unsubtle scene only fit for a child impressed by vastness. The young woman beside me would have been entitled to think I had nothing behind my face but a series of blue ridges with perhaps a few Australian-looking paddocks on the far side of me. And I had no business filling any girl friend of mine with the hills and valleys of tourist photographs.

I tried emptying myself of all my Australian landscapes. I felt frail again, with transparent skin enclosing nothing worth looking at. But then I thought of the green zone on the bookshelf in my room: the massed spines of my Thomas Hardy novels. That small patch of green did what the mounts of the Upper Yarra would never have done – even after some young woman and I might have held hands and whispered alone together on Donna Buang. The green of the Hardy books matched a certain colour that I saw inside myself – a colour that must have been inside me even before I looked at my first landscapes.

One of my teachers at secondary school had once said something about Hardy. The public examinations syllabus allowed us in a certain year to study either *The Mayor of Casterbridge* or *Great Expectations*. The teacher, a religious brother, had said we could learn nothing from Hardy. The man was an atheist and a pessimist; in his last years he had suffered from a terrible despair. Our class had read Dickens, but now the peculiar gloomy green of Hardy was displayed in my own room.

It was then, on the asphalt of the basketball court, that my revelation took place. I saw I had no more need of Australian or even American scenery. I would never be either a Catholic monk or a philosopher of hedonism. I would perhaps not be an atheist, but I was certainly destined to be a despairer.

I tried to imagine the contents of the row of green volumes. They were books about the countryside of pessimism, and even my knowing vaguely about that countryside reassured me that I still stood on the earth; that I had not disappeared for want of a landscape.

I knew the English countryside from my reading but I had never wanted any of it for myself. If I had considered England that night on the asphalt it would have seemed a little larger than a double page in an atlas, outlined by white cliffs and beaches where the sea sighed among the shingles and situated far away to the north-west of me, over the shoulder of the world, with its private patch of sky alternately sunlit and clouded. In the lower right-hand corner of England, red-pink and swollen and throbbing, was William Cobbett's Wen. In the far north Catherine and Heathcliff bestrode a hilltop, with the wind whipping their clothes against their legs. In the north-east, and hidden from Wuthering Heights by a shower of rain and the peaks of the Pennines, was Wordsworth's cottage and lake. Down in the south-west Jane Austen was pouring tea in a medium-sized mansion near Bath. The rest of England was a forest of oaks and elms, with occasional clearings of green fields. Oxford and Cambridge each occupied one of these clearings; in another was Anne Hathaway's cottage. Now I saw, in a district of England I had hardly thought of, the woodlanders creeping among their dripping glades with shoulders bowed by pessimism. I saw the mayor of Casterbridge with his face in his hands.

The moment that changed my life was when I muttered a solemn phrase that had suddenly become rich with meaning. I said the words 'literary landscape' as though I was naming my lost homeland, announcing a destination I was about to make for, and explaining the oddness that others seemed to see about me. There was even a title of Hardy's to suit the occasion. 'The Return of the Native,' I said, guessing that a man admired by Hardy had already come to a decision like mine and arrived home ahead of me in the green landscape of despair.

I whispered 'literary landscape' again, and with more force. The puffs of steam that the words formed near my face became the smudge of an out-of-focus leafy branch that was allowed to obtrude into the foreground of certain photographs of landscapes. For once, I thought of myself as on the far side of that blur – a part of the landscape rather than one of the observers. Still on the cold asphalt, I tried to feel greenness seeping into me. It passed easily through my porous adolescent's skin. On the uncongenial surface of my soul it was forced into droplets and ponderous globules. But before it drained away from my sight I found a place for it to settle.

I thought of the word 'ducts' and then the word 'glands'. All I knew about my ducts and glands was that they were small and well hidden and able to exert a powerful influence. Most importantly, I believed they were outside the provinces of theology and philosophy. I thought of them as green-tinted because I had stood as a boy beside my father cleaning the inside of fowls and being warned to watch carefully for the gall bladder and the drops of dark-green, potent bile which might spill inside the carcass and leave a bitterness that could not be washed away.

In my green glands, I decided suddenly, was the source of the strange-tasting stuff called poetic emotion. My glands gave rise to the moods that came over me sometimes as I read poetry or the last pages of certain novels. (Those moods were therefore not brief lapses from my real life into a state of illusion but my being recalled to my innermost workings: the trickling and dripping through me of the essence of emotion.)

That was the moment I considered for twenty-three years the most important event of my life: the moment when I decided that my glands and ducts were more important than either my soul or my skin and that I would devote my life to poetic emotion rather than philosophy or theology. From that moment I was much less anxious about my Catholic soul and much less interested in golden pagan skin. I felt myself filling up with all the branching greenness of the English literature I was going to read. I wondered how I had not noticed them before – the green fronds and tendrils uncurling all through me and reaching out towards the landscapes of literature.

There was more to be pleased about. Skin and soul could be inspected. My pimpled face and my pale chest and arms would have disqualified me from the Outer Banks. My soul was nearly always unsightly in the eyes of God. But the green groves of my glands were far away in a Dorsetshire of my person. I could feel already the sadness of Hardy, and of all the other despairers I would later read, spreading from a point near my throat inwards and away from the surface of me.

I was not rebelling against my church or turning away from women. But I saw that I would never become a priest or monk to tend the bland silveriness of my soul. And I was not going to adopt the philosophy that only led to sunlit lawns and dunes and bare female shoulders. I would never see the woods of Kentucky or the Outer Banks. I would never experience the refined joys of asceticism or the fierce pleasures of philosophical hedonism. I would indulge in pleasures that were morally neutral. In literary landscapes I could neither save nor lose my soul.

That night I packed away the books I had been pretending to study to prepare me for the university or the seminary. At lunchtime next day I left the State Offices and sat in the Treasury Gardens reading *The Woodlanders*. I chose a seat in front of a mass of shrubs. It pleased me that I could not have named any of the plants tossing behind me as I read. I faced a seat where a clerical officer no older than myself clutched at the hand of a girl typist because he had no landscape that offered scope for his emotions. The couple, whenever they looked up, would have seen me alone against a many-layered grove that was the visible counterpart of the twining emotions inside me. I wanted the couple to feel sorry for me, in their simple-hearted way, because I had only a book and no typist for company. I believed that the pity or even the scorn of such people would nourish the greenery I was cultivating.

When I walked into Cheshire's of a Saturday morning I saw the contents of the thousands of books around me as a large and uninviting map of all the landscapes imagined by authors to relieve the tedium of their lives. It was my pleasant task to look across those undistinguished grey continents, with their swarming cities and glaring beaches, in search of the trickles of green – the streams marked by willows and the valleys with copses in their depths. And so I strode past counters overlaid with repeated patterns of Australias and Americas and stood beneath the signs LITERATURE and POETRY, ready to inspect the sad scenery of literary England.

The lives of writers began to interest me as much as their own works, and I soon found fault with Thomas Hardy. He seemed to have been too bound up with the people around him, too ready to see his dull neighbours as heroic dreamers. If I was going to follow his example I would have to rejoin the YCW and pretend that the basketball men went to Donna Buang and such places to see into the grey-blue heart of Victoria. But what clearly disqualified Hardy was his having been twice married. I could not accept that the purest green could spring from a man who had spent most of his life as a fond husband.

Searching for books that would extend the zone of green between myself and my surroundings, I could hardly have ignored a collection of poems with the title, *A Shropshire Lad*. The morning when I bought the little volume was almost as decisive for me as the evening on the basketball court. The book was bound not in green but at least in a yellow that could have been called 'willows-in-autumn'. I had learnt half the poem by heart within a week. I was not so taken by the war-poems, the elegies for lost young men. But the other poems, when I recited them aloud, sounded like the first true account I had given of myself.

I recited them under my breath while I weeded the garden for my father on quiet, cloudy Sunday afternoons; while I walked from Flinders Street station to the State Offices my lips were moving faintly; and at lunchtime I paced the Treasury Gardens to the rhythm of a lament by a young man exiled in London, far from his true, green home and the girl he had lost for ever. I was reconciled to my life at last. Seeing rain-clouds bearing down on my suburb or spring sunshine spreading over all Melbourne – neither of these could disturb me. I no longer experienced changes of mood. A greenness had filled up all the spaces inside me. The same greenness was all around me. I had found the means to live continually in a landscape of literature. If I happened to see the building where I worked or the street where I lived, it was only because the wind had parted for a moment the drooping foliage in front of my face.

Every day I reviewed my past life, finding events in it that seemed vaguely alluded to in Housman's poems. I saw myself in earlier years wandering in what I had thought at the time was an unrelieved drabness of cream or white houses and grey paling fences and failing to see that the drabness was thoroughly interlaced with hedgerows and streams and bordered by blue, un-Australian hills: that my misery itself was a landscape I could not as yet recognise because I knew no poetic equivalents for my emotions.

I was even able to fit into this view of my life the

landscapes I had mistakenly dreamed of before I found my true bearings. I did not despise them; they remained somewhere behind my furthest blue hills, as even America and Australia were somewhere behind the Welsh Marches. But I thought I saw not them but their images, pale and somewhat askew because the light that disclosed them was refracted around the world. The autumn sunlight over Melbourne and the dunes of the Outer Banks were a similar faded gold like the covers of the *National Geographic*s that I would never need to open again. Thomas Merton and the monks of Kentucky still chanted their prayers on winter evenings, but the landscapes of heaven that they saw waiting for them had been tilted a little from the plane of the earth. Girls returning from Sunday picnics around Melbourne peered through misted windows of buses and found themselves already back in their own suburbs when they had expected to see for a little longer around them the foothills of mountains. The students in the seminary on the flatlands west of Melbourne felt themselves suddenly closer to the suburban presbyteries where their evening meal would be kept warm over steaming saucepans while they, curates or parish priests, stood beside basketball courts arranging bus trips to ensure the YCW men married NCGM women and settled in suburbs within sight of the Dandenong Ranges. And girls at the university of Melbourne wondered why their studies in philosophy and psychology had not brought them quite the revelation they had expected in their first autumn term when they sat bare-shouldered on the lawns and gazed at the windows of the library.

None of the people in these scenes could have known why a melancholic haze had settled where their horizons had once been. They could never have guessed that a young man sitting alone in the third bedroom of a suburban house twelve miles south-east of the city of Melbourne saw all their lives from behind a hundred miles of greenery. All the places I had once looked at were on the other side of Shropshire as it appeared to a poet looking west from London in the late afternoon.

A few of the young women of Melbourne came close to learning what had happened to them. They were the women who came into Cheshire's bookshop on Saturday mornings in the spring of 1957 and approached the sign, POETRY, where a stern-faced young man stood reading.

If the young man had not once looked up at them, the women could have dismissed him as someone who had lost touch with their world. But he never failed to notice them. He looked once at every young woman who came within reach of POETRY. He looked cautiously but intently into her face and then briefly at the rest of her before he turned back to his page. He believed that his looking proved he was still well aware of a city outside the bookshop – a city where young women were preparing to bare their shoulders through one more summer and autumn when hedonists would practise their philosophy and ascetics would turn away their eyes towards distant monasteries. But his turning back to his book proved that he saw their world framed by green; that for him bare skin or leafless woods were only parts of a larger, more satisfying scheme. If any of the women had cared to learn what this scheme was, she need only have stepped up and looked at the title of the book that he held obligingly at arm's length, and afterwards bought, *A Shropshire Lad.* But so far as the young man knew, no woman ever discovered that a little volume of poems on display in Cheshire's bookshop comprehended all the unhappiness she was bound to suffer.

I soon found the Penguin edition of the collected poems of Housman. The later poems of the Master meant even more to me. Learning them and linking their themes to my own life I was still too busy to learn the story of Housman himself. When I began to look for books about him it seemed a fateful coincidence that a review appeared in the *Age* of a new biography. (If, as Anatole France is supposed to have said, the only exact knowledge consists of the titles and publication dates of books, then the reader of this work of fiction is here given the first of the two items of exact knowledge in it. *A. E. Housman: A Divided Life* by George L. Watson was published in London by Rupert Hart-Davis in 1957.)

What I learned from that biography should have disappointed me. I had supposed *A Shropshire Lad* was written by a young man not much older than myself, a young man who had loved and lost a frivolous girl in his native district and then languished in London, regretting the landscape that had once seemed a promise of contentment. I learned from Watson's book that there were no lost young women in Housman's life. He had avoided all females except his favourite sister and a plain-faced spinster ten years older than himself who had befriended him as a child. If he had loved anyone he had loved his mother, who died when he was twelve, and a manly fellow-student at Oxford who had kept Housman at a distance and later left for India, married and fathered a family. The biographer argued cautiously and wordily that Housman was one of those homosexuals who can barely admit to himself his true feelings and that the tension of his constricted emotions gave rise to his poetry.

It took me only a few hours to accommodate this new Housman in my scheme of things. Not only that, but I decided the man I had just read about was in fact the worthiest possible exemplar for me. It did not trouble me that when he wrote the bulk of his poems he was a professor of Latin, nearly forty years old. I saw now that his poetry was a coded message – the same kind of message that I wanted to send to the world.

After reading the biography at one sitting I went back to the poems. They seemed, even more clearly than before, a landscape so green and dense that no one could have said where the foliage of glands and ducts gave way to the leaves ahead of the poet or behind him. This was just the sort of landscape I had felt growing over myself.

I decided I was fully qualified to be a poet. I began a notebook. I filled the first pages with an account of what I had already lost. I tried to explain that the girl who had bought *The Woodlanders* in Cheshire's was no mere girl but a great slice of the country that might have been mine; I would never know the pleasure of talking to a woman about the landscapes we had seen in fiction. Likewise, the NCGM girl I had never met had taken away with her thick folio of Australian scenes that might have had herself and me in their foregrounds.

But writing about the poems I was going to write, I realised that actual young women would be better left out of them. I thought I ought to follow Housman's example and not reveal the specific causes of my unhappiness. My poetic landscape, like his, would keep its secrets. I would have liked to buy up the complete edition of Watson's book to guard my privacy and Housman's.

I resolved to live as Housman had lived: to take him as my model. Like Housman I would never declare my love for any woman or man. My glands and ducts would still operate. But only my readers would connect the greenery around me with the stuff that choked me inside. When I began to write my poems, the bare space around me – the space that I kept free of people – would become an English sort of landscape. Mile after mile would fill up with Wenlocks and Ludlows for every young woman I saw in Cheshire's and every busload of picnickers that pulled away from the churchyard on Sunday morning while I was on my way home to my room.

In that room I would sit as Housman had once sat in his lodgings in London, surrounded by a green landscape that I saw as limitless because it lay in the wide spaces between myself and every separate woman or landscape or event that had ever moved me. More than that, my landscape would multiply and prolong itself as soon as I recited a poem of my own or one of Housman's and brooded over the grief that had prompted it and saw the green distance filling up around that grief. I could see all my future as a poetic landscape unrolling towards some unimaginable western place – a sort of Shropshire shifted almost out of sight by sorrow and regret.

Living the life of Housman I stopped bothering about what had once been familiar landmarks. I read poetry on the train to the city every morning and recited it as I walked towards the State Offices. At morning teatime I took out my Housman (sometimes, to vary my landscape a little, it was Swinburne or Robert Bridges or Richard Church) and read at my desk, shielding my eyes against the goings-on around me. But the drudgery of my work – checking sick-leave applications from teachers – and the stares of the other clerks and the typists had their place in my landscape. They became the suburbs of London between Hampstead, where the young Housman had lodged, and the first green fields of Middlesex or Buckinghamshire. The more uncongenial my nearest surroundings seemed, the greener was Shropshire.

My favourite time of day was early evening. In certain twilights I felt qualified to walk in the path of the Great Sufferer himself. I stood, trying not to seem self-conscious, on a hill near London with a view across most of the West Country. I had turned my back on all conventional pleasures and joys. All I wanted that evening, while other young people sought one another's company, was to catch sight of Shropshire. I recited aloud, pretending to believe I was alone on my hilltop:

Where shall one halt to deliver
This luggage I'd lief set down?
Not Thames, not Teme is the river,
Nor London nor Knighton the town:

I stood there, feeling my luggage press down on me. Only one other man had felt such a weight on him. And just then I heard that man approaching. Our paths had crossed in the twilit landscape. The poet had been out walking in the maze of overgrown lanes that wound like tunnels through the outer suburbs. He spoke with the voice of a middle-aged professor of Latin: a voice that was calm but by no means without emotion:

'Tis a long way further than Knighton,
A quieter place than Clun,
Where doomsday may thunder and lighten
And little 'twill matter to one.

I wanted to meet the man whose works I had learned by heart, but I was afraid some word or gesture of mine would be unworthy of the occasion. If I reached out a hand too promptly or looked too boldly into his face, I might seem to be hoping we could be close friends. Even if I kept my eyes lowered and shrank from touching his pale, scholar's hand, he might think I was affecting a sort of coyness. If I spoke out and told him how I had found my way to that landscape, he might cut me short as soon as I mentioned young women.

The meeting as good as took place. Somewhere between reading and dreaming I faced up to my hero. But Housman barely glanced at me. After reciting the last stanza of his poem he stood silent. In the silence I heard again the lines of the poem and the peculiar emphasis he seemed to have given them. I understood what a difference there was between us – even between the rich plangency of his voice and my own reedy complaining. He seemed to have looked even beyond poetry in his search for landscapes; to have followed the greenness of things past borders I might not cross for many years yet. He expected nothing but further refinements of greenness on earth or anywhere else. He was, I remembered from his biography, some kind of atheist.

I was still some kind of Catholic. I could still hope for a Catholic heaven and a God who would finally disentangle my soul from the greenery I had trained over it, and would tell me He took no exception to the workings of glands, and might even whisper (to my shame) that He had known all along my trouble was only a slightly unusual form of loneliness. Housman, though, had no destination but poetry. Compared with him I was a coward. When he stood beside me, staring past the furthest places that his poems had disclosed, I must have seemed to him a mere verse-maker embarked on a rural ramble that would end at dark with glowing tobacco-pipes and foaming jugs of ale in the firelit lounge of the Knighton Arms where young bachelors complained of having been crossed in love. Housman's voice in his last stanza was asking me had I considered how far I would still have to travel even after my collected poems had been published.

I bought a thick, plain-ruled ledger and resolved to fill it with nothing but poetry. I saw the dark-green cover as the lower left-hand corner of a landscape that reached well past Knighton. And I began to work on the first draft of the poems that were meant to fill the book.

When I looked into that ledger at the time of my reading Graves's biography of Housman – the incident described near the end of this story – I was surprised at how little I wrote during the seven hundred and more evenings that I had always remembered as given over to poetry. I felt what I supposed was the usual embarrassment of a man in his forties looking at his own scribblings from more than twenty years earlier. I believed that if I included any of those boy's verses in this story the reader would turn against the writer as I had often turned against the writer of a memoir who first claimed to be embarrassed by his juvenilia and then including a sample, hoping – I was sure – that the reader would find the early work not at all worthless and even a precocious indicator of the mature writer's talent. Then I remembered that I had been even more annoyed by those writers who referred to embarrassing texts but would not quote from them.

I decided to include the poem below in this story when I understood that the young man who wrote it was not myself but a character in a work of fiction and that as soon as I began to write about him I became an author of fiction. (Since the previous sentence is part of a work of fiction, a certain young man and the man he might have become are doubly difficult to imagine anywhere but in fiction. [The sentence just ended is also part of a work of fiction, as is this sentence…])

Here is the best of the poems by a young man of nineteen years who was arrogant enough to suppose that he might create what he called a poetic landscape around himself, but just humble enough to concede that other kinds of landscape might encompass what his poetry created.

Small wonder if my time
Of happiness was brief;
She thought that life was joy,
But I said it was grief.

Now, since she spoke her heart
One freezing winter night,
I know that she was wrong
And what I said was right.

But, oh, my greatest grief
Is that, her whole life long,
She'll think that she was right
And I was in the wrong.

When I seemed to be failing at poetry I tried even harder to live in the style of Housman. I had already noted strange correspondences between the Great Man's life and my own. The young Housman had failed his final year at Oxford under the strain of finding himself in love with his roommate and not daring to declare himself. He had then gone to work as a clerk in Her Majesty's Patent Office in London, studying the classics by night in his bachelor's lodgings to redeem himself as a scholar. I had failed my matriculation exam because I was in love with a landscape (even though I did not know where it was). Now I was a clerical officer in the Education Department of Victoria, living as a hermit in my parents' house. I had no ambition to study but I could be as dedicated to my poetry as Housman had been to his Latin.

By day I kept in mind the young civil servant Housman, as Watson had described him. (He was coldly polite to his workmates and rebuffed any intrusion on his privacy. His only relaxation was long walks through the suburbs of London.) Every Monday the man in charge of my office asked me loudly and cheerfully what I had scored on Saturday night. If I could have been as strong as young Housman I would have stared at Warwick Whitbread and asked him to explain himself.

But I inwardly excused myself from acting like Housman on the grounds that the public servants of Melbourne in the 1950s did not respect scholarship and solitude as Housman's colleagues had. So I merely answered that I had spent my weekend rather quietly, just reading or visiting friends. And I lapsed even further from Housman's example by hoping that Whitbread did not consider me one of the queer, emotionally stunted young men who were talked about and teased in every office of the Public Service. (A clerk on the same floor as ours was famous for using the stairs to avoid being alone with girls in the lift, and for spending all his weekends making a scale model of the Melbourne Cricket Ground out of dead matches.) Later I would hear Warwick Whitbread telling his mates how he had worked in his garden on Saturday and then, on Sunday, driven his wife and children to the Peninsula or the Dandenongs. I felt a keen pity for

Whitbread and his kind. Their struggling to grow lawns and shrubs and their visiting what they called scenic spots beyond Melbourne proved that even they felt an obscure yearning for landscapes.

I had first learned this on my Sunday walks. I used to pass the house of a young police constable, a man so poor that I had seen him sometimes at church wearing the trousers or jacket of his police uniform for want of better clothes. Every Sunday afternoon I saw him, in overalls and a frayed police shirt, pushing a rusty hand-mower over his swampy lawn or pulling weeds from flower-beds edged with scraps of broken roof-tiles. The front gates of his yard were tied together with rags to keep his three young children in. The children dragged at the man's legs, whining for something he could not give them, or picked up and scattered pebbles from the driveway. I always dawdled past the house, hoping the wife would push open the front door with the torn fly-wire and show herself. Her face affected me (although I knew Housman would not have looked twice at it). I thought of the woman (might A. E. H. forgive me!) as a type of all the attractive young matrons of Melbourne who looked out on struggling gardens late on Sunday afternoons and wondered where was that happiness they had once been promised.

If only the policeman's wife, a few years earlier, had visited POETRY or LITERATURE in Cheshire's instead of going on picnics with her husband-to-be, she might have seen ahead of her not blue ranges repeating themselves to the horizon but green fields and hedges so close to her face that she could never lose sight of them. I was far from gloating over her wrong decision. I would have preferred to see her content and prosperous: to have her weatherboard house freshly painted and one more sign of what I had turned my back on. One afternoon, when I thought she looked at me across her miserable lawn, I let my shoulders slump and put on one of my abject Housmanesque faces – not to win her sympathy but so that she could console herself by thinking afterwards of the lonely roads that led past her house towards the country of poetry.

I had never met Warwick Whitbread's wife but he had shown me a photograph of her with their two daughters. Her face had moved me even more than the face of the policeman's wife. It was the face of Tess Durbeyfield or Marty South (before her hair was cut). It was perhaps even the face of a woman who had read a little of Housman and knew about the hardships of poets. I wondered how such a face could once have looked with admiration at a doltish public servant when it might have gazed at pages of literature. I hoped that Whitbread had told his wife a little about the mysterious young man in his office who read poetry in his lunch hours.

One warm morning in the spring of 1958 Whitbread caught up with me on my way across the Treasury Gardens. He talked so pointedly of what spring should do to a young man like myself that I told him at last what I thought he had been trying to verify: that I had no girl friend and no plans for acquiring one.

A week later he invited me to a picnic at Warburton. Two other couples would be going, he told me, and I would be welcome to travel in his family car. I would not give him a definite answer. That night I looked through Housman's biography to learn what Alfred Edward would have done in my position. There was evidence that the poet had sometimes relaxed in the company of his married sister and her family on his annual holidays. I allowed myself to accept Whitbread's invitation, but I prepared myself for the trap I thought he was setting; I expected he would invite his young unattached sister or sister-in-law and seat her in the back of his car with me.

There was no young woman in the car. I still thought she might appear from one of the other cars when we met at the picnic ground, but in our party there were only three husbands, three wives, seven small children and myself – the solitary. We all walked down to the creek and back, and then sat around a rug on the ground. Whitbread and the men opened bottles of beer and offered me a glass. Housman, I knew, had been fond of wine (the one sense he had not striven to curb, Watson had written) so I accepted, hoping my slight hesitation had not told them this was my first taste of beer. I drank four tepid glasses as fast as the men offered them to me. When the beer was finished the men went off to kick a football but I stayed where I was. The women said they would sit for ten minutes before they prepared lunch.

The beer had gone to my head. I leaned back against a tree-trunk and looked freely at the women. Whitbread's wife was just as poetic-looking as her photograph, and the others too had faces that I thought I should have seen in Cheshire's. The women's bodies were more comfortably posed than any I had observed in trains or trams. Their breasts – well used, I supposed, by the crawling children around us – were shaped quite differently from the almost conical solid that was my idea of the breast of the human female. The women had drunk very little, but I assumed they felt the same warmth and fellowship that I felt. One of them, I thought, was in no hurry to pull down again the hem of her skirt that a squirming child had dragged away from a solid thigh.

For the first time in many months I deliberately put

Housman and his country out of my mind. I decided to give Australia one last chance.

My hands were resting on the soil, the peculiar mixture of brittle leaves and straps of bark and sprigs of gumnuts and sparse tussocks that was the texture of the land I had tried for nearly a year to ignore. I had thought that as a poet I had to ignore that soil. Yet in the land of Australia I might have had an audience waiting for me. Whitbread's wife, seeing me lift a child gently to its feet, asked me how many years I thought it would be before I had my own children crawling over me. I was ready to answer her honestly. I wanted all three women to be startled: to see what a great distance separated me from their lubberly, insensitive husbands. Perhaps they might even see me as striding alone in some Australian landscape much stranger than any that their own husbands could show them. I wanted them to remember my name for years afterwards and to look each Saturday in the literary supplement of the *Age* until the day when my first book of poems was reviewed and they turned to their husbands, about to say that strange young man they had once met on a picnic near Donna Buang was now a real poet after all, but then paused and decided to keep the news to themselves rather than hear their husbands guffawing about poets and pansies, because they (the women) vaguely understood why that young man had chosen to live in the remote landscape of poetry – they remembered the day when he had almost explained himself to them.

So, under the influence of the first beer I had ever drunk, I told the three wives what I had meant to keep to myself until I joined Housman in the West Country. I told them I was a recluse for the sake of poetry. I wanted to turn my emotions into poems. My poems would be like landscapes. Those landscapes would be much more strange and lonesome than anything the women could see in Australia. (I surprised myself with the word 'lonesome'. I had heard the word 'lonely' about to announce itself but had cut it short. It would have sounded like a crude appeal to the women, as though I wanted one of them to say she knew just the girl for me: a young friend of hers who sat at home every weekend reading. So I said my poems would be lonesome, and the women might have thought I was writing the words for hillbilly tunes.)

I was not quite so full of my own concerns that I did not notice the women's embarrassment. They looked anywhere but at me. Then one of them stood up and said it was time to get lunch. Another discovered that her skirt had worked its way a little above her knees and pulled it firmly down again. Only Whitbread's wife, with her face that belonged in a setting of the purest poetry, hung back a little after the others had moved away and told me with mock sternness that she wanted to see me not too many years from then at that same picnic-spot with my own wife and children. I saw that for her my landscapes were only a roundabout route that would lead me through unusual scenery back to the pleasant hills overlooking Melbourne.

During lunch the men drank their last bottles of beer and I gulped down another four glasses. Afterwards the women tidied up and their husbands stretched on their backs and dozed. I walked back towards the creek at the bottom of the gully. I was going to find a sheltered place among the scrub and take to myself. But, as I whispered aloud for Housman to overhear, I was not going to do it for pleasure. I wanted to prove that I had not felt towards the women at the picnic a common-place romantic or sexual attraction. I wanted to prove I was still a poet. I wanted to confront the women again after I had spent myself at the creek, to look at their faces and their bulging sweaters but to feel for them only the compassionate interest of a poet.

I tried to find a private place by the creek. There I could have finished my business in less than two minutes, imagining the women were hurrying down the hill after me, anxious to win me back to breasts and thighs and to save me from a life of poetry. But the place I blundered into was overgrown with blackberries. The English weed had choked the banks of the creek and whatever Australian plants might once have grown there. I crept in among some overhanging canes and felt a miserable pleasure each time my right arm came up against a thorn.

Those were the last women I spoke to, socially, for four years. I stayed for two more years in the Public Service, but Warwick Whitbread soon lost interest in me and invited me to no more picnics. I spent my evenings and weekends reading, writing drafts of poems, and studying maps and photographs of landscapes, mostly English.

At the age of twenty-one I enrolled in a course that would qualify me, after only a year, as a primary teacher. Teaching as a job did not interest me; I wanted to get away from Melbourne and into a new landscape. All through my course I studied lists of remote schools and large-scale maps of Victoria and tried to decide where I would spend the forty years of my teaching career. I thought of my future as a series of not days but late afternoons. I had begun to drink daily before I left the Public Service, and I found that a certain amount of beer could usually set my glands working. Now I planned that for forty years as a teacher I would drink every afternoon between four and six o'clock with stolid working-men in a small town whose tree-lined main street trailed away into gently undulating grasslands. I would eat alone at a table reserved for me in the local cafe and then walk through the dusk to my lodgings – a self-contained bungalow behind the house of a silent elderly couple. In the bungalow I would sip more beer and write at my desk. The people in the town would suppose I was preparing lessons or simply reading. But I would be at my lifelong task of writing poetry. And every few years a volume of my poems would be published under a pseudonym and well praised.

I decided, as a trainee-teacher, that the town where my stool waited in a corner of the hotel bar would be Casterton. It was the furthest western town of the size I needed. But when appointments were announced at the end of my course I found I would not be leaving Melbourne. Early in the next year I began teaching at a school of six hundred students in the last of the suburbs that followed the south-eastern curve of Port Phillip Bay.

I was still able to carry out at Frankston some of my plans for living as an unknown poet at Casterton. I rented a sleepout behind a house and drank every afternoon in the only hotel that had no view of the Bay. I even found for company three other teachers who drank every day. They were all grey-haired men who had transferred back to Melbourne after twenty years and more in small country schools. The youngest was as old as my own father but they seemed to accept me – perhaps because I pressed them for stories of how it had been during all their years of quiet days looking across dairy farms or wheat paddocks towards modestly sized mountains. I had hoped at first that one of these men might have been a bachelor who had stared for so long at melancholy landscapes that he had become a sort of bush-Housman. But the men were all married and full of talk about their children and grandchildren; and the only poems they knew came from the Education

Department readers. The grey-haired men could imitate perfectly the tones of children commanded to recite *with expression* 'The Brook' by Alfred Lord Tennyson or 'Where the Pelican Builds Its Nest' by Mary Hannay Foote or 'Sea Fever' by John Masefield.

Sometimes, after I had left the hotel at closing-time (six o'clock in those days) and walked home with the sea wind stinging my face and eaten my boiled eggs and mashed potatoes and got out my poetry folders and my bottle and glass and then sipped and scribbled for three or four hours – sometimes I stepped outside at midnight and breathed the cold air and remembered the night on the basketball court three years before and thought all my glands and ducts were only a green encrustation on the far side of me: a faint smudge like the district of Clunton and Clun as I saw it just then on the dark shape of England, even further away than when I had first begun to write.

On other nights, after I had actually filled half a page with what looked like a publishable poem, I seemed to have travelled some distance across a green territory peculiarly my own and perhaps not quite on the road to Clunton. Then, if I had drunk enough, I would look up at Housman's picture on my wall (cut from the preliminary pages of Watson) and tell him politely but firmly that he was only a pampered English academic who would never have written a word if he had had to teach a grade of forty-five children every day and cook his tea on a single gas-ring.

On Sundays I woke about midday, sick and still half-drunk from the night before. All afternoon I drank milk and tried to read and sometimes remembered suddenly the beginning or the middle of a story I had heard in the hours I could not account for between strolling into the saloon bar soon after lunch on Saturday and being driven home at midnight by the old teacher who had invited me to his house to eat fish and chips and sip whisky in his kitchen. The stories were mostly about country football matches or race meetings, or inspectors of school creeping across paddocks to surprise alcoholic teachers asleep at their desks, and when Sunday afternoon faded on the other side of my drawn curtains and I saw my folders lying closed on the table I was too ashamed to look up at the man who had spent his evenings alone at his desk or conversing over a civilised glass of sherry with some renowned scholar.

On some of those Sundays my drinking had made me so restless and irritable that I could only press myself against a mound of blankets on my bed and fancy myself a sort of Dylan Thomas overwhelming (with confessions of my sloth and my alcoholism and my lust for her) one of the young woman teachers from my school (the same young woman that I passed each day in the corridor and refused to look at for the sake of an approving glance from old Alfred). That would at least send me to sleep for an hour, but I would wake up seeing nothing but greyness around me and thinking I had become already a grey-haired bachelor in a place on the other side of Casterton where nothing much would matter to me.

During my second year in the bayside suburb I sent some poems to magazines but had them sent back to me without comment. I told myself I was not discouraged and went on writing. But I was finding it harder to reassure myself, at the school or in the hotel, that I was secretly a poet, someone with a rich inner life. I wanted to give some hint to the people round me that when I turned away from them I looked across a strange district. Yet I was only qualified to pass myself off as a heavy drinker: a young man who performed in his spare time notable feats of boozing with a group of seasoned topers more than twice his age.

One morning as I passed the sugar across the staffroom table to one of the young women, my hand trembled slightly. I was delighted. I held the hand where it was, trying to put more strain on it to prolong the trembling, and looking for a way to make the spoon rattle in the basin. For weeks after that I thought I might console myself for failing as a poet – for losing some of my inner greenness – by seeming, especially to young women, to glow from inside me with a poisonous yellow: the colour of bitterness and self-reproach – and of strong drink. I might have been satisfied, I thought, if the only landscape that seemed my preserve was a dark and complex series of back lounges of hotels each framed within the other and stretching along a sort of tunnel within the ordinary cheerful daylight of Victoria from that bayside suburb to a remote western town, nothing of which was visible around the dark mousehole where I tossed down the last pinpoint of gold, the molten drop that dissolved what was left of my liver and killed me.

In my last months at that school, while I was trying to find the courage to apply for towns in the western district, I had what my only friend of those days claimed afterwards to have been a nervous breakdown. I called it privately a fading of my inner colours. It began one morning when I walked along the school corridor and saw coming towards me the young woman I thought most often of impressing. I became suddenly convinced that while a man resembling me still walked along the corridor, I myself was staggering, then falling in a heap against the wall. While the woman was still a little way off and aware, I supposed, of a familiar outline of a man in front of her, I felt myself cowering against the wall, a sac of grey-white flesh with nothing solid inside it. I was not quite afraid – more embarrassed at finding myself in a public place with not one gland or duct inside my shrivelled outer casing.

In the past I had found strength at embarrassing moments by murmuring my own versions of the so-called pious invocations taught to me as a child for warding off danger or temptation. Some of the young women teachers used to hire a taxi to the railway station after school. If one of them was away the others used to offer me the spare seat and let me out at my hotel. Pressed into the back of the taxi beside a stockinged leg and a powerful thigh, I used to fear I would turn suddenly misty and vaporous and that the young woman, when the taxi swung around the first corner, would fall sideways into the space where I should have been and start screaming. I used to keep myself present beside her by saying under my breath, 'Alfred Edward, preserve me'; or 'Housman, Poet and Virgin, have mercy on me.'

In the corridor, when I seemed to be colourless, I got no help from Housman. I saw his face, stern and unblinking above his Edwardian collar; I even met his eyes for a moment. But he gave me the cut direct. He looked steadily through me towards the only greenness that he acknowledged: the land around Clun. I had no further claim on him. On too many Sunday afternoons I had thought of consoling myself with young women instead of setting my face resolutely towards the west.

The young woman came up to me in the corridor, nodded and passed on. Apparently my ghostly outline was still visible inside my clothes. I struggled into my classroom before any other women teachers could see me with my colours drained away. The children I taught seemed to find me unchanged, and for the next few days I survived by keeping to my own classroom all day and waiting until the corridor was clear of young women before I stepped out into it.

In the evenings I put aside my poetry and looked among the dust-jackets and back covers of my books for some writer whose life could provide me with a stronger colour than the green of poetry. In Cheshire's on the following Saturday I bought *Memories, Dreams, Reflections* by C. G. Jung. Not much of the book made sense to me but I was taken by the coloured mandalas in the illustrations. Travelling into the city I had had to change carriages to keep away from young women who might have seen how watery I was inside. Travelling home with Jung's book in my hands I found I could comfortably bear the scrutiny of any female by thinking of something called my psyche that glowed like an intricate many-coloured diagram.

I carried a complexity of triangles and circles inside my chest on the following Monday and strode unflinchingly past all my female colleagues. I even noticed a subtle, new resonance in my voice when I spoke to the women, and attributed it to my psyche's being mystically superimposed over my lungs and larynx, so that the air for my voice set quivering the strings of an elaborate three-dimensional harp.

I did not feel bound to one mandala alone. I gathered from looking hastily into Jung's book that the possessor of a psyche might spend years changing details in his personal device. Each night alone in my sleepout I used to add to my colours and shapes. I had bought a record-player and some records of Sibelius. Hart Crane, so I had read, had got his inspiration from whisky and Sibelius. I was not at all sure now that I wanted to write poetry, but I listened to Sibelius and sipped whisky and leafed through my collection of coloured illustrations from the Art section of *Time* magazine. I tried to arrange these sessions so that I was properly drunk and looking at a certain painting by Ralph Borge during the last movement of Symphony Number 5. (I found just now in my filing cabinet the half-page reproduction of that painting but it had been separated from the pages of the magazine and even from the text that included its name. I found only the reproduction with the caption, *Ralph Borge, with meticulous realism, shows human folly, isolation and decay.)* Then I slumped in my chair and ground my teeth while circles and triangles and hexagons of rare colours stamped themselves into my psychic heraldry.

I called the new thing inside me my psyche but the word seemed vague and even pretentious. I wanted to link my psyche with some recognisable part of me so that it would never come adrift and I would never again collapse inwards and stagger in the presence of a young woman. I decided that the coloured pattern represented my nervous system, the manifold and delicate network that grew out of me towards the colours and sounds of the world around. For too long, I decided, I had been preoccupied with the melancholy moods brought on by my glands and ducts. It was time to appreciate the splendid and variegated world that my mandala-shaped nervous system was reaching for; to enlarge and complicate myself; to cultivate my aesthetic sense.

My life now seemed so full and promising that I would have admitted I had been mentally ill when I sat in my room and brooded over Housman's poetry or talked about country schools with the old fogeys in the saloon bar. As for literature, I resolved to write only prose in future; a poem seemed a stunted, greenish thing compared with a huge, tangled, many-coloured novel.

At about this time I read a review in the *Age* Literary Supplement of *The Tin Drum* by Günter Grass. The reviewer acknowledged that the novel had caused a sensation overseas but he found much of the book, so he said, distasteful. It described, I gathered, the squeezing of boils; a man's fishing for eels with a putrid horse's head; the prurient researches of a hunchback dwarf in and around the city of Danzig…I decided that *The Tin Drum* was a message to my nervous system from the teeming, glowing world outside my sleepout. I cut out and kept the review but I had no time to read the book itself. It was enough for me to know that a German with a resonant, evocative name had written a book to prove that everything in the world was worth looking at and touching. In any case, I had to begin my notes for a novel that would do for Melbourne what Grass had done for Danzig.

I was going to write – and live – by the light of my mandala. In its glow, any detail of the world might seem significant. From my classroom window each day I saw the sixth-grade girls' basketball team leaping for the net and baring their white pants stretched over chubby buttocks. A few weeks earlier I had flinched at the sight of that same pink and white and pulled a Housmanish face. Now I stared boldly and felt the tentacles of my nervous system attaching me firmly to the real world at last.

Instead of Casterton and the far west I applied for inner suburban schools. In 1963 I was teaching in Richmond and renting a room in Carlton. The room was sub-let to me by a man I called the Danziger. I had met him by chance in the summer holidays when I was walking from one hotel to another around the edge of the city, buying a pot of beer in each and looking around for a circle of drinkers who seemed like characters from *The Tin Drum*, whose clothes and gestures and words derived from elaborate mandalas. The Danziger and I had been to the same secondary school. But while I had been sighing over my poetry in the Public Service, he had lived with a young woman and then married her in the registry office and been disowned by his parents. On the day I met him we drank from noon to six, after which he took me home and made me repeat to his wife what I had told him of the novel I was going to write about Melbourne; the characters would squeeze boils, and vomit, and smash windows with their voices. The Danziger told his wife to tidy their spare room, and I moved in with my clothes and books next day.

For the first few weeks I made notes each night in my room, but then the Danziger asked me to buy *The Tin Drum* and I used to sit in his lounge room after tea, drinking beer and reading the book aloud to him and his wife. When that book was finished the Danziger, who considered himself a philosopher and an atheist, began reading aloud to his wife and me from *History of Western Philosophy* by Bertrand Russell. On Friday nights we played stud poker with three or four men, bachelors like myself, who admired the Danziger for having found so soon a good-looking wife with no objection to drinking or dirty jokes.

Every Saturday night the Danziger and his wife went to a party somewhere in the suburbs. They urged me to go with them and bring back a woman to their house. Sometimes I did go, and sat drinking in a corner, hoping some perceptive young woman would notice about me the faint aureole from my fiery pattern of nerves. But always, in the early hours of Sunday, I would go home in a taxi with just the Danziger and his wife.

The Danziger was a querulous drunk, and it angered

him that I would sit for hours in a room crowded with young people and speak to no one. I could not have explained to him the strange pleasure that I got from those Saturday nights. I sat alone with a last cold bottle in the loungeroom after the Danziger's wife had called him to bed. Every so often, in the quiet street outside, a car would roar past – driven, I supposed, by some dedicated fornicator such as the Danziger wanted me to become. My nerves would be so alert that their waving, whisker-fine ends picked up a sadness from the miles of dark streets around me. Fornicators hurrying to their double beds or solitaries sitting alone with their bottles – all of us would soon be overwhelmed by quietness. But the solitaries were a little less unlucky because their view was rather more extensive. I had seen the West of England fade into darkness; I knew what was all around the bright patterns of the thoroughfares of Danzig.

One warm day in the schoolyard I noticed the art teacher wearing a sleeveless dress remarkably coloured – hoops of two shades of red interspersed with bright orange. A few days later she was in shades of green and blue strangely mingled. Another woman at the school turned up in browns and purples and told me they were called wild colours, the latest fashion. I was reassured to think of the women of my own city clothing themselves in the same colours that lay just beneath my own skin. Perhaps, I thought, even the most frivolous people worked unwittingly to complete diagrams of themselves.

Seeing wild colours around me I decided that my own mandala was potentially limitless. I had already seen it as including all the shades of skin on the Outer Banks of the Carolinas, all the greys and silvers of rain and monasteries and theology, and all the greens of Shropshire.

Now I was ready to take up my life's work of searching for the many skeins still missing from the huge, coloured fabric strung between my nervous system and the world. I would be helped in this work by a young woman whose preferred colours could lie like wild stripes among my own. And the promptings of my nerves suggested that the art teacher was such a woman.

I approached her in an asphalt schoolground among blank walls of factories under a grey but changeable sky. She was wearing yellows and old-gold. In my hand was a copy of *The Tin Drum*. I had noticed that sometimes in her lunch hour she kept to her classroom and read a book when she might have sat gossiping in the staffroom. I told her I was acutely aware of colours and that the book in my hand – whose contents I had always seen as an arrangement of greys and golds – had made me alert to unsuspected colours in and around the city of Melbourne. I made her take the book.

I was patient with her. I dreaded her thinking I was just one more of the many men who approached her with some novel ploy but only wanted to take her to a restaurant or a cinema and to get into her bedroom afterwards. I talked to her at school for a month before I asked her to go with me to the races.

We sat all afternoon in a private box in the grandstand at Caulfield. I taught her the lore of racing colours, and we chose our favourite jackets while each field of horses paraded. We used the time between races to sketch in the blank pages of our racebooks our ideal sets of colours. I kept the drink waiter busy, and late in the afternoon I was bold enough to tell her about a scheme I had begun at the age of fifteen which I now realised was prophetic of my life's work. (I had worked nearly every night for a year drawing a large map of an island vaguely like Tasmania; describing its many different rural landscapes, its provincial towns, and the suburbs of its capital city; compiling a list of the hundreds of owners and trainers of racehorses and their addresses; and then devising for each of these men or woman a set of racing colours reflecting their character or the special quality of the place where they lived.) The woman seemed impressed. She invited me that evening to the flat that she shared in Balwyn and we talked and drank until past midnight. But I understood, from something she let slip, that she had a man-friend of long standing who happened to be in Sydney on business for that weekend.

I did not press her in the weeks after that. I wanted to persuade her that my nervous system was far more extensive and brightly coloured than anything her travelling salesman friend could boast of. But I waited for her to invite me to her flat when she was free to learn more about me.

On my second night at her flat in Balwyn I declared myself to her. If I had still thought of myself as defined by my emotions, I would have said I was in love with her. But I wanted to use words befitting my mandala of nerves, and so I gave her a prose-poem I had written for her. Its title was *Grey and Orange*; the grey was for the suburb where we had met, and for Carlton where I lived; the orange was for the strangeness that she and I would find together wherever we went. (I had chosen orange under the influence of the passage in *A Rebours*, by J. K. Huysmans, in which Des Essientes is described as choosing a colour for his rooms.) I also gave her a tiny pattern of racing colours I had made from grey and orange silk ribbons. I wanted her to pin the colours to the wall of her loungeroom, so that she might glance up at my emblematic pattern on some night when her boy friend had revealed his own inner drabness.

On the night when I gave her my colours and my prose-poem we were alone in her flat – the other girls, her flatmates, were somewhere on holiday. I lay beside her on the couch and talked to her and kissed her until almost morning. She went to her room at last and told me I could sleep on the couch. I suspected I had failed her, and after she had gone to bed I fastened my grey and orange to the wall and slipped away, sure I would have no further opportunity for talking seriously to her.

There was another art teacher at another school in an inner suburb a year or two afterwards. She dressed always in a uniform red or blue or yellow and tried to tell me that only the primary colours, and very simple designs, were fully satisfying. Thinking of impressing her, I turned over stacks of ribbons at a shop counter to find a single shade for my racing silks. (In racing terms, I would have had *all chartreuse* or *all tangerine*.) But nothing so simple could do for me.

I was never alone with this woman in our few months together. She was planning to go overseas, to get over (so I was told by her best friend) a long association with a married man. On our last night together she asked to go with me to my room in the Danziger's house – to see, she said, the desk where I worked at my great novel. I sat with her on the edge of my bed, dosing myself with Bond 7 and feeling ashamed that for all my talking to her about elaborate works of fiction and detailed mandalas and many-coloured cities, the only noticeable colours in my room were the spines of books on my shelf and the vague brown or amber of the whisky in my glass.

In the last few years before I reached thirty I thought much less about the colours and shapes that might have filled up a putative space inside me. I had become a Statewide relieving teacher, which put me at the disposal of the Education Department. I was sent for months at a time to country schools whose head-teachers had resigned suddenly or had nervous breakdowns. I left my books and notes in a room that I still rented from the Danziger. (I had stopped calling him openly by that name. I even pretended to him that I had given up writing the novel we had once talked about. He and his wife had bought a much better house in Carlton and joined the Australian Labor Party; they gave all their free time to what they called grassroots politics.)

I lived now in country hotels with only a suitcase of clothes and a pad of blank pages as my possessions. In some hotels I stayed for as long as two school terms, but I always kept my room scrupulously bare. Except for a few clothes hanging in the wardrobe, the room always looked as it had on my first day in it. Even my shaving gear and toothbrush stayed all day in my suitcase, along with the book I was currently reading. The pads that I used for my own writing rested under my pillow by night and under the seat of my car by day.

I drank every evening with travellers who were booked into the hotel or with the local after-hours boozers. In those shabby hotel lounges I was more nearly contented than I had ever been. I belonged where I was for the time being but the place had no claim on me. The local people knew I was only passing through. They could not resent my not joining their clubs and committees. They could not even wonder why I had no girl friend, since I drove out of their town nearly every Friday afternoon and did not come back until late on Sunday night. (I grinned and tried to look secretive when they asked me in the hotel lounge on weeknights about my playing up, as they called it, in Melbourne. I tried the same show of secretiveness with the Danziger when he first asked me of a Saturday night about my social life in the country. But he saw through me and said there was no hope for me and I could rot in my room if that was what I wanted.)

In my first year as a relieving teacher my weekends had been spoiled by the Danziger's disapproving of my solitariness. After that I perfected a way of life that lasted me for nearly five years. I arranged my movements so that I was a stranger almost wherever I went. I in my months as head teacher by the Loddon, for example, I left my school at four each Friday and drove south-east but stopped well short of Melbourne at Ballarat or Daylesford or Kyneton, usually within reach of a race meeting. Sometimes I did return to Melbourne and quietly let myself into my room and told the Danziger when we met at last on Sunday morning that my movements were now unpredictable. He might well have imagined me alone of a Saturday at some country race meeting or football match and then drinking afterwards with the town's outcasts. But what mattered to me was that he had to *imagine* me. Sitting over our Sunday beer I was a man with something of a map defining me. Even if the Danziger saw nothing more than an outline of me intersected by a few wandering lines for the roads of north-central Victoria, I was satisfied. So was I satisfied if some mother of one of my pupils, a woman hardly older than myself, watching me lock the front door of my school and fasten the front gate and walk through drizzling rain towards my car, saw the grey margins of some approximate diagram of a nameless suburb of Melbourne protruding from behind me like a rudimentary aura.

I no longer tried to conceive of a unified image

for what comprised me. I had stopped wondering about anything so vague as a space inside me to be filled with something distinctive. I thought it was a sign of my maturity that I could entertain paradoxes and contradictions in my thinking of what I was. And I could even suppose calmly that the inner or real part of me was somewhere out on the back roads of a map of Victoria. No one talking or drinking with me in a particular town could guess which other town it was where I became myself at last. I enjoyed imagining a road junction like many I had passed carelessly through in the late afternoon, where two approximations of myself happened to meet for a moment (not driving cars but striding through the straw-coloured roadside grass like parodies of some English poet out for his daily stroll). They met, and barely paused before they went their different ways. But their passing at a place marked by no township, under a fading sky, and with no word and not even an understanding glance between them – the image of their passing like that and then going their ways towards even lonelier junctions where they might meet up with and pass still other men resembling themselves was an image that saved me from straining to imagine the one man I should have become. My skin and soul and nerves had long since stopped bothering me. If I needed to think of my ruling faculty I thought of my imagination – not as something with any colour or shape but as a space wide enough for a system of roads to intersect in it and then diverge and then perhaps meet up again by way of strange branchings and detours.

The life I actually led did not seem harsh or empty. Sometimes I was posted to a larger school in a suburb of Melbourne or a provincial city. The men teachers on their Friday night drinking sessions would defer a little to me.

I was a man who had not been trapped by marriage (as they affected to think they had been) and was not burdened with mortgage payments and lawn-mowing and home handyman jobs. When I named some town or district from my history as a State-wide reliever they assumed I remembered it as linked with the name of a young woman and memories of sexual adventures.

At some of these larger schools I would carefully approach one of the young woman teachers, finding her alone in her room just a little more often than could happen by chance or talking with her just a little more warmly than a teacher would talk to a colleague. When I mentioned to her a few of the towns I had passed through, I meant the names to sound like code-words for moods that had steadily settled over me: successive layers of quiet disappointment, mild regret, gentle cynicism. But, inevitably, she would say something trite, and I would go away thinking how far my tracery roads must have been from the sites of others' imaginings. For the rest of my time at her school I would treat with her politely but coolly and sometimes imagine a young woman somewhat like her in a town on the far side of roads I had still not even seen. (I saw my roads as leading always west, but during all my years at the mercy of the Education Department I had never been sent within a hundred miles of Casterton.)

At the age of thirty-four I had a story published in a magazine that lasted for three issues. *Charlie Alcock's Cock* had begun as a section in the huge novel I had not even half-finished. It was a mostly imaginary story about a man I might have been if things had gone differently with me. Yet I could foresee myself one day handing a copy of that story to a woman in a district not far short of Casterton and saying it would tell her more of the truth about me than any words I might speak to her.

As the author of a published story and of occasional articles in a country newspaper (whose proprietor had drunk with me five nights a week), I began applying for jobs where I might meet what I thought of as literary people. I was appointed an assistant publication officer for the Department of Main Roads. I was no longer a teacher with all of Victoria as my territory. I worked every day in an office in Melbourne and lived in a flat in South Yarra.

A senior man in my office had had a book of poems published. I tried to impress him as a writer who had learned his craft scribbling on a cheap writing-pad in the lounges of small-town hotels, with a pot of beer in front of him and his free hand pressed to his ear to keep out the din from the drinkers around him. Now, I told the man, I wanted to be stimulated by meeting other writers.

The poet invited me to a small gathering at his house. It was in one of the better parts of South Yarra; from a corner of its front balcony he could see the elms of Fawkner Park. (I lived in the cheaper quarter south of the Toorak Road post office.) He sat beside a woman he introduced as his girl friend, but I understood that he lived alone and had never been attached to any woman.

I told the man and his guests that I had come to live in South Yarra because I had learned that I belonged on the margins of things. I wanted to live as a tenant in a suburb of mostly transient people. The sound of the Dandenong trains at night brought my childhood as near as I wanted it. The wind from the sea sometimes was enough to warn me away from the bayside suburbs, where I had once spent two miserable years. And walking past the venerable trees in Fawkner Park told me all about the western districts I had always meant to cross.

When I mentioned the western districts the poet told me about a writer he very much admired, a man who lived alone behind his married sister's house in Malvern and wrote scholarly histories of early Victoria. This writer had been working for two years on a study of certain remote districts during the pastoral age. He spent his days in a book-lined room, deaf to the noise of traffic along Glenferrie Road and hearing, perhaps, only the sounds of quail and plover on the wide plains towards Hamilton.

After that night I asked the poet often about the solitary scholar. I was told he was a warm, even a passionate man, but that he guarded his privacy and disliked gatherings of people. And then I was told, finally, that the scholar had announced he would like to meet me.

Just the three of us had dinner at the poet's house. The man who wrote about the west had a fine, sensitive face. He looked at me guardedly, as though he preferred to wait for me to cross the plains between us. Later, relaxed a little by wine, he told me that he wrote because the idea of his published works filled a gap that he had always felt in himself.

While the two of them talked, in their leisurely and knowing way, I looked at the scholar. That aloof and somewhat effeminate man, only a little older than myself, was almost certainly the most likely person – of all the women or men I might meet – to understand my story. So I thought, and was then driven to play the boor in front of him.

I told both men that all my journeys across Victoria had been in search of a certain young woman. When I had not found her in this or that town I had dreamed about her in a town further away and then gone on drinking – drinking beer and not the wine we had been delicately sipping that evening.

Later in the evening I went uninvited to the poet's fridge and helped myself to the cans that he might well have been keeping as a treat for me: a midnight libation to be poured when the three of us had edged a little inwards from our widely spaced watching-posts. I gulped the cans in front of the two men. And in the last hour before I blundered out of that house and across Toorak Road (to vomit behind the nearest tree in Fawkner Park) and then home, I told them I had not finished my travels: I could still see myself in some town far to the west after all.

Yet I thought sometimes, for a year or two after that evening, that when I had passed the age of fifty and perhaps had a slender book of my fiction published, the scholar and I might drift together. We might share separate wings of a large white weatherboard house, with verandas running all around it and tamarisks in a row along the front fence, in a side street of Mortlake or Skipton (where he would be at the heart of the plains he wrote about, and I could look up for the rest of my life at huge patterns of clouds and feel I was at least halfway towards the vague destination that still floated to the west of my thoughts). Our wings of the house would have to be quite self-contained. I would have told him frankly that I was sexually neutral – something I had told no one else, although I might have hinted at it sometimes when I was hopelessly drunk in the company of dedicated womanisers for the odd distinction it seemed to give me. We would be two greying bachelors, reticent with one another because we had long since decided to save our words for the writing that was supposed to take us towards the places we dreamed about.

Now follows the second piece of exact knowledge contained in this story. In 1979, just as I turned forty, *A. E. Housman: The Scholar-Poet*, by Richard Perceval Graves, was published in England by Routledge and Kegan Paul. Waiting for the copy I had ordered from my bookseller, I was by no means intimidated. It was a lifelong bachelor (in practice, if not in spirit) and a published writer (of at least one short story) who mounted the stairs to a remote room in an outlying wing of Cambridge University. If I lost my way among the colleges and chapels I was not going to apologise. My place was Melbourne and its hinterland to the north and west. (I had never been anywhere else; my hair was turning grey and I had never crossed the borders of the State of Victoria.) I would not have a professor of a dead language talking down to me, as though it was part of my duty as a man of culture to know my way around King's or Balliol, and part of his not to know even where Melbourne was.

If my opening the parcel from my bookseller was my rapping at Housman's door, then my reading of Graves's biography was my finding the Great Man's rooms empty. I thought at first he had declined to meet me. I thought he had slipped away rather than confess that his solitariness was a sham: that the man from the colonies who had once been his disciple knew more about hardship than he did. I thought this after reading in Chapter 8 of the paper found, long after the poet's death, between the leaves of one of his books. The paper listed the dates of his visits (when he was a man in his fifties) to male brothels in Paris, and the varieties of pleasures he enjoyed there.

Later I thought differently. And my later thoughts were my turning away from Housman's door to look westwards for the last time across the Cotswolds and the Vale of the White Horse and the Thames Valley, and whatever else my vague geography should have taken account of, towards the furthest place I was entitled to imagine. I saw the quiet town of Clun. I saw it not too dimly because I had read enough twentieth-century fiction and heard enough jokes in bars to know what a middle-aged professor from Cambridge might enjoy when he submitted his pale, pudgy body to a muscular young Frenchman.

But I could not imagine the place on the far side of Clun, the place that Housman could still have thought of after he had paid off his boys and made his notes and folded them away between the pages of the book that would not be opened until after his death and put it on his shelf.

I put my own book on my shelf. On the cover was a coloured photograph of huge beech trees in some unidentified English landscape. Once, during a family game, the adolescent Housman had been asked to name his special tree. He was then not quite as old as I had been when I discovered the greenness of what I called poetic emotion. He had announced that his tree was the beech.

I could have been still standing on a rectangle of asphalt, a road cut off at its beginnings, while I went on looking at the thick trunks and the many layers of leaves in the place that was more quiet than any I had known.

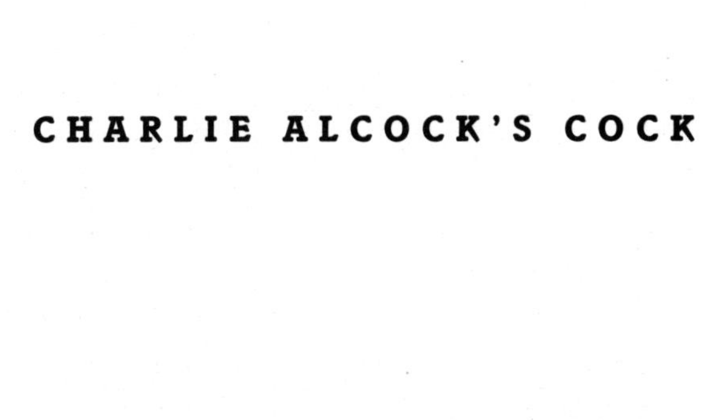

CHARLIE ALCOCK'S COCK

One of the first things I discovered about the world was that I seemed shut out of the best part of it. I had learned soon enough how to put a fence of mud and twigs around a clump of jonquils and a colony of slaters in a corner of my backyard and to tell myself that someone somewhere else was anxious to see behind my handmade barrier and to learn the private meaning that I gave to what I hid. But I knew that my hiding-places were too far along disused paths and too far into corners – they were the very places that a thoughtful searcher would set out for. I would have liked to learn the adults' trick of hiding their secrets in places I passed every day or even in objects I handled.

When my mother had gone to the bus-stop after warning me to be quiet and not to answer any knock at the door, I used to run to the drawers and cupboards in my parents' bedroom. I never doubted that I would find them all unlocked. But even before I put my sweating hands on the first of the cool, silvery handles, I knew that what I found inside would be only signs of further mysteries. On the afternoon when I opened one after another of the boxes on the floor of the wardrobe and drew out at last from layers of tissue-paper the long, casually coiled and flesh-coloured tube with a nozzle at one end and a swollen bulb at the other, I should not have expected too much from my discovery. Yet I pinched and bit the nozzle and squeezed the tube and tortured it into loops and thought I was about to learn something years before I was meant to. Then I gripped the bulb between my thighs and let the tube and nozzle dangle to my knees and turned to the mirror as though I would see there a face turned suddenly knowing.

I never found the rubber thing a second time. I believed it was still in the bedroom but behind some panel set flush in an innocent-looking wall. Long after I had given up searching my parents' room I remembered that I had once found something strange in my own house: had even gripped it ineffectually in my hand but then lost sight of it again. I went on searching for whatever else was hidden and yet within reach of me. I repeated to myself conversations that had stopped when I entered a room. Glancing at a shelf of books, I could nearly always pick the one that was not thought suitable for me.

My first ten years were spent in a suburb of Melbourne so quiet that I believed no people could have survived on the far side of their trimmed privet hedges unless their wardrobes and cupboards were stuffed with rubber or clay or painted tokens of another world altogether, a world that poked up into Melbourne in the dark corners of bedrooms and the shadowy spaces under fruit-trees and behind fowl sheds in backyards wholly hidden from the street. On many a Sunday afternoon when my mother took me on long trips by tram to visit some aunt or great-aunt and I had to sit for the first half-hour in the front room, I looked around me for some detail of a painted landscape on the wall or some gesture made by a porcelain figure in the crystal-cabinet or some pattern in the threads of an antimacassar that seemed the nearest sign of the other world. Then, when I was allowed to go outside, I would always find a certain kind of place – the patch of rotting leaves under the tree fern on the blind side of the house; the clump of arum lilies between the garden shed and the back fence; the corner of lawn just beyond the last flagstone in a path that had seemed likely to lead to something much more definite. I would stand in that place and stare, and wonder what word I had to learn the meaning of or what other person I had to turn myself into before I could recognise the doorway that must have been somewhere just in front of me.

The aunt that we visited most often lived in Hawthorn. At least once a month my mother and I left the tram on the corner of Riversdale and Glenferrie Roads, turned in among the narrow side-streets, turned again finally at a front gate, walked up a path between two identical beds of standard roses and poppies, climbed three wooden steps between two stuccoed columns, and stood on the oxblood-stained boards of the veranda. My mother called, 'Ooh-ooh' – the cry of a woman from the back streets of Melbourne at a door she was entitled to enter without waiting. Then she went through to the kitchen and I stepped across to the low wall of roughcast stone that bordered the veranda. If the dark-green canvas blinds had been rolled up, I could inspect either of two cement troughs resting on the broad top of the veranda wall.

I had three cousins in that house. The older two were girls, five and six years older than myself. Each girl had what she called a cactus garden in one of the cement troughs. Tiny gravel paths wound among dwarf cactuses and buttons of moss and painted pebbles; a painted wooden cottage, smaller than a matchbox, stood beside a pond that was a piece of broken mirror. I was always annoyed when I looked at the miniature gardens as soon as I arrived but found no evidence that their owners were embellishing them – no new plant inserted among the pebbles and no new turning given to a pathway.

Inside the house, while my mother sat at the kitchen table all afternoon with her sister and the two or three obscurely connected women who were always at my aunt's for Sunday tea, I was expected to amuse myself with the third of my cousins: a boy three years younger than myself.

In later years the boy had boxes crammed with comics under his bed, and I used to read all Sunday afternoon while he pleaded with me to play Test Match or Happy Families. But when I was seven or eight, and he was four or five, I still hoped he might help me to find what I was looking for. I used to take him to the cave of shadow under the lemon tree in his backyard. On the way, I reminded him of the strangeness of the place we were going into, hoping he would blurt out when we were there some secret of that house of mostly females.

Sometimes I would get his mother's permission to take the boy for a short walk. With my hand around his, I would pause at points among the half-dozen streets in the north-eastern right angle between the Glenferrie Road and Riversdale Road tramlines, waiting for him to tell me something that would cure my strange unhappiness as the afternoon turned to evening and the houses and yards still gave nothing away. There was one street named the Boulevard, with a cypress hedge and a laneway of bluestone pitchers on one side where a footpath should have been. I made the boy walk with me along the uneven bluestones, between the hedge and the grey paling fences at the sides of houses. I wanted to hear what a woman or a girl might cry out in a backyard, on one more afternoon that seemed to have come to nothing, when she forgot for the moment that her side fence adjoined the street with the strange name and the dark hedge. In another street we knelt in the very middle of the deserted roadway, putting our heads against an iron grating to hear the trickling and gurgling of unseen sluggish water on some unthinkable route. And at the furthest point of our walk we came to the junction of the tramlines.

The northern suburb where I lived had grown up around a tram terminus. A pair of tracks came to a dead-end at a T-shaped road junction. Any tram I saw was either arriving from the city or setting out for the city along the same straight route. But Hawthorn, east of Melbourne, was crossed by more than one tramline. I stood with my young cousin and studied the complexity of a right-angled junction with sets of points that could have sent a tram suddenly swerving out of its straight route around a corner – passing strangely close to footpaths and shop windows – and onto another route altogether. On those Sunday afternoons of the late 1940s, when the noise of motor-traffic was only the variously modulated throbbings of separate engines approaching and then passing and then fading away, I could sometimes watch one of the green and yellow trams out of sight over a hill and still catch the last rattlings of its wheels or the lingering hum in the wires overhead. No tram that I saw turned left or right at the crossroads. Yet I took pleasure from the signs of their destinations above the drivers' cabins: ST KILDA BEACH, KEW COTHAM ROAD, BURWOOD, WATTLE PARK ELGAR ROAD. I had never seen any of those places, but their names all sounded of open spaces and trees. I hardly bothered to remember which destination was in which direction. Instead I rolled all four names into one and thought of all the trams I saw in Hawthorn as bound for some quarter of an immense, park-like landscape.

When my boy-cousin was still much too young for comics, my mother and I came to live for a month in his house. (During that month there was no distant suburb I could consider as mine. My father had had to sell our house, and he was still looking for a new home for us while he boarded with one of *his* aunts.) While I stayed with my cousins I slept not in the boy's room but on a stretcher between the beds of my two girl-cousins.

On my first night I tried to stay awake until the girls' bed-time. I wanted to feign sleep and to peep at them from between my eyelids while they undressed. But I woke to see the walls strangely shadowed from a nightlight outside the door and the girls' beds with humped bodies under the blankets. I thought I might have learned something at least from studying the girls' faces while they slept, but each had turned away from me.

Hardly a car passed in the streets around, but the trams were still running regularly. The night was so quiet that I could hear the pairs and pairs of steel wheels bumping over the right-angled crossing at Glenferrie and Riversdale Roads. When a tram gathered speed I tried to decide which route it was following. The rattling and the whining might have come from just beyond the back fence. I could hear the whole length of the tram trundling over the bluestone pavement of the laneway where I was not supposed to walk with my boy-cousin because my mother said it was too lonely. At the end of the lane was the Boulevard, the street whose name sounded at night like the call of an owl. I listened, and then heard with ease what I had wanted to hear: the tram swung into the secret part of the Boulevard – the space between the cypress and the side-fences of yards.

In my bed, in the long shadows of my cousins' knees and shoulders, I remembered what was strangest about the Boulevard. It was a street that curved. Of all the streets I had seen in Hawthorn, only the Boulevard did not fit neatly into the commonplace grid surrounding it. When a tram in the night went by way of the Boulevard I could think of it as following the queerest of routes. One tram that I heard travelled easily through every dark space under the lemon tree, and then through the dark space under every tree in a hundred further backyards. Another tram went underground, through tunnels that were anything but straight, and rose again, startlingly lit, in the least expected of places.

Before I fell asleep again I was almost reassured. I had sometimes feared that the streets wherever I went would be too simply arranged to lead to the mystery that hung over certain afternoons. Now I could think of streets riddled with strange by-ways and short cuts needing years to explore. And I could hope to hear faintly in my sleep the sounds of trams multiplied, the patterns of their routes made more complex, and all their destinations called into question.

Each night, in the intervals of silence between the comings and goings of the trams, I stared at something on a high shelf at the far end of the girls' room. Under a tiny dome of glass a figure of a woman stood in a pale landscape. Sometimes I thought she was Our Blessed

Lady rising through fluffy white clouds on the day of her assumption in to heaven. Sometimes I took her for Saint Thérèse of Lisieux, posed among the shower of roses she had promised to send down from heaven after her death. Once, I thought the woman was a pagan goddess and the white stuff at her feet was the heap of veils she had thrown off while she danced until only one last layer was lightly draped around her.

In the mornings I lay in my bed while my cousins rolled and twisted and struggled to dress themselves under their bedclothes. I preferred not to listen to the trams by day and not to look at the woman under the dome of glass. I was sure that if I showed any interest in the woman, my cousins would lift her and her glassed-in scenery into the wardrobe and out of sight for good. Even if the girls had allowed me to press my nose against the glass, when I turned to ask them about the woman I would have caught them winking at one another.

On a few afternoons, when they had come home after school, the girls would invite me without warning to go walking with them. They led me by the hand to a neighbour's backyard where I crept slowly up to the canaries' cage – but never surprised the birds making their nests in the salmon-tins nailed near their roof. Or I was led to another yard and allowed to peep into a greenhouse full of orchids – but never to study the shapes of their pink and purple inner parts. Or the girls took me to the house they called the Hollywood mansion, where I stood at the front gate and stared at the gaps between the water-lilies in an ornamental pond and agreed that the red blob I saw was a beautiful goldfish. My cousins showed me these treats, as they called them, and I always thanked the girls afterwards. But I believed I was being tricked: the girls were trying to persuade me that I had seen everything worth seeing in their suburb. They wanted me to think that nothing more significant than canaries or orchids or goldfish was hidden between the back fences of Hawthorn. They wanted me to see no more than a child should see. They supposed I knew nothing about the insides of wardrobes or the dark spaces undermining their house and their suburb. The younger girl even grinned at me one evening when I saw her through the half-closed bathroom door tucking her skirt into her pants before she stood in the bath to scrub her knees and feet. She mistook me, I saw, for a child: someone who would do no more than squeal foolishly and try to splash her if she allowed him into the bathroom with her.

That was all I heard my boy-cousin doing every night in the bathroom. He sat naked, I supposed – in the shallow water while his sisters in turn stood above him or sat on the edge of the bath and leaned over and wiped between their toes or around their ankles. I listened through the walls to the boy's laughing and spluttering and wished I could have burst into the room and punched him in his moon-face and dragged him out of the water and stripped off my own clothes and sat in his place.

I could not have said what I wanted to happen after that. My lying there exposed would have been only the beginning. The girls, still with only their long legs bare, might have despised me at first or pitied me. But in time they would have come to trust me. I might not even have asked them to uncover their own bodies so long as they revealed their deeper secrets. I wanted to know what they talked about when they stood at the corner of their street of a morning, waiting for the tram to take them far to the east along Riversdale Road to one of those suburbs where the dark-green of hedges seemed to meet in the middle of the roadway and events sent a faint humming towards me through the tram-wires. I wanted to know why they stared for a long time at certain pages in magazines but held those same pages up to their faces to keep me from looking. I wanted to know what they kept in their cupboards, especially what they might have wrapped in tissue-paper in the darkest corners of their wardrobes. In return I would have explained to them what I had discovered about their backyard and their corner of Hawthorn. I saw the three of us walking of an evening in the Boulevard following its gradual curve, and myself stopping them well before they saw where the curve was taking us and describing all they should expect ahead of them.

The bathroom window overlooked the back veranda. The window was nailed shut and the glass coated with a thick brown paint. There was an hour on nearly every weekday afternoon when the girls were at school and the boy was lying down and his mother and mine were talking over cups of tea; it was the hour when blowflies blundered against window-screens and the leaves of the lemon tree were gently lifted and let fall again by twos and threes. At that hour I stood alone in the backyard and wished someone else as well as myself had the task of keeping in mind all the promises of things about to be revealed in all the quiet places of that suburb. One day at that hour I scratched furtively at the paint on the bathroom window. My fingernail took away only a few grains. I put my eye to the scraped paint and realised that I could never make out anything of my cousins on the other side. But I did not forget the blur of amber that had occupied all of my eye for a moment. It was private scenery for me alone to admire. If I could not carry out my scheme for bursting in on my cousins while they washed or undressed, I could plan instead to tell the girls about a strange place they would hardly recognise where two girls they did not know lived in a rich, golden twilight.

There was another place where the uncommon light would always start me wondering. At the same hour when the buzzing of a fly or the swaying of a leaf was most noticeable, I sat on the closed seat in the lavatory at the northern end of the veranda. The weatherboards in the wall were so thin that they glowed at their edges like my fingers when I held them against the sun. All around the walls were pictures of film stars cut from the coloured pages of the magazines that my girl-cousins bought every Saturday afternoon in the foyer of the Glen Theatre, Glenferrie. Veronica Lake, Yvonne de Carlo, Alan Ladd, Gene Tierney, Cornell Wilde, Rita Hayworth – they smiled and looked knowing, but their eyes were aimed past me no matter where I stood or crouched in that peculiar light. And yet I could imagine either of my girl-cousins resting easily on the seat with her pants around her knees and looking into the eyes of any film star she fancied and understanding something as remote from me as the groves and terraces and pools behind the real Hollywood mansions.

On a certain afternoon I decided I could wait no longer. The dark place under the lemon tree was where the tunnel began that would bring me out into a different sunlight in a place I had not quite expected. I led my boy-cousin in beneath the stiff green leaves and the spiky branches and the unpalatable fruit. I sat him down and told him we were being shut out of the best places around us. (My mother was shopping somewhere in Glenferrie Road; my aunt was lying down with her door closed; the two girls were at their school somewhere along Riversdale Road.)

I told the boy that his sisters were hiding things from

us. They were hiding scenery behind glass in their bedroom; they were even hiding something between their legs when they stood in the bath with him of an evening. To put him in the right mood I opened my trousers and showed him all that I had between my own legs. I persuaded him to do the same. I wanted the two of us to sit there, each with a hand between his own legs, feeling an occasional trickle of breeze on our bare skins and hearing the rumble of a distant tram, until my cousin began to share the urge that I had to explore some part of the elaborate network of the places just out of our reach. I hoped he would agree to meet me there on the next afternoon and tell me what he had seen when he tore his sisters' clothes from them in the bathroom, or describe the strange shape moulded from pink rubber that was kept in the girls' wardrobe, or repeat the exact answer of each girl after he had asked what she dreamed about when she sat in the lavatory on a hot afternoon and stared into the eyes of film stars.

But I must have understood that the boy was too young for all this. And I could hardly have been surprised when all he wanted was to grip the thing between my legs and to ask what I called it. He knew his only as a tommy; he had never heard the word I told him – cock. He said it aloud – cock – and he liked the sound of it. He began to repeat it more loudly – cock; cock. He made a chant of it and even shouted it, and grabbed at me. All I wanted by then was to get the two of us dressed again to shut the little idiot's mouth before someone heard him.

A noise came from just outside our shelter. It was the prolonged gurgling of the cistern in the lavatory in the backyard of the house next door. I could see the top of the little wooden building, overgrown by stringy branches of a yellow-flowered creeper. The boy beside me heard the noise and stopped his calling out. But when he knew where the noise had come from he shouted a name: Charlie Alcock. Then, while I listened for the footsteps of someone crossing the neighbouring yard from the lavatory to the back door (but heard nothing), my cousin set up a new cry: Charlie Alcock's cock: Charlie Alcock's cock.

I punched the boy and wrestled with him until he was quiet at last and properly dressed. There was a long silence all around the lemon tree, but I sensed that people had been listening to us and were still listening. I knew of Charlie Alcock only that he was old enough to have left school and gone to work. (I had never actually seen Charlie in all the years I had visited my cousins; my aunt and Charlie's mother were said to be not speaking.) If it was Charlie who had pulled the chain in his lavatory, and if he was still hiding there under the mound of green and yellow creeper, then I knew I had cause for shame. I saw Charlie sitting back at his ease in the greenish light under the arbour. The walls around him were thick with coloured pictures of film stars, some of them naked in gardens where the pathways alone would have taken a whole afternoon to understand. When he heard the sounds from under the lemon tree, he sneered at the boy who had searched for weeks and found nothing more than the little pink tube and bulb of his baby cousin.

I went on waiting for Charlie to come out from under his fronds of creeper and to jeer at me, but it was my aunt who broke in on the silence. She had been listening from just inside the back door, and she came out to rescue her son from me and to say that she would tell my mother everything. When my mother came home she took to me with the strap from one of our suitcases. In the pauses between her slashes at my legs, she told me it was bad enough that I had been rude myself but much, much worse that I had tried to put rude thoughts into the mind of my innocent young cousin.

It had nothing to do with my escapade under the lemon tree, but my mother and I left the house in Hawthorn a few days later. My father had found a house for us in an outer suburb among sandy paddocks and factories built of galvanised iron and cement-sheet. The house was a mile from the railway station and ten miles by train and tram from Hawthorn, so that our Sunday visits became rare events. But when I was fourteen I was enrolled at a secondary school near Hawthorn, and a year later my cousin waved at me from the ranks of the new boys, with his uncrumpled maroon cap pulled down to his eyebrows and his initials stamped in gold on his brand-new Gladstone bag, and looked hurt when I barely acknowledged him.

In the summer of that year my aunt rented a holiday shack in the tea-tree scrub near Seaford, and my mother and I were invited to spend a day and a night there. My mother had always assumed that a day at the beach was a treat for me. Perhaps as a very small child I had once squealed with pleasure when the waves curled against my shins. But all I remembered of any beach was my trying to get out of the glare of the sun and to wipe the gritty sand from between my toes, or struggling to keep the water away from my eyes whenever someone tried to teach me to swim. At fourteen I had another reason for hating all beaches. I considered myself a strange kind of pervert because I thought of nothing all day but the breasts and groins just beneath the bathing-suits of the hundreds of females all around me (from the girls of ten or eleven to women with greying hair like my aunts and yes, even my aunts themselves) while those same females lay back with their eyes closed and their legs apart or leaned far forward for some innocent purpose as though they had never heard of such a thing as a teenage sex-maniac.

At Seaford that day I crouched in the shallows among grandmothers in tucked-up dresses and screaming toddlers. I hugged my skinny white arms around my knees and watched the boy, my cousin. He was out where the water reached his thighs, laughing with one of his sisters who had once stood over him in the bath-tub at Hawthorn. (She was now a young married woman with a baby that she breast-fed.) The boy dived under and grabbed his sister's leg and tried to topple her. She caught the boy and tried to duck his head. While they struggled his head was pressed for a moment against her huge dugs. The thoughts that came to me seemed still more proof that I was a monster. There was nothing for me but to go off into the scrub with the pretence of dressing but in fact to handle myself to the point where my desperate mood would be suddenly resolved, and I trembled and whimpered and was disgusted with my own spent body and could hardly believe I had been so bothered a few minutes before by such things as protruding breasts and lumpish thighs, and vowed never to notice them again – and would keep my vow for three or four hours.

While I gathered my clothes together I heard my cousin behind me saying he was going to get dressed too, and when I left the beach he followed me. In those days the foreshore had not yet been levelled for carparks. I pushed through the tea-tree into a sheltered hollow and then stood drying my shoulders with my towel. I heard my cousin still close behind me but I kept my back turned to him.

It seemed to me, at fourteen, another proof of my sex-mania that as soon as I found myself in an empty paddock or clearing in the bush or even a corner of a tree-shaded backyard, I thought of the place as the setting for a sexual orgy with myself and at least three women romping naked together. I could have marked twenty crosses on a map of Victoria to show the quiet places on my uncles' farms or just off the walking-tracks in State forests or behind the fowl sheds in my friends' backyards where, in the past two years, I had turned aside from some family outing or some innocent visit, found myself suddenly alone among leaves and grass and insect-noises, and become for no more than sixty seconds (timed by my wrist watch) the grunting, straining male monster I believed I was at heart. I called these places collectively my landscape of lust and I was ready to leave my besmirching mark on the foreshore at Seaford except that my cousin was still dogging me.

I had decided long before that day that the boy was pathologically innocent; that he had never opened a wardrobe in any room but his own. If he had been left alone in his parents' house on some hot afternoon he would have pored over his stamp collection. Six months before the day at Seaford, on his front veranda, I had found in a *Lone Avenger* comic a line drawing of a young woman washing the dust from herself on a riverbank (and about to be surprised by the hero of the story). The woman was naked, but only her upper half intruded into the frame of the comic strip; and the artist, as I had learned to expect from artists in those days, had drawn a butterfly with wings outspread in the near foreground so that the woman's nipples were well hidden. I left the comic, open at the picture of the butterfly and the woman, where my cousin had to see it. From the corner of my eye I saw him look at the page calmly, then close the comic-book and slip it under the stack I had already read. He was not hiding it for himself. He had not stowed it carefully away to gloat over it alone afterwards. He was hiding it from me – I was certain of it. Whether or not he thought I had seen the picture already, he was making sure I would not see it in future. He was guarding me from temptation, trying to save me from dreaming of a lonely river in America where a woman would appear quite naked as soon as a butterfly had flitted past her.

I had wondered on that Sunday afternoon (and I still wondered while he undressed behind me at Seaford) whether he remembered our afternoon under the lemon tree. I supposed he remembered just enough to make him think of me as a sex-maniac from my earliest years. And I believed he himself had grown into the sort of Catholic boy who would think it his duty to rescue his unhappy cousin.

I dried myself and dragged off my bathing trunks and began to dress, still keeping my back to my cousin. The secluded place, or the squeal of some female sounding faintly from the beach, or the memory of something I had seen a half-hour before made me stiffen in the usual place, but I pulled my underpants tightly against me and tried to ignore my trouble. Properly dressed, I turned and saw my cousin still naked. His towel was dangling from one hand. He was looking slowly all around him, although he did not meet my eyes, and he seemed somewhat bewildered yet not at all unhappy. The thing he had once called his tommy was pointed towards me at the same angle as the barrel of the memorial cannon I had once lifted him astride when our mothers had left us to play in a little roadside park while they went on with their shopping. (And in the instant before I looked away and strode out of the clearing I had time to be surprised by the size of what he aimed at me; it seemed far larger than my own in spite of the three years' difference between us.)

I stopped on my way to the beach and almost turned back. I foresaw myself becoming his teacher and advisor. I had heard of such things happening. In a parish near mine a man had recruited boys into the Legion of Mary. Afterwards he had visited them one by one in the school holidays when their parents were out and shown them pictures of naked women and taught them what to do with themselves when their organs became too stiff for comfort. I might have taught my cousin what he had almost certainly not yet learned. In return he could have sworn a pact with me. Each of us would tell the other whatever he learned when he ransacked wardrobes or found certain paragraphs in books he had been advised not to read. My cousin's unmarried sister still lived at home. He might have drilled a hole in his bathroom wall and let me look through it.

But I did not turn back, because I remembered the boy's calling out under the lemon tree. I heard the exact tones of his childish voice calling for Charlie Alcock, and I imagined Charlie himself – a man who sat tugging at himself in his lavatory on lonely afternoons when he should have been out looking at women – pushing his way through the tea-tree and into the clearing and smiling a twisted, pervert's smile when he saw the naked boy teaching his naked cousin, and sitting the two boys down to teach them some disgusting tricks of his own.

That night in the holiday shack I had to sleep head-to-toe with my cousin in a single bed. I waited until he seemed asleep and then turned myself carefully over to face the wall. I began my nightly routine. I thought of my married cousin as I had seen her that day with her motherly breasts and her huge buttocks straining out of the bathing suit that she complained was much too small for her. To make my imaginings more lifelike, I allowed my boy-cousin into them. But he was hardly the boy I knew; the world I saw with my eyes closed each night was peopled by bodies and faces with no other purpose than to provoke me. I was about to have both my cousins behave so preposterously that I could not have looked them in the eye for most of the next day. My memory of the boy wrestling that afternoon in the water with his sister drove me to imagine the three of us in an absurd tableau. I had found the boy naked among the tea-tree shrub, wondering how to relieve the strange mood that had come over him. While I performed a demonstration for him, his sister found the pair of us and took pity on us and said there could be no harm in her doing for us just this once, what she was about to do because we were all part of the same family and bound to help one another.

My cousin's voice interrupted me. He asked me why I was burrowing in my bed like a rabbit. I could picture the moronic grin on his face in the darkness. In the hollowed-out kapok mattress our bodies had rolled against each other, and his buttocks were pressed into the small of my back. The shape of them reminded me of his sister's breasts, and for a moment I thought of going on recklessly with what I was doing and letting him learn whatever he would. But I decided he was so stupid he could have asked his mother or even his sister next day to explain what I had done to myself, and I fell asleep that night as chastely as the fool cuddled up against me.

In my years at secondary school I kept away from my cousin. He was one of the boys that my own friends called 'pies' – boys who played with chemistry sets or model railways or joined in mixed doubles with Catholic girls at tennis clubs when they might have been telling dirty jokes or reporting how they had got a hand up the sweater of a St Kilda moll. (My friends sometimes accosted fifteen-years-old working-girls on the ice-skating rink at St Moritz.) But I was always uneasy when I met my cousin in the schoolground. Perhaps I feared he might let slip to his mother that I hung around with a group known as the dirty boys. (She, nodding solemnly and making a note to tell my own mother, would remember a hot afternoon years before when I had shown a precocious interest in filth.) Perhaps I wondered how often the boy himself thought of our childhood and interpreted afresh what he remembered about me.

I was beginning to suspect there was something wrong with me. The years were passing, and yet each Monday morning when my dirty friends reported their latest skirmishes with females I could only quote for them some description of breasts from a novel I had read at the weekend. If my cousin happened to walk past my group he would look calmly at me and I would drop my eyes. (Once, in my last year at school, he had stood behind me before I noticed him and had almost certainly heard me composing for the benefit of my friends the text of a letter of sympathy we talked of sending to one of our pretended heroes. This was a commercial artist and photographer who was on trial in Sydney for having taken a group of young women models into French's Forest and stripped and raped them. I did not learn until long after the man's trial and conviction that as a young commercial artist he had drawn the *Lone Avenger* comic strips, which I had assumed – when I read them as a child at my cousin's house – to be the work of an American.) I feared my cousin's thinking of me as still prying into wardrobes, peering at pictures in twilit toilets, dreaming of impossible streets and tram terminuses while he had easily acquired a body of knowledge that made my own investigations seem irrelevant and foolish. From the look of him I decided he had still not laid a hand on himself; in a barber's shop he probably sat on the copies of *Man* and *Man Junior* that I searched frantically for their pin-up pictures. And yet he had learned something that had quite escaped me. He moved easily through the world, never dreaming of any part he seemed shut out of – perhaps not even of my little corner that I tried to shut him out of.

In the year when I had left school and gone to work as a clerical officer in a State government department, I heard through my mother that my cousin was planning to become a priest.

I had stopped going to mass and confession. But this was in the late 1950s, long before it became fashionable for Catholics to speak against their Church. My friends and I, young men nearly twenty years old, used to dress for mass on Sunday morning (in our separate parishes), walk out of our houses at an appropriate time, and then sit for a carefully measured hour in some milk bar, hoping not to be noticed by some friend of our parents. When I heard the news about my cousin I foresaw at once a day when he fixed his eyes on me and tried to see into my soul as St John Vianney, the Curé of Ars, had seen into his parishioners and learned their shabby secrets. I told myself I would defy my cousin when he confronted me in his black suit, hoping to make me drop to my knees and blubber aloud that I had not really lost my faith, that I only stayed away from church because I was ashamed of my relentless habit of solitary sin. I would force myself to look the young priest in the eye, confounding his theories about the sly mannerisms of Onanists. He might tell me his strength was as the strength of ten because his heart was pure. I would answer, I hoped, that his so-called purity was only the ignorance of a child who had sat vacant-eyed under a lemon tree and never suspected that his backyard and his neighbourhood were full of signs of a mystery that he ought to have spent a lifetime investigating.

Two years later, when he was in his last year at school and it was public knowledge that he was going in the following year to the diocesan seminary at Werribee, my cousin phoned me with a strange request. He had helped to re-organise, so he told me, a branch of the Young Catholic Workers' Movement in his suburb. The branch was now running a Saturday night dance, and he thought I ought to drop in next weekend and meet a fine bunch of young people.

I was on my guard at once. I told him, for a start, that I had never learned to dance. He was prepared for this excuse. He told me that volunteers from the National Catholic Girls' Movement ran a learners' class for an hour before the dance itself began. I was not brave enough to refuse him outright. I asked for time to think about his invitation.

I guessed that my mother had told his mother how I spent my weekend locked in my room. I had told my parents I was studying to prepare myself for a part-time university degree, but mostly I wrote long entries in my diary or read the biographies of twentieth-century writers. (I had begun to think I might become some kind of writer myself.) I still came out of my hideout on Sunday mornings and allowed my parents to think I was going to mass, but I spent the hour striding through distant streets, looking over front fences for sights of young wives in slacks. (My nightly imaginings had become less outrageous to the extent that I now dreamed of myself as a married man.) I suspected a plot between my mother and her sister to have the future-priest introduce me to a nice girl who would bring me out of myself. I would have liked to meet such a girl. (I had not spoken socially to a female since the days when my school debating team had competed against girls' schools and I sometimes passed around the tea and biscuits afterwards.) But I was not going to have my cousin looking on smugly when I met her. Yet I agreed to drop in at his precious dance.

My cousin was the only person I knew in the hall. He led me into the back room where the learners' class was going on. The only other learner I could see was a man who looked at least thirty years old, and I was heartened – until I saw his feet doing things that mine could never have done. My cousin was laughing at the centre of a group of girls. He led a rather pretty girl towards me, told me her name – which I did not hear – and asked her to take me in hand. She asked me what experience I had had. I told her not a great deal. She suggested we start with the modern waltz. She seemed to think I only wanted to brush up on my steps. I did not want to shock her by saying I had never before been on a dance floor, or by telling her that I had never heard of the modern waltz until she mentioned it just then and that she was about to become the first young woman I had ever laid hands on.

I did my best to follow the girl's patient instructions, and even tried to make a joke against myself when my cousin looked across at me and called out that I was doing just fine. But I had never felt so miserable and incompetent in all my life. When the lesson was over and the dance proper was beginning, I went into the hall and stood for a few minutes with the other solitary males. I saw my cousin among the dancers, gliding into some complicated routine with the girl who had tried to teach me the modern waltz. As soon as his back was turned to me I fled.

The tram I caught in Glenferrie Road was almost empty. The conductress was not much older than me, and when she looked at me I thought she might have worked out exactly why I was going home alone at that hour in my good suit. I caught a train at Malvern station. I was the only passenger in my compartment. At every station I leaned my head in my hands in the pose of a man recently betrayed and hoped a young woman would open the door timidly after fleeing from a dance, and swearing never to dance again, because her partners had only wanted to maul her. But through the cracks in my fingers I saw only a black-on-white nameplate (CARNEGIE, MURRUMBEENA, HUGHESDALE…) and moths and beetles gliding round and round a light-globe.

I wondered once again whether my cousin was a complete simpleton who had no idea of what he was giving up to become a priest, and who only danced with pretty young women to set an example for the young Catholic men of Hawthorn, or whether he was fiendishly cunning. In that case he would have arranged the whole evening in the hall to teach me that I and not he was the bumbling incompetent: that he could take the world or leave it, while I was still burrowing in my dark bed and trying to tunnel through to the brightly lit world where young people danced innocently together or frolicked on beaches.

The railway line from Malvern to my suburb ran straight for mile after mile. Looking out into the darkness I could have been one of the travellers I had wondered about whenever I heard the rattling of wheels in the darkness somewhere outside my girl-cousins' window in Hawthorn.

But my route was fixed; it would take me only back to the room where I scribbled in my diary, while the repetitive patterns of streetlights for miles around me marked out the routes taken by people who had met at dances and fallen in love to the rhythm of the modern waltz.

My cousin's course at the seminary was to last for seven years. His mother and mine, and the women who sat with them over afternoon tea on Sundays at the Hawthorn house, loved to roll the magical number around their mouths while they held their chunks of Swiss roll or their iced boats poised between plates and faces. Seven long years, they liked to say. And their other favourite phrase was 'giving up the world'. He was giving up the world to become a priest.

I sat in the background when I happened to be at these gatherings. In the year when my cousin entered the seminary I left home to live in rented rooms not far from Hawthorn. (I had grown tired of walking my parent's suburb while ten o'clock mass was on, and tired of hiding my diary in my wardrobe every morning before I went to work.) At afternoon tea in Hawthorn I sat in a corner and studied my two women-cousins. They were both married and mothers by then. They talked about new washing machines or their children's visits to the doctor. I tried to slip away before their husbands came to collect them. I felt childish and tongue-tied beside the car salesman and the insurance representative, each in slacks and casual shirt, who jingled endlessly in their hands the keys to their station wagons and wondered, I supposed, what to say to the boy-man in the outmoded sports coat and grey Stamina trousers who had no car or television set or girl friend and therefore nothing to talk about.

I despised the men most when they affected a mock-bullying way with their wives to hurry them into their station wagons and when they drove off just a little too noisily into the streets of what they thought was the only world. I wanted a roadway to cave in some Sunday evening beneath their cars so that they would never reach their homes in East Burwood or Vermont but would struggle all night through dark sewers and stormwater drains and stagger out next day into some side street of a suburb they had to admit was strange to them. Such was my crude dream for proving to their literal minds that there truly was another world: that their plump wives had once been slender schoolgirls in sharply pleated navy-blue tunics and long-sleeved white blouses who found meaning in the windings of pathways through tiny cactus-gardens or the fixed gazes of film stars through an amber twilight and who might have hidden in their bedroom things so mysterious that I still dreamed of finding them or of my old dreams of having found them and been at last inside the other world and looking outwards.

I visited the seminarian once a year. A crowd of visitors sat around him in the garden, but while they took their afternoon tea he made a point of strolling with me for five minutes around the paths. He asked me cheerfully how things were going. Since it was always Sunday when I visited him, I was always able to tell him truthfully that I had a painful hangover. If I was particularly anxious to tell him of achievements that he could not hope, as a seminarian, to equal, I would describe the precise location of the spot where I had vomited in the early hours of that morning. Usually I mentioned arriving home at dawn from a party, which was true enough. I did not add that I had gone home alone from the party or that it was not so much a party as a drinking session arranged by a group who were mostly bachelor card players. Made gloomy by alcohol, I guessed that he surmised these things anyway.

He was already learning to pose as the priest that no confession could shock. He never urged me to mend my ways or asked me how often I went to mass. He simply said that he remembered me in his prayers every morning.

A year before he was due to be ordained I turned up on a visiting Sunday with my first girl friend. My cousin could not help giving me a nod of satisfaction when I announced her Irish-sounding surname. I sat back and let the two of them talk. (She knew some girl whose sister had once played tennis with my cousin, and he knew a nun who had been to the same school as my girl friend.)

I let them talk but I was angry that he seemed so pleased with the girl. I supposed he thought that his prayers had been answered: that I had had enough of alcohol and poetry and freedom (my Diabolical Trinity, as I had once called them when he and I walked together in the seminary grounds) and was now turning back to the safe refuge of a Catholic marriage.

The girl had come to work in my office two years before, when she was just out of school. I had watched her every day. I watched the particular way she hung her coat in the locker in the corner that was protected by the angle of her desk. I watched her opening the top drawer of her desk and putting her keys and cigarettes and matches inside. I followed her a distance when she walked in the Treasury Gardens at lunchtime, and I drew diagrams afterwards of the routes she had followed. I found out that she boarded with an aunt in South Caulfield, after which I drew the pattern of the Number 64 tram route that took her home.

One day I heard her saying she was going to share a flat with two other girls in Hawthorn.

I was only a few years short of thirty. I was rather tired of trying to keep in mind all the half-lit corners and out-of-the-way streets I had once thought signs of a city within a city. When I first studied the new girl in my office I believed she dealt in plain surfaces, regular angles, direct routes. What she hid she kept still within reach. If she became my wife she would answer all my questions plainly and honestly. Being married to her I could have my own backyard and plant my own tree – a grove of trees, if I liked – and watch the branches gradually overshadowing a little patch of the lawn and making a sort of cave. When I heard that she was moving to Hawthorn I knew I had to approach her. If I could sit with her on some Sunday afternoon in her flat, within sound of trams, I could pretend I had travelled by all the roundabout ways I had once dreamed of – and still arrived at a somewhat surprising destination.

When I first took my girl friend to visit the seminary we were not officially engaged but she had agreed to marry me. She came away from the visit saying what a fine man my cousin was and how nice it would be to have him perform our wedding ceremony after he was ordained.

This was not what I had planned. It would have seemed to me some sort of disgrace if my cousin became a priest before I acquired a wife. I had often imagined the day of his first mass, the day when his family would arrange the traditional celebration for him. My aunt's house in Hawthorn would be overflowing with guests. My cousin would stand in state on the back lawn near the old lemon tree, or on the veranda where we had once read comics together, and the people around him would make a point of calling him 'Father' and asking for his blessing before they left. But I would not once address him by his new title. Nor would I kneel to have his hands pressed on my head. I would deal with him politely, but he would see that I was not in awe of any supposed powers he had had conferred on him. He might have been qualified to hear confessions and to touch the insides of chalices and ciboriums and to murmur the miraculous words of consecration at mass, but I would always know him as the boy who failed to notice the true mysteries of the world.

From the day when I knew that my girl friend was going to marry me, I had looked forward to celebrating my cousin's ordination for the pleasure of drinking the free beer and seeing my wife flit around in her best clothes and telling myself I would be watching her that evening taking off layer after layer of those clothes while my cousin was going down on his knees by his single bed, trying to fix in his mind an image of the god or the heaven he believed he was suddenly so much closer to.

My girl friend told me too, after her first visit to my cousin, that we ought to visit him more often. The sting in this was that Sunday (the visiting day at the seminary) was the only day in the week when my girl friend's flatmates were always away. I had taken to calling at the flat every Sunday in the early afternoon, a few hours before I was due to go with my girl friend to mass. Those few hours were all the time I had for the enterprise that I described to myself at the time, with what I thought was wry amusement, as laying siege to her virtue. (Writing this, nearly fifteen years later, I can still think of no better words, but they no longer amuse me. I did act and think in those days like a character – already, perhaps, overlaid with an author's irony – in some work forgotten among the back streets of fiction. And the young woman I thought I was besieging really was, whether she knew it or not, defending something invisible. Now, knowing what I know about the man who wanted in those days to capture what was merely of the body, I am content to call that thing a virtue, and I try to use that word quite without irony.)

It was hard for me to keep up my siege knowing the girl and I would be sitting together in church a few hours afterwards. I did not want her to think of what we did (or what I wanted us to do) as sinful. I did not want to make her unhappy. But I was much more afraid of her deciding afterwards that she ought to tell a priest in confession what had happened (or what I wanted to happen) between us. I thought of her being questioned by a young priest with my cousin's view of things. I heard him telling her she was being unfairly used; that I was a man who had rather lost his way and wanted to see her as his corner of some shadow-suburb, to stand between her and the sunlit thoroughfares of the world. Sometimes I saw myself again creeping beneath trees and through wardrobes and past the walls of lavatories. I followed a tunnel upwards towards a hint of strange sunlight. But the outlet of the tunnel was barred by the wire grill in a confessional booth in the Church of the Immaculate Conception in Burwood Road, only half a mile from the backyard where I had first gone underground.

My girl friend never forgot which Sunday of the month was visiting day at the seminary. On that day, after lunch in her flat, she went on chain-smoking her cigarettes to keep me at bay and then asked, as though she was proposing some rare treat for both of us, whether we couldn't drive out to see my cousin. An hour later she would be smiling and chatting in the cluster of matrons around the seminarian while I sat a little apart and knew we would still be an engaged couple – that social oddity –

when my cousin was strutting around in the fullness of his priestly powers.

On the Sundays when we were alone together I went on with my siege. I still hoped it might end suddenly with her locking her arms around me when it was time for us to leave for church, and announcing that we would stay where we were, that she would not care if she never saw the inside of a church again. She would fall asleep beside me, and I would watch through what had always seemed the hardest hour to bear in any week: the hour when Sunday afternoon turned into Sunday evening. The fading of that particular Sunday would persuade me that I was still following one of my routes around the margins of the accepted world. When it was quite dark the young woman beside me would open her eyes and be startled. But I would tell her she was quite safe in a place not at all strange to me.

In her flat of a Sunday, if I was not trying to corner her on the couch I was preaching to her. I tried to explain to her that I had turned my life into a quest. I was searching for something I had first divined as a small child. From my earliest years I had hoped to find an actual place where the mystery would reveal itself: a suburb at the end of an unmapped tramline, a street bordered with hedges and curving in on itself like a pathway in a maze, even a corner of a backyard or a cupboard in a room made sombre by the sunlight of late afternoon. There was something fateful, I declared to her, in our being alone in that room in Hawthorn every Sunday afternoon. I was destined to find with her what I had been looking for all my life.

When this had not impressed her I preached on a different theme. I spoke darkly about the powerful forces that drove a man towards a woman. I confessed to her that for ten years before I met her – the very years when those forces were at their strongest in me – I had sat quite alone every night reading and scribbling in my bachelor's room. I even told her a censored story about the man who had drawn the *Lone Avenger* comics, as though it was somehow linked with my own story.

This sort of posturing always had the same result. She asked me would I care to explain how my cousin was at that moment going calmly about his duties in the seminary, preparing for a life of celibacy and not trying to undress a woman in the loungeroom of her flat. My cousin had played in the same backyard with me and looked at the same comics, but he had not dedicated his life to searching for a twilit love-nest in Hawthorn.

One of our quarrels ended with my saying I was not going to church with her again. After she had gone I locked the front door of the flat and went quietly into her bedroom. It was the first time I had been there. I was careful not to disturb any of the clothes on the bed or the hairbrushes and cosmetics on the dressing table. But I gently slid open one after another of the drawers and pushed back the sliding door of the wardrobe. The floor beneath the hanging coats and dresses and blouses was a jumble of cardboard boxes with labels from women's clothing shops. I knelt down. I looked back once over my shoulder, wanting to see through the curtains that the daylight was fading and so to reassure myself that I was still the child who had expected to learn all that mattered when he reached at last, in the late afternoon, the innermost of the places he had been shut out of.

A corner of a mirror showed me the face of a man who knew surprisingly little. I knew that the young woman and I would end our quarrel when she came back from church; that we would announce our engagement in a few weeks and marry a year afterwards; that I would soon have no cause for saying I was shut out of any part of the visible world. I knew all this, but I preferred to fix my eyes on the furthest of all the boxes on the floor of the wardrobe and to use my trusty right hand on myself to console me for never knowing what such a box concealed.

Not all my Sunday afternoon preaching ended badly. After we had become formally engaged my cousin gave us as a present a little book on the spiritual meaning of marriage. One Sunday I made my fiancée smile when I read aloud from the book in a nasal voice meant to imitate not, I assured her, my well-meaning cousin but some old, Irish-educated priest of her childhood and mine.

From the first contact, then, between lovers, the thing that desire obscurely strives after is the spiritual reality of man, the unique and eternal soul.

But then I stupidly lost my advantage by showing her the frontispiece I had pasted into the book. It was part of a picture I had cut from a very different book bought in my solitary days from Sewards in Bourke Street: *The Encyclopaedia of Sexual Practice*. It was an annotated cut-away diagram in muted, old-fashioned pinks and greys with the caption: *Cavernous bulb and shaft engorged prior to intromission.*

My cousin was ordained in St Patrick's Cathedral and said his first mass in his parish church on a fine morning in late winter. After the mass, he and some of his seminarian- and priest-friends came back to the house in Hawthorn to celebrate with forty and more of his family and relations. The house had been altered and renovated a few years before. New rooms filled the space where the back lawn had been. One of these rooms had been set up with trestles and tabletops for the meal. My cousin sat at the head table, flanked by his parents and the clerical men in black. Just behind him, filling the wide window, was the dark-green mass of the old lemon tree where I had thought I was giving him his first lesson in exploring the world.

The meal and the speeches made me think of the wedding reception that my fiancée's parents were already planning for her and me. For a moment I tried to feel sorry for my priest-cousin: when his celebration was over he had to go home to a single room and take his pleasure from invisible things. I looked around and tried to enjoy a foretaste of my own pleasure on my wedding day. But then I felt the shudder that always passed over me when I stood in a crowd of revellers. When the drinking and laughing came to an end, what then? How long would it be before I had learned all I could learn about my wife, and then had to go back to wondering about nameless things?

There were tubs full of crushed ice and bottles of beer on the back veranda. My rather wowserish uncle and aunt had done the right thing by everyone. I settled myself in a patch of sunshine with a bottle at my elbow and watched my cousin posing for the people with cameras. But then someone wanted my fiancée and me to pose with the newly ordained, and I was shown to a spot against the lemon tree.

So far as I could judge, my cousin and I were now standing as near as we could have got that day (the branches having grown lower and ourselves taller in the past twenty years) to the place where we had sat on the afternoon when I tried to interest him in female bodies. He grinned at me from the other side of my fiancée, and the people clicked their cameras. Someone asked me to shake Father's hand.

I tried to get the stronger grip on him to remind him that I was still the senior of us, but he grabbed me first and squeezed my hand in his. There we stood in our old spot, or if not quite that spot then as though we had just struggled out from under the tree and into the sunlight. (The cameras would register a sunlight rather less rich than the light I remembered from the day when I had tried to convert my cousin to my way of life.) More cameras clicked. In photo albums in homes I would never see, during the years while one of us made his way towards an idea of God and the other went on looking for a certain suburb in a Melbourne of dreams, the young priest would smile confidently at me while I peered at him foolishly (I could feel myself doing just that) across the frank, untroubled face of a young woman.

I sat down with my beer to wonder what my cousin might have been thinking while he and I stood with hands clasped just beneath my fiancée's breasts. But the point of this story, 'Charlie Alcock's Cock', depends on his having thought none of the thoughts I attributed to him then and none of those I might still attribute to him now while I look at a photograph of myself standing awkwardly beside the only two human beings whose sexual organs I have touched and the only two who know enough about me to surmise why I am as I am today.

When a few of the guests had already gone and I was well settled beside the tubs of beer, and during a lull in the talking and laughing and the fizzing of bottles being opened and the clatter of plates from the kitchen, the people in the backyard heard the loud gurgling and cascading of a toilet cistern suddenly emptied – a noisy, old-fashioned cistern that should have been replaced years before. Some child in our party tried to force a giggle; some adult half-turned towards the side fence past the lemon tree and then pretended not to have turned. I saw the old outdoor dunny in the next yard, still under its dome of creeper. I asked the husband of one of my cousins what ever had become of Charlie and the Alcocks. I heard that after Charlie's mother had died he had turned into an eccentric bachelor who hardly left his house except to go to his cleaner's job at the tram depot. My aunt had invited him to drop in for a drink later in the day but of course Charlie couldn't be expected to change his ways.

That was all I needed to know. The people in our yard had gone on with their talking but I could still hear the last splutterings of the cistern. I turned to the man who had just told me about Charlie. I winked at the man. He looked at me blankly but I was not put off. I took a few steps towards the Alcocks' fence and cupped a hand at my mouth (and was pleased to notice a few people now looking at me). I aimed my voice towards the heap of greenery and the small yellow flowers above the old dunny and kept it not so loud that I would seem to want to reach anyone still under the green and yellow. I called out:

'Are you still there, Charlie? Come over and join us.'

I waited for a moment. Then I said with mock-disappointment in my voice:

'Ah, well; stay down in your burrow then, Charles.'

Then I backed into the crowd and poured myself more beer.

My fiancé walked past me, hissing at me from the corner of her mouth that I was a childish, drunken idiot and that she was going home at once by tram. I sat quietly drinking and composing the explanation I would give her later. I would try to tell her that the flushing of the old lavatory had made me hear again the sounds of Hawthorn twenty years before: the tricklings from deep below the grilles in streets where no car passed for hours and all the window-blinds were drawn against the afternoon sun; the grinding of trams on their way to distant groves where schoolgirls smiled and whispered out of sight from boys; the gurglings and chortlings from the pipes in the twilit lavatory where Lauren Bacall and Myrna Loy were all smiles to my face but secretly planning to torment me for years afterwards. Hearing the solitary bachelor on the other side of the fence, and knowing that one of the crowd around me was a young woman whose body, encased for the moment in costly clothes, was almost within my grasp, I had decided I was looking at Hawthorn at last from the secure vantage-point I had always wanted. I had crawled out of the long dark tunnel that had been my life for the past twenty years and found myself in the green and sunlit world that had once seemed the preserve of girls and women and secretive adults. And still poor old Charlie, who must have been nearly forty by then, sat in the shadowy cave of his backyard lavatory.

In the first years of my marriage I rather enjoyed my cousin's visits. He came to our flat for tea once a month from his parish in the western suburbs where his curate's job, so he said, had opened his eyes to the spiritual needs of the ordinary lay person. I was sure now that I was his better. I sat back after our meal and admired my bookshelves and the titles boldly displayed of books I had had to hide from my parents when I first bought them. I opened my well-stocked fridge and offered my cousin more beer. I helped myself to the drink that had once been my only consolation of an evening but was now a spice to the pleasure I enjoyed in bed. And the bed itself was in his view – I made sure always that his was the chair facing across the little hallway to the bedroom of the flat. Before each of his visits I hung some of my wife's pantyhose over the shower-screen in the bathroom. I wanted to remind my cousin that it was his turn now to be shut out of the wardrobes of the world. I was not too vindictive. I would not have displayed bras or pants. (My wife would probably have taken them down in any case before the priest arrived.) But I could not forget that he had once roamed a house where girls' wardrobes were left unguarded on almost every afternoon and the bathroom door would have swung open if he had had the wit to blunder against it in a feigned fit of absentmindedness.

As a married man I believed I saw clearly at last. Shadowy landscapes interwoven among actual streets and suburbs – I had once searched for such things but only because I was baffled by the strangeness of females, having no sister and not even a girl-cousin of my own age who might have sat under her lemon tree with me. Now, with my wife beside me, I wanted my cousin to see the gaps and dark fissures in his own view of the world.

On each of his visits he wanted to tell my wife about some or another young priest who was doing great work around Melbourne. I kept mostly silent to show that I found his talk irrelevant. But my wife could have talked all night to him. We had reached the late 1960s. It seemed that Catholics everywhere – my wife among them – wanted to argue with their priests, mostly about the morality of contraception. Only ten years before, I had quietly stopped believing because I was no longer brave enough to go on for month after month whispering to an unseen priest in the confessional the tally of my furtive and solitary sins. And I had skulked in milk-bars and dreamed of leaving home so that my parents and Catholic neighbours would not know I had stopped going to mass. Now my wife was sitting with her legs boldly crossed and looking a young priest in the eye while she quoted to him from a chapter called 'Contraception and Holiness' in some book by an American Catholic.

One night while the two of them argued about the intrinsic goodness – or otherwise – of sexual pleasure I went into the bedroom and closed the door behind me and quietly opened the bottom drawer of my wife's side of our wardrobe. I took the packet of condoms from where it lay clearly in view on a stack of her pants. I opened the packet and took out one of the sheaths from its foil. I unrolled the thing and held it up by its open end and looked at it dangling helplessly in the bright light of the bedroom. I put the packet back where I had found it, but the limp rubber in my hand I slipped far back under the shoeboxes and travelling bags on the floor of my own half of the wardrobe.

In the third year of our marriage my wife and I moved to our own house in an outer suburb. We were still childless, but contraception was no longer a debating topic. My cousin had become interested in the charismatic movement; he talked to us about the enormous power of love in the world and the joy he had found in learning to express freely his love of God and of his fellow men and women. Now, when he came to our house he pressed my hand between his two hands; and he put an arm around my wife's shoulder and kissed her lightly near her ear.

One night, during his charismatic period, he sat with me while my wife painted the insides of the kitchen cupboards. He was telling us about the natural tendency towards goodness and wholeness that he now recognised in the world. My wife was listening, but she was squatting on the floor and reaching with her brush into the lowest cupboard. I looked down and saw that her sweater had come away from the top of her slacks and exposed above her buttocks a broad band of naked white skin with all its downy hairs picked out clearly by the kitchen light.

I got up and strode across the room and stationed myself squarely between my wife and the priest. I stood there, on some pretence or other, until my wife got to her knees to reach a higher cupboard.

I was not troubled by anything so crude as a suspicion that my cousin was my rival. (I may even have considered for a moment letting him look his fill at the bare skin so that he might have had to struggle against the memory of it for days and nights afterwards.) I stood where I stood to keep my cousin from seeing too easily into my territory. Both he and I had seen the same signposts years before in Hawthorn, but only I had tried to go where they pointed. The route I had followed was much longer and more circuitous than I had expected; and I had seen on the way none of the landmarks I had hoped for. But I believed I occupied – as a man with my own backyard and my own wife – a territory not unlike the place I had kept in mind for so long. Especially when I looked at the backgrounds of photos of my wife as a schoolgirl, and made her tell me what she had seen beyond the paths and streets she had once had to keep to – especially then, I seemed to be somewhere near the end of an unpredictable tram route or a street that lost itself among hedges. If my cousin had chosen quite a different route, that was his business; but he had no right to creep towards my territory from an unexpected quarter – to travel across country through the grounds of presbyteries and monasteries to the back corners of my dream-district.

I had stepped forward boldly enough to block

my cousin's view. But I could not quite meet his eye while he went on talking about the great love he was still discovering. I thought just then of the dunes behind the beach at Seaford where he had stood facing me with his tommy quivering uncertainly in front of him as though he wanted me to take it and point it in the right direction: towards the place that was Hawthorn turned inside out, with its wardrobes and shady places wide and green and bare to the sun.

Although I was ready to defend my wife and my house and backyard as the territory I had travelled so far to reach, I was not sure that I had come to the end of my private journey. One of the landscapes I had seen as a child still lay beyond me. I had never seen myself in the Spanish Mission mansions and the velvet-draped penthouses that my girl-cousins admired on the screen of the Glen, Glenferrie. Now, in the early 1970s, I had begun to bring home copies of *Playboy* and *Penthouse*. I kept them in my wardrobe, but I took them out on certain nights when my wife and I lay in bed reading. I accepted her laughing at the pictures of the women absurdly posed, but sometimes (mocking myself – or pretending to mock) I recommended to my wife what I had once supposed might only be done in the depths of some Hollywood mansion. Then I seemed about to enter the scenery that my girl-cousins had only gazed at: a vast palace of rooms opening endlessly onto further rooms and vistas of rooms – an indoors continent of the size and shape of the USA. Its carpets, preposterously deep, and the miles of fluted draperies on its walls were coloured in the unwavering pastel shades of the backgrounds I had once noted behind Linda Darnell and Evelyn Keyes and the others of my cousins' favourites.

At my desk in the city in those days, I would think of the stack of magazines in my wardrobe and see my territory extending endlessly in a direction I called, for convenience, inwards. The American palace would always disclose further systems of rooms. But just as often, I would overhear some conversation among my workmates and understand from it what was happening among the young people I could still call, stretching a point, my generation. Then I seemed to be surrounded by blank, pastel-coloured walls with bright sunlight and all that mattered on their farther side. And I had to concede that all my so-called travels had occupied a space no wider than a backyard and had lasted no longer than the few hours of an afternoon in which the sun shone directly against the thin weatherboards of a lavatory wall.

While my wife had been painting the lowest cupboard, she was crouched in one of the postures of the women who were supposed to be waiting all through the endless afternoon that overhung the far Dakota-wings and the Iowa-courtyards of the pleasure palace. But there on the kitchen floor, with her head hung low and her buttocks spread, she had seemed for a moment like a victim weighed down by all the stories I had made her listen to; by all the imagined places I had tried to describe to her. Perhaps I had got to my feet and tried to distract my priest-cousin because the woman bowed almost to the floor, with not even her face visible, was all I had to boast of after all my years of following my own path away from him. I might have feared he would see what a little space in the world I had used for what were supposed to be the dreams that distinguished me.

Five years later my wife and I had a son and a daughter

and my cousin had a considerable reputation as a marriage counsellor. He had been transferred from his parish to a diocesan office that arranged conferences for married couples. (Ten or so couples would occupy a motel for a weekend and look into their hearts and talk honestly to one another and renew their marriage vows.) One Saturday afternoon he arrived unannounced at our house. My wife was trying to spoon some mush into the mouth of our younger child. I had just come inside after trying to tire my son so that he would sleep soundly when we put him down for his midday nap. My cousin wanted to talk to my wife. He had been called on suddenly to deliver a paper on the woman's view of marriage to a conference of priests, and he urgently needed some first-hand opinions.

He began to ask questions. My wife answered him in between spooning the mush and wiping the child's face, but with no sign of impatience. I went outside again with my son; I could not go on listening. The priest and the woman were talking the same stuff that I had once read aloud from the book that was my cousin's engagement present to us: the same stuff that had made my fiancée smile in the days when I was still only preaching at her or pawing at her.

Outside, I coaxed my son into a shady place in a far corner of the yard and then slipped quietly away from him. I wanted to stand by the kitchen window, hidden from my wife and my cousin but hearing more of their strange talk. The kitchen window was partly overgrown by a passionfruit vine. When I heard my wife's voice through its layers of leaves I seemed to be in my rightful place after a long time away from it. She was telling a priest about a way of life she had always dreamed of, a way of life I knew nothing about. I was hiding among dark-green leaves and trying to make sense of her words. Behind me was no ordinary backyard but an outlying peninsula of the district that still had a claim on me: the green labyrinth that had grown so much more complex and extensive in the years since my childhood.

In later years my cousin still visited us occasionally, but I preferred to find some excuse for being out of the house – my son had to be at football training, or I was making notes in the local library. I no longer considered myself happily married, although I could not have explained why. In the office where I worked, and among the few friends I had, more than a few marriages were – in the phrase of those days – breaking up. Even in my priest-cousin's family, his two sisters – the girl-cousins of my childhood – were no longer with their first husbands. I thought often of slipping quietly away from my wife and children to some room where I could write the truth about myself at last. All that stopped me was my feeling that my marriage was so unusual – I had crept so slowly into the sunlight of the conventional world from such a dark corner – that I should not escape from it in so ordinary a way.

When I thought of leaving my family I had no other woman in mind. I had actually come to envy the life of my priest-cousin. I was not interested in his religion, but I would have liked to live as he did in a building that was clearly different from the suburban houses around it. I had begun to make a study of the presbyteries of Melbourne. Each weekend I selected five or six from the telephone directory and drove to inspect them.

Saturday afternoon was my favourite time for looking over presbyteries. It was easy then to imagine most of the people of Melbourne at football matches or listening to horse-races while the presbyteries were quiet and forgotten. Many of the buildings I looked at adjoined their parish churches. When I visited these I went into the church for a few minutes, as though to pray, and then walked slowly out by the door that gave me the best view of the grounds and the side windows of the presbytery. I was especially pleased when I saw a long side-veranda screened by creepers, or a backyard enclosed by tall fences with only treetops visible above them, or an upstairs window with a view that could not have been had from any of the humble houses around.

Seeing one of these buildings I put out of my mind the memories I had of the inhabitants of actual presbyteries – of sour-faced housekeepers and tired, grey-haired parish priests – and imagined the place in front of me as a little community of like-minded men. They were solitaries who kept mostly apart from one another, but they had in common that each was engaged on some elaborate project that had kept him a bachelor or obliged him to live away from his wife and children. I was as vague about these projects as I was about the great task that would have taken up my own time if I could have ensconced myself behind one of the ivied upstairs windows. But each man would have been bringing to light something that had been for years unremarked by the thousands of people who thought the word 'Melbourne' referred to no more than what they would see looking to left or right on a journey along every street, or looking around from the top of the tallest building in the central city, or looking out from the front windows of every suburban house, or even looking each of them into the eyes of the one person in all of Melbourne who claimed to love him.

Under shaded desk-lamps in corners of high-ceilinged rooms, night after night, still more details were added to fantastic maps. Somewhere, on a vast table-top, hundreds of photographs of unidentifiable foliage were being fitted together, row by row. And behind the highest of all walls, in the least travelled of all streets, a man painted grids of street-patterns on clear glass panes and alternate surfaces of systems of mirrors, preparing to fulfil the dreams of those who had always wanted to see themselves somehow a part of the maps they had pored over.

For one set of reasons I had come to despise the Catholic religion, but for quite other reasons I admired the sites and structures and surroundings of the homes of Catholic priests. I could have wished for a presbytery in every street of every suburb: a place to vary the repetitive pattern of houses of married couples, to hint at other patterns imagined too late to occupy the hills and flatlands of Melbourne.

One Saturday afternoon I met my cousin at my own front gate. I was arriving home after one of my tours of presbyteries and back streets; he was leaving after visiting my wife and children. He gave me a long and rather sorrowful look and said that his marriage counselling program was not just for practising Catholics, that perhaps I should talk to my wife and the pair of us attend one of the weekend sessions that had done so much for other couples.

I gave the priest some evasive answer and resolved never to let him know my address after I had left my wife and children. The man who thought he knew all my secrets could spend some of his seemingly ample free time searching for the presbytery-like place where I had gone into hiding.

For some time my cousin had been mentioning to my wife and myself a woman that he called his dear friend.

He seemed as eager to bring her name into our conversation as I had once been to mention the name of the young woman who was then my first girl friend. My cousin's dear friend was a widow with a small child. How he had met her and become attached to her was a long and detailed story. He had wanted to tell the story to my wife and me but I had so far avoided hearing what I expected would be a tedious account of the working out of divine providence.

Of course I had been hearing for years about priests being released from their vows to marry their female parishioners or former nuns. But my cousin, it seemed, was following a much more roundabout course. He and his lady-friend had agreed to love one another but never to be alone together in circumstances that might tempt them (as the priest had put it) to fall. When I heard of this I told my wife I would offer my services as chaperon, but she was hardly amused.

Nor was my aunt, the priest's mother, amused when she heard of the affair. Her two daughters, the cousins who had made me miserable thirty years before, were both divorced and remarried – for which she had finally forgiven them. But she had expected something better from a priest, as she told my wife.

She complained to my wife on a hot Sunday afternoon in the house in Hawthorn. For the first time in years I was back in that suburb. While my wife and my mother and my aunt sat over their teacups in the redecorated kitchen and my son and my daughter watched the colour television in the front room, I wandered out into what was left of the backyard.

There was just room enough for me to have crawled in under the lowest boughs of the old lemon tree. I was going to sit there, with no solemn purpose in mind, but I could hear my aunt still complaining loudly in the kitchen about priests who gave scandal, and I was actually afraid that she might come to the back door and see me loitering under the tree and blame me for having first put rude thoughts into her son's mind.

At that very moment my cousin was at Portsea, on the Mornington Peninsula, in his lady-friend's beach house. (Her being wealthy was something else that angered my aunt.) I had never met the lady-friend, but my cousin had shown my wife and me a bundle of coloured photos taken at the Portsea house. There were other couples and their children in the photos, but it was only the young widow that I stared at. She was in bathers. She had the fetching look of a schoolgirl with something to hide, but her body had the relaxed plumpness I had observed about young mothers on beaches long ago. The priest had been in some of the photos too, but never in the foreground. He was where I would have preferred to be in any beach party; he hung back, forcing himself to smile and trying to look relaxed in his t-shirt and long trousers.

Standing alone beside the lemon tree, I imagined my cousin at the moment trying not to look too closely at the young woman sprawled beside him on the sand. I wanted to assert my superiority over him once again: to make clear to him that he had travelled such a long way and yet arrived only at a place like Seaford to be tormented by sights of buttocks and breasts. Remembering the young widow's face from the photograph, and feeling the tension that hung about the group on the beach, I was ready to slip behind the lemon tree and undo my trousers and resolve the matter for the time being. And I might have done so, except that my wife came to the back door just then and called me inside for afternoon tea.

In my own house my cousin talked more and more warmly about married love and what his new friendship, as he called it, had done for him. Sensing that I was now estranged from my wife, he took me aside one day and began to advise me about women. They needed constant love and reassurance, he said. From his own experience he could tell me that a woman needed to have the man she loved put his arms around her every day.

I made some effort to see the world as he saw it – throbbing with the heartbeats of lovers or glowing with the radiance of contented women. In that world I was one of the odd or the timid, puzzling alone over private visions and illusions when I should have been talking to people. I was the small boy in Hawthorn believing that something was kept hidden from him and creeping into dark corners to find it. My boy-cousin under the lemon tree, calling out joyfully to Charlie Alcock, knew instinctively what I had never learned. We should all of us have got together in the sunlight – Charlie and my boy-cousin and I, and my girl-cousins too, and talked frankly and kindly to one another; then there would have been no mysteries to puzzle me.

In my cousin's world, the dark spaces I had seen as a private map inviting me to undertake strange quests – those dark spaces were no more than the shadows cast by other people, and those people would have welcomed me into the sunlit spaces between them if only I could have trusted them and loved them. In that world the backyards of Melbourne were filled every Sunday afternoon with parties of people confiding in one another. Bedroom cupboards lost their mystery as groups of guests strolled in to throw their coats onto the beds. The tramlines of Melbourne kept their rightful appearance; they were a rectangular grid of the most direct routes for people wanting to visit one another.

I told my wife at last that I was about to leave our house and to live as a single man in a building that would seem not a part of the suburb around it. What she said is no part of this story, but when my cousin heard of what I was doing he rushed to our house and made us sit down for what he called a conference.

At first I told my cousin only that I wanted to live as a solitary for the sake of my writing. (My scribbling had developed. I was on my way to finishing what later became my first published piece of fiction: *Landscape With Artist*, a story about a man who had travelled backwards and forwards over his territory whereas I had circled around my own.) But my cousin provoked me by saying that he had lived a solitary life for many years and he thought I was not the man to survive it.

I answered him then – provocatively, as I thought – that my first destination was the backyard of his old house in Hawthorn, that I was going to begin there at last my real life: the life I should have led for the past thirty years if only I had been true to my own insights. If I had not been overawed by people such as himself and his sisters, I would never have conceded that the dark half of all I saw was only a part of the sunlit world that I had not yet understood. Now I knew that those dark spaces were part of myself. They were a huge projection of some intricate pattern behind my eyes, and it would be my life's work to explore those dark spaces and to interpret the pattern that gave rise to them. The dazzled and half-blind people of Melbourne's suburbs would lose sight of me. Only now and then someone might pause in front of a wardrobe door, hearing a scuffling noise that could have been myself among the boxes and the tissue-paper. Or someone in the front seat of a tram in the last sunlight of an autumn

Sunday might see a likeness of me in a man walking close to a hedge, in the one curved street in a suburb of right-angles. Or someone else, squatting comfortably on a toilet seat, might look up uneasily as though a face stared inwards through a wall of the same disturbing pastel shade that Linda and Veronica and Gene had once posed against.

My cousin did not ridicule me. He claimed to understand me, even to sympathise with me. He talked of our childhood together and confessed that he had always looked up to me and wanted me for a brother. I thought for a moment he was going to admit to remembering our afternoon together under the lemon tree, or to mention a certain day at Seaford. But he only went on to say that I belonged with him, with my wife and my children, that wherever I hid myself I would hear the people who loved me calling after me to join them.

That was when I chose to see what would always keep my cousin and the others from finding me; when I recognised around me the green and yellow of the untrained creeper that had made my little cubicle into a dim cave. Knowing where I was, where I had always been, I could rest my head in my hands and lower my eyes while I heard the voices.

They were muffled voices, and they reached me at long intervals. I heard the words they said. I had even made out a sort of refrain in them. But I did not answer them. I would not give myself away.

LANDSCAPE WITH ARTIST

I am in the backyard of my three-bedroom house in the City of Heidelberg, on a gentle slope that I insist is the first of the foothills of the Kinglake Ranges. I have chosen this house, where I mean to live for the next twenty years, because it is near enough to half-way between the centre of Melbourne and the district of Harp Gully.

As often as I am half-drunk, I tell my wife or my friends that I belong at Harp Gully. I unfold my favourite map (Broadbents Number 222: *Melbourne's North-East Hill Country*) and I point to the line I have plotted from the inner northern suburb where I was born to the outer north-eastern suburb where I now live. I explain that the line shows me to have been moving all my life in a north-east direction at an average velocity of 0.75 kilometres per year. I move my finger slowly across the map to show where the line will have taken me by the age of fifty. I am stationary in my suburban house at the moment, I say, because my wife wants our children to have what she calls a good education. But in 1990 I will catch up again with the projection of the graph of my life. I will settle at Harp Gully, on a dry and stony hillside in the rain-shadow of the Kinglake Ranges – in clear sight of the dark-blue escarpment that was the first shape to make me wonder, as a child, about my native land. My wife, of course, will be welcome to join me.

I am planting a wattle seedling. The wattle is the last of the little clump of Australian trees I have arranged in a corner of my yard. I have been told that wattles grow quickly and then decay and die long before other trees, but if my grove lasts for twenty years it will have served its purpose.

I hammer a stake into the soil and loosely tie the green, supple plant to the stake. Then I sit down and press my palms against the soil and lean back slightly as though the wattle has already grown and its trunk is supporting my back while the rest of the grove hides me from view. But I feel uncomfortable, first because I think I might resemble some character in a work of fiction, affecting to draw strength from the Good Earth, and then because I remember sitting in this same pose on a stony outcrop behind a house at Harp Gully, on a certain Sunday morning in 1960.

I get up from beside my young wattle late on a Sunday morning in 1970. I am badly hung over. I have no headache, but what I suppose are my nerves seem to be twitching uncontrollably just beneath my skin. On the previous night I sat alone in my kitchen drinking beer. My wife had gone to bed at seven after I said something harsh to her. I had put my son and daughter to bed soon afterwards. For a while the beer had inspired me to make notes in the margins of the manuscripts I had worked at for ten years. I had considered again one of the problems that had kept me from showing my manuscripts to a publisher. I tried to decide whether they were a collection of short stories or whether I could combine them and unify them to make a single novel. But long before midnight I had put my writing away and told myself that when I moved to Harp Gully, when I was no longer bothered by children howling and crawling around my feet, I would sit in a study with a view of the Sugarloaf at Kinglake and devise a new form of prose fiction – neither short story nor novel – with a shape to match the pattern of my life. After that I went on drinking calmly in the kitchen and reading and looking at maps; then I slept soundly on the couch in the children's playroom.

At midday I walk in through the back door, thinking that only some decisive bodily event can stop the shuddering under my skin. I count the bottles and cans in the fridge, but then I think of getting into bed beside my wife – assuming she has forgiven me for whatever I said to her last night.

Her door is still closed. Before I reach it I hear my daughter and son behind their closed door: the girl talking and the boy babbling (I had put them to bed at eleven after they had been up for six hours.) The children fall silent when they hear my footsteps near their door. I stand still, waiting for them to wail. They wail. I let them go on wailing for sixty seconds by my watch, knowing their mother cannot fail to hear them from her room. When my wife has still not appeared after sixty seconds I let my daughter out of her room and lift my son from his cot. I change the boy's wet napkin and give slices of apple to each child. Then I open the first of my cans for the day, and with the can in my hand I lead my daughter outside to show her the wattle tree and warn her not to damage it.

I sit on the back veranda of a weatherboard cottage on a hilltop district of Harp Gully. It is early afternoon on a midwinter Sunday in 1960. If I climbed onto the roof of the veranda and looked to the south-west I could make out, on the hills around Heidelberg, the outer edge of what journalists call the suburban sprawl. I vaguely remember having stood on that roof in the early hours of the morning with a flagon of sherry in my hand, leaping and capering and jeering at the faint lights of the creeping suburbs of Melbourne. But in the early afternoon I sit very still, staring at the dark ridge of the Kinglake Ranges a few miles to the north.

I think of what lies beyond that ridge. For the Kinglake Ranges are part of the Great Divide, and on their other side inland Australia begins. I think of the inland as the setting for long journeys that I might soon make as a solitary hitchhiker. I have just read *On the Road* for the second time, and I carry the book in my bag wherever I go. (My drinking wine on the previous night was part of my program for imitating Jack Kerouac.) I believe that of all young men in Australia I am the closest in spirit to Kerouac, and that his other Australian followers have not even begun to understand the Great Man.

At the hotel in Russell Street, Melbourne, where I drink every weekday afternoon, I stand among young men who wear beards and dirty clothes and are proud to be stared at in the streets. They talk of having hitchhiked to Sydney to borrow a certain jazz record and then having set out ten minutes afterwards to hitchhike back to Melbourne. They cadge money from anyone known to have a job, and they live on toasted sandwiches and flagons of wine and sleep on the floor in filthy rented rooms. A few of them have lank-haired girl friends who never blink when the word 'fuck' is used in front of them.

The bearded young men seem to want it thought that they devised their way of life spontaneously. They call themselves Scrags, although I suspect that even if I dared to ask them they could not say where the word came from. Yet I court the scrags; I buy drinks for them and listen to their mumbled stories of having stood for three hours in the freezing night air beside the Hume Highway near Yass on some desperate trip to Sydney, or of having been pushed around and questioned by the police when they sat in some Melbourne park for a warming sip of wine on their way home from the hotel. I would like to be fully accepted by the scrags. As a scrag I could almost see myself on the long roads across the Great Plains States.

I try to think of the scrags as distinct from another group in the hotel – the artists. The scrags, for all their pretences, are the nearest Australian equivalent to the Beats of the USA. The best of them are dedicated to feeling the qualities of particular places and moments. The artists seem to me nothing but pretenders; they assume that anyone who paints or sculpts is obliged to behave outrageously. Many of them do no more than dab with a brush at a piece of masonite once a week. But when a man says he is an artist he announces it fiercely, tilting his bearded chin forward and squaring his shoulders.

Probably no one but myself worries about this distinction between scrags and artists. The two groups mix freely. Many a young man with wild hair and paint-spattered trousers would regard himself as both artist and scrag. And the three or four genuine artists who gather sometimes in their favourite corner of the bar, remembering the rebel-artists of the 1930s and 40s, might see all the drinkers around them as hangers-on and mere talkers about art and unspecified revolt who owe nothing to any American upstarts but follow unthinkingly an old tradition of the back streets of Melbourne.

I consider myself a scrag. But on the veranda at Harp Gully I ask myself why I envy the self-styled artists. Each of them seems to stand comfortably in his surroundings, as though he can see around him all he needs for his life's work and as though the saloon bar is not a room filled with jabbering wild-men but the detailed background of 'Tattersall's Hotel, 1960, with the Artist Defining Himself'.

Even drunk I am never comfortable among the artists. I think of myself as a writer, and yet nothing I see around me seems to belong in my writing. What I write (during the few hours each week when I actually write) are things I call landscapes of the mind. They are a sort of prose-poem made by arranging words from a private collection I have begun to compile.

I have collected, in a thick notebook, nearly a thousand words so far. I expect to have a total of about five thousand when I have finished going through my *Concise Oxford Dictionary*. On days when I cannot face my writing, I tell myself I am doing a writer's work by turning page after page of the dictionary and selecting or rejecting words. I reject outright any word that is alleged to denote an abstract idea. (I myself have never had a so-called abstract idea, and I believe the term is self-contradictory. I believe that all thinking is done with sensible entities. I believe that people who claim to have abstract ideas either lie or fail to recognise that their abstract-seeming thoughts are composed of the sounds of words or the shapes of letters of the alphabet or pastel-coloured clouds or even holes or gaps in the dark screen where their thoughts usually appear. I call this belief of mine my Writer's Manifesto and I sometimes try to explain it to scrags who are not artists.) But I do not collect *all* the words commonly agreed to denote concrete things or ideas. I want to write in what I think of as a dialect of the north-eastern hills: a refinement of English in which every word has a perceptible effect on my emotions. I cannot define this effect or assign terms to its gradations; I can only recognise it – or its absence – and say that this or that word does something to me.

Out of these words I try to compose my landscapes of the mind. I arrange the words in obedience to tremors and impulses too subtle to be explained in any other way than by pointing to the arrangement of words they provoke. (Two years later I will read for the first time the poems of Dylan Thomas and believe that I devised quite independently, at the age of twenty-one, a way of writing at least comparable to his.) All of my pieces, even the most complex and abstruse, have clearly accessible titles. A work whose first words are:

pennants of memory decline to flutter by thorns so
blue ago

has the title: *Journey by Railway from Prince's Bridge Station, Melbourne, to Hurstbridge; May 1960.* I choose the title first; it refers to some place where a certain mood has come upon me. The body of the work is meant to record (in my purified language of the hills and the emotions) all the variations of that mood. I set down clusters of words from my private collection in response to what I call my inner promptings. I compare the pen in my hand as I write to an instrument recording on paper the faint trembling of the earth or the wavering of the wind in the landscape of my mind.

But I do not enjoy looking back at my finished pieces (the few that I have in fact finished). I cannot see in any of them any sign of the place named in the title. If that were all, I might cheerfully tear up my writing and stand with my back to some place I had written about and pose as a man with an interesting background behind him. But at some time I would have to look over my shoulder at the gap between me and the scenery behind me. There is an uncomfortable space between me and what others might see behind me. This is the gap that my writing is meant to fill.

The only writers I know are those whose photos I see each week in the book review pages of *Time.* I envy most the men who pose against trunks or branches of trees, patches of unkempt grass, or corners of old buildings. I assume that these photos are the same ones that appear on the dust-jackets of the men's books. I imagine this or that photo facing me on the rear cover of a novel or a collection of poems. I see the author standing easily in the foreground of the landscape he has chosen to define himself. I postulate the existence somewhere in the depths of that landscape of a horizon too fine for my eyes to make out, the horizon between the end of that landscape and the beginning of the landscape which is the equivalent of the contents of the book. Last of all, I speculate about the subtlest of all horizons. This quite imperceptible boundary would mark, if anyone saw it, the beginning of the furthest of all landscapes, the place that the writer once looked at in the days before he composed his book. And although I read about these writers and their books, and dream of becoming such a writer myself, I do not read their books. I do not read them because I do not want to be reminded that the scenery on the far side of the books is hardly different from the scenery in the books themselves: that the first page of each book (the first page, because I think of a book as showing me first its rear cover with the photograph of its author in a landscape and last of all its first page) merges easily into the places where the author once dreamed of posing for photographs.

Sometimes, while drinking, I announce that I will read no more books apart from *On the Road*, which I intend to look into every day of my life, because only Jack Kerouac understands that a writer has to compose long sentences leading like roads away from the country that presses against the back of his neck, roads from which the South Platte valley seems almost lost to view and Wyoming only in the sky.

I announce this in the hotel in Melbourne to some or other hairy man, but then he tells me he has a studio up in the hills past Hurstbridge, and I drop my eyes and note that he stands squarely and easily on the stained carpet. I see the carpet stretching away behind him and meeting smoothly, at the doorway into Russell Street, the asphalt that stretches back to Heidelberg Road and further back and upward, to the yellow, friable soil of the north-eastern hills, which meets neatly on a certain hilltop the slabs of his studio floor, which reaches to the far end of his studio where his latest painting rests with the soil of its foreground neatly abutting the stone slabs.

And then I become confused and wonder whether I should take up the life of a simple scrag and walk to

Harp Gully making notes as I go, in whatever words best fit the weather and the sharpness or dimness of the hills, or whether I should go on collecting my private words and still try to describe some landscape that separates me from what I see.

I am at Harp Gully in 1960 (and for the first time in ten years – since a bright winter Sunday when my father drove his wife and his ten-years-old son through these hills to see the wattle in bloom) as a result of my meeting a man who prefers to be called the Existentialist. I met him for the first time in Tattersall's Hotel on the previous Friday afternoon. He told me quietly that we were standing just then among the dregs of Melbourne; that the real artists are all up in the hills to the north-east. The real artists live in huge mud-brick houses with stained-glass windows; they despise the people of Melbourne and call them tourists for their driving up to the hills every weekend to look for cheap paintings of gum trees and wattles. The Existentialist impressed on me that he was by no means a tourist himself, despite his suit and tie. He was a sales representative in builders' hardware, and he had helped some of the artists with deals at wholesale prices. In return they had let him have some of their best paintings at genuine prices. He had lately bought a rundown shack and five acres at Harp Gully. He and his girl friend were going to spend every weekend there until the place was properly repaired. Then they would live permanently in Harp Gully, and he might even do some painting himself after having dreamed of it for years. I was welcome at his shack whenever I pleased. I could sleep on the couch in return for helping with the repairs.

On the Sunday, sitting behind the Existentialist's shack, I stare at the line of mountains to the north and try to recall the Saturday afternoon and evening. All Saturday morning I helped the Existentialist, measuring and cutting masonite to line his inside walls. While his girl friend was away shopping he told me he was very fond of her and would probably marry her after her divorce came through; but he was not going to knock back any other opportunities that came his way. Most of the real artists changed their women every year or so; there were always women available in the hills. He and I should get ourselves invited to the wild parties that went on every Saturday night.

On the Saturday afternoon the Existentialist and his girl friend and I sat for three hours in the Harp Gully Hotel – in the lounge where the artists were known to gather. The Existentialist pointed out and named three or four artists for me. He caught the eye of one of them, and the man nodded, but the Existentialist said it was a little too early yet to go barging in on them.

Towards closing time the three of us walked over with our glasses in our hands to the artist who had nodded at us. He was one of a circle of a dozen men and women. They seemed to me true artists and not mere scrag-artists and pretenders. The men had shaggy but well-kept hair and monstrously thick pullovers or bulky jackets; they roared and laughed at one another across their circle or sprawled back in their chairs and drank sternly and thoughtfully. They were plentifully supplied with women.

What I noticed most about the artists was their sureness of themselves in their surroundings. Even their images in the plate glass at their backs rested comfortably among the dark shapes of trees outside – one more of the landscapes that arranged themselves behind artists while they themselves barely glanced over their shoulders.

I remember, hunched in my chair on the Sunday,

a moment just after closing-time when the artists were somewhat pressed to empty their row of jugs and the woman nearest me turned in her chair and poured the last of a jug into my glass so easily and naturally that I decided I was from that moment welcome among them all. I saw the Existentialist talking to the artist he knew and the artist listening earnestly; I saw an artist with huge, knobbed silver rings on his hand – and the ringed hand itself stroking the hair of the Existentialist's girl friend. I told the woman who had shared her beer with me (she was ten years older than me and in the custody of an artist, of course, but she would surely have known women of my age and invited them to her parties) that I was a writer and planning to settle in Harp Gully.

We were invited to no party on that Saturday. The three of us stood in the frosty night air in the hotel car park holding our carton of beer and our flagon of wine conspicuously until ours was almost the last car. But late at night, drinking by the fire in the Existentialist's shack, we agreed that we would very soon be part of the artists' circle.

The Existentialist comes out to the veranda with a cold bottle and two glasses. He and I drink until late in the afternoon. We see successive rainclouds obscure the Sugarloaf. Once or twice a shaft of weak sunlight reaches a slope of the ranges and picks out folds and complications in what had seemed earlier a simple grey-blue barrier. The Existentialist tells me his shack was built many years before by two old ladies who fancied themselves as artists. They thought an artist was someone who set up an easel in front of a few trees, and so they had chosen this site because it had the best view for miles around. The Existentialist says Christ alone knows how many pretty little tourists' landscapes they must have painted before they died.

Late in the afternoon I announce that as soon as my writing is being published regularly I will give up my school-teaching job and move to Harp Gully. (I estimate that this could be at any time from six months hence.) With the Existentialist's permission I will build a small shack of my own in the thickest part of his bush. The Existentialist tells me I am crazy if I don't start using his shack right away. I ought to bring up here to Harp Gully one of the little teachers from my school – bring her up in the school holidays when he and his girl friend are in Melbourne.

He walks to the tankstand and shows me a spot where he can leave the keys of the shack for me to find. I pretend to be interested. But even drunk I cannot imagine myself approaching a young woman from the suburbs. I believe I could never persuade such a woman to give up her hopes of marriage and a house and garden just to consort with a man of the road, even if he was a published writer. And yet I have decided that this place, Harp Gully, these close-set timbered hills still in sight of Melbourne but having in their soil the toughness of the spine of Victoria – Harp Gully will be the place where I take my first woman. I can hardly imagine how the deed will be done; but I resolve that it will be done out of doors, out on the dry soil on a pleasant mat of dead grass and straps of bark. When I set out on my last journey from Melbourne to Harp Gully (I will walk it; I will make a pilgrimage on foot) she will be waiting for me. She will have read a little herself of the book that I carry always in my bag. She will know I am on the road: that I am heading towards a place much further than Nebraska. But as we sit down together at Harp Gully she will ask me to stay with her there in that South Platte Valley – to pose there with my back to the trees and with all the texts of my published works reaching into the distance.

The afternoon ends and the Existentialist says he must sober up for the drive back to Melbourne. I know that having got drunk again so soon without recovering from Saturday, I will shortly have what I call the dry horrors, when I cannot sleep or even sit still and all I can bear to do is pour cups of water down my throat and walk around touching walls and chairs and even the skin of my own arms and hands because every surface I see seems to be twitching and trembling.

I would prefer not to have the dry horrors at Harp Gully. I pack my bag (and stow in it a wine flagon of cold water), explain things to the Existentialist and his girl friend, then set out to walk the few miles to the railway station at Hurstbridge.

I am standing outside the railway station at Hurstbridge on a clear, frosty night in June 1980. My twelve-years-old son is beside me, wearing a hiker's pack on his back and talking about our expedition. To please him, I set out walking with him along the road to Harp Gully although I know the Artist is on his way to meet us in his car.

This is my first night away from Melbourne since I moved out of the house where my wife and my son and daughter still live. I am tired of asking myself why I left my family. I have prepared a story for anyone who might ask me tonight at the Artist's party. I am going to say that one night, when I was drinking, my wife asked me did I have no ambition left. I told her that in 1990, when our children had left home, I was going to set out alone and on foot for the hills around Harp Gully and live in a hut on the Artist's property and stare at the Kinglake Ranges and try to write something of value after all. My wife, according to the story, invited me to set out that very night.

I obliged her, and here (I would say at the party) I was.

Walking away from the meagre lights of Hurstbridge and into the dark countryside, I am astonished by the symmetrical pattern of my life. I think of writing – now, in 1980 – a story of a man who took twenty years to make a journey that he had first thought would last a day or so and to write a story that he had hoped to finish within a day days afterwards. Yet looking around me, I feel the same uncertainty that kept me, twenty years earlier, from writing. The trees ahead and the gravel under my feet seem solid and real, but I cannot find the words to make them into anything but the scenery for an imagined or dreamed-of journey. I try to make use of the notion that I am a character in a story that I tried to write twenty years ago, and that I could not finish *that* story because I cannot now imagine how I should have finished it (that is, how I would write it now, as part of my story of 1980).

I cannot follow my thinking through. I blame the freezing air and my son's chattering beside me. I think of the advantage I will enjoy at the Artist's party, announcing quietly to some young woman who only discovered Harp Gully in the 1970s (when the fashion began for a new generation of artists and their camp-followers to build mud-brick or colonial houses on five-acre blocks in the hill country and to keep horses or goats or donkeys and spin wool and grow herbs) that I was there as long ago as 1960. When the woman asks me what I do I will say I am a freelance writer. (This is almost true. I have had three feature articles published in supplements of newspapers. And three years ago I resigned from my teaching job to do small editing assignments for a publisher of textbooks. I called myself, on my taxation return, a freelance editor and writer and set myself up with a desk and a filing cabinet in our spare bedroom. Between editing jobs I did the housework and minded the children while my wife was out at her own work. But I earned far too little from my editing. I took a job as a security officer at the university near my home. This is still my job, although I have still not given up working on the fiction that has never yet been published. I sit all day in a glass-walled booth by the gates to the university car park and look at the strange species of eucalypt in the wildlife reserve and tell myself I have left the suburbs of Melbourne and entered the forests of the Great Divide. I take a notebook into the booth each day, but I cannot bring myself to write in it, and I wonder whether this is because I have found a somewhat congenial landscape at last or because I am now a solitary man with no woman to explain himself to.)

My son hears a car-engine far ahead of us. The beam from the headlights sweeps the trees like a searchlight. We stand where the driver will catch sight of us – a man and a boy at a gradual bend in one of the lesser roads from Melbourne to Kinglake.

The Artist roars and guffaws while we climb aboard. He pretends to believe we have walked all the way from our suburb, and he says we will be heroes at his party. He reminds me of the four unattached women he has invited and warms me he will not let me leave Harp Gully until I have won for myself at least one of these nubile nymphs of the hills, as he calls them.

I wonder how much of this my son will take back to his mother. I remember her saying on my last night in her house that I was free now to go and live with my pretentious wife-swapping friends in the hills and to find a floosie there for myself. I remember staring at her and wanting to ask her only where she had heard or read the word 'floosie'.

Sitting beside the Artist (bear-sized in his sheepskin jacket) I agree with my wife. The people of the hills are mostly pretentious. And the Artist has been through two marriages and who knows how many affairs. But whenever I visit the Artist or drink with him in the Harp Gully hotel, I seem a little nearer to the man I have wanted for twenty years to become. The land itself affects me. The trees do not overshadow me. The spaces between them are not choked with the undergrowth of rain forests. I step easily from any driveway or veranda into the territory of skinks and pardalotes, and I take up easily and naturally the pose of a writer of fiction in a photograph on a dust jacket.

I secretly despise most of the artists of the hill country; I believe their work only reproduces the appearances of things and that none of their paintings or prints or sculptures will ever make my throat tighten or my eyes water as a novel sometimes does. But I envy the artists for finding their subject in the same world where they walk and drink and eat. When I step out of the Harp Gully hotel with a group of them, and all of us pause and blink around us at the late sunlight on the hilltops, I believe they see already some detail of their future work while I know I will never read in any book of my own this paragraph of my own story – even if something of mine is published years later it will be the story of a man I have imagined.

The Artist himself is two years younger than me, although I find myself always deferring to him as a man of much wider experience. I met him first in a hotel in a suburb where he was a swaggering high-school art teacher and I was a drudge in a primary school. I know, in 1980, that his reputation is already secure, that art critics call him one of the boldest of the younger generation. I sometimes dare to tell him that I am artistically illiterate and quite unable to appreciate his work. Once, after drinking all day with him, I showed him the typescript of something I had written. He read a little of it and I told him how I despaired of writing publishable fiction because as soon as I began a story or a novel I lost sight of my subject and wrote page after page trying to explain what was wrong with me as a writer, which was that I hardly noticed people and things around me because I was always looking for some kind of ideal scenery that would correspond to obscure places in my thoughts.

I wanted the Artist that day to agree that all of us – painters and writers – were bullshit artists: too weak to shape the solid world to our liking, we scrawled and scribbled our daydreams of a more compliant world. He scratched and scraped (I said to him – rather hesitantly for all that we had drunk together) in wash or tempera, or whatever the fuck it was called, the twisted bodies of women because he knew he could never build on his five acres the hundred-roomed harem he desired. I began one draft after another of the same story because I was too timid to leave Melbourne and to look for the place where I belonged or the woman who would listen to the story of my travels.

It was a dangerous thing to have said to him. He squared his shoulders and took a first step towards me. I was ready for him to hit me; I was going to take the blow and then walk away saying over my shoulder something about the outworn tradition of the artist as bar-room brawler, jabbing his fist in the face of anyone who saw through his pretensions.

It had not come to that, but we never talked again about painting or writing except as our work – something we each had to get on with in the intervals between our drinking together.

For so long as I avoid talking too seriously to him, the Artist and I enjoy a subtle understanding. Whenever we have drunk a certain number of bottles together he asks me to tell him once again some story from 1960, when I thought I was Jack Kerouac and wanted to walk to Harp Gully and then over the Kinglake Ranges to Nebraska and Christ knows where else. The Artist has never read *On the Road*, but in 1962 – after I had left the scrags – he sat through poetry-and-jazz sessions all around the inner suburbs of Melbourne with people who dropped the names of Ginsberg and Ferlinghetti. The life he led in his twenties was much more scrag-like than mine; yet I am sure I have drunk more than he has, and that even if he gets to have a hundred of his paintings and prints displayed in every important gallery in Australia he will still be far from knowing what I almost knew on certain nights in the winter of 1960 when I staggered away from the fireplace in the Existentialist's shack and out in the frosty night, and looked at the throbbing stars over the Great Divide and the inland and then at the timid lights twinkling on the edge of Melbourne, and ran or blundered from one tree to another down the hillside until I found myself on some level patch of grass that could hardly have looked different from any other in the darkness but felt like the place I had travelled all my life to stand firmly on at last, and stood there convinced that I was about to see with utter clarity a vision of the woman who had been waiting for me all her life in her hilltop fastness among the back roads of Harp Gully or of the complete text of the work of fiction that had waited for all time in a universe of possibilities for me, its author, until suddenly I was aware of nothing but my body doubled over and all the beer and wine I had drunk since three o'clock that day in the Harp

Gully hotel spewing out of me and my face wet with a sort of tears yet also the hope that my misery just then was part of the ritual I had to undergo before I came into my own and the puddle of muck at my feet a sign of something I could surely pass beyond.

In the car, in clear view of the Artist, I take out my flask of vodka and swig from it. He laughs and says his bath is filled with enough cans and bottles to last us the whole weekend. I tell him I am starting early so that I can overpower with my eloquence as soon as I meet her the best of the women he has procured for me.

I see that I have made him a little uneasy, and I am pleased. He suspects I might be going to perform in his home what I once confided to him was my favourite trick in the 1960s – talking crazily to a woman for half the night, then going outside to urinate or vomit, then passing out on the back veranda or in a spare room and not waking until morning, and then talking for weeks afterwards of the woman who had been the first to understand my story but who disappeared before I could learn even her phone number.

I take out the vodka again, unscrew the top with exaggerated haste, and throw my head far back as I drink. As the road winds into Harp Gully I deliberately compose again the scene I have imagined every day since the Artist first told me about this party. The scene is as it would appear to his eyes. I have left the party with a woman. Hours later, when everyone else has gone home, the Artist walks around his veranda and sees a light in his studio (a bluestone building, as large as a suburban house, a hundred metres away among the trees). He looks through a window of the studio and sees the woman leaning back in a corner of his padded velvet couch. He sees me pacing the floor in front of her, waving my arms (even the right arm with the beer can at the end of it) more forcefully than he has seen me wave them in all our sessions of drinking and discussion. Sometimes I confront the woman, and seem to be saying something about myself or her or both of us. Sometimes I turn to the massed array of his prints and paintings and sketches and sculptures and wave and gesture towards them. Sometimes I walk in among his works of art, appearing and reappearing unpredictably at some gap between them or at the end of some pathway leading almost back to the far end of them. He knows from the woman's pose that I am talking ceaselessly, that even when I am out of sight in the maze of paths and tunnels my voice still reaches her from somewhere in the jumble of his works. Then he sees the woman sit up a little and listen more intently. She calls out a single word – my name, he presumes. She calls the word again, then listens a little longer, and then turns to the couch and draws up her knees and closes her eyes and sleeps.

I cannot decide whether he then walks back to the house or whether he steps quietly into the studio to find me collapsed in the shadow behind some almost-finished landscape or some half-formed female nude.

The Artist's front door opens into a huge room with a mezzanine around it, a massive open fireplace, and a stained glass window at one end. But all I see when he flings open the door is the crush of men and women talking and shouting above the taped noise of Little Richard. The Artist himself shouts at the people nearest us that here is a man he found on the road walking all the way from Melbourne to the party. A few people look at me with mild interest and then look away again. I turn to tell the Artist that I have to make up a bed for my son, but he has already pushed his way into the crowd to fetch me a can – and perhaps a woman or two as well.

I am sitting in a hotel lounge in a northern suburb of Melbourne. It is 1960 and I am not among scrags or artists. The drinkers are decently dressed working class men and women. And the people at my table are some of my fellow-teachers from the primary school where I teach, decently dressed, from Mondays to Fridays. We are celebrating the last day of the winter term. This is the first time I have drunk with teachers; normally I take the tram to the city every afternoon to drink at the scrags' hotel.

This is just what the teachers are asking me about – where am I in such a hurry to go every day after school? I am drunk enough to answer them all boldly, but my answer is aimed at the young woman who has seated herself – deliberately, I believe – beside me.

I have talked to the woman sometimes at school without being attracted to her. But drinking near her this afternoon I have rested my eyes often on the smooth, clear skin of her face and the oddly grouped freckles low on her throat. While I answer the question about my doings she keeps her eyes on my own face, and I notice what I believe is a wistfulness about her.

The hotel lounge is a warm and pleasant place. Its frosted windows shut out the noise of tyres on the wet road just beyond them. When the sun outside shines between the spring showers, I see a rich yellow glow all around me, and I decide that this room on this afternoon represents the comfortable refuge I might have found in the suburbs if I had not been called to a life on the road. The young woman with the freckles at her throat represents all those small-minded but not ungenerous females who might have been content to do the dishes at night and sit in front of the television set and keep me supplied with cold bottles while I went on writing in my room.

My reply to the teachers' question is long and detailed. I describe myself as a Jack Kerouac or a Sal Paradise, moving continually between the squalid inner suburbs – where no respectable teacher would dream of living – and the hill country around Harp Gully – where the average teacher would be classified as a tourist, a gullible buyer of pretty pottery and framed landscapes. I say that the jagged hills of Harp Gully are the source of my inspiration as a writer, where I spend my weekends drinking with artists and wild-men; my bare room in Fitzroy is my monkish cell where I write until long after midnight during the week. At Harp Gully I walk among the landscapes of my spiritual home. Then from my upstairs eyrie in Fitzroy I see those landscapes in the distance, remote and intricate.

No one interrupts me. I make a show of gulping from my glass. I talk about the artists at Harp Gully; about parties in mud brick houses from whose upper windows I see the faint lights of Melbourne far below. As I talk I take off my sports jacket and tie and take out of my carry-bag the dirty sweater that changes me every afternoon from a teacher to a Beat writer.

Later, the young woman beside me asks quietly what I happen to be doing on this coming weekend. I take this to be her last desperate attempt to rescue me from my life on the road. I tell her I am walking this very evening all the way to Harp Gully; I will arrive about midnight and drink with a man called the Existentialist; on the Saturday night I will be at a party in the home of the most famous artist in the hill country. (I name the Famous Artist and she nods gravely.)

About half of these statements are true. The

Existentialist first told me about the party weeks ago. It should properly be called a musical evening; a classical guitarist is performing. The Famous Artist has invited dozens of wealthy tourists from Melbourne. (He is calling them for the time being not tourists but patrons of his, or art lovers.) A second category of guest will be asked to pay at the door. The Existentialist, as a resident of Harp Gully, belongs in this category. A third category of people will be driven away forcibly if they so much as come within sight of the door. These are the scrags. The Famous Artist knows all about the scrags. He keeps them at a distance whenever he and his artist-friends favour Tattersall's Hotel with a visit. He knows that a scrag will hitchhike half the night to find a party he has heard a whisper about in the hotel – and to grab at the food on the supper-table and guzzle the free beer and wine and sleep on the floor and stay for days afterwards.

I explain to the girl that I am a scrag at heart and therefore not welcome at the party in the house of the Famous Artist. But I tell her I am not overawed by any artist; I will get inside the Great Man's house and drink his beer and look his paintings over and score a victory for Beat writers over pretentious painters. I admit that I may have to approach the Famous Artist's door as a guest of the Existentialist; but I will not disguise my scraggish appearance, and once inside I will insist on behaving scraggily. I am supposed to meet the Existentialist outside Tattersall's Hotel at closing-time, to be driven to Harp Gully. But I announce to the young woman, I have decided to walk from Melbourne to the hills. The time has come for me to make the grand gesture I have always dreamed of. While she still listens patiently, I divide the miles between Brunswick and Harp Gully by the miles per hour of my average walking speed. I decide that I have to set out at once. If the young woman cares to slip away from the others for a moment, she can watch me as I walk away into the dusk.

I tell her this is no mere walking trip I am about to undertake but a pilgrimage. The Famous Artist, so I have heard, keeps the great hall of his house as a gallery, with some of his own best works on the walls. In the heart of the north-eastern hill country is a mud brick and bluestone shrine where the people of Melbourne are sometimes permitted to look at framed images of landscapes they could never see or imagine for themselves. I am going to penetrate to the heart of that shrine, but not necessarily to venerate the images there. I am a writer; I can see further into things than a painter sees. I speculate continually about places far beyond the meeting-point of all the lines of perspective in all the painted landscapes of Australia. I expect to write soon the story of my journey from Melbourne to Harp Gully; and in that story the Famous Artist and his baronial hall and all his celebrated paintings will be a mere dot in the landscape. And he need not think I will allow him to restore the balance between us by painting my portrait after I have become a recognised writer, and showing me with a tiny, misshapen book in my hands and some of his favourite gum-trees towering at my back.

The young woman persuades me to have what she calls a drink for On the Road. I sit at the table while she goes to the bar. Somewhere behind the bar a radio is suddenly switched on. I hear what I suppose is one of the latest hit-tunes: *Poetry in Motion* sung by a pleasantly insipid male voice.

I have reached the degree of drunkenness at which things even a little odd or unfamiliar can seem strange and remarkable. As the young woman walks towards me the song reaches its high point. I see that her buttocks and breasts, under her skirt and twinset, are a little too large for the rest of her. Her motion with the tray of glasses in her hand is hardly poetry. Yet I am sure something surprising is about to be revealed to me as I watch the approach of her chubby body to the oddly jarring accompaniment of the song from the radio. While we drink I feel obliged to tell her about the Woman of the Hill Country – a composite of all the forbidding women I have glimpsed in the Harp Gully Hotel or imagined in the houses where the Existentialist and I will soon be welcome. Then suddenly I know that if I were to stay here until closing-time, drinking and talking seriously with this young woman of the wistful eyes and the pear-shaped body, and humming to myself the asymmetrical melody I have just heard, I would see the spaces between once-familiar things widen before my eyes: gaps would open between the walls of the hotel, between the close-set buildings in the street outside, between the northern suburbs themselves; the young woman would walk through one of those gaps and I would follow her, each of us singing like wise zanies the queer music of our theme song, and I would never even set out for the hills.

Then I feel, just as suddenly, sad and miserable. I walk towards the street-door, knowing the young woman is watching me from behind. It occurs to me that my journey to Harp Gully may be not so much a pilgrimage as an attempt to provide myself with a background in the eyes of a young woman I have never seen clearly.

Outside, I sling my bag over one shoulder and walk eastwards towards Nicholson Street. The clouds have cleared and the sun is still not quite down. I am a strong walker, and the bag is light on my shoulder, but twice in the first half-hour I lose time searching among laneways for a place to urinate. It is cloudy again and almost dark when I reach Heidelberg Road in Clifton Hill. I find myself trying to walk to the rhythm of *Poetry in Motion*, but then I find the uneven rhythm is holding me back. Soon afterwards the effect of the beer begins to wear off and I stop to sip from my flask of vodka that I keep always in the side pocket of my bag.

Light rain falls as I cross the Darebin Creek into the city of Heidelberg, and the sky is quite dark. I sip more vodka to help me over the hills in front of me. Somewhere among those hills, on a slope that I decide is the first of the foothills of the Kinglake Ranges, I calculate that I am barely half-way between Melbourne and Harp Gully and I decide that I cannot go on. I walk a little further, looking for a football ground with a covered grandstand or a park with a thicket of trees. Then a car passes me slowly and stops at the roadside. The Existentialist's girl friend leans out of the front window and calls to me. I climb into the back seat between two male scrags I vaguely know, and the Existentialist drives me on towards Harp Gully.

I ease myself between the knots of people, looking for the one corner of the room that I remember as having bookshelves built into it. I hold two cans prominently in front of me as I nudge the shoulders of tall, crowing men or mumble apologies into the hair of laughing women. The two cans are to save me from having to cross the room again too soon and to suggest that I have a companion waiting in the corner – a woman who drinks beer from cans and prefers to talk intimately with the man who has studied Harp Gully for twenty years rather than stand with a circle of swaggering artists who only joined in the rush to these hills in the 1970s. I reach the bookshelves and turn my back to the party to examine the fifty or so spines. But then I realise that of course these are books about art and artists. I arrange myself carefully, leaning against the side of the fireplace, still with a can in each hand and now with the chequered pattern behind me of books I decline to open.

Much later I am visited for a few minutes by a man and his wife from the suburb where I lived for more than ten years with my own wife and children. The man is a cabinet maker who once fitted out the Artist's studio; he talks of moving one day to Harp Gully and becoming what he calls a real artist. Otherwise I am left alone. But towards eleven the Artist himself comes to throw logs on the fire and asks me – trying to seem amused rather than annoyed – what the Christ I'm doing there by myself. I answer, trying to seem quite drunk, that I am trying to see the past twenty years of my life as a work of art.

I am pleased when the Artist can find no ready answer, but a little later he comes back with a woman and tells her I am one of the pioneers of the district and leaves her with me.

The woman tosses her long, blonde hair away from her face and asks me why I am not dancing. (I had not realised that many of the close-packed bodies are in fact dancing; I had thought they were only moving with a little more animation than before.) I tell the woman I do not belong among the cavorting artists and their audience. Those people exist in a three-dimensional world of figures against backgrounds, but I perceive a deeper meaning behind a scene such as this – and I hold out my arms and taper them slightly towards a point far away from me, as though she and I and all the people in the room and the paintings on the walls and even the bush outside were all included in some many-layered vista.

She does not turn away, as I had expected she would, but asks me to tell her more about myself. I tell her I am a writer, but one whose best work is still unpublished. I say my writing is too complex to talk about. I write fiction in order to discover the pattern of myself and my life. At first sight, a piece of my fiction might seem to describe only a few figures in a landscape; but on closer inspection it reveals extraordinary depths – another dimension perhaps. If she read my fiction closely, I tell her, she would seem to be stepping inside a painting of a landscape with one or more figures and walking back as far as the furthest painted detail and then seeing still further off other landscapes rising to view. (I am aware as I talk that nothing I have written fits this account; that I have never before given this account of my writing; that I may well forget before tomorrow what I have just been moved to tell her about non-existent works of mine.)

Still she does not turn away, and I believe I may have made some sort of sense to her. I go outside to urinate. In the fiercely cold air I mutter aloud that I will soon occupy my true country at last. Here I make my stand, I tell myself aloud, dragging the toe of my shoe around in a half-circle in front of me. Somewhere behind me are the bluestone outbuildings that the Artist calls his colony. (He has plans for teaching his way of art to young men and women who will live for weeks on his hilltop and drink in his words – especially the young women.) Tomorrow, I decide, the Artist will turn over to me a modest room in his colony. I will move into that room with my desk and my bookshelves, a refrigerator and a camp stretcher. I will never leave. The Artist will know that I have not settled there to learn how to daub landscapes or nudes on flat canvas; he will steer a wide path around my cell whenever he hears the rattle of my typewriter. Yet every Saturday evening he will tramp through the trees and knock firmly but respectfully at my door. (Before he knocks he peers through my uncurtained window and wonders yet again how any man can need so many books around him.) The Artist will lead me back to his house, to have tea with him, as he says. His current wife will have withdrawn discreetly to the bedroom with a portable television set. The Artist will fling open his fridge and show me the stack of cans, which he says is our tea. I will remind him of the stack of cans in my own fridge, which I say is our supper and breakfast. We will sit by the fire and drink. He will play continuously in the background his tapes of hit tunes of the late 1950s and early 1960s. We will talk all night, and I will force him to concede a little more ground: to retreat a little further towards his shallow paintings, seeing how much more of the hill country now belongs in my sheaves of typed pages in the room that has only spines of books to decorate its walls. On the Sunday afternoon, when I have begun to tremble a little from the after-effects of the alcohol, and even to doubt myself again, another knock will sound at my door. The woman with the long, blonde hair – or someone very like her – will have arrived for her weekly visit.

I step carefully inside the house again, expecting the woman to have gone from the corner by the fireplace. She is still there, but some shaggy-haired artist is talking to her, pressing his fist against the wall just beside her head. I take up my position in the corner and try to look indifferent, with my thoughts on the deeper themes of my life (twenty years of solitary journeys between Melbourne and Harp Gully; twenty years of making notes for the story of those journeys) while the latest of all the women I have tried to impress is about to go off with an artist to admire the latest landscape he has dashed off.

But the woman sends the shaggy man away and turns back to me and asks what we were discussing before we were rudely interrupted. I ask her who the shaggy man is. She tells me he is just a guy who was crapping her off so much she had to be rude to him.

I am pleased to have her to myself again but not so pleased to hear 'guy' and 'crapping me off' from her mouth. I hear these as the fatuous speech of filmgoers and diners-out from the trendy suburbs of Melbourne. (I use the word 'trendy' to myself in quotation marks.) I make a note to convert her in time to a pure, hill-country dialect in which every word asserts that the speaker sees only what he or she sees and only from the peculiar angle of a hills-dweller.

Seeing her prepared to stay beside me for the rest of the night, I decide to tell her everything. I explain that I have dreamed of Harp Gully for half my forty years; that as long ago as 1960 I planned to walk from Melbourne and live in a shack on a hilltop; that I am now free at last to fulfil my dream.

She says she had never heard of Harp Gully in 1960; that she lived there for five years until a few months ago but now lives in Melbourne and cannot imagine going back to the hills.

I think of asking whether she herself is an artist, but I fear to embarrass her if she has failed at art. Then she tells me that she was at Harp Gully for those five years because she lived with a painter after she left her husband.

She reaches down from the shelves behind her a small book with the words 'modern' and 'Australian' as part of its title. She turns unerringly to a certain page.

She holds in front of me a coloured plate with the caption *Landscape Unspecified, Number 1* and asks me do I see there anyone I know.

I see a patch of the sort of bush I am used to seeing in Australian paintings. Far back among the trees a naked woman walks across a clearing. Her face is hidden behind her tossing hair, but her stride makes her seem intent on something amongst the furthest trees and quite unaware that an artist might have seen her as part of one of his landscapes.

I tell the woman jokingly it is a remarkable likeness. I make a note of the book's title and publisher and tell the woman I will search all the bookshops of Melbourne on Monday to buy a copy and remove the plate and hang it on my wall. I try to sound a very different man from the one who has already resolved to pore over the tiny painted blobs of breasts and buttocks, preparing himself for the awesome moment when he may have to confront their originals – and certainly quite unlike the man who will wonder endlessly after tonight what the artist did with her after he had thrown down his brushes and stepped behind his easel and followed her into the place she had found behind his furthest trees.

She asks me somewhat seriously what I think of the painting as a painting. I tell her I am an ignoramus in the field of art; that all Australian landscape paintings look more or less the same to me; that as a writer I am only interested in whatever the woman in the painting sees but the onlookers and even the artist are prevented from seeing. And I boast that as a writer I do not see the painting as the end of the matter: that I can see myself enclosing the painting and all it is meant to reveal in something I will yet write.

I hear above the noise of the party Richie Valens

moaning the words of *Donna*, which I first heard late in 1959. Somewhere on the other side of the crowd, the Artist has switched on the tape that he knows is my favourite. I can only suppose he has been observing me in my corner with the woman he sent away. I ask the woman to stop talking because a miracle is about to take place. In a moment I am going to hear my theme music: the tune that winds in and out of my life and makes a pattern of the past twenty years. She thinks I am trying to amuse her; she says that the Artist has been playing his tapes of golden oldies for hours but I was so busy talking that I hadn't noticed. I tell her I know nothing of so-called golden oldies; all I know of popular music is what I heard from 1959 to 1961 when I spent my Sunday afternoons alone in a room in Fitzroy or working as an unpaid carpenter or house-painter in a lonely shack with a view of the Sugarloaf at Kinglake. On those Sundays I was always ill or depressed from my Saturday's drinking, and the tunes I heard sounded to me like the last, dwindling cries from a city I was about to leave for ever, a city whose people still enjoyed the simple pleasures I had turned my back on.

I forbid the woman to speak while Jimmy Jones sings *Handyman*. Near the end of *Alley Oop*, by the Hollywood Argyles, I ask her has she heard of a man named Marcel Proust. She says she has not, but she says it pleasantly and expectantly as though she only waits for me to take her across the room and introduce her to my friend with the French-sounding name. I tell her to call at the Artist's house tomorrow when I am not so drunk and to ask me about the uneven paving-stones or a certain little phrase of music. Then I tell her I have to leave her for a few minutes. I have to be alone while I hear the music that tells me I am still on the right road.

I am alone on the Artist's veranda. The woman has not followed me. (I wonder whether I would have stopped her if she had tried to come with me.) I hear the first notes of *Poetry in Motion.* I close my eyes to concentrate on the music, but then I teeter on my feet and see the flashing lights that warn me I am close to vomiting. I set out walking along the veranda (which extends, in the best colonial tradition, all around the four sides of the Artist's house). Sometimes I stride; sometimes I take quick little fairy footsteps; sometimes I stagger and veer with what seems an inspired craziness. Whatever I do, I find myself moving in exactly the rhythm of the music from inside the house.

I make almost a circuit on the veranda, and then the song ends. I listen for some other howl or wail from my scrag-years, but all I hear from the house is the roaring and shrieking of the mob of artists and their women. Then the first notes of *Poetry in Motion* sound again. Someone has wound back the tape. The woman has understood that this sacred music of mine is a serious business, even if I seemed to joke about it. Or the Artist, my friend of nearly twenty years, has seen me leave the house and knows how I want to look back into my past – and to impress the woman – and so he sends my tune all over the hill country (the volume is much louder now). Best of all, perhaps, the woman has gone up to the Artist, and the only two people who have almost understood me are sending their message to call me back from the darkness.

I pause in my circuit and perform my ritual movements, my poetic motion, in front of the largest window, which is filled with the work of an artist in stained glass. The Artist, my host, once boasted to me that his house has been decorated by the leading artists and craftsmen in Victoria. Painters and printmakers and sculptors each gave one of their works when the house was being fitted out, and a famous stained-glass man designed a window for the main room. Now I advance poetically towards the glass panels, trusting my destiny – that force which has brought me back to Harp Gully to discover again the music and the woman and the sense of mission that first drew me to my sacred hills twenty years before – trusting my destiny to guide my dancing feet so that anyone happening to look out from inside will see a strange shape of a man appearing suddenly out of the darkness and the vague tree-shapes, looming up against the esteemed glass pattern as though he meant to walk on through it: to burst into the room and to stand in sight of the artists with chunks of the precious, smashed work still falling behind him at odd intervals from the edges of the man-sized gap he has opened in it, a shard of acid-green still wobbling on his head, a chip of flame-orange sliding down his sleeve from his shoulder, and in his outflung hand something purple-red that might be a slab of the glass or the spreading stain of his own blood – but then stopping suddenly and gracefully just short, so that his face almost presses against the other side of one of the more significant zones of the pattern.

And so it happens. I stop suddenly and, I feel, gracefully. I look in for a moment at the richly coloured room where heads nod and arms point and mouths open and close. Then I dance backwards to the edge of the veranda and the first of the shadowy trees, and forward again rapidly and menacingly to the coloured glass.

For the first time since my arriving that night at Harp Gully I am sure I am in my rightful place. The artists have their place, but I have mine; and mine encloses theirs. And while they shout and strike poses between their decorated walls and artfully tinted windows, they can see nothing of the man who moves easily among the shapes of trees on the other side of their framed landscapes and patterns. Striding or staggering or strutting up to the coloured window, I wish again that some artist, preferably *the* Artist, could happen just then to peer at the glass, annoyed that he can see only darkness behind it when he suspects there is much more to observe. I want him to come close enough to see my face for just a moment – but not to identify it. I want him to know that some man he cannot name sees not only his precious glass with the light behind it revealing its pattern – such as it is – but the little enclosed world of artists shut in the narrow space on the wrong side of their works.

When *Poetry in Motion* has finished I step back from the veranda and feel earth and grass under my feet. This time I want the blonde woman to peer out through the glass. I suppose that a woman who has consented to pose naked among the trees of Harp Gully believes herself somehow attuned to the landscapes of the hill country. I want her to have to imagine me out among the dark masses of the bush, to wonder why I stayed out here all the while my music was playing, to wonder what I find alone in the place that her artist-friend would have assured her was the setting for a man's dream of a woman.

I remember a passage from *The Great Gatsby*: a description of a house on Long Island surrounded by a green lawn that seemed to rush towards the house and to break against the walls in a wave of creepers and vines. I see the landscapes of Harp Gully advancing over the hills to engulf the house where the arrogant artists have gathered. I station myself at the head of the advancing landscape, I, the only man on that hilltop who has tried to see twenty years of his life as a kind of landscape.

I feel a tremor in my stomach. I have just time

enough to turn and reach the nearest tree before I begin vomiting. Afterwards I find I cannot walk steadily or focus my eyes. I wash my face at the tankstand and creep in at the Artist's back door to get my sleeping-bag from the laundry. I stumble away from the house to one of the studios. I find the key in its hiding-place under the eaves and let myself in and lie down to sleep among dark shapes of canvases or easels or printing presses – all the strange equipment which the Artist once took great trouble to show me but which now I cannot even name.

I walk out from between thin saplings of second-growth forest. I climb through a wire fence and step onto the road. I follow the road towards the township of Harp Gully, which I know to be just around the next hill. I look back and see the two scrags coming out of the bush far behind me. I slow my walk, waiting for them to catch up.

It is mid-morning on Saturday. I have crossed sodden paddocks and stumbled through dripping bushland to avoid the roads. When the scrags and I left the Existentialist's house he was still asleep. But he had warned us while we drank with him on Friday night that he would come after us in his car if we tried to escape on Saturday morning. We are supposed to work on his shack all Saturday. In return he will take us as his guests to the Famous Artist's musical evening.

Time and again while we sat around his fire the Existentialist told us the Famous Artist was going to bar all scrags from his house. And if we three pissed off to the Harp Gully pub before we had done our fair share of work on the Saturday, the Existentialist was going to sit back among the artists at the party and say not a word while he watched us being manhandled at the Famous Artist's door.

The scrags and I woke one another early on the Saturday and agreed in sign language that we were all crazed with thirst. I led them by way of a short cut towards the Harp Gully township. We have told one another that the hotel will be sanctuary for us – the Existentialist could hardly try to prise us away from the bar, and once we have got him to have a drink himself he will be one of us again. And we have agreed that after a day of quiet drinking we will find the right words to get us into the Famous Artist's house.

I feel today a bond between myself and the two scrags. I still think of them as ignorant bastards who never read books or worry about theories of art or the imagination as I do. But I am glad to have two scrags with me as I walk towards Harp Gully on my way to the Famous Artist's house. I admire the scrags for what I have decided to call their instincts and their intuition. I suspect that this will be the weekend when I penetrate to the truth about the hill country; when I break through the layers of my own delusions and the mumbo-jumbo talk of artists; when I see my own vision of my own place. Today I want scrags for my companions. I am on a quest that perhaps only a scrag can undertake.

I see it as significant that I have emerged from among trees onto the road and that the road winds through the heart of Harp Gully. I wish that some artist might have passed along the road just as I appeared from the bush with two scrags stumbling after me. The artist would have been startled, I think, to see that a scraggy writer has somehow found his way in through an aperture on the Melbourne side of the landscape that should have been the artist's own preserve.

But the main street of Harp Gully seems deserted.

We three scrags push open the door of the hotel and breast the bar. The barman seems not at all pleased to see us. We order pots of beer. He takes his time serving us, and the beer, when we get it, tastes badly. One of the scrags asks the barman cheerfully is there somewhere a man can shower and have his clothes cleaned up and pressed. The barman looks the scrag slowly up and down (we have all slept in our clothes on chairs around the Existentialist's fireplace) and walks away from us.

Later, when three farmers arrive, the barman makes a point of talking warmly with them, his trusted locals, at the far end of the bar. But by now the beer has settled in our empty stomachs and we do not care. One of the scrags asks me loudly what I am going to order for breakfast in the hotel dining room. The other talks equally loudly of going to the Famous Artist's for breakfast and to help get the party started early. The locals hear the Famous Artist's name mentioned, and one of them asks the barman did he know that So-and-so (presumably a local bruiser) will be one of the men at the door tonight to handle any gate-crashers from the city.

More local men arrive and station themselves at a certain distance from us. I know that only the beer inside me keeps me from feeling afraid. I look out through the windows. A few cars have arrived in the main street. A new-looking truck drives slowly past and the driver waves to someone in the street. The driver is the Famous Artist himself – unless all the drinking I have done since yesterday has brought on already what I call my persecution horrors (when strangers all around me seem to be whispering my name and gradually forming themselves into a circle that will close in on me).

I drink my next pot rapidly to try to explain to

the scrags that we are about to take part in scenes such as we watched as boys in Western films. There will be a showdown very soon in these hills. Already the camera is moving swiftly from one to another of the little bands of determined men who will come together at last. (I say 'the camera' but I have the exhilarating feeling that my own eyes can see all over Harp Gully at this moment.) Watching cowboy films as a boy I was always annoyed that I could never see the *whole* landscape of the final scene spread out like a map with the protagonists converging from its far corners. Today I can look down on the forested hills, the grazing paddocks and orchards and poultry farms, the narrow dirt roads, Harp Creek winding down the valleys towards the Yarra. I see a group of scrags leaving the train at Hurstbridge station and setting out – perhaps too late – on their long, steep walk towards Harp Gully. I see the Existentialist waking in his shack and telling his girl friend he must warn the Famous Artist that three dangerous scrags have escaped from custody and are heading across country towards the party. I see the little bands of locals among their fibro-cement sheds full of sickly white-leghorns, blowing down the barrels of their squirrel-rifles and taking their stockwhips down from the nails where they hang coiled. Word has reached these men that the Famous Artist needs them. They are no great friends of the Famous Artist but of course they will close ranks with him against a threat from outside their territory. (They are desperate, disgruntled men. Their fathers came to these stony hills during the Great Depression when there was no work in Melbourne. The fathers built the fibro shacks and sheds and called themselves farmers but died as poor as when they first arrived.) I see the Famous Artist himself returning to his hilltop after spreading the word that a notorious scrag, a desperate prose-poet, has sworn to break into the shrine of art and to see through the sacred paintings kept there. The Famous Artist sets a local man with a rifle at each window of his Great Hall and walks around hanging tarpaulins over each of his paintings. An eerie silence falls over the bush outside as the Famous Artist goes from one to another of his men with a few last words of encouragement. He reminds them that they are fighting for the sacred images of their home district. Each man turns his stubbled face over his shoulder towards the walls where the landscapes and nudes hang veiled in black, then looks out again through the window and fixes his caved-in mouth into a straight line and squints along the barrel of his rifle towards the bush.

With the beer in their blood, the scrags complain of being hungry. The barman tells us to do ourselves a favour and buy something from the store down the road. We walk through drizzling rain towards the shop. A woman with a pinched face tells us it is past midday and the grocery department is closed by law. We buy loaves of sliced bread and bottles of milk. The woman warns us not to eat on the premises.

Outside we notice, in the opposite direction from the hotel, a weatherboard building with its floor-level high above the ground at one corner where the land falls away. The building is obviously a hall, but one of the scrags insists on calling it a church, and when we crouch on the soft yellow dust under its floor he says we have descended into hell. We stuff the sliced bread into ourselves and drink the milk, and the two scrags curl up in the dust and sleep.

I go on sitting with my back against a foundation-stump. I am afraid that if I fall asleep we will wake up sick and sober after six o'clock, the pub closed, and us with nothing to drink for the rest of the weekend. The rain falls steadily outside our shelter, but the bread in my stomach cheers me a little. I am anxious to get back to the hotel. I believe I could soon overcome the sullenness of the local men if I confronted them alone without my insensitive scrag hangers-on. I would show the locals that I can hold my beer; and I would tell them quietly that I have more to offer them than any painter. I would declare that I am a writer who will soon be settling permanently in their district. They would hardly want to know about my writing, but they would surely have a native respect for the Word – perhaps even a crude oral tradition of ballads and songs from their long years of struggle with the land. They would gradually accept me into their circle, and after I had built my hut on the Existentialist's property I would walk into Harp Gully every Saturday to sit with them and talk and listen. (I with my circle in the public bar, while the artists roared their inanities in the lounge.) In time, as my works become published, I would be known among the locals simply as the Writer or even the Famous Writer. Sometimes they would ask me what my books were about. I would tell them simply, in their own language, how the hills around us were a source of poetic inspiration for me. At last the hotel would become for me what his Great Hall is to the Famous Artist – my shrine, but a shrine sacred to the invisible scenery of poetry whereas his is dedicated to the merely visible stuff of painting.

The scrags wake up and tell me it is time for a pre-lunch drink. They creep out from under the hall without bothering to dust themselves down. The scrag who owns a watch says we have three hours of drinking-time left, and we walk through heavy rain back to the hotel.

The bar is crowded. The barman (the same one)

serves us silently as though he has never seen us before. The drinkers spread themselves out just enough to keep us from leaning comfortably on the bar. One man stares at the coating of dust, now strangely striped by the rain, on the back of the scrag nearest him. I wish I could ask the yokel what he sees so odd in a man who has nowhere to rest but on his native soil.

One of the scrags looks through the doorway into the lounge and tells us to follow him. Other scrags have made it to the hills. Around the tables in the centre of the lounge are men and women from Tattersall's Hotel. They assure us that every able-bodied scrag will be at the party tonight. When Tatts closes in a few hours a cavalcade of cars will set out for Harp Gully.

I notice that the locals occupy all but a few central tables of the lounge. They watch us from along their walls and out of their shadowy corners. I make one last gesture towards these people who will be my neighbours next year. I take my beer and sit alone at the last unoccupied table – at the edge of no-man's-land.

An hour later I am still drinking at my table but with two men who belong at the edges of scragdom. One is a New Zealander who has told me he is wanted for embezzlement in Invercargill and who recites, whenever I ask him, from the poems of James K. Baxter. I think it clever to call the New Zealand man Enzedder. The other man is a public servant who wears his suit and tie defiantly into Tattersall's every afternoon and sometimes pesters the young scrag women. Enzedder says he has no money. The public servant and I take turns to buy his drinks. I try to persuade these men that we three look respectable enough to get into the Famous Artist's house. I urge them to slip away from the scrag-pack a little before closing time, to buy three flagons of wine, and to walk the mile to the Famous Artist's and shelter among his trees until seven-thirty when the official guests will be arriving.

A man I know only as Bob the Poet sits down beside us. Bob is grey-haired and haggard but perhaps no older than forty-five. He is respected as the Grand Old Man of Scragdom, and sometimes he reads at poetry-and-jazz sessions in St Kilda from a long work he says he has been writing for the past twenty years. But his company is hard to bear; he is an alcoholic who becomes quite incoherent after only a few beers. When he joins us he is already far gone. He leans almost sideways in his chair and hits out at us when we try to straighten him. He talks to himself. The public servant puts an ear to Bob's mouth and tells me the old fellow wants a whisky. When I bring it back from the bar Bob is sitting on the floor with his back to a leg of the table, but he has lost his alarming tilt. I hand him his drink where he is.

Now the locals are all watching the three of us. At some of their tables the voices have dropped to whispers. They seem especially bothered by Old Bob, who goes on continually with his semi-human speech. I finally become angry with the locals. I am ready to stand on the table and address them all and demand to know why they drink and talk in a pub if they can't abide the sight of a man who has devoted his life to drinking and poetry. We all three become angry. Enzedder announces loudly that he is wanted by the police in Te Awamutu for kicking a man's head in a pub very like this one. The public servant leans back in his chair and blocks the path of a teenage girl walking past and asks her would she like to come to a party with him. Then two small children walk past and Old Bob comes out from under the table on hands and knees and confronts them. I am sure he is trying to greet them kindly, but even to me he sounds like a dog barking at them. The children back away, and I have no doubt that the people whispering at their tables have reached the end of their patience.

I hurry to the bar to buy another round. The barman tells me he is ordering me off licensed premises before witnesses and would I please take my three disorderly friends and go at once. I ask can we buy some flagons of wine before we go. The barman says he can make an exception in that case and asks me what I want. I call the public servant to the bar and tell him what is happening. In a schoolboy's imitation of an upper-class English accent he warns the barman he will be hearing from his (the public servant's) solicitors before a week is out. Then, considering the long wet evening ahead of us, we buy a flagon each of port and sweet sherry and dry sherry.

Outside, the sky is dark but the rain has stopped. I tell Enzedder and the public servant we can shelter under a hall down the road and sip our flagons to keep warm. But they howl me down. They want to phone for a taxi and get to the party at once. Even Old Bob seems to have understood our talk and to be against me.

While he rebukes me in his strange language I resolve that on no account will I approach the Famous Artist's door with Old Bob in my company.

We set out for the public phone box beside the store. Old Bob has begun to lean again, and we find that he wants to go down on hands and knees. We move forward very slowly at the side of the road, with Old Bob crawling beside us. When I phone the taxi service I am told there will be a long delay, as the car has to come from Eltham.

We sip from our wine on the steps outside the store

until the taxi arrives. The public servant and Enzedder take the back seat with the flagons safely between their knees. I hold the front door open for Bob, hoping he will get in and sit normally. But he struggles in on hands and knees and crouches on the floor of the car. I perch on the corner of the front seat and swivel myself into the car, resting my legs gently on Old Bob's back. The taxi driver watches all this from the corner of his eye but betrays no sign of surprise or amusement. I ask him to take us to the front gate of the Famous Artist's property and he drives off calmly. If I could talk freely in front of the others I would like to ask him his name. I would like him for a friend when I come to live in Harp Gully.

At the front gate, in the twilight, we can see nothing of the Famous Artist's house – only a driveway leading over the shoulder of a hill. Enzedder and the public servant cry out to be driven to the front door of the house, but I take out the money for the fare and beg the driver to let us out where we are.

We stand hugging our flagons to our chests. Old Bob whimpers and whines at our heels. I insist that we must not approach the house so early. I lead the way to a plantation of wattles on the hillside above the driveway. The public servant keeps a hand on Bob's collar to guide him through the long grass. Rain begins to fall just as we reach the trees, but under the lower branches the ground is still dry.

We sit and drink our port and sherry, not forgetting Bob. I become cheerful again and talk of staying there all night under the trees, telling one another our life stories instead of fawning on the Famous Artist. Enzedder and the public servant tell me to shut up.

A car approaches the front gate; the first guests are arriving. My companions cheer. Then the headlights of the car shine directly into my eyes. I look around me and see our little huddle of scrags brightly lit by the full beam from the lights. I realise that the driveway curves unpredictably from just inside the front gate, so that our shelter-spot is directly in front of any approaching car for perhaps twenty seconds. I would like to move to a more concealed place, but I know better than to say so to the others.

More guests arrive. As each pair of headlights shines on us, Enzedder and the public servant wave and flourish their flagons. One driver, invisible to us behind his lights, toots his horn. Another driver stops his (her?) car, perhaps taking us for hitchhikers or travellers who have lost their way, but we wave him (her?) on again.

Then I find myself alone. Enzedder and the public servant have set out along the driveway, each with his flagon in one hand and the other hand slung across Bob's shoulders, supporting him like a wounded soldier. I still believe they will be turned away at the door, and I wonder how I can make my own attempt on the party without their spoiling my chances. I sit a while longer and drink. A few late cars aim their lights at me, and I wonder what the art-patrons from the suburbs make of the solitary figure in the lower foreground of the dark landscape.

At last, I follow the driveway to the house. The front doors are ajar, with no one guarding them. I cannot believe I am free to walk straight through. I stand outside and cough. A man looks out and asks me mildly do I have ten shillings. I pay him, and walk with my flagon into the Famous Artist's mud brick mansion.

Around the floor of the enormous main room perhaps a hundred men and women – well-dressed, with some in evening clothes – sit or sprawl on rugs or cushions. In a little clearing at the centre of the crowd a woman in a long black gown is sitting on a stool with a guitar in her lap. Every face in the crowd is fixed on the guitarist. No one hears me enter.

I slink towards an unlit corner and find another crowd quite separate from the guitarist's audience. All the shadowy zone of the room is littered with scrags. Some are dozing with their arms curled around their flagons. Some are still drinking. Most are eating. They have somehow got at the supper already, and they tear at rolls of bread and slabs of cheese and handfuls of salad and meat. I see Enzedder and the public servant and all the scrags from the Harp Gully hotel that afternoon – and others who must have come directly from Melbourne. All of them have got through the Famous Artist's door before me and made themselves at home.

I sit quietly in a corner and wait for some food to be passed my way. It occurs to me that I have not seen Old Bob, and I wonder if he at least has been barred from entering. But a little later, when the guitarist has just finished a piece and the official guests have clapped politely and she settles herself for the next item, the gruff, babbling voice comes from the very centre of the room. Bob's strange half-speech sounds oddly impressive, like a funeral oration delivered in an unknown tongue. But the audience look around them and the guitarist raises her eyebrows and I press myself further into the shadows. Then the Famous Artist himself gets to his feet at the edge of the crowd. I put the top on my flagon and prepare for the road again. This, I suppose, will be the moment when the Famous Artist calls on a gang of his artist-henchmen to clear the room of all the scrag-barbarians who have ruined his evening. But all he asks is for the guitarist to please wait a moment while he gets a drink for Bob. Which he does, pouring a large scotch and water from a trestle-table at the side of the room and stepping in among the guests to hand it himself to Old Bob, who makes one last, pleased barking noise and falls silent.

I sit against the mud brick wall and try to appreciate the fact that I am in the home of one of Australia's leading artists. I can touch with my own hands the walls that the artist's hands have shaped from the tough yellow soil of the north-eastern hill country. I can see around me the spaces that the artist has decided will be not wall but landscape – the extra layer of scenery he has chosen to surround him on all sides. If I wish, I can bring my eyes close to the backgrounds in paintings I have seen before only as prints in books; I can stare at the least detail of the man's distinctive scenery – the wallabies as tense and upright as fenceposts, the white bones of cattle like roads leading out of sight, the plumage of bronzewings like eyes glinting.

I feel again my sense of mission. Here on this hilltop something has been made visible, something of the essence of my special territory. I must look hard at it, and yet I must not accept it. It is too easy to stare at paintings. It is even too easy to paint paintings. I am called on to do much more. I must speak or write about what I see.

But as yet I cannot find the words. I pour more of my sweet sherry into myself. I eat my share of the chicken legs and spring onions and cubes of cheese. When the guitarist finally ends her recital and the guests break into noisy groups, I begin to talk.

I talk first to the scrags around me, but they are tired after their hard day. Many of them have curled up to sleep in the warm room. I walk among the other guests, looking for someone to talk to. I talk a little to the Existentialist and his girl friend, who have apparently forgiven me for running away from their shack. I even talk a little to Old Bob, who is upright now, and able to walk a few steps, although he strains his throat horribly to make the merest growl. Then, much later in the evening, I talk to the paintings.

I begin a slow circuit of the room. In front of each painting I take a mouthful of sherry and whisper a few words. I am not aware of time's passing, but the room is vast and there are many paintings on the walls. As I reach the third corner I realise that the crowd has thinned and that I have been hearing for some time the noises of cars starting outside.

Half-way along the last wall I see the painting that cries out for my most eloquent address. It is a portrait of a woman naked to the waist. I remember having seen the woman herself on that very evening; she is the current wife or girl friend of the Famous Artist. But I have nothing to say to the woman in the room – the woman in the painting is the one I am driven to talk to.

She leans slightly back, with her hands resting wide apart on the rich texture of a fallen tree-trunk. Behind her the background is thick with trees. And through the trees, I know, is the place that even the Famous Artist can only hint at: the orange-gold core of all the hill country, the place where all its meaning might become apparent, the place I am destined to write about.

The woman's eyes are fixed on me, but I cannot meet their challenge. I lower my own eyes; but there, at the very centre of the painting, violet and pink against white, the nipples of her strouting dugs are aimed directly at me.

I try her with soft words at first. I explain that I bear her no malice. I ask her why she has placed herself between me and the heart of the landscape; why she bars my way to the one place I am urged to write about.

She does not answer, of course – only goes on staring with her eyes and bailing me up with those deadly breasts.

I speak more harshly. I accuse her of intruding on the sacred preserves of art and poetry. I begin to compose threats against her. I hear my words sounding wonderfully sonorous. I hear from myself a voice I have wanted for a long time to hear.

I am aware of being escorted out of the house by the Existentialist and his girl friend, and then of being bundled into the back seat of their car. I am aware that they are very angry but inclined to blame the scrags for having tempted me away from the shack that morning and sat with me under hedges in the rain and filled me with cheap sherry.

I wake with my face against a scattering of charcoal lines that could have been an early sketch for one of the Artist's finished nudes. My son is standing over me, telling me it is late in the morning. I brush my clothes down and wet my face at the tankstand outside and go into the house.

The Artist's wife is making toast for her small daughter. She asks my son and me what we would like to eat. I say I will wait a little until my stomach settles.

In the bathroom I see at least a dozen cans still lying unopened among the melted ice-water. If I knew the Artist's wife better I would ask her to find room for some of the cans in her fridge. Instead, I take two tepid cans outside to look for the Artist.

I find him dragging dead branches towards the house for firewood. He refuses a can and takes a chain-saw to the branches. I sit and watch, and I open a can.

The Artist tells me not to drink too much because my lady-friend from the night before may be calling after lunch. I cannot remember my last words to the blonde woman, but I say nothing to the Artist, not wanting to reveal how drunk I was last night.

I ask him about the woman. He chooses his words carefully. He says she is a lady of many talents. I ask where she lives and who she lives with. The Artist says she seems to live mostly in Fitzroy, although she often appears of a weekend in Harp Gully, where she still owns a mud brick house and a fair patch of bush on the road to Kinglake; as far as he knows she lives alone.

When the wood is cut and stacked the Artist asks for his beer, but I have emptied both cans. He laughs and tells me to fetch his emergencies from the fridge. I excuse myself to his wife and find six cold cans hidden behind the stacks of food. I sit with the Artist in the shelter of the woodshed, in a patch of winter sunlight, and we share the cans.

When the beer has revived me somewhat, I say I will declare myself that very day to the woman with the patch of bush and move myself and my books and manuscripts into one of her mud brick rooms and sit all day looking out over what has always been my rightful territory. I offer to share with the Artist the worthy task of exposing to the world the profound spiritual truths that lie among these folds of hills; as Writer and Artist we will sit together every Sunday morning over cold cans and report to one another on our work-in-progress. The Artist puts an arm around my shoulder and swears to the pact.

The Artist and I rekindle the fire in his main room. His wife serves us spaghetti beside the fire. The bottles and glasses and plates and food-scraps from the party are all around us. I offer to start cleaning up, but the Artist's wife tells me the mess can wait, that my lady-friend is quite used to the customs of Harp Gully. I take my son outside and arrange for him to ride a borrowed bike around the roads with the Artist's son and to tell me afterwards if he would like to spend every weekend at Harp Gully.

Before the woman arrives I open a can but the Artist says he will wait a little. Suddenly I feel coming over me what I have not felt for nearly twenty years: what I used to call my caving-in horrors. I seem in danger of having my skin collapse inwards and my body shrivel to the floor. I take my can outside and perform the exercise of imagining the beer as liquid ballast, filling me out and keeping my surfaces firm. After a second can I am almost comfortable again.

The woman arrives. She seems rather taller and heavier than when I saw her last night, and certainly more so than the figure in the painted landscape. (I have wanted all morning to look at that picture, but I could not do it with the Artist and his wife watching me.) She accepts a small glass of wine and sits opposite me and crosses her solid thighs.

I ask her something about her property on the road to Kinglake, but she says she would prefer to hear me finish what I was trying to tell her last night when we were rudely interrupted.

I try to recall what I might have left unsaid. She laughs and says she was rather drunk herself last night. I cannot tell whether she says this to make me easier or whether she would like me to forget anything *she* might have said at the party.

The Artist and his wife say that have to catch up on their sleep. They excuse themselves and leave the room.

I have drunk enough by now not to fear for the time being my caving-in horrors. The woman opposite seems quite happy to sit and talk. But I want her to leave me alone. I am suddenly afraid she will ask me to visit her Harp Gully house – if not this afternoon then on some other Saturday or Sunday when I am struggling with one or other of my horrors. She will conduct me to a spacious room: the sort of room that writers are supposed to covet, with a view that reaches from the Sugarloaf at Kinglake to the lookout tour at Kangaroo Ground. She will leave me there at a massive desk with a typewriter and a ream of blank paper. Before she leaves (and locks the door after her), she will invite me sweetly to write something for her – something such as I talked about at the party where we first met, something such as I have talked about all over the hill country for twenty years. Only after she has gone will I notice the paintings on the walls around me. From every sort of landscape the image of the woman looks out at me, tossing her hair from her eyes, pointing her bare breasts at me, striding towards me with well-muscled thighs – and always quite at her ease in front of whatever scenery a painter has assigned to her. I will sit in my room and wonder. Is the woman in the paintings to be my reward for writing cleverly about some scenery she has never imagined? Or am I obliged to include her and the spurious scenery behind her in some more extensive landscape of my own devising, so that when she comes back and unlocks the door and reads my typed pages she will learn what new poses are required of her?

I am most courteous. I know I am to blame for bringing her out of her house to sit with an alcoholic failed writer on this darkening winter afternoon. I offer her more wine. I make all kinds of small talk to disguise the fact that I know neither what she wants from me nor what I want from her. Then, when she looks at her watch and says she really must be off, I am so anxious not to leave the space between us undefined that I ask for her postal address, which she gives me. I explain that I want to send her a copy of the best thing I have written in twenty years as an unpublished writer of fiction. The character in it is only an imagined version of myself, but if she reads the story carefully she will know as much about the man sitting in front of her now as any other woman or man has ever known.

I wake in my clothes, huddled on the couch in the Existentialist's shack. I know from the taste in my mouth and the pain in my head that I have vomited somewhere during the night. I lie for a long time without moving. I try to guess what time it is from the grey sky outside the window, but I cannot think consecutive thoughts.

I become aware of noises on the other side of the masonite wall. I am fairly sure of the cause of each noise, although I have never been in bed with a woman. The noises grow more rapid. I turn my face cautiously towards the window. There is no rain in the sky, but clouds have covered the spine of the Kinglake Ranges. I try to calculate whether this is the nearest I have yet been to a copulating couple; I try to remember certain nights in scrag houses when vague noises awakened me for a few moments while I lay on floors behind couches. Then the noises in the shack die away and I decide that the two behind the masonite are going to sleep again, which means I can sneak a cold bottle from the fridge and go outside.

I step carefully between the trees with my opened bottle. When I am out of sight of the house I sit down and lean back against a tree and drink. But then I am suddenly afraid. I recognise an attack of what I call the freckled horrors. I have to roll up my sleeves and stare hard at the dark-brown marks on my forearms. If I do not stare at them they will tear themselves away (trailing ragged little patches of skin behind them) and drift through the air and attach themselves firmly to trees or walls or any pale surface within my view.

I try to stare at my arms and wrists and to drink from my bottle at the same time. Then I hear the Existentialist calling to me from the back door of the shack. I stumble further into the trees, stop to drink, and stumble on again. I am suddenly anxious to press myself against a tree – perhaps to keep the marks on my skin in place or perhaps to prevent an attack of what I call the sexual horrors.

I reach a clearing among congenial-looking trees. I drink the rest of my beer. I note that the skin on my arms is now stable, with the freckles all in place. But I notice a section of a mottled tree-trunk shaped vaguely like part of a female body. I lean against it with my head against my wrist in the pose of a child gone 'he' for hide-and-seek. I tug at myself until a miserable trickle of seed arrives. I leave the stuff smeared against the tree like a pale, unhealthy sap.

The Existentialist also needs beer before breakfast; he shares two bottles with me. But nobody speaks in the shack and I know I have worn out my welcome. After lunch I say I will walk to the station at Hurstbridge, but the Existentialist offers to drive me. He puts three cold bottles in my bag, saying without smiling that they will keep me quiet until I am too far towards Melbourne to think of turning back.

I am the only passenger in my compartment of the train. I drink furtively from a bottle and write a draft of a letter to the young woman who walked in the hotel in Brunswick to the tune of *Poetry in Motion.* I write that I am writing beneath a tree somewhere between Harp Gully and Melbourne; that I am tired of scrags and artists and drunks; that I want to spend my time in future sipping quiet beers with a sane young woman like herself for company; I will show her sometimes a dark-blue line of hills far away across the northern suburbs and explain that those are the Kinglake Ranges where I will take her one day when I have become a published writer and established a territory for myself.

Around Heidelberg, where the suburbs begin, I put away my writing for the time being.

I go on sitting alone in the Artist's room. The sun has almost gone behind the Great Divide at Kinglake, but some of the last light reaches the stained glass window. Irregular patches of pink and watery green appear on the earth-yellow of the wall behind me, and one of the Artist's paintings seems oddly enhanced in the changed light.

I hear the Artist climbing down from his bedroom under the eaves, but I cannot find any pose to disguise the fact that I am absolutely buggered.

The Artist seems surprised that I have not gone off with the woman. But he has nothing to say to me, and he waves away the can I offer him, and I understand it is time I left. He says that of course he will drive my son and me to the station in Hurstbridge, but then I ask one last favour of him. I want him to give me an hour's start and then to drive after me with my son. I explain that I want to clear my head by walking.

I set out, in fading twilight, in the direction of Melbourne. The road at first is deserted – just a track of rutted gravel and clay winding down the side of a steep ridge. Every hundred yards or so I pass a front gate and driveway but the houses they lead to are hidden by trees or slopes of the land. I know that the people in those houses are anything but artists, and that they had never heard of Harp Gully when I first dreamed of living there. But I choose to think of them all as accomplished painters of landscapes and nudes and intricate abstractions, as people who know they appear always against a distinctive and recognisable background.

I ask myself what lies behind me.

If I mean to answer my question literally, I might mention a photocopied typescript of a piece of fiction called *Landscape with Freckled Woman*. (It lies in the pack on my shoulders. I brought it with me to Harp Gully because I imagined myself – before I set out – sitting on the Sunday afternoon with a woman I had met at the party and her wanting to read the best of my writing.) But I find it easier to see myself on a road through Harp Gully with behind me a rich and varied pattern of forested hills and among those hills houses with their inner walls hung with paintings of landscapes and in those landscapes figures and one of those figures myself – painted at last by the Artist, my drinking companion of nearly twenty years who watched one Sunday afternoon as the outline of me dwindled on the road to Melbourne and saw something about the failed writer and his repetitive journeys that was worthy of a place in a painting.

But as soon as I imagine that figure walking away from the Artist, I want to have the man he represents imagine something that will be always out of sight of the Artist. And so I imagine him planning to write a piece of fiction in which this view of him is described and something added to it.

Yet I have read enough to know that such fiction would seem nowadays merely modish, that my self-conscious narrator would seem only a figure of artifice and not a means of telling the truth. And so I decide never to write such a story. And I keep to my decision.

Dear readers,

As a publisher of shamelessly literary books, in addition to bookshop sales, we rely on subscriptions from people like you in order to publish in line with our values.

All of our subscribers:

- receive a first edition copy of each of the books they subscribe to
- are thanked by name at the end of our subscriber-supported books

BECOME A SUBSCRIBER, OR GIVE A SUBSCRIPTION TO A FRIEND

Visit andotherstories.org/subscribe to help make our books happen. You can subscribe to a selection of the books we're in the process of making. To purchase books we have already published, we urge you to support your local or favourite bookshop and order directly from them – the often unsung heroes of publishing.

OTHER WAYS TO GET INVOLVED

If you'd like to know about our upcoming books and events, please follow us via:

- our monthly newsletter, sign up here: andotherstories.org
- Facebook: facebook.com/AndOtherStoriesBooks
- Instagram: @andotherpics
- TikTok: @andotherbooktok
- X: @andothertweets
- Our blog: andotherstories.org/ampersand

Barley Patch

Gerald Murnane

¶ A few weeks before the conception of the male child who would become partly responsible, thirty-five years later, for my own conception, a young man aged nineteen years and named Franz Xaver Kappus sent some of his unpublished poems and a covering letter to Rainer Maria Rilke, who was by then a much-published writer although he was only twenty-eight years of age.

'He is without question both the most original and most significant Australian author of the last 50 years, and one of the best writers Australia has produced.'

EMMETT STINSON
The Guardian

Inland

Gerald Murnane

¶ I am writing in the library of a manor-house, in a village I prefer not to name, near the town of Kunmadaras, in Szolnok County. ¶ These words trailing away behind the point of my pen are words from my native language. Heavy-hearted Magyar, my editor calls it. She may well be right. These words rest lightly on my page, but this heaviness pressing on me is perhaps the weight of all the words I have still not written. And the heaviness pressing on me is what first urged me to write.

'The most ambitious, sustained, and powerful piece of writing Murnane has to date brought off.'

J. M. COETZEE
New York Review of Books